THE
INESCAPABLE
CONSEQUENCE

ISBN 978-1-952320-42-2 (Paperback)
ISBN 978-1-952320-43-9 (Hardcover)
ISBN 978-1952320-44-6 (eBook)
The Inescapable Consequence
Copyright © 2020 J.D. Belcher
Cover art by Yamile Quintero

Yorkshire Publishing
1425 E 41st Pl
Tulsa, OK 74105
www.YorkshirePublishing.com
918.394.2665

Printed in the USA

THE
INESCAPABLE
CONSEQUENCE

J.D. Belcher

TULSA

For Dad

Contents

Prologue   xi

Part I: The Dreams

Chapter One   1

Chapter Two   23

Chapter Three   54

Chapter Four   69

Chapter Five   87

Chapter Six   122

Chapter Seven   133

Chapter Eight   157

Chapter Nine   171

Chapter Ten   193

Part II: The Angels

Chapter Eleven   217

Chapter Twelve   232

Chapter Thirteen   251

Chapter Fourteen   273

Chapter Fifteen   298

Chapter Sixteen   313

Chapter Seventeen   331

Epilogue   351

Afterword   355

Scenes

The Prophet	11	Transition	99
The Bat	23	Azazel	102
Adam	27	Yousef	110
I Love You	30	Perfect Papa	126
Monica	35	The New Mafia	141
The Keys	39	YMCA	157
Two Chairs	41	Angelina's	171
First Accident	49	Fuck Buck	198
The Fire	77	Timing	209
The Raven	80	Do Not Touch	212
The Magistrate	92	Second Accident	218
Mister Reddy	94	Tulpehocken	219

Auras	225	Two Steps Behind	314
Third Accident	232	Demonic Attacks	318
Ubiquitous	238	Baldheaded Midgets	325
Avaloni	241	Prophecy Fulfilled	328
Hospice	246	Chip Activated	334
Frogs	248	Confirmation	337
Fairies	251	Back to Normal	338
Fourth Accident	264	South Side	339
Sami	269	The Elders	342
Threesome	278	The Initiation	343
Tableaux	282	Coincidence	349
Astral Projection	290	Evidence Disposal	350
Enough	300	Sleep	350

And Azazel taught men to make swords and daggers and shields, and breastplates. And he showed them the things after these, and the art of making them; bracelets and ornaments, and the art of making up the eyes, and beautifying of the eyelids, and the most precious stones, and all kinds of colored dyes. And the world was changed.

Book of Enoch, 8.1

Prologue

IF YOU ASKED Cashemente Tomás Alvin how it all started, the moment when the proverbial Peter Pan came knocking on his bedroom window to take him off to Never Neverland, he would tell you that it began during a warm, early October evening, when for the first time in his life, he witnessed, of all things, a gruesome murder. He and his on and off girlfriend, a cute Egyptian named Kia Alawi, whom he met years before while attending college at Pitt, had shacked up together in a one-bedroom apartment in Mount Lebanon on the south side of town. They both were graduates, he with a degree in creative writing, and she in psychology, but couldn't find full-time jobs in their fields. Until they figured out what they were doing and where they were going to do it, she worked as a waitress less than a mile from their home at Eat'n Park, a restaurant chain known for selling the best home cooked meals in western Pennsylvania. He delivered pizzas for Coccelli's, a popular shop on West Liberty Boulevard, searched for work online and wrote in his journal when possible, which was hardly ever.

The evening he parked his red 1997 Ford Ranger across the street from 1352 Tennessee Avenue had been like all the others. It was already less than a year and he had perfected the art of the delivery; to stop and observe his surroundings at each residence, to find the door, to make sure he had change and a pen, to lock his car and above all, to be courteous, no matter what. He remembered peering out of the passenger side window and squinting through the tall bamboo that filled the yard next to him, noting how rare it was to see that type of plant in someone's yard. The thought, *Who grows bamboo in Pittsburgh?* had gone through his mind as he eyed the rows of ringed stalks, so thick and high, it was difficult to see the house behind them. *Probably some Vietnam POW trying not to forget the 60's or something.*

Chatter from a flock of starlings hidden inside the clusters of skinny, knotted green rods could be heard from the lawn. Splatter of bird poop painted the car in front of him, and the grass and sidewalk next to the miniature patch of forest. But he was going in the other direction, across the street. Cashe took a sip from his Coke, then inspected the address that had ordered. He was in no rush, only tired, and couldn't wait to go home after he finished his shift.

On the seat next to him, hot steam slowly rose from the openings of a worn-out hot-bag. He re-checked the receipt.

Two 12-piece orders of buffalo wings, extra sauce. One large pepperoni pizza. A 2-liter bottle of Diet Coke.

He scooped up the food, waited for an approaching car to pass, then crossed. Again, he checked the information, making sure it matched up to where he was going.

1352 Tennessee Ave, Apt. Front 1.

As he started toward the steps, he noticed how the vehicle that went by parked about three houses up on the right. Out the corner of his eye, he saw the guy: an older version of himself, with dark hair and olive-toned skin, wearing blue jeans and a white T-shirt. The man exited the car and approached fast, almost running. *Great,* he thought. *Here's the weird shit again. It's always something. I bet he's coming over here.*

Strange was the last word he imagined using as a description for this job after he first got hired. It was supposed to be simple. Deliver the food, get the money, and then come back for more.

How wrong he had been. Every shift, there was always something *peculiar* going on. Addresses and telephone numbers missing digits. Incorrect toppings on pizzas. All those inexplicable free dinners that resulted from cancelled orders. And, of course, the bizarre customer encounters.

The brick porch of the house, spacious and empty except for a beat-up burgundy office chair, didn't have a bell. He truly hoped the guy was going to an address across the street or *somewhere else*, but instead, the man slowed his pace and walked up *his* steps. Cashe had never been robbed, yet in that instant, he felt as if this intruder might pull out a gun, take the food and all his money. The way the job had been going as of late, he believed anything could happen.

Why isn't this easier? he thought. *Why is this guy even in the picture at all?* Standing next to him, still holding the hot-bag and soda, Cashe casted a sideways glance in his direction and realized the man was probably thinking the same thing. *Fucking pizza delivery drivers. Always in the way.*

"You can go ahead," said Cashe, letting him through.

At first, neither moved. They both just waited for a few seconds, which seemed like an eternity. The man didn't smile—barely blinked. He only wore an intimidating, angry expression, like someone had just smacked him hard in the face with a shoe.

"Is that for Lisa?"

He pointed to the hot-bag in Cashe's hand.

Cashe looked at the receipt, fumbling it, now feeling nervous and threatened. He could hear keys making a clinking sound in the guy's hand.

"Yeah, Lisa."

"How much is it?"

"It's $18.32."

The man dug into the pocket of his jeans and yanked out a wad of money with a purple rubber band slung tight around it.

It reminded Cashe of the same roll he brought home after a busy night of deliveries. He wished his shift were over now.

After unsnapping the band from around the folded bills and thumbing through them for a long second, the guy pulled out a twenty. That's when Cashe noticed the ring. It was gold, studded with a shiny blue gem and distracted him from looking at the man's hands and the money he was giving him.

"Step inside and I'll get you a tip," he said, scratching his head and finally going past Cashe, the ring sparkling on his hand in the waning sunlight like a hypnotizing charm. It was beautiful and desirable, like a piece of sweet, hard candy. The only thing missing was the plastic wrapping. When Cashe regained his senses, he realized he had accepted an invitation that he shouldn't have, but it was too late.

Here we go again. Always dealing with this crazy crap.

His mind started to race as he followed the guy inside. Something was off, but he couldn't quite put his finger on what it was. Several different questions and explanations about what might be going on came to him at once.

Why didn't he just give a tip on the porch? Maybe he has too many big bills. Who the hell is he anyway? Maybe he's Lisa's boyfriend.

They went into the apartment through the porch entrance, walked inside and immediately stopped at a door with a chrome sticker labeled #1. Reggae music blasted from the other side of the wall, and the smell of marijuana hung thick in the air.

Before using the keys in his hand, the guy tried to turn the knob. It clicked and the door silently swung open. Cashe only had a partial view of what was going on in the room, but what he saw made him involuntarily take a step back. A white woman, on her knees, was bent over the lap of a black man who reclined on a leather sofa. They both were butt naked, except for a baseball cap on the black guy's head. Blonde hair covered and hid the woman's face but couldn't mask the unmistakable sight of her bobbing head.

Flashes of more images he wasn't accustomed to seeing on a delivery quickly came into focus. Side boob mounted with a puckered nipple. Smoke rising out of an ashtray. Scraggily pubic hairs. The lonely tilt of the Pittsburgh Pirates hat the naked man wore.

"What the fuck?" yelled White T-shirt, looming erect and tall in the entrance, the epitome of judgment day, a thousand chickens coming home to roost. "What the fuck is *this*?"

Cashe, supernaturally frozen, watched him as he reached into his waistband and lifted out a gun. The woman pulled back, still on her knees, and screamed. She shook both of her hands, spreading out all ten fingers in shivering horror, then lifted her voice a second time.

The guy in the white T-shirt walked over and kicked her in the ribs. It wasn't a quick, clean type of connection one might see in a kung-fu movie, but rather an awkward thud that landed square underneath her armpit and hanging breast. The woman's shrieks were immediately silenced as she fell over onto the coffee table, spilling a mound of cigarette butts on the floor. Then, White T-shirt turned toward the couch. The man wearing the Pirates hat pushed himself back further into the sofa and raised a right hand, as if that might somehow stop the bullet that blew off a finger and the top right section of his forehead. White T-shirt pistol-whipped the man on the couch one hard time, and blood splattered onto the curtains in the window behind him. He turned, paused and stood over the woman as she lie on the floor.

"You know I don't like that motherfucker, and you're going to do *this*?" he asked, sounding sad, a slight quiver in his voice. He kicked her again.

Cashe finally thought about himself. He was stuck. His body was paralyzed as he continued grip the pizza and wings, clutching the Diet Coke to his side. Just as he began to consider that he might get shot if he ran, the guy in the white T-shirt threw the gun on the couch next to the dying man and swung around. Cashe stayed put in the doorway. When he thought about it all later, he understood that it was the unnatural peace in the room that kept him there.

White T-shirt dug into his pocket and revealed the wad of money again. Amazingly, Cashe took the pizza and wings out of the hot-bag and handed them and the 2-liter soda to him.

"Here," the man said, setting the food on the ground. He separated a single one-hundred-dollar bill from the rest and handed it to Cashe. A bloody fingerprint was smeared across Benjamin Franklin's face. The blue jewel on his finger sparkled from the light above the door.

"Thank you very much," said Cashe. "Have a nice day."

PART ONE

The Dreams

Chapter One

CASHE BOUNCED UP the three flights of steps to his apartment that night exhausted and excited to be alive, knowing Kia's imagination had probably gone haywire wondering about his vague text message: *I'm at the police station. I'll give details tonight.* He unlocked the front door and upon entering, saw her standing in the bedroom at the far end of the hallway.

"Why were you down at the police station?" she asked coming towards him, sleepy and disheveled. "Did you get robbed or something?"

"No, worse," he said. He recanted everything—that he saw a shooting, the man who got shot in the head had died, and how a news reporter showed up at the pizza shop afterwards to interview him.

"What? That's freakin' crazy!" she said in euphoric disbelief.

They sat on the sofa and he gave a more detailed recollection of the events. He told her that somehow, miraculously, he was able to walk away from it all not only with his life, but also a $100 tip.

"You actually said, that?" she asked. *"Have a nice day?"*

"Yeah, I did," he admitted. "It just came out. I didn't even know what I was saying."

Kia let out a playful laugh, but then caught herself, and shook her head. "You're such a goofball."

"When I said that to the cops at the station, I wanted to be serious but couldn't stop smiling. I tried to hold it in, but it didn't work. I hate when that happens."

She threw her arms around Cashe and kissed him as if he had actually done something, like he had been the hero in all of this. Foreign women did things like that, he learned, and he loved it. He could tell she wanted to have sex.

"Stop!" said Cashe, pushing her away. "I didn't do anything but stand there. I'm just blessed to be alive."

"No," said Kia, "You *did* do something. You reacted calmly and handled the situation *very* professionally. I'm sure your manager said that to you, too, didn't he?"

"Nah, he was just glad I didn't get shot. He liked all the attention they got from the news, though. It's good for business. Let's see if they show it on TV tonight."

He grabbed the remote control from the coffee table and changed the channel to the news. It was a couple of minutes past 11 o'clock, and after the usual disheartening national blurbs—a militant with a backpack full of grenades had blown himself up at a Ku Klux Klan rally down in Louisiana, some nut opened fire with a AR-style assault rifle at a high school football game in California, half of the Amazon rainforest was on fire and Iran launched a missile into downtown Tel Aviv—sure enough, the incident ran as the lead local story. To Cashe, it all felt like a high he couldn't come down from.

"Oh, this is perfect timing," he said.

A reporter named Teresa Witowski, an attractive brunette wearing a lavender business suit and dangling earrings, stood under camera lights next to the house on Tennessee Avenue. Their towering antenna and a satellite dish decorated the top of the production van behind her. The anchor from the newsroom gave an introduction about a shooting death in Dormont and then Teresa took the baton.

Teresa:

…That's right, earlier this evening, a gunman entered this house on the 1300 block of Tennessee Avenue in Dormont, fatally shot one man and brutally beat a woman, both of whose identities have not been released pending further investigation. A bystander, a pizza delivery driver from Coccelli's just down the road from here witnessed it all go down.

The video cut to Cashe, talking with his undeniable smirk, briefly recalling what had happened. He giggled when he saw himself on TV.

Cashe:

I was just standing there with the pizza, waiting for the guy to give me a tip, and all of a sudden, he started screaming at the lady. Then, he pulled out a gun and shot the dude on the couch and turned back to the woman and started kicking her. I'm just happy to be alive…

The video cut once again, back to the reporter.

Teresa:

The driver was able to get away unharmed, but get this, the shooter, who police arrested hours later, gave him a $100 tip before leaving the scene. This is Teresa Witowski, live…

"I can't believe I just saw myself on TV."

"Oh my God," said Kia.

"They cut a lot out. And they didn't play the part with me talking about how they were naked or me mentioning the $100 tip," said Cashe. "And, oh, that reminds me. Look at this."

He opened his wallet, took out the one-hundred-dollar bill, and handed it to Kia.

"Eww, there's blood on it."

"I'm not going to spend it. I'm just going to save it as a souvenir and then eventually frame it. Or maybe I'll keep it in my journal."

She gave the bill back to him and he put it into his wallet. The blood on the money made him feel sticky and hot and dirty, and suddenly he realized how tired he was. He had been in the car all evening, down at the police station and then interviewed by the news. It truly was the strangest day of his life, and it all weighed down on him like a wet blanket.

"I'm going to take a shower."

"Okay, I'm going to lie back down," said Kia, getting up from the couch.

The steamy water cleared his mind, and after smoothing lotion on his body and slipping into a fresh pair of boxer shorts and a T-shirt, he slowly slid underneath the covers, cupped his chest and groin to Kia's back and buttocks, and softly kissed her neck. Immediately, he felt her *want* for him as she turned around and returned the affection, heartedly. He undressed himself first, thinking that he probably should have just gotten in without clothes instead of wasting time with the underwear and shirt, as they both were quickly flung across the room. He took off her panties and tank top and they made love. The sex had been passionately lethargic, and when they finished, an odd thing occurred.

Most nights after indulging in one another, they simply fell asleep. Cashe called it being 'hit with the sleepy stick', an imaginary weapon used by the infamous Sandman that left his victims incapacitated and instantaneously knocked unconscious. However, tonight, following the surreal sequence of the day's events, they lay wide awake underneath the comforter, holding one another.

"Let me ask you a question," said Kia. "The guy who shot up that house in Dormont, what race was he?"

The question kind of caught him off guard. It jolted him much in the same way his revelation about getting the $100 tip must have done to the police officers.

"Um, I don't know," he finally answered. "I guess whatever race I am."

Kia stayed silent, letting him talk.

"Ever since you came into my life," Cashe went on, "I've been considering this whole race thing and I'm not quite sure what to make of it."

"What do you mean?"

"Well, remember the first time we met?" he asked.

"I'll never forget it. That day Kumi and I were standing outside washing windows at the Brugger's Bagel café on Forbes Avenue."

"Yeah, and I started talking to you and asked for your number."

"You chose me over Kumi."

Cashe smiled. "Hmm, I never thought about it that way, but I guess I did. You're right."

"Boy," she said, teasingly pulling him closer, "you can't resist this!"

He smacked her behind. "I know, but listen. My point is that when I first saw you, I would never have guessed you were Egyptian or Kumi was from Oman."

"What did you think then?"

Cashe squeezed her breast and delicately kissed her pink nipple.

"Honestly, I was just thinking, *damn, you're fine as hell*."

She smooched his forehead, put her arm back around him, and turned her head to the side, as if she had just been mentally hijacked.

"No, but really, it was the same with this guy. He could have been a lot of different things. Venezuelan, Cuban, or even Egyptian. I honestly don't know what race he was."

Until college, Cashe never *seriously* considered these things. For whatever reason, it just didn't seem important. He remembered hearing his grandfather talk about back in the day when there were entire communities of *us,* until the white man put an end to it all. There really was no clarification about who the *us* were, but from what he gathered, he had a basic understanding. They were the light-skinned folk with Indian in them. His grandpa called them Mulattoes and Creoles. He always talked about how white peo-ple looked down on them because they really weren't white and how black folk viciously hated them because they believed, in their minds, that the lighter-skinned people thought they were *better* than them.

Cashe's parents technically consisted of some type of multi-racial mix, but to be honest, his mother didn't look much different than Kia. She wasn't wrapped up nicely into a term like Egyptian, Tunisian or Libyan, although she probably could have been if she lived over there. And though his father also looked North African, neither he, nor his mom or his grandparents had ever been to the continent, as far as he knew. But it had to add up to almost the same thing, he presumed.

Then, of course, all those genes had trickled down to Cashe. Even as a child, he knew he was different. Kids know these things. His extended family was a conglomeration of different pigmentations and colors, literally from white to black and everything in between. And because of that, he always viewed himself as a true American mutt, but in a good way. But others didn't always come to that conclusion. Year after year, like a glitch in the world's system, the same old question was presented to him, no matter at what age or what school he attended. Everybody wanted to know *where* he was from. Kia had even asked him that question the first day they met.

"So, where are you from?" Kia asked long ago, after introducing him to her friend Kumi, a browned skinned girl with long Hindu hair and a sub-Saharan nose.

"I grew up here in Pittsburgh," he answered, thinking that she had been another out-of-stater from Maryland, upstate New York or Ohio. Every once in a while, he'd meet someone from *really* far away, like Oregon or Florida who decided to attend school in Pennsylvania.

"Well, where are your parents from?" she asked again, continuing to press into it.

"Both of my parents are from North Carolina," said Cashe.

"No, that's not what I mean. *Where* are they from? *Where* is your family from? *What* country?"

That's when it would start to sink in, and he knew where the conversation was heading. He had learned how to play the game of giving people what they wanted: his classification. They needed to put him into something more palatable and easier to digest.

"Cuba," he had said, testing the waters.

"Really?" asked Kia, raising her voice an octave.

"No, I'm just joking, I'm from Puerto Rico."

He was tempted to settle on that final lie, to put an end to all the *Jeopardy!*-like categorical guessing, but as usual, he always knew he'd run into roadblocks not supposing where to take it from there. Finally, he just told her the truth, knowing the fun was over. She wouldn't believe him, but he answered the best and only way he knew how.

"Honestly, I'm just an American," he said softly, with quivering lips, waiting for her response.

"No, but you have something in you," she said. "You know, you shouldn't be ashamed of your heritage, Cashe."

The more he began to consider it, the more he began to understand that yes, by looking at himself through the lens of a world perspective, there were quite a few slots into which he easily could fit. Especially after he started following the news. Like how most African Americans could look to black Africa, stare into that cross-Atlantic mirror and see themselves in places like Ghana, Nigeria, or the Congo, and how whites could do the same in Caucasian European countries like Norway, Sweden and Ireland, Cashe too tried to view himself in many of the *yellow* places around the world. He paid attention to the wars in the Middle East, read stories about drug cartels in Mexico, the political atmosphere in China, the dictators in South America, and the miracle of Israel and her neighbor Palestine. It had turned almost into an obsession to digest those pictures streaming in night after night, scanning their faces on the computer screen as if searching for a long lost relative.

"Where are *you* from?" he had asked back, turning the table.

"I'm Egyptian. My parents are from Egypt," she answered easily.

He could hear the pride in her voice, the confidence that came with inherently being part of a people and a nation. The word *Egyptian* seemed so pinpointed and exact, while the term *American* could almost mean anything. Defeated, he let the conversation about all that drop, and after a brief chat about random nothingness, asked for her telephone number while Kumi turned away and continued to clean the storefront window. The next day, the two met at Starbucks, drank Chai and he fell into an irresistible love. Not too long after, they routinely took long strolls through Schenley Park after class, often hiking down the winding flower-filled path to Panther Hollow Lake, holding hands. In the evenings they'd visit each other in their off-campus apartments, smoke cigarettes, drink Turkish coffee and watch sexually explicit foreign films checked out from the Carnegie Library. He shared the story of his life, the pain of living as an only child, his parent's early deaths from a car accident, and the difficulty of being knowingly thrown into adulthood prematurely. She told of her experience of never having her mother around and growing up just down the street from a gigantic university campus under a super-strict Egyptian father, who, to this day, she refused to introduce to Cashe out of fear of his traditional beliefs concerning arranged marriages and dating. She thought she might end up kidnapped and stoned to death.

At times, it seemed insane that after two years, he hadn't so much as even shaken her father's hand, but now that they lived together, he sensed its foreboding imminence.

Meanwhile, he had done his fair share of spying, discretely gathering information about her childhood home, fantasizing about who this man could be. Often with Kia totally unaware, he'd drive past her father's home, a three-story row house on the corner of Bates Street and the Boulevard of the Allies, and watch her outside digging and shoveling through the dirt, indiscriminately picking out weeds by the roots and throwing them aside near a tiny patch of garden at the bottom of the steps. On the porch, he'd see an enigmatic old man sitting in a chair underneath the shade, staring out into the traffic, the person whom he assumed was her father, though he was never quite sure.

Living together had been Kia's idea. She initially surprised him by announcing that she moved into a new place—alone. At first, Cashe was crushed, and didn't understand why. Maybe deep down in his heart he envisioned them doing it *together*. And even after she made the offer for him to join her, it didn't provide the right remedy to balm his wound; in his mind, it just wasn't the same.

"I found an apartment in Mount Lebanon for only $600 a month," she revealed while they were sauntering down a path through the park near her father's house, the one they used to roam when they'd first started dating.

"And it's right across the street from the T-Station," she had said, selling the idea. "I thought you'd appreciate that since I know you like riding the train. Do you want to move in and pay half of everything? That way, we both can save a little money."

In a month, the lease to the apartment he rented in North Friendship would be ending, and like Kia, he was in desperate need of work. Although it wasn't exactly the way he wanted things to go, the timing couldn't have been better. They both were anxious to clean up their lives and venture out into the world beyond university life, so he hesitantly accepted the invitation, thinking this was their opportunity to launch. He sold most of his college furniture online and put the rest in the garbage, bringing only a few of his belongings: some clothes, a couple of pairs of shoes, a sleeping bag, the keys to his truck, his journal, a Bible and the *ring*.

It was a gold engagement ring, set with a two-carat pear-shaped diamond. He bought it after his parents had died, not sure who he'd give it to. What worried him most was that it wouldn't fit once he'd found someone, until the salesman at Kay Jewelers said he could always bring it back to get it *sized*, oblivious to the fact that they did such things. The square velvet box was small enough to hide into the tiny zipper on the side of his backpack, tucked away for the love of his life. But first, he needed to find another job.

A sign pointing that way came after he ran into Murad Gilauri, a friend from school he encountered one Saturday at the Giant Eagle grocery store, who suggested that he quit his $10 per hour part-time gig as a telemarketer and try something he never thought in a million years he'd be doing—delivering pizza.

"Dude, I make $600 a week, just in tips!" said Murad. "How can you say no?"

It didn't sound like respectable work, but after Murad bragged about the money, Cashe thought he'd give it a try. He applied and the same day got hired a few blocks away, as a driver for Coccelli's Pizzeria. His earnings in a month turned out to be more than enough to pay his share of the expenses, even giving him a little extra left over for an occasional, *just occasional*, visit to the Tavern Bar around the corner to catch a football game and have a couple of drinks. He had decided that his New Year's resolution would be to stop his random smoking cigarettes and sporadic partaking of a beer or two altogether. The idea was to get over the depression of his parent's deaths and not use alcohol as an excuse to escape. More and more he was beginning to believe that it was time to get earnest about his life, his relationship to God and a future commitment to a family, and that Kia was the one he wanted to do it with.

One of the positive things about living together was that it provided a setting where they both could get to know each other better. Though they did spend many hours on the job, whenever they were off on the same day and not ridiculously tired, they stayed pace with doing the things that kept the relationship going. They shopped, usually at the thrift stores, which was Kia's favorite thing to do, especially for furniture. She had a way of discovering great pieces at rummage sales and flea markets which made their apartment look like they bought everything at IKEA or Levin's. And they watched movies, *tons* of movies. Cashe's preoccupation with current events made it easy for him to always discuss the news, but she seemed more comfortable with keeping simple conversations, usually about her father or a new living room item she'd found. She cooked for him—and he *loved* her Middle Eastern cuisine—couscous with beef and vegetables, and *béchamel*, a macaroni in a milky white sauce were his favorites. Overall, their arrangement seemed to be working out well, in Cashe's opinion, headed in the right direction. That was, until suddenly, like a symptom from some exotic disease, something began to go terribly wrong.

The Prophet

IT HAD BEEN the movement of Kia getting up, the squeaky fall and rise on her side of the bed and then the silent, empty space of crumpled blanket that awakened Cashe. Too tired to speak, he squinted through the dim cover of his eyelashes and saw that the bedroom light had been turned on. He lazily rolled away from it all, threw the comforter over his head and instead listened to her scurrying about the apartment. In his mind, he saw a mental picture of what she might look like preparing herself for work. When he heard clothes hangers scraping against the metal bar in the closet, he knew she was hunting for her Eat'n Park uniform and trying to match the right pair of khakis to wear. He could hear her climbing into the pants she'd chosen, then shuffling through the dresser drawers, most likely searching through them for a bra and the right necklace and earrings.

The sounds of her rushing footsteps creaked the carpet covered floorboards as she left the bedroom and went into the bathroom, hurrying, and not making any effort to keep quiet. The opening and shutting of the medicine cabinet, the flushing of the toilet and the trickle of the faucet prevented him from entering back into the deep sleep he desired. After all the noise had quieted down, he felt the light turn out, and then the sheet being gently pulled away from his face.

"Bye, Cashe. I'll see you tonight," she said after kissing him once on the cheek. "I love you."

"I love you too," he said, yawning. "Have a nice day at work."

"And get your ass up and do something, don't just lie in bed all day."

"Yeah."

He listened to the front door open then slam, the click of the deadbolt lock, and soon the hush of the room and the warmth of the bed were just enough to push him back to sleep.

An hour later, he woke up again, but this time sat on the edge of the bed, craving bacon and tea. The heaviness of having nowhere to go made him lie down and sit back up several times before he finally forced himself into the bathroom for a shower. When he finished bathing, he went to the kitchen and made breakfast. Amid the savory smell of pork fat and the crackle of the teapot, he thought about what he might do on his day off. He needed to get away from the apartment for a while and decided on the brilliant notion of taking a trip on the T downtown, and afterwards catching a bus into Oakland to visit the park. Perhaps he could carry his journal and write some poetry and an entry for the day. It was something he wanted to do since the move but didn't have time for until he and Kia finished settling into the new place.

On the television, a giddy meteorologist forecasted the weather as partly cloudy and 52 degrees, so after eating, Cashe threw a windbreaker over his plum-colored polo and made sure to grab his backpack before leaving. The air outside was freshly brisk in his lungs, and he filled his chest, tasting the sunlight, the clouds and the breeze rustling through the leaves of the trees above. It was no doubt one of those days that seemed especially made for a trip like this, as if God Himself had set the stage. Every now and then he peered into the slanted storefront windows on West Liberty to check his clothes in the reflection, loosening the stray cuff in his jeans or zipping up his jacket a few more inches.

From the top of the steps, just before the descent to the loading platform, he saw a blonde woman ahead of him, wearing an ankle-length brown dress and tan cowboy boots, clicking her way to the ticket booth. When Cashe arrived, the transit worker behind the bulletproof glass smiled and said hello as he paid his fare. After taking the transfer, he leaned up against one of the massive cement columns holding up the roof overhead, stared down at the parallel steel tracks, and then off into the dark, menacing tunnel to his left. Haphazardly, the woman settled onto the bench to his right and crossed her legs surprisingly close to a man in black slacks, a blue dress shirt and red tie. Seeing the two of them together made him think of Kia, and he wished that they could have enjoyed the day together. The slow rumble of an approaching train became more and more pronounced as the screeches and squeals of its brakes echoed, and the lights of the engine came into view.

When the train halted and its doors clanked open, he took a seat near the back. The two passengers who had been waiting on the dock came into the same car. The woman in cowboy boots sat five seats in front of him, while the man distanced himself to the left side and scooted into a window seat near the exit. They rolled forward, and before each stop, he watched commuters gradually crowd around the unopened doors of the train, noticing the dull anticipation on their faces as they prepared to board.

The lulled motion of the ride made him tired, and if it weren't for the frequent breaks at each station and the arrival of new passengers, he might have fallen asleep. He tried to enjoy the scenery, but the beauty of the city only relaxed him more. Out the window, flashes of subway lights streamed by, one after the other, as they sped through the shadowy burrow underneath Mount Washington, until the metallic skyline of downtown Pittsburgh exploded on the other side. The sparkling brown Monongahela River crept along tirelessly below the towering yellow bridges that connected each shore.

At the underground Wood Street station, he cautiously rose from his seat and followed the meandering flow of traffic up the escalators, then outside to the bustling street. Instantly, as if she had specifically been waiting for Cashe outside the revolving doors, a limping, toothless beggar shook a white Styrofoam cup in his face, rattling the few coins inside.

"Change?" she asked through a thick, lisping tongue. "Do you have any spare change?"

His first instinct was to say "no," and ignore her, but for some reason he felt generous, dug into his pocket, grabbed the three quarters that were there and dropped them into her cup.

"God bless you."

"God bless you too, sir," said the woman, and immediately she turned her head, waddled a few feet away, on to the next person coming out into the street.

The number of homeless people Cashe saw in the city always astonished him. Once, while riding his bike through a cluttered pedestrian tunnel near Point State Park, the expansive floodplain where the Allegheny, Ohio and Monongahela rivers meet, he found one of the places where they slept at night. There were rows of dirty sleeping bags and piles of clothes pushed up against one side of the wall. He remembered the trash mingled among all their belongings, how pigeons randomly pecked through them, eating whatever scavenger birds feast on in those places, and his fear that a dead body might be lying somewhere underneath all the mess. As he passed by, what struck him as odd was not only how quiet the tunnel was, but also that not a soul was there. Then, it occurred to him that the homeless, like the rest of the proletarians downtown, must leave for work to go about the business of begging, only to retreat at night to sleep under the shelter of the passageways.

Cashe slipped into the lunch hour crowds on Wood Street, navigating through the heavy congestion on the sidewalk. He looked above him at the spiring skyscrapers overhead, then back at the street, wondering what kind of jobs these people had during the day. The men, wearing slick suits and silk ties alongside women in fashionable business attire and designer sunglasses almost made him jealous, but when he thought of the bag lady with her cup of quarters, he pushed away the idea and thanked God for what he had. He and Kia were by no means rich, but they had everything they needed.

After taking in a half hour of the downtown scene—the street vendors, the aroma of hotdogs and sausages, and the muffled vibration of hip-hop music that slowly but surely loosened the nuts and bolts of a pimped-out Cutlass stuck beside him in traffic—he was ready to catch a bus into Oakland to visit his old campus and walk around the park for a while.

When he arrived at Fifth Avenue, there was a street preacher holding a Bible into the air, screaming at groups of commuters on the corners who waited at the bus stop:

He who overcomes shall be clothed in white garments, and I will not blot out his name from the Book of Life; but I will confess his name before My Father and before His angels!

Cashe crossed the street, stepped into an empty spot between two teenagers standing in front of PNC bank, and rested his back up against the wall. He put his hands into the pockets of his jacket and watched the man preach; the way he turned in all directions, not speaking to anyone in particular, but rather to everyone at once. How he snapped his arm whenever he emphasized a point, or raised the Bible over his head and smiled when he said something about how Jesus had saved his chosen from sin.

A few blocks away, several buses lined up one behind the other in the transit lane at a red light, all of them announcing on their golden marquees that they were going through Oakland. He wasn't worried so much about boarding the wrong bus, but rather finding a seat. Most of the crowd crammed into the first one that arrived. Foreseeing the same with the second bus in queue, he went to the third, and as soon as its doors slid open, he climbed on and took a window seat.

The bus, now twice as packed since the time it departed downtown, meandered up the steep incline of Fifth Avenue and into the University of Pittsburgh's campus in Oakland. A happy group of girls loaded down with oversized book bags had taken both the vacant seat next to him and the two spaces in front. College students packed the middle aisle and held on to the straps that hung from the chrome bars overhead. They looked as if they might fall over one another like a row of dominoes every time the bus came to a sudden halt.

When the automated voice announced the arrival of Bigelow Boulevard, he pulled the hanging cord in the window, sounding the bell to request his stop. After following the girl who sat next to him and her two friends to the fore, he squeezed past a mosh pit of passengers, gave the driver his transfer, and then steadily exited the bus.

Just ahead, he could see an open field on a hillside in Schenley Park, and the gathering of treetops at the summit where he planned to sit underneath. As he walked by many of the classroom buildings he used to frequent during his collegiate days, he couldn't help but reminisce about rushing to class to take exams and eating in the cafeterias. In many ways, he considered himself a phantom, a dead man revisiting an empty place that used to have so much life. All the people he once knew were now gone, and all the spots he used to frequent were filled with faces he no longer recognized.

When he reached the entrance to the park, he saw another reminder of his past. A tall, red-bearded man with unkempt hair matted down to his shoulder blades became visible from behind a row of bushes across the street near the Phipps Conservatory. Two adult German Shepherds, one at each of his sides, lazily sniffed the grass below. This was the man who Cashe had personally named "The Prophet" during his days on campus. The guy looked exactly what he imagined a true messenger of God to be, a tramp drifting around the deepest woods of the park, living off wild honey and grasshoppers like Elijah the Tishbite of Gilead.

The prophet stopped under an apple tree on the side of the building, and with a wave of his hand, both dogs sat down on the lawn, stood at attention with straightened ears and awaited the next order from their master. Cashe glanced about to see if anyone other than himself had just witnessed the prophet's amazing display of control over the animals, but no one else was around. It appeared to be almost magical, and it wasn't the first time Cashe had seen him in action.

While en route to a sociology class during his junior year, the prophet and his dogs, out of nowhere, had come near the entrance of the Forbes Quadrangle building next to a crowd of students. In order to avoid a scene, he pointed to a secluded spot on the lawn close to a set of bushes and yelled, "*Over there!*" Immediately, both of them darted to that exact location, laid down head over paws and waited. The prophet stood motionless until the last student went by, tilting his head to the sky as if he were receiving instructions from an invisible voice above.

The lure of this unnatural man who became somewhat of a legend on campus, like the strange guy who lived in a closet in an old 80's film Cashe had seen called *Real Genius*, surrounded his breakdown and apparent lapse into insanity. According to the stories Cashe had heard, he had once been a reputable professor of astrophysics. Then one day, for no obvious reason, he cracked and had gone missing for over a year until he was found by a colleague who spotted him in the park. They committed him into the Western Psychiatric Institute, just a few blocks away from where he used to teach and conduct research. When he was finally released, he totally rejected all norms of society, and became one of the many supposedly mentally ill homeless people who could be seen around the city.

At the top of the hill, Cashe found a bare patch of ground beneath one of the huge oaks that lined the tip of the field. He sat down, stretched out his legs and took in the view of all the campus buildings, hospitals, and the downtown outline looming in the horizon. From his vantage, the campus seemed as if it was a city in of itself. The thought of smoking a cigarette had crossed his mind, due to an old, instinctual reflex. He had smoked many under this very tree, but with the habit now broken, the minuscule craving no longer had an effect.

The prophet and his dogs ambled from the lawn of the conservatory to the bottom of the hill on Cashe's side of the road as he took out his journal and a pen from his backpack. At first, there was quite some space between them; the length of the field made the trio small enough to crush between his thumb and forefinger, and he did so several times in jest. But as they made their way up the hill, he noticed how they were coming in a straight line towards him. Butterflies fluttered inside his stomach as the prophet came closer and closer. More than anything, Cashe wondered what the man could possibly want from *him* as he scratched his back up against the trunk of the tree, satisfying an itch in the middle of his spine.

There had been other times like this when he received superfluous attention. Perhaps it was just paranoia, but it always seemed that elderly people at the grocery store took pleasure in asking *him to* take a product from off the uppermost shelf because they couldn't reach it, or someone always stopped in the middle of traffic to ask *him* directions. It was perplexing, and sometimes he felt as though he had a sign on his back that read "Ask Me".

When the prophet and his dogs crossed the halfway point of the field, Cashe began to notice details about them he couldn't see from afar. Blackened feet inside the prophet's flip flops looked like they were covered in engine grease, and his swollen ankles were like the bulging knots of a tree's twisted stump. The tattered bottoms of his slacks made him look surreal, like he was wearing a costume and the park was his stage. Both of the German Shepherds were healthy and well fed, but seemed thirsty, or was it *hungry* as they panted, slopping up their wet tongues every now and again?

About ten feet away, the man paused, and the dogs with him. Cashe thought about moving, just to get away from the craziness of it all, but his curiosity told him to stay put and see what might happen next. The prophet dug into his pockets, mumbling words that couldn't be heard because he was still too far away. When he stopped speaking, he raised his head, looked at Cashe, and took a few more steps forward. His eyes, like green balls of flames set inside deep creases of crow's feet on either side of his temples, were kind, but also sharp and dangerous. He waved his hands at the dogs, and once again, they obediently lay in the grass.

"Hello," the prophet said simply, in a soft voice that made him sound more like a gentle professor than the deranged lunatic he seemed to be in exhibition.

"Hi," answered Cashe. "How are you?"

"I'm fine thanks, yes, but um, I was wondering if I could ask a favor from you?"

Cashe thought he might want money, or for him to buy a meal, but for some weird reason, he didn't feel imposed upon. He couldn't stop staring at the prophet's long, strawberry blonde beard and his rough hands which were the same complexion as his feet.

"Well, I guess it depends on what you're going to ask," said Cashe, noticing how both dogs were now staring at him. "I'm not going to make any promises though."

"Don't mind the dogs, they won't bite you," said the prophet. "What I need is a place to put my shoes."

Though his request seemed a little off, there was something genuine about what he asked which made Cashe want to keep listening. He looked down at the man's flip flops again and stared at his feet.

"You need a place to put those?" questioned Cashe, pointing.

"No, not these. I have a really nice pair of boots this young lady bought for me the other day. I have them hidden."

"Why are you hiding them?" he asked, just going along with conversation, being careful to keep a safe distance from making any obligations.

"Because the police keep stealing them from me. Every time a get a pair of shoes, they come and take them!"

What he said wasn't making much sense, but at the same time it did. A part of Cashe believed him. *But why would the cops take shoes from a homeless man?*

The prophet went silent with the same peace as his dogs lying in the grass, waiting for a response. On the inside, Cashe didn't want to decline his offer, but he wasn't ready to enter into a deal either. The sound from the engines of a commercial airline rumbled overhead. Cashe lifted his head to the sky and watched the jet bank at an obtuse angle. He knew he was misunderstanding the man's request, or lacked access to an important link of information which would put all of this into perspective and bring wisdom to his plea for help. The words, like the plane, flew over his head and he couldn't get at what it was the prophet was asking. There was more to it, he just didn't know what "it" could be.

"Wait a minute, I don't understand. Why would the police steal your shoes?"

"Because they're assholes!" he screamed, startling Cashe by his sudden outburst.

In that instance, he genuinely believed the prophet and felt sorry for him. He knew that there really were evil people in the world capable of these types of pointless, random acts of foolishness. Over the years, he had seen it happen. He even had known friends who occasionally picked upon the less fortunate, just for the hell of it.

"I can't help you with that," Cashe said, trying to stay honest as possible. "I don't live around here."

The prophet turned toward the dogs, and they slowly rose to their feet. The three began walking around the side of the tree, until he stopped and began digging through his pockets again.

"I'm really sorry," said Cashe, truly wishing he could do something. The man seemed to be in a terrible situation, apparently harassed by those who were supposed to uphold the law. His mind raced as he tried to think about a place where the guy could go for help.

At the bottom of the field, a young couple holding hands began unashamedly gawking at the prophet and his dogs as they came up the hillside. Their presence made Cashe feel uncomfortable, as if they were beginning to violate the private space he and the wild man had just created, interrupting their intimate moment together. But at the same time, another part of him didn't want anyone to see him talking to a homeless person in public. Out the corner of his eye, he noticed the prophet coming towards him again. He held out his right hand and directed a calloused finger at Cashe.

"They told me *Azazel* has been released and is coming for you," he said, and then let out a giggle.

"What?" asked Cashe.

"The Watcher. He's coming to see you."

As the couple approached, the girl pulled her lover close and whispered into his ear. Cashe wanted to finish the conversation, to know more of what the prophet was talking about but didn't ask.

"Oh, really?" he answered, now distracted by the intruders arriving all the more closer, humoring the prophet's seemingly strange remarks.

"Yes," he said with a smile, and suddenly Cashe saw his jagged, pearly brown teeth, "They told me to tell you that the lot has been cast. Azazel is coming for you."

Chapter Two

The Bat

AFTER EATING A SLOPPY sandwich which consisted of corned beef, sauerkraut and French fries for lunch at Primanti Brothers in Oakland, Cashe hopped a bus downtown, did some window shopping, then caught the T back to Mount Lebanon. When he arrived home, he noticed that the apartment was freezing cold.

"Cashe, is that you?" Kia screamed from the other side of the shut bathroom door.

"Who else would it be?" he asked, jokingly. "Is there another person who has a key to the place and just shows up unannounced? You're talking crazy!"

He looked around the corner into the bedroom and noticed that the windows were open, screens and all, flooding in the chilly air from outside.

"And, why do you have the windows open? It's cold in here. What are you doing?"

"There's a bat in the apartment!" she yelled again, and the statement took a while to ring the right bells inside his head. *Bathroom floor mat. Baseball bat. Bat. Oh, the animal. A bat.*

"A bat?" he asked, now confused. "Where?"

He had never seen one up close except at the zoo. There were many different kinds, from teeny tiny common house bats to other, larger varieties. Some, like the mega fruit bats from the Philippines, were *really big.* They were gigantic, big as opossums with wings; he thought they looked like little flying dogs.

Not knowing what to expect, he began searching the apartment. In the bedroom, he scanned every detail of the room, paying attention to the blinds, the top of the doors, underneath the bed-frame and the corners of the walls, but didn't see anything. As he turned around to investigate the living room, a black, dark blur the size of a sparrow fluttered past his head like a leaf falling from a tree and made him duck low to the ground. Up near the ceiling, he saw it change course back toward the bedroom in its choppy, awkward, moth-like course. Hunched over, he crawled into the hallway, sat down on the floor across from the bathroom, and leaned against the wall as if he were in a combat position. The bat flew again into the living room, making a figure-eight pattern from one end of the apartment to the other.

"I see it, Kia, it's flying back and forth!" he yelled at the bathroom door. The thought of how she locked herself inside tickled him, and he felt a laugh coming on.

He had caught and killed many types of bugs and wild animals in his lifetime. Most were simple jobs. Spiders that showed themselves on the walls or in the bathtub, he easily took care of with one simple swat of a shoe. Black-eyed, mangy mice would always get themselves stuck into glue or in the harsher metal spring traps. Once, a sparrow had flown into his old apartment in Friendship on the East Side and hid behind the dusty water cooler closet near the kitchen. He was able to shoo it out the front door with a rolled-up newspaper. But a bat was of a different genre. Not only could the mammal fly, but it had teeth and could bite. Cashe had never heard of a bat trap, and even if there was such a thing, he didn't know where to buy one at this time of night. The risk of getting some type of an infection, like rabies, floated through his mind as he tried to find a solution of how to get it outside.

He stood up as fast as he could and pulled the unopened windows in the living room and both the front and back doors ajar. Crouching, he stayed below an invisible four-foot mark so that the bat wouldn't fly into his face, then hid under the dining room table among the chairs and waited.

For five long minutes, the bat refused to change course. The animal flew in what seemed to be an endless pattern from the living room and into the bedroom. It passed by the open doors and windows as if it didn't know that there was a way out. He thought of the adage *blind as a bat.* His plan wasn't working.

"Kia, how in the world did a bat get in here?" asked Cashe from underneath the table.

"I don't know," she answered. "Just get it the hell out of *my* house!"

"What's going on in the world? This has been two days of insanity!" said Cashe in complete wonderment.

It was nearing the end of the fall season, and not too long ago, he had checked and made sure that no opening or crack existed in the apartment to better hold in the heat. Given that there was no way the bat could have come in through a closed window, he began to consider other scenarios as to how it might have gotten in.

Maybe it had snuck in behind someone at the building's entrance and flown all the way up the staircase, he speculated. *Then, perhaps, it crawled in under the space beneath the door. But what are the chances of that happening?*

The place was getting colder and Kia still hadn't made one move out of the bathroom. Just when he began to think that he was running out of ideas, the bat mounted upside down, of all places, on the edge of the table, directly in front of him. Cashe froze and stared at the animal, face to face. He watched as it licked its bat lips and then made itself comfortable, wrapping its silky wings around its furry body like a shawl.

Never in his life had he seen such an ugly creature. It was in no way similar to the cuddly rodents which made housewives jump on top of chairs in the kitchen, like in the old *Tom and Jerry* cartoons. Up close, mice were cute, furry and familiar. They were kept in glass boxes on top of kid's bedroom dressers and given workout equipment. A bat, he thought, was horribly grotesque. Not one drop of adorable charm emanated from its demonic body. At the tip of its wings were claw-like hooks, and below its skin, he could see protruding joints and a thin, chicken bone skeleton. Its face, snout-nosed and wrinkled, was the stuff scary movies were made of.

He pushed the chair behind him at the other end of the table out with his foot, and at the same time slowly retreated away from the bat, so not to startle it. After crawling backwards a few feet, he remembered his netted laundry bag hanging in the closet and figured it would be the perfect instrument to use to entrap the bat. Without making too much noise, he quickly dumped out the dirty clothes onto the floor, then carefully approached the animal, inching ever closer and closer, one step at a time. He opened the mouth of the bag, surrounding the bat so that there was nowhere else for it to go except inside. And that's exactly what happened. It dropped and became entangled in the mesh holes.

"I got it!" he declared to Kia. She kept silent in the security of the bathroom. He knocked on the door to show the fruits of his labor, but was only met by more of her dramatic antics.

"Don't you bring that thing in here!" she screamed, so seriously, that she frightened him more than the struggling bat had done, and so much so that for a moment, he had almost forgotten why he was outside the bathroom door and what he had in his hand.

"I'll be back. I'm going to let it out outside."

After tying the bag in a knot, he placed it on one of the dining room chairs and closed all the windows in the apartment. Then he took the bag, went out the door and into the hallway, holding it before him with an outstretched arm. When he reached the bottom flight of steps, he walked out into the cold, laid the bag on the ground, untied it and spread it open. He pulled the drawstring as wide as it would stretch and watched as the bat fluttered up and away into the starlit sky.

Adam

THE NEXT MORNING, he and Kia sat at the dining room table and ate breakfast together, saying nothing about the bat. He filled up a bowl of Raisin Bran with vitamin D milk while she drank coffee, spooned up mouthfuls of yogurt and nibbled on toast spread with Country Crock and strawberry jam. Cashe suddenly realized that amid all the commotion the night before, he failed to mention to Kia that he saw the prophet in the park.

"I forgot, there's something I wanted to tell you," said Cashe, directing his spoon at Kia. "You'll never guess who I ran into at Schenley Park yesterday."

Her face scrunched into a frown, as if the question had smacked her across the cheek. She quickly dabbled around the inside of the plastic container of yogurt, licked the spoon and then took a sip of her coffee.

"Who?"

"Remember that bum who used to walk around campus when we were in school? The one who had those two big-ass German Shepherds with him all the time."

"Yeah, I do," she said. "The guy with the beard."

"Yup, it was *him*. He came up to me while I was sitting on top of the hill across from the conservatory," said Cashe. "And he said the strangest thing to me. Something crazy like, a gazelle, or a *zazel* is coming to get me—whatever that means. What the hell is an *azazel*?"

"Azazel? I think that means the devil," said Kia, then laughed.

"No it doesn't."

"I swear to God. I think it does."

"What, in Arabic?"

"No, not in Arabic. In Arabic, the devil is Shaytan, the same as in English. Or Iblis. I'm pretty sure Azazel is a Jewish word. I'm positive I heard it somewhere before. Look it up."

A chill literally ran down the back of Cashe's spine, and fear welled up from his stomach.

That couldn't be what he said.

But it was. He knew it was. He not only had heard what the prophet said clearly in the park, but he also recalled his mouth full of crooked teeth after he smiled about it.

"Okay, don't mind if I do. May I use your computer for a second?" he asked, rising from the table to put his dishes in the sink.

"Go ahead."

But before he got the chance to press the power button on the laptop and open up an Internet browser, he was distracted by a telephone call someone made to Kia.

Immediately, he perceived that something was amiss. Kia didn't respond in the way he thought she might by taking the call, but stood frozen, holding a spoonful of yogurt in her mouth, gazing down at the phone before her as if trying to solve a puzzle. It looked like she was thinking about whether or not to pick up. Just before the phone went to voicemail, she answered. Cashe pretended to ignore her, but listened to the conversation until she rose from the chair, left her food at the dining room table and went to the bedroom for privacy.

He faked like he had to use the bathroom, keeping the door cracked just enough to hear her talking in the bedroom: *Oh my God!*

How have you been? Where are you now? It's so good to hear from you. Yeah, yeah—I'm living in Mount Lebanon now. He's fine, just getting old. We'll have to get together soon. Ok—Yeah, you too. Yes, I have it now. Talk to you later. Bye.

"Who was that?" Cashe asked, suddenly coming out of the bathroom and into the bedroom where Kia sat cross-legged on top of the bed, obviously pleased, thumbing through her cell phone.

"What?" she asked, as if he had no right to question her.

"I said, who was that?" he asked again, now insulted for having to repeat himself.

"It was an old friend of mine."

"Who?"

"Damn, why?"

"I'm just asking a question. What's your problem?"

"It was my friend Adam. He went to Pitt. You don't know him."

Cashe hadn't even thought that the person *could have been* a woman she was talking to, but intuitively guessed right. It *was* a guy. Now, he was both curious and hurt, but played off how much he was bothered by leaving the room.

"Oh," was his only response, though he wanted to say more, and forgot all about using the computer to research what the prophet had said.

For three days, that telephone call ate away at his insides. He toiled over whether or not he should delve further into who this Adam was, or if he was making a big deal out of nothing. No doubt, he noticed that a subtle change had begun to take place within Kia. He wasn't sure if it had something to do with them moving in together, or some crazy indirect correlation about him witnessing the murder. Perhaps, he was just being paranoid. Briefly, a thought floated through his mind that the Azazel demon truly had come to torture him. Whatever it was, the feeling of uncertainty pulled and tugged at him so hard that it had begun to affect his sleep.

I Love You

THE FOLLOWING WEEK, on a day when both he and Kia had off, Cashe sat in the living room watching Steelers football highlights on ESPN, waiting for her to return from checking on her father. He thought she might want to go for a walk or watch a movie together, like they usually did when they both didn't have to work. A stroll through the park sounded like the better option. As he reminisced about getting back into shape, the *real* shape he used to be in, not just being able to trek up and down the steps without getting winded, the door creaked open and Kia came through carrying several bags of groceries.

"Why didn't you call so I could help you bring some of that up?"

"I got it," she said, in a high voice that sounded more like *I understand*, than *I don't need your help*, then disappeared into the kitchen. "I'm just dropping this stuff off and leaving again. I'll be back in a couple of hours."

"Where are you going? I thought we were going to hang out."

"Um, I ran into a friend today while I was driving through Oakland on the way to my dad's," she spoke slowly, in chopped up portions, in between segments of opening the refrigerator and shutting cabinets as she put the food away, as if she were trying to distract herself. "We're going to meet up for coffee."

Here it was again. He knew Kia was attempting to keep a secret, like with the telephone call. Cashe wasn't fooled in the least bit.

"Oh really, what *friend*?" he probed.

"I thought I told you. His name is Adam and look—he gave me a gift card to Trader Joe's!" she said, coming into the living room as if it were no big deal. "Wasn't that sweet of him?"

He didn't look at her, didn't even turn his head, but stayed seated on the couch, letting her know that it *was* a big deal. Maybe she didn't think so, but it was. More and more, all this just seemed to be her womanly way of providing an intentional confession to burst his bubble, allowing the poison of his righteous jealousy to gradually ooze out into the atmosphere. Kia hardly ever said anything just for conversational purposes. This had been a calculated attack. Meanwhile, a piece of his heart broke off and dropped somewhere next to his stomach. His body literally *twitched* from the news.

"Oh, did he?" answered Cashe, not at all sharing in her enthusiasm, trying to remain as calm as possible. "*I get it*. You mean he gave you a gift card to his penis, huh?"

"You know what Cashe? Fuck you!"

As if on cue, her cell phone rang. It was *him* again. The two talked about a meeting time and location, and after she hung up the phone, Cashe did finally turn his head to look at her, zeroing in on the smirk that was camouflaged beneath a composed expression of guilt on her face, as if she were playing some cruel game with his feelings and enjoying it.

"I'll be back," she said coolly.

"Wait!" Cashe tried to shoot back calmly, though his chest was visibly heaving. "Has it entered your mind that going on a date with him might be a little out of the bounds of our relationship?"

"I told you he's just *a friend,* nothing else!"

"And I think you mean to say your old *boyfriend*," he said, standing up. "Am I right? Did you ever fuck him? Don't lie, because that makes a huge difference if you did."

Kia didn't answer. All he saw was that stupid grin on her mouth. It was the same one he had worn when the reporter questioned him about the shooting. Only now, it was Kia being questioned while he got murdered by her actions.

"Don't you think that there is something *wrong* with accepting a gift from another man?"

"Damn it Cashe, no!" she screamed and began to cry.

"Oh my God. I don't get this! Why are *you* mad? I'm the one who should be upset."

Her phone rang again. Adam had called back, right on cue, and Cashe couldn't believe the things he saw and listened to. If was as if he was observing a stranger who had taken over Kia's mind, body and soul. She wasn't herself. He had no clue who this person was strolling around the apartment, speaking on the phone.

"Adam, I really need to talk to you," she said, sobbing, gravitating back toward the bedroom. "I can't take this."

Then he heard it. It was like the pebble that started the avalanche. The straw that broke the camel's back.

"Yeah, I know you do," she said, and before shutting the bedroom door behind her, those piercing words made their way to his eardrums, "*I love you too.*"

Hearing Kia tell another man that she loved him had been a first. He shook his head in disbelief as his intellect refused to process the information. Instantaneously, he found himself in some other sphere, like studying a new subject in the school of life—Relationship Geography 101. It was like being on a field trip, traversing through rough terrain in an uninhabitable, desolate region that he never knew existed and really didn't care to visit again. Her treatment of him had been cold and empty as Antarctica. Cashe felt as if he might pass out.

I love you. Though her back had been turned to him, it was brazenly done right in front of his face. The phrase echoed in his mind repeatedly, as if his brain were a deep cavern. She had often used those same words to genuinely express her apparent affection for him. But now, a higher law had been violated, and immediately he sought for a solution to what she had done. He felt an urge to report the problem, to call the cops, the FBI, or the CIA. Some type of special task force or global tribunal needed to meet in emergency deliberations to deal with her actions. He wished she would have said those words to Adam in secret, in the privacy and seclusion of some place of her own, but not before him, where he was forced to witness the whole thing go down. It was—*disrespectful*.

Sticks and stones, whatever, he thought, paralyzed. Her words hadn't broken bone, but something had shattered, and for the first time in his life, he actually *sensed* her leave him, though they were still physically present in the same place. He knew his precious dove had no doubt flown to another man. The empty feeling left a fiery hole that burned like a hot furnace inside of him, and he didn't know what to do with the pain. He wanted to take an axe, go into the woods and swing at the largest tree he could find. Finally, he exploded.

"You love him? What the *fuck* is that?" he asked, darting down the hallway, yelling at the bedroom door.

Kia burst out of the room past Cashe, almost knocking him over. A brown coat hung lazily halfway off her shoulder and a scarf was sloppily thrown around her neck. She slammed the front door and the mysterious woman was gone.

Forty minutes later, she quietly returned, much earlier than expected. Her next actions would further contradict everything he thought he knew about his girlfriend, and serve as proof that indeed, his world with her was beginning to show the first signs of going topsy-turvy. Kia sat next to him on the couch, grabbed the remote control from the coffee table, and turned off the television. She wrapped her arms around him and kissed him on the cheek. It seemed like a toddler with a soiled diaper was holding on to him. He tried to nudge her away, but she held on tight.

"I'm sorry, Cashe," she said, "I was thinking about what happened and you're right, I should never have said that to Adam in front of you. I don't know why I did it."

"But you *do* know why. You said it because you meant it and because you purposely wanted to hurt me," he said, turning towards her, looking her in the eyes, first staring into her left, then her right, somehow able to contemplate how they were the exact amber color of brown as his.

She kissed him on the mouth, and that ridiculous involuntary smile showed up once more on his face, the kind a baby gives when his father does something silly to it, like lift both of its feet into the air, or make farting sounds by blowing into its belly.

"You don't know him. Adam and I have always said that silly kind of crap to each other," she said, and he saw the ubiquitous hint of a grin form on her face too. "I know it sounded bad, but it really isn't that serious—"

Cashe was beginning to hate that smile and didn't see what was so damn funny. They were like aliens who invaded their conversations without warning. This was a serious matter, and he couldn't let it get away so easily. As he thought about her blatant disrespect, the pang and that awful burning in his chest returned. He was beginning to believe it might never leave. His calm and resolve lie on the surface of chaos, like a thin layer of rock on top of molten lava. It only had to be stirred a little to be swallowed by the heat.

"So, what did you buy at Trader Joe's?" he asked out of plain curiosity, searching for untold information that she might be hiding. It all still seemed a bit *fishy*.

"Nothing," said Kia throwing the gift card on his lap like it was a magical charm with a hex attached to it, the object and focus of their trouble. "We never met. I didn't buy anything. You can have it. I don't want it."

"I don't want it either," said Cashe. He took it and threw it on the coffee table. "It was a gift for you. Go and fucking buy something."

Monica

MOVING IN TOGETHER had once been a fantasy in his naïve thinking which, in theory, appeared flawless, with the exception that some extreme occurrence, like both of them losing their jobs or getting into a car accident, might prevent it from ever continuing on. But now, Cashe was learning that again, he was wrong, and how even the subtleties of life could do just as much damage. He also began to understand that in life, there seemed to be a tit for every tat, and his tat for Kia's tit, surprisingly, came in the form of their attractive neighbor. A woman named Monica.

A week later, he came home in the late evening after a slow shift of driving—only making $55 in tips—and noticed someone he had spotted several times coming in and out of their building, a chick who always used the entrance to the back stairwell, never the front. From several clues he gathered over the past couple of months, he surmised that she was his next-door neighbor and lived with a foreign man who seemed to be somewhat of a recluse. He always caught glimpses of her going inside the apartment beside his on their floor, but rarely, only perhaps once, had he seen her roommate. Through a little investigation and a keen eye, he also found out she drove the navy-blue Audi coupe parked in the rear lot. Like trapped in some divine clockwork, they always magically arrived home at nearly the same time after the end of his shifts.

He wasn't sure why, but from the very first time he laid eyes on her, he had been *drawn* to her in a devilish kind of way. Those fleeting thoughts he'd never speak and those innocent desires he knew would never manifest offered glimpses of pleasure for his *alien smile,* whenever he saw her alone. Comparatively, of course, she possessed those feminine attributes that Kia lacked. Thinner legs. Smaller feet. Auburn hair. She was a bit more stylish. There was a seductive air about her, from the way she approached dangerously close to him whenever they met at the back door entrance, to her teasingly mischievous habit of always turning back to grin as she climbed the staircase. It was like she purposefully took her time up to their floor ahead of him, hypnotically swaying her hips, making his imagination wander and muse about naughty thoughts while lying in bed next to Kia.

Kia was posted at the television on the couch, sitting cross-legged on top of her feet when Cashe came through the back door. He still sensed the uneasiness, mistrust and uncertainty of what exactly she wanted from their relationship, and every time he juxtaposed her invitation for them to move in together alongside planning to go out on a coffee date with another man, it made him only want to get in his truck and drive off into the sunset. To reinforce that the barrier between them still existed and wasn't going anywhere, he ignored her, showered, changed into sweatpants and a T-shirt, then carried a load of laundry into the basement.

The shock of seeing his neighbor taking clothes out of the washer and stuffing them into the dryer offered multifarious considerations, from the extreme of how tiny the red shorts were she was wearing, to him possibly having some type of supernatural power which allowed his bawdy thoughts to become a reality.

"Hi," said Cashe, simply. "How are you?"

"I'm good," she answered heartily with *that* smile. "Tired, but good."

Cashe set down his laundry bag and began loading the only available washer, the one which happened to be right next to the dryer she used, inwardly excited by the fact that he rightfully could stand so near. Though it was the closest he'd ever been to her alone, other than in the stairwell, and the first time he'd ever seen her in the laundry room basically in her underwear, he remained cautious because of the setup. He was no fool. Her roommate or boyfriend—or whoever that guy was she lived with—could show up at any moment.

"My name is Cashe. What's yours?" he said, nervously holding out his hand. "I know you're my neighbor, but we've never formally met."

"I'm Monica," she answered, taking it. "Nice to meet you."

"You live with—is that your boyfriend, I'm assuming? I've seen you two out back a couple of times."

"Actually, that's my husband. His name is Kareem."

He had tossed around the possibility of them being roommates or boyfriend and girlfriend, but for whatever reason, it didn't come to mind that they might be a husband and wife.

"Oh, really? How long have you all been married?"

"We just tied the knot last year," she said, grinning, tilting her head. "He's from Morocco."

"Moroccan—nice," said Cashe, paying attention, but also trying to decide if he should wash his laundry bag too, since he just used it to catch a wild bat. He could tell by her accent that Monica was a hometown girl. Her English was clear as Giant Eagle bottled water.

"My girlfriend and I live together, you've probably seen us around," said Cashe. "She's Egyptian."

"Are you Egyptian too?"

"Me?" he asked, then playfully responded, "No—I'm American. What about you?"

"I'm from here," she said. "I grew up in Sewickley."

"Oh, yeah? I'm from Monroeville."

The similarities between them produced a natural tendency in Cashe to stray, especially after what Kia had said and done. He secretly wished that Monica was also miserable at home, married to an adulterous husband who went on clandestine coffee dates. Perhaps they were meant to be together, right here, right now.

For you, Cashemente. For you.

He continued to speak to his neighbor, after deciding that the laundry bag *should* be washed, and even after loading up her clothes, putting in the quarters and starting the dryer, Monica stood next to him listening, but at the same time it seemed—he wasn't sure—waiting for something to happen. Or, for *someone*, like Kareem or possibly even Kia, to show up. It was a real possibility. And though she wasn't moving, to him, it also looked like she was undulating ever closer in waves of taunting vibrations. He had been tempted to grab her by the waist, turn her around, yank down those hot red short shorts and lace thongs (the kind, he bet, that she most likely was hiding underneath), and start donkey lunging away. Honestly, and he didn't quite understand why, he *wanted* it. Nevertheless, he denied himself, and half-drunk with desire, clumsily put his quarters into the machine and stuck to the business of washing clothes.

He also had received and accepted another clear message after seeing it for the first time there in the dimly lit basement—a sparkling diamond on Monica's left hand. Because she was a married woman, there was no way in hell he would cross that line. It had never been in Cashe to tread upon someone else's property, regardless of how often those thoughts came knocking on the door. It was something his parents had instilled in him long ago, morals and commandments that wouldn't even allow an attempt at anything which might appear remotely close to that kind of a breach. Unfortunately, he couldn't muster up enough control to stop himself from thinking it.

They left at the same time, and after he said goodbye, Cashe watched from behind as she carried her basket up a wonderful three flights of stairs, promising himself that he would never mention to Kia that he had spoken to Monica in the laundry room. *If she wanted to have her little rendezvous, why couldn't he do the same?*

The Keys

THE NEXT EVENING, Cashe and Kia snuggled on the couch underneath a blanket, trying to read the subtitles across the bottom of the TV and at the same time follow the plot of *Le Fantôme*, a French movie she had brought home from the library. They both faced each other, legs and bare feet entwined in a bundle of warmth. Suddenly, Cashe heard someone whistling up the steps in the hallway outside their front door. Whoever it was had oddly stopped, pulled out a set of keys and began jangling them, intentionally it seemed, as if attempting to send some type of signal.

Cashe turned to Kia, giving her a "What in the world?" kind of stare.

"Who is that?" he whispered.

"It's Azazel coming to suck your blood," she said in her best Dracula voice, then laughed out loud, before they heard it again.

He didn't want to move from his comfortable position on the couch. When he started to get up, she held him down with a heavy leg, and put a finger to her lips, motioning for him to stay still. The bubble of peace and serenity they shared quickly burst wide open as the clinking of keys from the other side of the door grew louder and more obnoxious.

The sounds changed from metallic rattling to hoarse coughing, and then, laughter. When he heard the heavy accented cackle, Cashe figured that it might be Monica's husband Kareem and immediately he wondered if she had said something to him about their friendly encounter in the laundry room. Perhaps Kareem was upset because Cashe had spoken to his wife, and this was his childish way of showing disapproval. Kia scooted closer to him on the couch. Cashe's mind froze and entered some kind of purgatorial state of uncertainty. He realized that though the activity in the hallway outside their door *seemed* directed towards them, there was a possibility that it wasn't. Kareem, if that's who it was, might as well have been trying to gain the attention of Monica, and he and Kia just happened to get caught in the crossfire. Perhaps he was just being overly paranoid? What if it wasn't Kareem at all, Cashe thought, but the 'other' neighbors across the hall whom they had yet to meet, or even better yet, just some random stranger standing out there, fumbling his keys and laughing while listening to someone from the other end of his cell phone? He wasn't sure what was going on, but it was making him dizzy. As he considered this, all of a sudden, Kia did something very strange.

"Cashe, look what I found," she said, picking up her phone off the coffee table, no doubt trying to distract him from what was going on *out there*. "I have Tetris on my cell phone."

She quickly hit a few buttons and the game's ringtone chimed loudly into the air. Kia pushed off the couch and began to twist her hips to the music, blocking his view of the television, matching the distraction in the hallway on the other side of their front door with her rotating body. He wondered what Tetris had to do with French movies and loud people in the hallway as she moved around like a belly dancer. It was probably yet another one of those 'foreign things' she sometimes did.

Like for example, she had a habit of asking a question to something he already answered. For instance, he might say, *I'm thirsty*. Then she would immediately ask, *You're thirsty?* She'd say it in a high falsetto, and it always seemed to Cashe that she was talking not to him, but to some invisible Shinigami spirit standing behind him, trying to use his body and emotions like a parasitic host before lifting him off to the netherworld.

"That's nice, Kia," he said, giving his attention back to the TV. "But I thought we were watching a movie?"

Though addictively cute, he was unable to share in her unexpected jubilance. He stayed under the covers stationary, listening to the jingling keys and coughing on one side, while watching Kia dance to the music coming from her phone on the other. It wasn't clear how, and there was no way to prove it, but *he knew* all of this had connections to his conversation with Monica in the laundry room. Now, part of him wished he had never spoken to her, especially if it meant he had to endure what was turning out to be an exotic form of 'psychotic' payback.

"Party pooper," said Kia and after all the giggles and gyration stopped, she disappointingly returned to the couch and Cashe, who sullenly attempted to concentrate on the movie's English subtitles, again. On the screen, a man sat at a table in a café with his girl-friend, while another guy across the aisle made subtle glances at his woman. The lady basked in the moment, being admired by two men at once, both having her cake and eating it too.

When he finally heard a door open, then shut outside in the hallway, Cashe got up, went to the bathroom and locked himself inside. He felt like he needed to get away and be alone, to enjoy a bit of old-fashioned peace and quiet. At the sink, he stared at the mirror into his own eyes, studying his corneas, watching his pupils dilate. After splashing his face with warm water, he saw that the doorknob tried to turn at his side.

"I need to use the bathroom," said Kia. "What are you doing in there?"

"What do you think I'm doing?" he answered.

"Why did you just get up like that and leave?"

"Just give me a minute," he said. "*I'm using the bathroom.* I'll be out in a second."

"Well, hurry up and come back. I want to finish the movie."

Two Chairs

ON A RANDOM AFTERNOON after work, Cashe totally ignored the back steps, and decided to walk around to the main entrance of the building. He really wanted to see if the person with keys would show up again, but after climbing the three flights of stairs to the apartment, he came to his floor and noticed instead, the strangest thing. Two wooden chairs sat back to back in the middle of the hallway, just outside the front door. He thought Kia had most likely been shopping at the Goodwill thrift store on Carson Street, as she often loved to do, or that maybe she bought the chairs from someone on Craigslist. *But why were they in the hallway?* He decided not to bring them in right away, figuring that there must be a good reason as to why she had left them there. He studied their craftmanship for a second, admiring the gloss and noting the patterns of fine grain on the smooth wood.

Inside, the apartment was empty and still. He took off his shoes and placed them on the floor mat beside the door. Arching streaks from his poor job of wiping the top of the coffee table and the screen of the television set while cleaning the day before remained in view, now exposed in the afternoon sunlight. *Next time,* he thought, *it's Windex and paper towels.* He began to think about the chairs again and started to inspect the rooms more closely than he normally would, searching for clues, as if a crime had been committed on the premises. *Detective Cashemente Alvin on the case.*

In the kitchen, he found two mugs left in the sink—a used tea bag in one, a minute layer of water in the other. He tried to recall, but couldn't remember whether or not there had been any dishes in the sink when he left for work in the morning. In the bathroom, two pieces of balled up toilet tissue were nestled on the floor next to the maroon wastebasket, which also seemed odd. The plastic container was empty, still lined with a fresh grocery bag. It was the epitome of laziness, he thought. *So close. Why not just place them in the garbage?* In the bedroom, he could see how Kia had rushed and forgotten to make the bed, and decided she wasn't picking up after herself today. A pair of her Nike tennis shoes tilted sloppily in the middle of the floor.

As he finished examining the entire place, he hung up his coat in the closet, and again heard the sound of tinkling keys on the other side of the front door. He began to believe that it was the infamous jingler again until Kia pushed through, carrying several pale blue plastic bags filled with groceries. Struggling, she shoved the door open with her right foot, and then leaned up against it with her shoulder. Finally, she dropped everything onto the floor, sighed heavily, closed the door and slumped on the couch. She hadn't even bothered to take off her coat, scarf, gloves or hat. Her moves seemed exaggerated, as if she were giving a performance, and Cashe was tickled by this. Nonchalantly, she stuck out her feet and rested her head to one side as if she had just given up the ghost.

"Kia, can I ask you something?"

"What?"

"Why didn't you call and see if I was home before you decided to carry all this stuff up the steps by yourself?" he asked, taking his cell phone out of his pocket to make sure he hadn't turned it off by mistake. "I told you I can help you with these things."

"I don't know," she said, still breathing heavily, "There's more in the truck if you feel like you have to."

He reopened the closet and put his coat back on.

"I need your keys," he said, standing next to her on the couch. She took them out of her coat pocket and dropped them in his hand. As he entered the hallway, he glanced once more at the chairs outside the door. He turned and opened his mouth as if to comment on them but decided to wait until he finished bringing the rest of the groceries up.

Cashe walked outside contemplating how even though Kia drove her father's Ford Explorer, by virtue of his old age and her being a daddy's girl, as she so often pointed out, she was allowed the privilege of unlimited access. It was basically hers. In the back of the SUV, she left four bags, mostly lightweight stuff—a couple boxes of Special K cereal, and cleaning items, including a few packs of green Brillo scrub pads and a bottle of toilet bowl cleaner. He grabbed them all, slipping his hands through the flimsy plastic handles, and carried them upstairs. When he reached the top flight of steps he noticed that the chairs were gone, and when he entered the apartment, he saw that Kia had placed them up against the wall next to the dining room table.

They didn't match anything in the room. The ones in the dining room were made of darker wood and had arched backs. These new pieces of furniture were square. They just didn't belong. There was no place to put them in the living room because there wasn't enough space. And he couldn't see Kia placing them in the bedroom, they would just get in the way. When holding his tongue became unbearable and it was impossible to hold back any longer, he jumped at the chance to finally make his remarks.

"Kia, where'd those chairs come from?" he asked as he set the bags down. He thought about putting the groceries on the new chairs, but he didn't want to touch them, like they had been cursed or had the "cooties" disease.

"Oh, the maintenance man left them for me," she said, taking a box of cereal from the table.

"What?" He stopped in his tracks, wanting to hear more. His suspicion that something screwy *was* going on again had been instantly confirmed. "What do you mean he left them *for you?*"

"The other day I saw him unloading furniture out of a truck and carrying them to the basement storage. The chairs were on the sidewalk at the bottom of the steps and I mentioned that they were cute. I guess he remembered what I said and left them in the hallway for me."

Here it was again—that same familiar splurge of hot burning anger rippled through his chest, and he thought of Adam. He turned his back to her and stepped toward the couch, feeling an urgent need to—break something. It seemed as if the world was closing in on his life with Kia, choking out the very breath of their relationship. Attacks seemed to be coming from every direction. First, from an old friend, and now, the maintenance man.

"I don't like what's going on Kia," he finally blurted out.

"What's going on, Cashe?" she asked casually, brushing off his concern as if whatever speculative theories churning in his mind were nothing but delusions.

"What's going on is—and I'm going to be straight up with you," he promised, "you are opening yourself up to everyone else but me. You act like it's *nothing* for you to talk to your ex-boyfriend and flirt with the maintenance man."

"Cashe," Kia said in the most even and plain tone, while placing the second box of Special K into the cabinet above the sink in the kitchen, "I really think you have some type of mental problem. You need to see a doctor."

He put both of his hands on his hips and just stared at her. She stopped stocking the cabinets, crossed her arms and stood opposite him in the kitchen, pouting.

"Oh, I get it. So *I* need to see a doctor because *you* are telling ex-boyfriends that you love them right in front of my face, and accepting gifts from strange men, absolutely showing no respect to me? It's like—it's like I'm a piece of shit to you or something."

"I don't need this," said Kia uncrossing her arms. She blew past him and headed towards the bedroom.

"Yes you do! You do need to hear every word I'm saying and stop pretending as if it doesn't happen," demanded Cashe, following her down the hall.

"Get away from me," she said, sounding like a sister annoyed by her pesky little brother.

"I just want to talk to you, Kia," he said, placing both hands on his hips again. "But obviously, if you keep acting as if nothing is going on, I can't. I might as well talk to the wall. That's all I seem to do with you anyway—is talk to the damn wall."

Kia paused and turned towards him.

"What did you say?"

"Nothing," he said and left the hallway. Kia went to the bedroom and shut the door. He returned into the living room, sat on the couch and turned on the TV. More than ever, he began to wish he had his own pad again, or even better yet, an underground hideout. A spot he could escape to for a while whenever she started to behave unreasonably. But the not-so-pleasant truth was that he had nowhere to go. He felt like he was trapped inside a hot oven and she had her hand on the dial, steadily turning up the heat.

Kia came out of the bedroom, completely ignored him, went into the kitchen and prepared dinner for herself. It all seemed hopeless. He wanted to just give up. Yet, in the midst of his frustration, he began to entertain a thought, one that offered a bit of calm and made sitting before the television while his girlfriend paid no attention to him in the other room tolerable. He wondered if they would ever marry. It had been a prospect he examined quite a few times and came to the conclusion that he was willing. He just wasn't sure if Kia was ready to take such a step. A lot of their problems, he thought, might be solved if they were. Things could go a lot smoother. Like, instead of sitting on the couch, waiting for his turn to cook in the kitchen, maybe they would eat together more often.

Yet on the other hand, he couldn't overlook her sudden erratic behavior either. He decided that it had something to do with them moving in together. In the past, they argued, but it had been nothing like this. Deep in his heart, he didn't want to think of them being apart, and though it hurt, he *had* to be realistic and consider himself. His mother and father were no longer around to fall back on, and if he and Kia truly were unable to make it through these periods of instability, staying together might not be such a great idea. Numbers began to float through his mind as he added, subtracted and divided how much money he would need to save up to put a deposit and first month's rent down on a new apartment. The names of places in the city arrived as he brainstormed what part of town he could move to alone, and nearby states like Maryland, New York and Ohio surfaced as he fancied about what region of the country he could get into his truck and drive to.

Cashe pondered all of this, looking down into the creases of his hands, observing the patterns made by the hundreds of wrinkles and lines on his skin. He pushed back the dry, overgrown cuticles growing over his fingernails, and noticed how the food from the kitchen was beginning to smell really good.

He turned his attention back to Kia, watching, as she paced back and forth from the dining room to the kitchen, sometimes making quick stops in the bedroom and bathroom while she continued to prepare dinner for herself. She was a woman hard to reject. Her sandals made soft smacking sounds at the bottom of her heels when she exited and entered each room, and it was like intoxicating music to his ears, leading him away from what in this instance seemed to be unreasonable notions of abandonment. Her curved body delicately called him as she placed her dishes on the table.

Come Cashemente. Come here now.

Kia's breasts jiggled under her bra-less T-shirt as she put the food on her plate. Black curls fell out of the grouped bundle on the top of her head with perfect timing, covering her left eye. Cashe was uncontrollably beginning to turn into another man, and like Kia had just waved a magic wand over his head, he began to forget the inflating troubles which arose over the past week. He didn't know if he was hungry or horny.

Yes, an apartment all to himself might alleviate many of their temporary issues, but he had to weigh both the negatives and the positives. He was a reasonable man. Kia wasn't a bad girl, just one who took things to extremes, he convinced himself. Their relationship was either very good or very, very bad. But even in all her pomp and circumstance, he told himself, he wouldn't be entirely fooled. Regardless of how sexy his girlfriend appeared tonight, he knew their problems couldn't be so easily forgotten.

After she sat down and began to eat alone, he went to the kitchen, opened up the refrigerator and searched for something to cook for himself. He didn't have any of the salmon with green beans and almonds she had been munching on for the past five minutes, in fact, there was nothing on his side of the freezer except a frozen pound of ground beef. He matched the hamburger with a box of Hamburger Helper Lasagna, placed the frozen meat on a plate and began defrosting it in the microwave.

Cashe found himself reminiscing about a day, years ago, when they met not too far—and not too close, either—from her father's house in Oakland. Now, she looked no older than she had in college. Her ebony hair, much like his own, if he would ever let it grow, was still the same length as it had been years ago. She even dressed the same, always wearing a prism of different colored tight T-shirts which brought attention to her God-given voluptuousness. Her onyx eyes were still framed with kohl and the sandals she wore continued to expose the perfection of her mauve tinted toenails.

Over and over again he thought of her smile, of how they laughed and joked with one another blocks away from that esoteric man's home, always careful to keep their distance so to not be seen. Even as he made dinner and ruminated over last week's arguing, he still missed her and wanted to be with her again. He was in love and wanted to talk, to communicate the way they used to. All of her correspondence only concerned this evidently intentional separation from him, ever since the whole Adam incident occurred, but he wanted her back.

He leaned up against the sink and crossed his arms in the same manner Kia had done earlier while listening to his barrage of complaints, attempting to find the right words to say—that was— until he was interrupted. On the other side of the back door, he heard the sounds of footsteps and singing rising up the stairwell.

"Hey baby, I'm home!" screamed Kareem. His voice permeated the room.

Cashe could hear him opening the back door to his apartment.

"I missed you, baby!" he said, as clear as day to Kia, it seemed, until at last his giggling voice was cut off by the shutting of his door.

First Accident

CASHE HADN'T SMOKED a cigarette in over a year, but a week later, he sensed the sudden urge to remind himself why he'd quit. Kia was sneaking them again in her father's truck when he wasn't around, he knew, because she had been coming home with the faint smell of Marlboro Lights and marijuana in her clothes. After a certain amount of pressuring, she finally gave in and told him that she was hiding a pack in her purse. While her back was turned, he stole two cigarettes, threw a scarf around his neck and announced that he was walking up to a place called *The Tavern* to have a drink.

"Wait, do me a favor before you leave," she said.

"What?"

"Roll a joint for me."

He sat down at the dining room table while Kia dug through her purse, pulled out an unopened dime bag and Tops cigarette paper and slid them to him. Though he thought about who she might have bought it from—the name *Adam* immediately came to mind—at first, he refused to ask. He didn't feel like getting into an argument tonight, but wanted to know.

"Who'd you buy the weed from?"

"This dude named Kris. I know him from school. He lives on McKee in Oakland.

"I took two cigarettes from your purse," said Cashe.

Kia shrugged. It had been some years since they smoked pot together. In college they did it more often, though Cashe never really liked to get high as much as he enjoyed having a drink. And when he drank, he liked to have a cigarette. He finished rolling two joints, tied up the remainder of the weed into a tight ball, and wiped the surface of the table clean with his hand.

"I'll be back. I'm not going to stay long."

The bar, like many of the other hundreds of drinking holes in Pittsburgh, was decorated with every trinket having to do with the city's sports history imaginable. Autographed pictures of athletes from each of the 'Burg's' three professional organizations, the Steelers, Penguins and Pirates, adorned the top of all the restaurant's tables underneath a thin layer of glass. Even odd objects like cornhole boards, horseshoes and rowing oars hung from the walls. Cashe found an empty stool at the bar, ordered a Heineken, and lit a cigarette. To make the beer last as long as possible, he took tiny sips. Two blondes sat beside him, both emanating dangerous amounts of libido. He tried his best not to pay any attention, and after ten minutes of ignoring them, ordered another beer. Acting on the illicit thoughts entering his head brought on by the alcohol—specifically, a ménage à trois in a room at the Marriot down the street—was out of the question. There was no reason to stay. When he finished the beer and his first cigarette, he left a two-dollar tip next to the empty green bottle and threw his scarf around his neck. Outside, he reached into his breast pocket, took out his final smoke and placed it into his mouth.

What the hell am I doing? he thought. *I'm an athlete.*

He cupped a hand around the flame to protect it from the November wind, then left the Tavern, walking back up a virtually empty West Liberty Boulevard toward home.

Just past the light at Florida Avenue, he took a shortcut through an alley. The dark, narrow path led to a flight of broken concrete steps that declined and ended near the three parking lots at the back of his apartment building. Two were side by side, but the third lot to his far right was raised about ten feet above the middle lot, creating a wall, with no fenced-in barrier to separate them. When people parked their cars in that upper lot, he always thought how easy it would be for someone to put their vehicle in the wrong gear by mistake, or to press the gas pedal instead of the brake and make a *Dukes of Hazzard* jump on top of another car in the lot below. As he approached closer, he saw how that was exactly what must have just happened.

He took one last drag from his cigarette, snuffed it out under his shoe and stared at the scene before him. The end of the normally shadowed passageway was lit by red, white and blue flashing lights. Screeching static from radio dispatch filled the air. Four police officers were posted at the far end of the first lot. He could see their thick black belts and hanging handguns. In the center lot, an ambulance and a mammoth dark red fire truck glistened in the night.

The back door was blocked. He walked forward, not only trying to figure out the best way to get inside the building, but also how to get a clearer view of the accident. A gray Jeep Cherokee had taken a dive over the railless separation and landed on top of Monica's Audi, crushing the roof and shattering all the windows. Both she and Kareem talked to an officer who was holding a clipboard, writing down information. This was the first time he had been able to get a good look at the *intruder* who lived on the other side of the door. Surprisingly, he was short and thin, wore jeans and a T-shirt out in the cold, and had a dark brushing of stubble on both sides of his face.

The commotion forced Cashe to go all the way around to the left side of the building and enter through the front entrance. Monica looked over at him as he passed, but didn't speak. Once inside, he sensed his appetite mixed-in with the excitement from the action out back and the beer. Smelling a tinge of weed smoke in the air and a pungent stick of lemon incense burning in the living room, he went straight to the kitchen, scarf and all, and began to season, then brown slices of raw chicken breasts from the fridge. Staring into the pan, he made careful flips with a worn-down wooden spatula. Kia had unplugged the computer, which she usually kept on the dining room table, and taken it into the bedroom. He heard her close the door just enough to keep out the noise he was making in the kitchen, and decided to wait a moment before telling her what he saw in the parking lot.

After he turned the stovetop temperature to OFF, he crept down the hall. Through the crack in the door, he stopped, like a peeping tom, to admire her. Everything about her was beautiful, in its own way, he thought, from her eyes squinting at the computer screen, to how her breast rested between her arm and stomach as she reclined against the wall while sitting on the bed. He wanted to stare until she knew she was being watched, and waited for the turn of her head to confirm it. Since they moved in together, he *had* gotten to know her better, amassing tidbits of information here and there, picking up on her idiosyncrasies. For instance, he knew her favorite color was purple because a fourth of her closet was stocked with clothes of that particular hue. More than anything she hated waking up early in the morning. The spot she enjoyed most in the apartment was the kitchen window.

Exactly as he hoped, Kia's head turned. She seemed shocked, but he guessed it might have been pretense. *How could she not know that he was gazing at her through the door for the past minute?* Her face conveyed a woman's pleasure—the instinctual satisfaction of being the one adored. He felt dizzy from the beer.

"Why are you standing there staring at me with your coat on?" she finally asked, looking at him, then just as fast, giving her full attention back to the computer resting on her lap. By her bloodshot eyes, he immediately realized she was high.

"I just wanted to talk to you," he said stepping through the door, taking off his coat.

"Oh, *now* you want to talk?"

"I've always wanted to talk. You're the one who's been quiet with me over the past couple of weeks. Was it something I've done?"

He sat on the end of the bed, grabbed one of her bare feet and began rubbing it.

"No. Cashe *never* does anything wrong," she said, mocking him.

"If I've done something to offend you, just tell me. And if I'm wrong, I'll admit it."

"Like I said, Cashe *never* does anything wrong," Kia repeated, heavy with sarcasm.

"I don't want to fight with you, Kia, especially over perfection, because both you and I know that no one's perfect." He kissed her foot.

She didn't respond, but listened, focusing her eyes on the computer screen.

"Anyway, I meant to tell you, you're not going to believe what's happening in the back parking lot," he said, secretly happy that the accident might shut Kareem's mouth, yet at the same time, feeling sorry for Monica and her car.

"What?"

"You know our neighbors next door?" he said, whispering as if they might hear. "Somebody's Jeep dove over the side of the lot and went right on top of their Audi."

"It didn't happen near my truck did it?"

"No."

"Hmm—that's strange."

"Yeah, it is. Their car is probably totaled," whispered Cashe. "I'm just glad I wasn't parked there either because that's a space I usually pull into. Even you've parked there sometimes."

They both fell silent.

"I'm making chicken tacos. Do you want some?"

"No thanks, I'm going to cook something for myself later."

"Fine, I'll leave you alone with your computer," he said and left the room.

Chapter Three

WHEN CASHE ARRIVED at Coccelli's Pizza Parlor at 12:00 P.M. sharp, just as his manager Lenny Smith had asked him to do, he found Rick Morgan and Harry Torrelli, the two daytime drivers, working on a crossword puzzle next to a cryptogram in the *Pittsburgh Post Gazette*. Lenny had said he didn't want Cashe to drive today, but rather put in a couple of extra hours hanging flyers in the area.

"Hey, hero!" called Rick with an upside-down pencil gripped in his right hand. He scrubbed out an incorrect answer from the squares in the eight-down section of the puzzle. "Come 'ere for a second."

The word *hero* stuck him like a prickly thorn; for some reason it was annoying in a way he couldn't quite explain. It was as if Rick was describing him, or naming him, like he was a tree, or a shoe, or a hero submarine sandwich, but not a human being. He might as well have said, "Hey, Fido! Come 'ere. Come on buddy!" Cashe tried his best to ignore the statement, and not address it with a kick to the side, like the guy in the white T-shirt had done to that lady sucking dick in the soon-to-be murder scene.

"Hey guys, what's up?" he asked, smiling. "And believe me, I'm no hero."

"That's not what I heard. It's starting to get around that you saved that lady's life," said Harry.

"No, that's not what happened at all."

"What's a six-letter word for *Lee's Books?* It has C for the first letter and C for the fifth letter."

After a quick glance at the crossword, followed by an enlightened flash of both fresh jubilance and uncertainty, Cashe spoke.

"Comics?" he suggested, and Rick filled in the word. He watched the grin on his face widen.

"Oh crap, why didn't I think of that?" he asked. "Yeah, Stan Lee, Spiderman and Superman and all that shit. Cashe, you're a genius too!"

In the back office, Lenny was turned away from the door, his head level with the computer monitor in front of him. The office décor consisted of unopened boxes of various Coccelli paraphernalia: coupons, flyers, posters, black polo's and beige baseball caps donning the shop's logo—a dark-haired man with a very thick mustache that curled at the ends, holding two large pepperoni pizzas in each hand. In a *Penthouse* calendar above the computer screen, a blonde woman gripped her own breasts with both hands. They were tanned and shiny and polished as if they had just been dipped in Canola oil. She looked down to the top of Lenny's head. Yellow Post-it Notes with the scribbled messages *Jason can't work on (12-13-16)* and *Ted needs next week off,* among other things, hung from a bulletin board to the right.

"What's up, Cashe?" greeted Lenny over his shoulder. "Give me one second here, I'm trying to wrap up next week's schedule."

"Is mine finished yet?" he asked, taking out his cell phone from his pocket.

"Yeah, yeah. Yours is finished," he said and quickly highlighted Cashe's week on the screen. "You work tomorrow, ten to nine, you're off Wednesday and Thursday, and then you work Friday through Sunday, five to close. Is that cool?"

"Yeah, no problem, I just need to put it into my calendar before I forget."

Lenny made a few more additions, stood up from his seat, stretched his back out with a series of popping sounds, yawned and then rested his hand on the back of the swivel chair.

"The flyers you'll need are in that box there, next to the hats," said Lenny. "Wait a minute, I'll get them for you."

Lenny walked over, slid the box out from the metal shelf and pulled a purple pocketknife from his pants pocket. He made a clean cut down the center of the clear strip of tape on top. After opening it, he grabbed a stack of about 300 glossy door hangers advertising the month's specials and handed them to Cashe.

"Let's go take a look at the map."

Cashe followed him out of the office, past Rick and Harry, who were still working on the crossword puzzle, to the front of the shop. To the left of the registers, a large Rand McNally featuring South Pittsburgh hung by four gold thumbtacks.

"This is the area I want you to cover," said Lenny, running a thick pointer finger across the color-coded lines. "Start here at the corner of Pioneer and Fordham. Go all the way down to Queensboro, Bayridge then to Sussex. From there, make your way back up, hitting all the streets in the middle until you come to Berkshire, then circle back to Pioneer. After you finish there, cross over West Liberty. Door hang on Potomac and the streets off of it, Glenmore, Broadway, Connecticut…"

Cashe took out his pen and wrote down the major intersections while Lenny spoke.

"But, whatever you do, don't door hang on Voelkel Avenue. We've been having some problems with a few houses on that street. They called and complained about not wanting any flyers on their doors, so fuck 'em."

Lenny talked like many of the men in the military Cashe had met during his brief stint in the Marine Corps after high school.

It was no secret that his manager served four years in the Armed Forces. He stood out like a sore thumb. Lenny flung a middle finger up at the map as if the entire street had personally insulted him.

"Got it?" he asked, adjusting his Coccelli's hat a little to the left over his forehead.

"I think so," answered Cashe. "I guess I'll see you in a few hours."

"If you run out of flyers, just come back and grab a few extra, but I think what you have should be more than enough. And stay away from people with guns!"

The statement made Cashe smile, but also wince a little as he imagined door hanging on all those streets, walking up and down steps, dealing with the problems of locked gates, secured apartment building entrances, barking dogs and whatever else might make this seemingly simple task difficult.

As he left the shop and began walking toward Pioneer Avenue, he noticed that the weather was perfect for the job. The temperature, a warm 55 degrees for November, made him think he probably could have gotten away with wearing shorts. The clouds created huge shadows over the city blocks, while patches of sun and heat provided a welcomed contrast to the shade in the streets.

Most of the homes he encountered were fenceless yards whose residents were either elderly, away working their day jobs or out of town. A lot of people had already taken down their Halloween decorations or combined them with Thanksgiving pumpkins, turkeys, Indian corn and pilgrims. After the first couple of streets, his eyes *opened*, and he gradually noticed what would have otherwise been insignificant details along the way; red shingles on every other rooftop, the chipping paint on many of the windowsills, and most of all, the different shapes, sizes and colors of *door knobs*. The majority of them were round, making it very easy to hang on. Others had gold or chrome handles protruding to the left or the right and didn't hold the flyers too well.

By the time he finished the first street, he had found a rhythm. At the few locked apartment buildings he encountered, he just slid the advertisements under the door or left a stack sitting any place he could find. To those residents who happened to be working in their yards, washing their cars, or sweeping their porches, he personally handed them the coupons. But he totally avoided homes with dogs, especially the miniature crazy ones that almost leaped over the railing of their gated lawns, violently barking as he passed by.

At Berkshire Avenue, he peeked at his cell phone. It was 2:45 P.M. Instead of finishing the other side of West Liberty, he decided to head back and call it a day. He didn't have to work until the next morning at ten and wasn't sure what he'd do for the rest of the night. Upon his return, he found out that Lenny had left to run some type of errand, so Harry clocked him out for the day.

When he got home, he thought about renting a movie from Redbox or maybe making a trip to Giant Eagle to pick up some snacks. He was surprised to find Kia tucked into the sofa, watching television. Her feet rested atop a pillow on the coffee table. At first, he was excited to see her, but his anticipation quickly faded away when he realized that she wasn't supposed to be there.

"What are you doing home? I thought you had to work today?"

"I quit my job."

"You quit your job! Why?" he asked.

Immediately, he thought of their finances. *Would she be able to pay her half of the rent and utilities without the nearly $100 per shift she earned at the restaurant?* He wondered, too, what might happen if she decided to move out because the apartment had been leased in her name.

"I know you said waitressing wasn't the greatest job, but I thought you were making pretty good money."

He set his keys on the coffee table, went to the hall closet and hung up his jacket.

"I just don't want to work there anymore. I'm going to try to find an office job somewhere or something," she said, turning in his direction. "I'm tired of working around food."

He could hear the uncertainty in her voice mingled with a tinge of fear. She sounded ambivalent, as if she wasn't sure what might come about because of her decision.

"Well, we need to talk," said Cashe. Maybe he was being paranoid again, but it seemed like she was only thinking about herself and not concerned for him in all of this.

"Talk about what?"

"Do you have any money saved up to cover next month's rent?"

"I have enough for next month. Listen, I really don't want to discuss this right now," she said, sounding even more bothered and upset. He wanted to do business. Obviously, she didn't.

"Whether you want to talk about it or not, the fact of the matter is that I need to know what's going on. I guess what I'm asking is, do I need to cover the rent for a while until you get another job? I might be able to pick up some extra hours."

"No, that's not necessary," she simply answered, avoiding the question. "I don't need you to stand there and lecture me like you're my father, Cashe. I know what I have to do."

"I don't doubt the fact that you know how to find a job, or that you won't find something, Kia." He emphasized her name. *Kia*. His voice naturally dropped into baritone, and he tickled himself as he realized that he *was* speaking like an old man.

"And I know I'm not your dad. I just want to understand what's going on."

"Are you deaf? Didn't I just say I don't want to talk about this right now?" she said, getting up from the couch. "Sometimes, you're just so fucking irritating!"

"Kia, I am not your father, I am your boyfriend," he said playfully, but could tell she wasn't in the mood. She was serious.

"That's right, you are *just* my boyfriend. You are not my father and you are not my husband," she answered, crossing her arms.

"Well, I would marry you, but you act like you are ashamed of me or something. You won't even introduce me to your dad."

"I can't. I told you, he is not like American moms and dads— I've *never* brought a guy home before. Do you hear what I'm saying?"

"You talk like you guys are some strict Muslims or something. You don't even wear the hijab."

"I don't wear it because I *choose* not to," said Kia. "Besides, what I wear has nothing to do with him. I mean, he's not as bad as he used to be, but he's sixty-eight-years-old and he's still old-fashioned."

"Well," said Cashe, "I just don't understand why you are so afraid of him."

He stopped, as if someone had plunged a hypodermic needle full of memory into his skull. Again, he reminisced about how Kia would never meet him anywhere near her father's home before they moved in together. They *always* met at his apartment, her place or a neutral location. The closest he had ever come to the house had been one night when he walked her a block away, up to Welsford Street, just around the corner. He remembered holding hands and how she kissed him on the cheek and said, *This is far enough, I don't want my dad to see us together.*

"I can't take this," said Kia, rubbing the sides of her temples.

Predicting the signs of a pending escalation, he decided to end the conversation. Cashe went to the kitchen and searched in vain through a near-empty refrigerator for something to munch on while she rushed into the bedroom. He caught a glimpse of her passing by in a green overcoat, and then heard the front door slam. In a way, he was glad she was gone. She always seemed to do a great job of bringing confusion into a perfectly peaceful situation when she wanted to.

Cashe took a few steps to the kitchen window overlooking Florida Avenue and tugged the string on the side of the horizontal blinds. He waited to see if she really would pull off in the truck or if she was just taking a walk. Maybe she was just bluffing and would return momentarily after smoking a cigarette. After a few minutes had gone by, he watched her SUV bounce out of the driveway from the rear lot and then make a right turn outside the building. Like Lenny's comment at the shop, her leaving did nothing but jab another sharp point of aggravation into his side like a sharp stick. He didn't understand what was going on. Maybe she didn't either. Perhaps leaving for a while would give her enough time to think about things until she could give him a straight answer. *But if that was the case, why couldn't she just say it?*

In the apartment building across the street, a gray cat jumped on the ledge of a windowsill and stretched its spine into an arch, standing tippytoed. It sat down, yawned, and then lazily looked up at Cashe standing in the window. He felt like that cat—trapped and bored, with nothing else to do but stare into an empty street at cars and trucks occasionally traveling through.

The silence of the room began to bother him. The annoyance of it grew until he could no longer take being in the apartment alone. That's when it occurred to him: he didn't have to be there. All he had to do was grab his keys, get in *his* truck, and—go somewhere. Anywhere.

Hastily, he went to his closet and changed into a pair of dark blue jeans and a hooded sweatshirt. He patted his side pockets for his keys, and when he couldn't find them, he went back to make sure he hadn't left them in the khakis he had worn while door-hanging. They weren't there either.

After digging through his entire bag of dirty clothes and searching the living room and the bedroom, the obvious answer to what happened began to bleep into range on his radar. He no doubt had set them on the coffee table.

Kia took them.

Cashe sped-dialed her number on his phone.

"Kia, did you take my keys by mistake or something because I distinctly remember coming home and setting them down on the coffee table?" he asked in a tone suggesting he already knew the answer.

"Yes, I have them," she responded back, plainly.

"Well, I need you to bring them to me."

"Cashe, I'm going to be gone for a while—I just can't do this anymore."

His mind froze. That pure, searing anger rose within him again. He was like a man who had been holding his urine for an hour and had to piss, *right now*. There was no time to talk about it, it was coming; his emotional sphincter was too weak, and he exploded.

"Wha-what?" he stuttered, "What do you mean you are going to be gone for a while?"

She didn't answer.

"I don't think you understand what I just said. *I need my keys!*" His hands were now beginning to shake.

"Cashe, I'm just telling you. I'm leaving for a few days and I'll give you your keys when I return," she said with the most calm, collective voice on the entire planet.

He hated *how* she said it, as though it made all the sense in the world. Like she truly believed that the sky was green. As if, she had every right to take what belonged to him. Listening to her talk made Cashe feel ill, and he knew that she was playing some type of idiotic game.

"So, you're not going to bring them back?"

He also knew that from this point on he had to be careful, both about what he said and how he said it. Forcing the issue might exacerbate her apparent lapse of sanity—yes, he truly understood that stealing his keys counted as a brief episode of craziness—and provoke her to do something even more ridiculous. She might throw them into the Monongahela River or down some dark, cold, flooded gutter to be lost forever. Raising his voice would only make the situation worse.

He began to weigh his options with instinctual, life threatening rapidity. No, she wasn't the type to skip town for a few days. She hadn't even packed any clothes, unless this was already planned out and she had prepared a suitcase in the back of her truck earlier in the day. Although she *did* quit her job, if she was telling the truth. Now would be the opportune time for her to leave. *But why would she steal his keys?* It didn't add up. Cashe decided to take a gamble and call her bluff.

"No."

"Fine, Kia. Whatever. That's fucked up, but whatever. See you when you get back," he said and hung up the phone.

He went to the kitchen, leaned against the wall and stared across the street at the gray cat, still in the window. Its head jerked back and forth at every small movement: a piece of paper floating in the wind, sparrows chasing one another like teeny fighter jets, toddlers walking beside mothers pushing empty strollers.

Cashe felt like Kia's pet, trapped in her little carrying cage. A giant man-toy. He knew that if he decided to exit the building, both the main and rear entrances would lock behind him. To get back in, he would have to ring a neighbor's buzzer. The doors to his truck were also locked and he didn't have a duplicate key. The more his mind toiled over every detail, every choice, every possibility to escape this circumstance, the more he wanted to call her again. He couldn't take it any longer. Knowing that she was his only way out, he pulled the phone from his pocket and dialed her number. She answered immediately and he reminded himself to speak tactfully.

"Hello?" Kia answered, nonchalantly.

"Listen, I know you said you need to leave and go out of town for a while, or whatever. But you have me stranded here like I'm in jail or something. Could you *please* come back and give me my keys before you drive too far away?"

His voice was composed, but on the inside, he wanted to reach a hand through the phone, grab her arm, twist it behind her back and forcibly take what was his.

"Like I said before," she said punctually, almost sounding as though she were singing the words, "Whenever-I-get-back-in-town, I-will-give-you-your-keys."

Cashe's hidden inner stockpile of combustibles detonated.

"Bring back my fucking keys, you fucking bitch!" he hollered, holding his cell phone in front of his face, yelling into it. "If you aren't here in one fucking hour, I swear to God I'm going to take all of your shit out of the closet, throw it into the fucking dumpster out back and fucking burn all of it. Don't fuck with me, Kia! You're fucking with the wrong person. I swear I will burn down this whole fucking apartment building!"

"Are you threatening me?" she asked. "Is that a threat?"

"You heard what I said," he answered. "Just bring back my keys."

The line had been crossed, and now he began to feel like he had spoken too much, too hastily, and too foolishly. He wanted to take back his words, and he *knew* she would somehow use what he had said as ammunition against him.

"If you touch any of my shit, I'm calling the police on your ass," she said, confirming his unction, and then hung up the phone.

The room, again silent, began to come alive, as he waited for what seemed like an eternity. The furniture stared back, tsk-tsking him while he stood there, guilty and scared of what might happen because of his foreboding declarations. But she started all of this. She had stolen from *him*.

He went to the kitchen and began snacking on Saltine crackers and then an orange, re-thinking every course of action from all possible angles, just in case he had missed something. In the opposing building, the gray cat had disappeared from the window, but now, he could see two black and white police cars parked back to back in the street. Their lights were off.

Kia's truck was third in line and he watched as his girlfriend hopped out of her vehicle. She paused while one thick-mustached, and another clean-shaven cop met her at the entrance of the building.

Cashe stepped away from the window because he didn't want the policemen to look up and see him spying on the scene. There was really nothing he could do, except maybe try and make a run for it, but he knew that would just complicate matters worse. So instead, he sat down on the couch and waited for them to come up the stairs and inside.

A few minutes later he heard a police radio echoing through the hallway outside, and then keys unlocking the deadbolt. For the briefest of moments, he thought about going against his own decision to stay and making a quick last-minute dash through the back door.

"There he is," said Kia, pointing to Cashe, who sat cross-legged with his arms folded, staring at a blank television screen. "He said he was going to burn down the building and throw all of my stuff in the dumpster!"

The cops looked him over, then turned their attention to the apartment. They surveyed the room, examining the couch and furniture, then peeked down the hall toward the bedroom.

"Can we talk in the other room?" the clean-shaven cop asked Cashe, motioning to the open bedroom door.

"Sure," he said, and the officer followed him into the room.

"What's going on here? Your girlfriend said you threatened to destroy her property. That is your girlfriend, isn't it?"

A smile grew on his mouth, those damn aliens taking over again, and he tried, unsuccessfully, to hold back a giggle. The question sounded so cynical. In a way, he didn't want to take ownership of her, and to be honest, right now, he wasn't so sure.

"Yes, she is, but I only said that because she stole my keys and said she was taking them with her out of town."

The cop went back into the living room and asked Kia if she had them. She dug into her purse and handed the keys to him. The cop, in turn, gave them back to Cashe. He noticed the keys to the apartment were missing from the ring.

"What do you have in this apartment that belongs to you?"

"Everything in the hall closet is mine. I have some food in the kitchen and some stuff in the bathroom, but that's about it," Cashe answered quickly.

The mustached officer came to the entrance of the bedroom door.

"She says she wants you to leave," he said, "So you have to go."

"What do you mean I have to go?" asked Cashe, and that nasty surge of disappointment rushed in. "I've been paying half the rent, half the utilities and my name is on the mailbox. What do you mean *I have to leave?*"

"Is your name on the lease?"

"No."

"Well, if your name isn't on the lease and she wants you out, then you have to leave. If you don't, we'll arrest you and you can plead your case before the magistrate."

Cashe looked past the officer at Kia, who was standing in the living room near the door. She looked away from him. He hated her and the fucking cop.

"I'm not so sure about that," said Cashe directing his gaze back to the police officer and his mustache. "I think I have some rights. I've been here for several months, and you're telling me, just like that, all she has to do is call the police, say I don't want my roommate here anymore and I have to go?"

"Like I said, I will arrest you *right now*, and you can take it up with the magistrate. Or you can just leave."

"Fine, I'll go," Cashe said finally. "Excuse me."

He brushed past the officer, opened the hall closet door and inventoried everything inside. There was a black crate where he kept his shoes, a blue sleeping bag, two empty gym bags, and shirts and pants hanging on wooden hangers. He pulled off his clothes, folded them as tightly as he could and stuffed them into both bags. After that, he went to the bedroom and took *his* pillow from his side of the bed, returned to the closet, grabbed his sleeping bag, and wrapped it around the pillow. In the bathroom, he packed a towel, a washcloth, a bar of soap and all of his toiletries. Something told him to check his backpack. He quickly unzipped the tiny pocket on the side. There, he saw the small box with the engagement ring.

Fucking ring. I don't know why I even bought it.

Cashe was surprised at how quickly he had managed to pack most of his things. It wasn't everything, but he didn't care. He just wanted to leave. As he threw both bags over his shoulder, tucked the rolled-up sleeping bag and pillow under his arm and attempted to lift the milk crate, the mustached cop came to his side.

"I'll help you with that," he said, and took the crate.

Cashe let him carry it.

The officer followed him down the back stairwell and out to the parking lot near his truck.

"Is there anything else you need to get from the apartment?" asked the cop after setting the crate down.

"No," answered Cashe.

Kia appeared on the side of the building with the clean-shaven officer. The mustached cop reached out a hand to him, as if a business deal had just been closed. Cashe instinctively took it, and thanked him for carrying his shoes. But as the officer walked away, he regretted what he had done.

Assholes.

After fitting the sleeping bag, two gym bags and the milk crate into the passenger side of the pickup, he started his truck and the strangest thing happened. It was something that seemed so far away and odd, but yet somehow, so right for this occasion. He thought about the prophet and his dogs in the park.

Chapter Four

CASHE'S MIND RACED as he made a right turn off Florida Avenue to Cedar, and then a left onto West Liberty Boulevard, passing through the pristine shops and businesses of Mount Lebanon. Unearthly yellows, oranges and purples dominated the evening skyline and illuminated the road and sidewalk, contrasting the shadows cast by the maple trees along the street. These details he normally overlooked, but now, they seemed to scream for his attention.

Where will I sleep tonight? What will I eat? How will I be able to work in the morning?

Just thinking about it all proved too heavy, so he parked at the Sunoco Gas station on Kelton Avenue until he could decide what to do. He shifted the truck into neutral, took the keys out of the ignition and sat for a moment, facing the storefront.

He wasn't super hungry, but could eat. Though he had *sort of* warmed his belly less than an hour ago before the cops showed up, he still felt like he wanted something, but didn't know what. It crossed his mind that he might need to go to the grocery store and stock up on chips, sandwiches and bottles of juice in preparation for a night of camping out in the truck. Perhaps, even for a few days. The next thing which occurred to him was that he didn't know how much money he had on his possession or in the bank, so he reached over into the black milk crate in the passenger seat, pulled out his burgundy checkbook, and found the number on the last page of the register. *$345.96.* After tucking it away, he leaned forward toward the steering wheel and took out the wallet from his back pocket. Inside was a twenty-dollar bill. There was no way in hell he'd find an apartment with less than $400 anytime soon, so that was out of the question. Hotels would just eat his money up, and he couldn't think of a single person he was comfortable enough asking to stay with for a few nights. Ironically, before they died, both his mother and father told him he should be careful about living alone in a city with no family around. They said one day he might need people. *But what good would that advice do now?* Fortunately, there were some positives working in his favor. He had a job. At 10:00 A.M. he had to be at work. Tomorrow's tips would add money to his stash and give him more time to figure out a plan.

Staying the night in the truck wasn't a bad idea, but not having a place to wash in the morning injected a tinge of depression into his system. In the front seat of the pickup, he began moving his belongings around as a test to see if he could find a comfortable sleeping position. He pushed up the center armrest, placed the milk crate on the passenger side floor and then put the gym bags on top. After contorting his body by lifting both legs from under the steering wheel, he laid on his side across the length of the cab. With the folded sleeping bag under his head, he guessed that one or two nights like this wouldn't be so bad. His mind was made up; he wouldn't check into a hotel and spend money he might need later. Now, he just needed to find a place to park.

Cashe sat up, started the truck, and drove back up West Liberty toward the apartment. He thought about Kia and wondered what she might be doing. The evening was beginning to set in, and the streetlights glowed in blurry halos that shot beams at the windshield. For the heck of it, he decided to drive past—if only for a look. As he approached, the warmth of the bedroom light permeated from the window, through the blinds and into his truck. It all seemed so surreal. Maybe, if he had just kept his mouth shut and stopped preaching to Kia, things would be different.

He slowed down and looked up to the third floor again. Secretly, he hoped to see the silhouette of Kia's head and shoulders appear, but knew it was time to break away from her. He had to force himself not to call. After the terrible thing she had done by violating her trust and commitment, there would be no turning back. At least not yet.

Quickly putting the thoughts of reversal away, he instead changed his focus to getting some food. The first and easiest place that came to mind was McDonald's. He drove to the one a few blocks away from Coccelli's, and as he passed the shop, entertained the idea of picking up a small pizza instead. Only he didn't feel like bull-crapping with the guys tonight; he just wasn't in the mood. As he cruised by the storefront, he saw Harry on the phone taking an order. Tomorrow he'd show up to work like everything was normal. What happened between him and Kia was really no one else's business and he wanted to keep it that way. And even if he had ever decided to talk about his personal problems, he knew the guys would do nothing but give him false sympathy, then afterwards shy away like he had some type of disease.

At McDonald's, the line seemed unusually long in the drive-thru lane, so he chose to find a space and go inside. He pulled a little too close to a beige Buick, and tried not tap the door as he slid out into the cold parking lot. As he climbed the ramp to the entrance, he saw that the restaurant wasn't really crowded at all.

In the far end of the seating area, a young father and his wife fed ketchup-tipped French fries to a sloppy-faced little boy and his older sister. All their coats were balled up both in-between and on either side of their booth. They looked like birds sitting in a giant nest made of opened cheeseburger wrappers, napkins and straw-topped soft drink containers. On the other side of a partition that ran through the middle of the diner sat an old man. He had a long, silver mustache, wore a red and white flannel shirt, blue jeans and sipped on a milkshake. The old man seemed to look past, yet in the general direction of another elderly guy two booths away, who wore a green sweater, had a chiseled shaven face, and slowly munched on a Big Mac. At first glance, it appeared as if the two were engaged in a staring contest or possibly studying one another. Like the man with the mustache had been counting the number of times it took the other guy to chew and swallow a bite of his sandwich.

As Cashe glanced around the room, everything began to remind him of what happened earlier with Kia. The two men made him think of the police officers who made him leave, and the people in the booth taunted him with thoughts of the family he might never have.

"I can help you here," said a young cashier, who bore a strong resemblance to Kia, only a younger version. Tonight, it would be impossible to get her out of his mind.

After ordering a combo meal, which consisted of a quarter-pounder with cheese, fries and a large sprite, Cashe waited a few moments for his order to be brought out. The Kia look-alike arrived at the counter and slid him a brown tray. Under his food, a flyer advertised a new cherry pie. He went to the condiments table and filled five small white paper cups with ketchup, then sat down near the back on the same side as the two old men who were engaged in the staring contest.

The restaurant seemed oddly quiet. He wondered if somehow God had silenced these people in some sort of divine way to give him a hint of peace, to make up for all the commotion he experienced earlier. Again, he thought of Kia, and wished he wasn't in this situation. It was all so unexpected, something that never could have been planned for ahead of time. Now, he was stuck with no place to sleep or shower, trying to figure out what to do with his life. Everything had just blown up, all at once. In a way, he wanted to blame her, but he knew it wasn't all her fault. He kept pushing when she said she couldn't take any more. Regardless, he wished she might have been more reasonable.

The fries were hot and salty and addictive, and he couldn't stop dipping them in the ketchup repeatedly, eating and chewing. He didn't even break to take a bite from the quarter pounder or sip his drink. Cashe looked at his cell phone to check the time. It was 8:30 P.M. and a heavy cloak of lethargy enveloped him like a sweater, the kind of tired that often arrives after consuming a good meal. He wanted to curl up in a bed, pull the covers over his head and sleep more than he ever had in his life. And he knew he longed for it only because he couldn't.

His body didn't want to move from the comfort of the cozy dining area, but he forced himself up anyway. After dumping all the empty containers and wrappers inside the trash flap of the garbage can, he placed the tray on top and slowly made his way back down the ramp and across the parking lot to his truck.

All of a sudden, he remembered, but didn't understand why *now*, how in the hurry of leaving the apartment, there were a *lot* of things he had left behind. They were random items he wouldn't need to use in the near future (and honestly didn't want)—garbage bags he had bought a few days before at Wal-Mart, a bottle of dish detergent, though he didn't have any dishes to wash, and all of his food in the refrigerator and cabinets. If Kia wanted to play rough, he wouldn't be giving her any free gifts. No, everything that was his, no matter how small, he wanted back. Though he said he wouldn't, resisting the urge *not* to call her was too hard to deny, like those damned McDonald's fries. Now, he had an excuse. He reached into his pocket, sped-dialed her cell phone number, and listened to the ringing on the other end of the line.

"Hello," Kia answered after the first ring, sounding very close, as if she were sitting right next to him in the truck.

"Kia, this is Cashe," he said, purposefully wanting to go directly to the heart of the matter, "There are some things I left in the apartment that I need, so I'll be there in fifteen minutes to pick them up."

"Come by tomorrow, and I'll put whatever you want to take outside at the front entrance of the building," she answered plainly.

"Why can't I come over now? I'm close and it will only take fifteen minutes to pick up my stuff and leave."

"Like *I* said, come by tomorrow and I will have it outside waiting for you," she said coldly.

His demands were powerless. He had to acquiesce to her terms and agreed to come back in the morning. The family that had been eating on the other side of the restaurant came out into the parking lot. They were all bundled up now, in hats and scarves and hoods tugged over their heads. As he watched them, he promised himself that he would never again give someone the upper hand with anything that belonged to him.

Cashe started the ignition and made his way down familiar streets in South Pittsburgh, recalling from his mental database areas he frequented while delivering pizzas at work, searching for the perfect place to park his truck. On the radio, he heard the DJ say that there was a chance of an inch of snow overnight. *Great*, he thought. *Perfect timing.*

He turned into a large complex off Greentree Road named *Carriage Park Apartments*. About a month before, in the early evening, he knocked on the door of a distinguishingly attractive woman with a heavy Indian or Middle Eastern accent who lived there. He remembered waiting for her to answer, how the food weighed heavily in his left arm, and thinking she *intentionally* and *purposefully* ignored him after pushing the bell a second and third time, yet receiving no response. He had been positive that someone was inside because the door was slightly ajar.

Just as he reached into his pocket to take out his cell phone to dial the number printed on the receipt, a husky, honey-skinned woman with flowing black hair came into view on the other side of the screen door. She wore a red sari trimmed with gold and seemed elaborately sophisticated in a way that fascinated him. After he gave her the food, she said slowly, with thick enunciation, "An dis iz for *you*," then proceeded to place a five-dollar bill in his hand.

Cashe not only envisioned the woman clearly, but even more so, could recollect what he saw that evening as he climbed back into his truck and exited the parking lot. A PAT bus stopped at a shelter near the road and droves of people who looked like *him* were coming home from work in professional business attire. Dark-haired, tan men held briefcases and women with wheat colored skin, wearing heels and colorful, professional pantsuits, dispersed in different directions throughout lot, perhaps finishing up after a long day's work. Of all the places he delivered to, he had never seen so many of *these* kind of people in one place on this side of the city. He realized that the yellow and brown residents could have been from any exotic and mysterious nation of the world—India, China, Mexico, Egypt, Tunisia, Turkey, Israel or even Palestine.

But what were they all doing here?

As he slowly drove around the lot, searching for a concealed parking space to pull into, he pondered those people who came off the bus that day on that faraway evening, and the memory made him feel even more frustrated and sad. The thought reminded him of Kia.

The wind pushed up against the windows of the truck as he completed a circle around the complex, still unable to find a place he was totally satisfied with. All the empty spaces had been too close to the buildings and he didn't want to draw attention to himself. The last thing he needed was someone passing by in the morning, peering through the windshield and seeing the eye sore of him splayed across the seat of his truck underneath a sleeping bag.

In the rear of the lot, near a large oak tree, he eyed an empty parking spot a good distance away from the apartment buildings and decided that it was there where he would park. He checked the time on his phone and saw that it was getting late: 11:14 P.M.

Snowflakes began to fall from the sky like white feathers spilling out of a torn pillow underneath the head of God. Cashe reached for the sleeping bag in the cramped hole below the glove compartment, took off his shoes and jacket, untied the string and slid in feet first, lifting the soft lining up to his neck. He folded his pillow in half and rested against the driver's side door.

Lying motionless, he faced the steering wheel and listened to a whistling sound coming through the crack in the cab window behind him, shifted positions, rubbed his legs together and stuffed his hands in-between his thighs to keep warm. The fluffy snowflakes had quickly covered most of the glass on the windshield and he gratefully anticipated a little snow piling up. Now, if someone did happen to pass by in the morning, they wouldn't be able to see that he was inside.

Sleeping in his truck had always been an enjoyable getaway, ever since he paid cash for the vehicle from a used car salesmen three years before. As recently as last summer, he and Kia had gotten into one of their stupid arguments about who was taking up more space in bed one evening when he had decided to sleep over. In utter frustration, he stood on top of the mattress with his head close to the ceiling in the early hours of the morning, nudged her on the behind with his bare foot and pointed out the problem. She had gobbled up more than two-thirds of the bed, leaving him with only a sliver of space between her body and the edge. He complained that his leg and arm hung off the side, when all the while she slept comfortably in a fetal curl. During the entire night, her buxom buttocks had steadily scooted him away.

He was so upset about her indifferent attitude when she refused to move that after snatching a pillow, he got into his truck and drove straight to Washington's Landing, a small, peaceful, marina island in the middle of the Monongahela River, just across the 31st Bridge. In his own stubbornness—later he second-guessed the rationale of his decision to come there instead of just going home, but he had been particularly morose about his parents being gone that night and wanted to be anywhere far away—he nevertheless crept into the parking lot underneath the bridge and lie outside in the bed of the truck. The air that summer night was just the right prescription, humid and soothing like a sedative; the crickets below and the stars above were like a lullaby, and his only worry was that some curious woman walking her dog, or possibly a police officer patrolling the area might interrupt his rest.

Cashe's thoughts drifted away inside the cab of the Ford Ranger as the snow continued to fall, and he digested those memories until the glow of his consciousness dimmed and he was floated off to sleep.

The Fire

HE DREAMT THAT A fire engine steered into the lot. Its sirens blazed and its flashing red and white lights illuminated the façade of the apartment building he had parked next to. In the dream, he looked through the rear window of the cab, and behind him he saw the chrome wheels and the polished red sides of the truck. Nearby were an ambulance and a few police cars. Static voices from walkie-talkies echoed across the tranquil court. The low murmur from a crowd of people standing in groups, some in coats, others in their pajamas, created a steady hum amid the background noise.

At first, he thought all the attention had been for him, as if everyone somehow knew he had no business sleeping there. Perhaps, someone had called the cops, and everyone had come out to see. But then he understood. Behind the fire truck, smoke billowed dark black clouds into the air. On the third floor of the building across the square, fire danced and jumped and lit up the sky. He could hear the snaps, crackles and pops from inside the cab.

He found himself opening the door and walking toward the crowd. It had stopped snowing in his dream. In the long-sleeved T-shirt he wore, he felt abnormally warm, as if the burning building had somehow made the outside temperature rise 20 degrees higher. Two women at the far end of the lot stood close to one another—one, in a black sweater, had a yellow shawl wrapped around her neck and the other wore a red pajama top and bottom. They whispered to each other, like women do, but as he approached, they stopped talking and turned their heads to look back at him. The shock of seeing their dark, lifeless eyes surprised him, but he kept going. Moving in what seemed like slow motion, he stepped in-between them, and they parted, allowing him space to get closer to the fire. He wove in and out among the people, giving "excuse me's," as he placed his hand on one person's back and on another's shoulder, making his way to the fore. On the side of the building, a crane had lifted two firemen high off the ground. One held a taut hose, and the other a chrome-plated spout as they sprayed a stream of white water onto the rooftop.

When he reached the head of the crowd, he saw an officer guarding a roped-off police line.

"You can't come in here," the cop said.

Cashe noticed his big, black glossy eyes. Similar to the two women, they had the blankness of an animal, like a dog or a deer. It was as if nothing lived inside of him, his pupils only serving as cameras, monitoring the scene for—*what?* The restriction sounded like he couldn't enter—not because he wasn't an officer or a fireman— but because he wasn't one of *them*. One of those empty people.

On the ground, lying on top of clean white sheets, were seven burnt corpses. Pink flesh peeked through the charred skin of their legs, hands and feet. The sight of them didn't shock Cashe as much as it had the women and others who stood by, as they cried into balled up tissues and held on to their friends and loved ones. He looked away from the bodies and glanced up to the third floor as one of the windows exploded from the heat inside.

"Back up!" screamed the police officer, pointing to a man who tried to cross the yellow tape separating the gathering and the burning building, "You! Get back on the other side!"

It began to snow and in all the commotion, he noticed someone standing across the police tape where everyone else wasn't allowed to go, leaning on the right side of the burning building. The man was all alone except for two dogs resting on the lawn beside him. It was the prophet with his panting German Shepherds. Facing the crowd, seemingly unaffected by the fire and activity in the parking lot before him, he looked directly at Cashe, smiled, and then pointed to a black bird overhead in the sky. A barely noticeable raven emerged from behind the building, cawed, and then alighted on the limb of a tree rooted at the edge of the lot. Seeing a bird flying in the middle of the night seemed odd, more than the previous sequence of events, and even more ominous than noticing the prophet. After Cashe watched the bird land, he saw something even more bizarre—a little black boy, dressed in what looked like a coppery, one-piece shiny robe, seated all alone on a thick bough hidden among the other crisscrossed limbs of the tall oak tree. The sight made Cashe forget about the fire, the prophet and the raven. He sensed a laugh coming on. For some reason, it initially looked comical.

But the feeling of humor quickly abated, and a chill traveled through his entire being when the boy looked at him. At first, he too, like the prophet, faced the crowd, but when the child turned his head toward Cashe, his eyes seemed to reflect the flames, or, were they too on fire? His stare and posture—the boy listed slightly forward, elbows bent with his hands on his thighs—was laced with aged seriousness, and Cashe thought it particularly abnormal coming from someone with such a young face. Then, as *Cashe's* eyes opened further, it all made perfect sense. Initially, the boy appeared to be partially wrapped underneath a thick quilt, part of it kind of sticking up behind him like a headrest, but Cashe realized that it wasn't a blanket at all. Black wings covered him, folded above either side of the child's shoulders, slowly twitching every now and then apart from his stoic body, as if trying to settle into the most pleasant position.

Oh my God, it's an angel!

The angel looked away from Cashe and turned his gaze to the building, took a heaving deep breath and blew. The smoke coming from the rooftop shifted direction as a blast, the color of cigarette smoke, streamed from his mouth and put out the fire inside the building. To everyone else, it was just a gust of wind, but Cashe could see its source.

The Raven

HIS MIND WENT BLANK, like someone had hit the power button on the TV of his brain, and Cashe woke from his dream, not knowing where he was.

"Kia," he said to no one, "I wonder if I should try to go over there?"

He opened his eyes and saw his own breath as he exhaled. The windshield was totally covered with snow, and the bluish-white glow of the morning highlighted the passenger side window. Gradually, he understood that he wasn't standing in a warm parking lot, nor underneath the covers in bed at the apartment on Florida Avenue, but rather sprawled on the seat of his truck inside a sleeping bag. Cashe laid back on his pillow and stared at the ceiling of the cab. The dream still lingered, clouding his reflexes, and for some reason he was frightened, in a mystified type of way, as if he had just been notified of some impending doom, certain that something bad was about to happen. He had never dreamt of an angel. Usually, by the time he was out of bed and into the shower, his dreams disappeared, but this one was different. Its details stuck around, and he wasn't sure if he had totally come out of it—if that were possible.

He thought about how he had always envisioned angels. From his manipulated understanding, (due to watching too much TV and reading too many comic books), they were the size of linebackers on professional football teams and had polished swords in their hands. They were enormous winged creatures who were invincible to mankind, perhaps like dinosaurs. But what he saw had been no older than a twelve-year-old boy. The dream was saturated and soaked with great power and importance—it wasn't just an unconscious vision, but a *communication*. It gave him the kind of feeling that came from listening to really good music after smoking a joint, leaving him drunk and wide open. He could barely move.

Cashe reached into his pocket and took out his cell phone to check the time. The display read 7:45 A.M. and he remembered that he had to work at Coccelli's at ten. Suddenly, he began to think of all the simple, yet necessary preparations to do before arriving to work, as if the dream had robbed him of the realities of his responsibilities, all the little things he had taken for granted before his girlfriend threw him out. Not only did he have to wash and dress, he also had to eat something and then figure out what to do about the few belongings stored in the cab of his truck. And, of course, he couldn't forget about picking up the rest of his stuff from Kia. He peeled the sleeping bag off his body and searched for his gray zip-up hoodie and shoes. When he opened the door of the truck, powdery white snow flew into his face.

As soon as he stood to his feet, something dark and shiny grazed his head and he instinctively lowered his body to the ground. Immediately, he thought of the bat that had come into the apartment. The sound of whatever it was that had flown by was like the shaking out of a handkerchief. The black shape hovered in the air, and then swooped over the rooftop of the building that had been burning in his dream. A raven. When it landed in the tree where he had seen the angel, another distant recollection came back into his memory—seeing the prophet, just like in Schenley Park with his dogs beside him, underneath the shade of the tree.

They told me to tell you that Azazel is coming for you.

With his heart pounding hard in his chest, Cashe slowly meandered across the parking lot—his hands dug deep into his pockets—and scanned the buildings, revisiting the front entrance where the firemen had carried the burnt bodies, and the place on the sidewalk where they had laid them. The third-floor window, broken by the intense heat and flames, was now intact.

He walked over to the large oak and looked up at the bird. It had perched on the exact same limb where the angel sat, now flapping its wings and screeching as if it were *calling* down to him. Around Cashe, a few people began exiting the buildings on their way to work, arriving to scrape the snow and frost off the windows of their cars. To avoid bringing too much attention to himself, and before anyone would begin to wonder why he was staring up into a tree at a screaming bird, he calmly turned around, went back across the lot and got into his truck.

In the driver's seat, he gazed at the windshield, dumbfounded and stunned by the feeling that continued to envelop him, unable to move, speak, or fully process what was happening. The caked-up snow and ice had made crystalline sparkles across the glass, so he reached for the scraper behind him. He unlocked the latch of his seat, tilted forward, and then grabbed the handle to wiggle it free.

Back outside, he immediately began to blend in with the scenery. A few cars down, a woman wearing a shiny bronze coat and black earmuffs dug into her windshield, spraying ice chips in every direction. *The angel's colors.* After he finished clearing his windows, he started the truck, turned on the defrost and drove out of the parking space.

Only about an inch of snow had fallen, and there were several places in the tiny yards of the buildings and along a narrow field near the entrance of the apartment complex where greenish-brown grass still peeked out from the frosty covering. As he came near the exit, the truck's engine began to stutter. He looked at the gas gauge and saw that the needle rested in the middle of the "E." Filling the tank had been yet another task he forgot to accomplish in the chaos of the past two days. Though he was just at the gas station, he hadn't thought to buy any.

Cashe coasted down the steep decline of Greentree Road, thanking God for hitting all the green lights while thinking of how the raven sat on the very branch where he saw the angel in his dream.

My Lord, a real angel.

As he turned left at the bottom of the intersection, he envisioned it over and over again; the black little boy, his clothes and twitching wings; the fog which flowed from his mouth and how it quenched the flames of the burning building like a giant fire extinguisher.

The truck jerked and the engine spat as he pushed the pedal all the way to the floor and made a left into the Sunoco gas station at the bottom of the hill. He parked at pump 5, and everything seemed to come together in one perfect place and time. His tank even faced the correct side. He made it.

Through the storefront window, he saw the answers to all his immediate problems—a bathroom sign where he could wash up, and a stand decked with coffee and pastries from which he could buy breakfast. As he pumped the gas, he examined his surroundings for any other signs or weird manifestations which might appear from his dream.

Everything seemed normal: two construction workers wearing flannel shirts readied themselves for a morning job by filling large stainless steel thermoses with hot coffee inside the store, and a red-headed woman in a beige overcoat pressed the buttons at the pump opposite him, making loud beeps on the electronic display screen. A stream of traffic flowed intermittently on Cochran Road in front of the station. The splash of melting snow in the street magnified the sound of passing cars.

Cashe finished pumping, got in his Ranger, backed up, and then pulled into an open parking space beside the store. He reached for his gym bag, stuffed it with a change of clothes, a washcloth and a bar of soap. When he stepped out of the truck, he tried to appear as composed as possible as he went through the glassed double doors and into the bright, rainbow filled aisles. Two twenty-something women wearing jeans and Sunoco smocks rang up customers in a closed-in booth near the entrance. After perusing the candy aisle, he went to the coffee and tea island to quickly examine what he might buy for breakfast, then inconspicuously made his way to the unisex bathroom near the back. He felt a sense of relief when he found the door unlocked, knowing he wouldn't have to wait in line, or awkwardly ask one of the attendants for some bathroom key attached to a miniature block of wood.

Inside, a framed painting on the wall portrayed a lonely woman under a tree. She sat on a blanket, resting under the shade next to a flowing stream, wearing a white dress and a brimmed straw hat, with flowers sticking out of its purple band. From her basket, a cornucopia of diverse fruits, vegetables and breads spilled out onto the spread, overflowing at her side.

The colors in the painting, too, seemed superfluously enhanced like everything else that morning—the chalky blue sky, the cloudy grays in the water and the spring greens in the lawn next to the stream all beamed with realism. He thought the painting was much too pretty to be in the bathroom of a Sunoco gas station and that the woman shouldn't have been having a picnic all alone. It reminded him of Kia all by herself back at the apartment, and he suddenly hated that she was making him go through this.

He locked the door, still drunk from the dream, took out the folded clothes tucked inside his bag and placed them on top of the paper towel dispenser on the wall opposite the painting. Carefully, he tore several lines of brown paper towels from the dispenser and made two layers on the dirty floor near the sink. When finished, he stripped naked, hung his jeans and jacket on the gold handle of the door behind him, stood on top of the paper towels and washed, then rinsed himself from head to toe. After putting on clean boxer shorts, khakis, a T-shirt and socks, he folded all the clothes he had worn overnight into the gym bag and cleaned out the sink.

Just as he began to change and clean up the floor, someone tried to turn the knob of the door.

"Be right out," said Cashe, wondering if he had somehow drawn attention to himself or taken too long.

"Oh, sorry," a man answered back, "Didn't know somebody was in there."

He glanced around the bathroom to make sure he hadn't forgotten anything, peeked one last time in the mirror, opened the door, smiled at the man standing outside and entered the brightness of the store.

After making a large cup of tea, he bought it, along with two granola bars and a giant chocolate chip cookie, from the younger of the two women working behind the register. In the truck, he blasted the heat and ate his food, then drove back to Florida Avenue to see if Kia had left his belongings outside the apartment. Finding nothing there, he headed down West Liberty toward Coccelli's and thought he saw her SUV ahead of him. When he read the license plate number, he knew it wasn't hers. With nothing else to do and nowhere else to go, he parked in the lot next to the shop and waited for his shift to begin. At 9:50 A.M. Lenny pulled up, waved and unlocked the store. Cashe gestured back, then reached into the bottom of his gym bag and took out his Coccelli's shirt and hat. At the precise moment he walked inside, his cell phone rang and Kia's name flashed on the display screen.

Chapter Five

WHEN CASHE SAW KIA'S NAME, number and grinning portrait illuminate across the screen of his phone, immediately, he hit the button on its side to silence the call. He figured she just wanted to tell him that all of his stuff was tied-up tight in a garbage bag, probably sitting out in the middle of Florida Avenue, waiting for him to pick it up. A few seconds later, the phone rang again, and again, he muted the ringtone. Then, it vibrated in his pocket, a sign that she had sent a text. When his phone chimed a third time, Cashe still didn't answer, but replied with a text.

Kia:
PLEASE call me back.
Cashe:
I'm at work, what?
Kia:
I need to talk to you, it's important.
Cashe:
Hold on.

He stepped outside, hit the phone icon under her name, and before the first ring ended, she spoke.

"Cashe," was all she said before he heard a moan at the other end of the line and several sniffles before finally realizing that Kia was crying.

"Hello?"

"I'm sorry, Cashe, I'm so sorry," she said between intermediate whimpers. "I won't keep you, I know you're at work. I just wanted to say I'm sorry for what I did and I want you to come back. I don't want to lose you. Will you please come back tonight?"

Cashe couldn't speak. He almost stopped breathing. What he needed more than anything was to sit down, or even better yet, to lie down. Emotionally, everything that had happened in the past 24 hours began to physically take a toll on him, and he thought about leaving the shop early.

"I thought you didn't want me there—"

"I do want you here. It doesn't make sense, I know. I'm so stupid. I know you think that I'm not a good person, and you're right for thinking that."

Cashe sighed deeply. It wasn't an over-exaggerated expression to purposefully bring attention to himself, but the long, genuine reflex of a young man who had truly come to his wits end. Kia picked up on this, and her response seemed just as sincere.

"Just stop by when you get off work," she said. "I'll make dinner and we can talk. I just want us to talk, that's all I'm asking of you. And if you don't want anything to do with me after that, I'll understand. It will be hard, but I'll understand."

During his entire shift, he thought about how there was no way to decipher what her intentions were, but decided he'd show up anyway. If she had called him last night, before he parked in some random apartment complex and slept in his cold truck during a snowstorm, he might have reacted differently. She knew he didn't have anywhere to go. The way she kicked him out put a tinge of indignation inside of him. Nevertheless, Cashe decided to try, to ride the wave to shore, to take this next event in stride and see what might come of it. *But why the sudden change?* He knew there was really nothing Kia could do but apologize, and though she had never done anything like this in the past, he considered whether or not she might be crying wolf. *Would she ask for me back if she truly didn't love me?*

Out of nowhere came a crazy idea. *Why not propose? Now.* If she really was serious about him returning and wanted to reconcile, now would be the perfect opportunity. And if she said yes, he would only ask for one condition; that they begin to search for a place where both of their names would be on the lease. If she said no, he would just move on and put all of this behind him.

At the end of his shift, Cashe drove into the parking lot in the back of the apartment building. For a second, he had a flash of nostalgia injected into his brain, and it seemed as though he were coming home just like he had any other night, like nothing was different. He unzipped his backpack and before pocketing the engagement ring, opened the case to take one last look.

Instead of using the stairwell on the side of the building—he couldn't because he no longer had the keys—he went to the front entrance like an outcast, remembering that what she had done by calling the police was *for real*, and a very big deal. Before he hit the buzzer, he paused and reminded himself that this was something he could just as easily walk away from and that he really had no obligation to return. *Just get into your truck, leave and never come back. It's that simple.* But yet, he also knew this could be God's open door, an opportunity he might not want to pass up so easily. Especially with temporary homelessness in the cards. Amid these contrasting opinions, he pushed the button next to her name and Kia buzzed him in.

At the top of the stairs, the door had been left open. He walked inside and took a spot on the sofa, forgoing any reconciliatory hugs and kisses, just as she began to busy herself by quietly setting the table. Cashe didn't expect much as far as conversation, and the only time she spoke before he sat down to eat was when she asked if he wanted ice for his cranberry juice.

Dinner had been one of those rare occasions when the alignment of the stars and planets in the universe allowed the two to meet at the dining room table across from one another and fork up mouthfuls of spaghetti in silence. While he chewed, he thought of the engagement ring that he had hidden in his pocket. Nervously—he wasn't sure if she was picking up on how he felt—he periodically looked up from his plate and studied Kia's face. He tried to read her expressions, to find some clue from her signifying if she sensed that something out of the ordinary was about to take place.

All of a sudden, after Kia finished half of her food, she put down her fork and started crying into the palm of her hands. It was then he *knew* that what he was about to do would be an absolute surprise. Obviously, she couldn't get her mind off what she'd done. Before she had the chance to speak—he didn't have much time if he wanted the marriage proposal to occur during dinner—Cashe stopped eating. After taking a sip of the cranberry juice from his wine glass, he put his hand in his pocket and palmed the velvet-covered case. Anxiously, he twirled the box under the table until, finally, he stood up. He took a step towards her, got on both knees at her side and wrapped his arm around her back. When she leaned into him, he revealed the ring.

She froze, wiped the tears from her eyes and squinted down with a frown, like her brain couldn't process what was before her, then put a hand to her mouth.

"Kia, will you marry me?" asked Cashe, smiling, watching her confused visage.

Snapping out of her hypnosis, she slowly rose from the chair and joined Cashe on her knees. Her eyes, round, onyx irises glazed with moisture, looked at him in befuddlement and with a hint of grief. She placed her hand around his and shook her head, crying and nodding yes. Finally, she spoke.

"Yes, Cashe," she said. "I will marry you. I love you so much."

He pinched the ring, lifted it out of the case and reached for Kia's left hand. It slid up her finger and loosely stopped just past her second knuckle. Not a perfect fit, but he thanked the Lord for 'resizing'. He kissed her once on the lips.

"Oh my God!" exclaimed Kia, holding up the back of her hand, taking another look, "It's so beautiful."

"We'll return it and get one that fits," he said. "I guessed the wrong size."

Cashe got up off his knees and grabbed her by the elbow. They hugged, and when he tried to let go, she held on to him. He kissed her again, then guided her back to her seat, as if she needed help, and sat down at the table.

"Listen," he said, speaking intensely, knowing she was about to flip out at his statement, "All I need to do now is go and talk to your father so we can begin planning the wedding."

"What? Are you crazy? You can't go and talk to my father," said Kia wiping her tears away and brushing him off as if he had just told a bad joke. "He might throw you off the porch."

Cashe smiled. "I knew you might say that, but I thought I'd give it a try anyhow," he said. "But, geez, I have to meet the man sometime Kia."

"I know," she said. "I promise, I'll introduce you to each other soon."

"Since I already know we won't be able to have a traditional wedding, I thought we could just pay a visit to the magistrate, if that's okay with you."

The biggest obstacle between the two of them, as far as marriage was concerned, had to do with a matter of culture and circumstance. She knew they couldn't have a traditional Egyptian wedding. No matter how much Cashe looked like someone from North Africa, there were still issues. He didn't speak the language, for one, and secondly, he wasn't a Muslim. With him being an only child with dead parents, and she, the one relative in the U.S. living within close proximity to her elderly father, both of their attitudes about the situation were basically, *Why have a wedding at all?* The courthouse seemed to be the best diplomatic alternative.

"Yes," she said. "That's perfectly fine with me."

"It just makes the best sense," he said. "Because I know you don't want to get married in a church."

"No, you're right. But, even if we did, who'd come?" she said, appearing to halfheartedly laugh and cry at the same time.

He paused for a minute and forlornly considered her question. "No one."

Neither of them had many friends. She came from a family of divorce with her parents marrying young, and then splitting up after having children. Kia's mother and father, Yousef and Karima Alawi, separated in the spring of her twelfth year, just before she started the seventh grade. Karima went back to Egypt, rarely keeping in touch, to pursue a career in education at the University of Cairo while Yousef remained in the States. He worked tirelessly for several years at the Ali Baba restaurant on Forbes Avenue, living with friends, before saving up enough to buy three row houses on the Boulevard of the Allies to become a local landlord. He made a killing renting one-bedroom units to college students who came from the Middle East to study at the many colleges in the area. Kia had made the choice to stay in the US, live with her father and help out with the business. She always spoke of Yousef's houses to Cashe, and every time he drove past the properties, his curiosity piqued as he imagined what might be happening on the other side of their doors.

The Magistrate

IT SNOWED ON THE DAY of their scheduled appointment to see the magistrate. With Christmas approaching, Cashe labored over the tug of missing his parents again, and because of that, had grown to hate not only this time of the year, but all holidays. Although he wished his mother and father were still alive to see his marriage, the fact that they couldn't made him feel even more content about settling for such a serendipitous occasion as this. He thought about wearing a suit but decided to go casual. Instead, he opted for a polo shirt, slacks and dress shoes. Kia put on a blouse and pants and spent a lot of time pinning up her hair in the mirror.

She had already begun searching online and in the newspaper for an apartment to rent and scheduled a viewing for them approximately an hour after the marriage would be finalized. It was a studio in Squirrel Hill she found advertised for $520 a month. The district judge's office happened to be in the same neighborhood, tucked in-between a dry cleaners and a four-story residential building on Forward Avenue. If it weren't for the sign in the parking lot, the place would have been virtually invisible. The secretary, an attractive brunette in her mid-forties arrived, handed them clipboards with applications attached to complete, then disappeared behind a door. They filled out the paperwork near the entrance to the judge's chambers in a modest lobby lined with mismatched chairs. All the furniture looked as if it had been manufactured in the 1970's—every other plastic seat cushion was a dull brown, orange or lime green. When finished, they both studied an array of Kodak Instant photographs showing other couples who had been married there over the years. Hundreds of these pictures were neatly pinned to a bulletin board on the wall, and it made Cashe feel like what they were doing was *okay*.

The secretary who had handed them the forms returned, took their clipboards, then told them to go inside to see the judge. The ceremony was simple and straightforward. At the front of the courtroom, black tape formed the symbols for 'male' and 'female' on the carpet underneath their feet, indicating where each of them should stand. Soft music played from behind a door to the right before it suddenly came to an abrupt end, and an old, bearded, Jewish man wearing a black yarmulke entered the room. In less than fifteen minutes, after he asked a few questions about how they met, what religion they practiced and how long they had been together, he told them to exchange vows, rings, kiss and just like that, they were officially husband and wife under the authority of the City of Pittsburgh. The judge offered to take their picture for the wall outside and they both agreed.

"Think of it, a Jewish magistrate marrying a Christian man and a Muslim woman—I have a good feeling about you two," the judge said before they left the courtroom. "I really do."

Mister Reddy

THEY HELD EACH OTHER'S hand in the truck as Cashe drove up to a hidden edifice on Shady Avenue, just in time for their appointment. He parked on a road that wound up the hill at a steep incline, stopping next to a young maple sapling planted in-between the sidewalk and the curb. The complex, built on a plot of flat land at the plateau of the block, consisted of three buildings. It made a U shape around a grassy lawn surrounded by flourishing bushes and spotted with enormous, branchy poplars and elms. Even though the neighborhood consisted of a high population of Jews, many of the homes had Christmas lights lining their windows.

"I think it was a good idea to go before a judge and not a preacher or an imam," said Kia from the passenger seat.

"Me too," he agreed as they left the truck and crossed the street. "I liked how he said that he had a good feeling about us."

Cashe looked at his ring, admiring the shined, white gold Kia had given him. Wearing it made him feel part of not only a marriage relationship with his new wife, but a member of the "married club," a conglomeration of all the wed couples on the face of the earth. He also couldn't stop looking down at her diamond as they approached the sidewalk across the street, and how it made her left hand even more beautiful than it already was.

On the opposite side of the road at the bottom of three flights of stone slab steps, four burgundy light posts stood at each corner of the entryway—two near the sidewalk and two at the top. As they climbed the steps, it almost seemed as if they were accessing the grounds to a private mansion.

"The landlord said we should go to apartment B-10," said Kia, looking at an address and telephone number scribbled in sloppy cursive on a yellow Post-It note. "His name is Mr. Reddy."

When they arrived at the top of the courtyard, the buildings came into clearer view. They were all identical—the three brick structures, made of various shades of tan, had flimsy metal ornamental balconies that matched the lampposts at each corner of the courtyard, designed for decoration rather than actually standing outside and smoking a cigarette on. Instead of patio doors opening out to them, there were framed windows.

On the building ahead of them, a giant golden letter "B" sparkled in the sunlight after a cloud shifted overhead. Cashe noticed how the entrance to the left had a letter "A" and the one on the right a letter "C."

"There's B," he said, and they both walked to the left and around the square. The main entrance was open, and when he immediately saw a door marked "B-2," he knew they would have to climb more steps.

"The place he shows us better not be on the third floor," said Cashe, "It's going to suck if we have to move furniture up three flights of stairs."

"No, he said the one he has available is on the first floor," said Kia. "And it's in Building A."

When they reached the top floor, a tiny gilded rectangular plaque with the inscription "B-10" had been centered on the door, underneath an equally burnished, gold-plated knocker. The name *Rajarwari Patel* was printed on a label and placed in the square slot above. Cashe banged three times using the handle, and they stared at each other with lifted eyebrows, waiting for a response. On the other side of the wall, the faint sound of scurrying feet was heard, followed by the jiggling of the knob and the unlocking of the deadbolt.

The door opened and revealed a thin, balding, bronze-skinned man. Atop his head, rays from the hallway window made a reflection about the same brightness as the smooth placard with the B-10 inscription, the golden door knocker and the giant glimmering letter "B" on the front of the building.

"Hello, Mr. Reddy?" Cashe asked, interjecting before Kia had the chance to speak.

"Yes," he answered, slightly bowing his head.

"Hi, my name is Cashe, and I think my wife talked to you earlier today about seeing a studio apartment for rent?"

Reddy looked at Kia and smiled.

"Yes, yes. Just one moment, I have to get the keys," he said with a thick Indian accent.

Reddy kept the door open and Kia and Cashe were left waiting again, looking at one another in expectation. After more foot shuffling, he returned with tinkling keys hanging from his right hand.

"The apartment is in Building A," said Reddy. "It is $520 a month and it is available immediately if you are interested."

They followed him downstairs as he led them straight backed and stiff shouldered into the courtyard. His brown sandals, stuffed with rusty wool socks, flip-flopped at every stride as they went through the beveled doors of Building A—each having one large rectangular slab of glass inside—walked down a narrow corridor, and then stopped at a door on the right. Reddy opened it and they stepped inside.

There were three rooms. The studio living room to the far right had dark cherry hardwood floors, a walk-in closet and two windows with a terrible view. Outside, there was a cement wall lined with air conditioning units, piles of branches, and loose weeds growing out from the cracks in the concrete. On the other side, the trunks of the giant trees which surrounded the building looked like brontosaurus legs. They were so tall that Cashe had to crouch his head close to the ground to see the tops of them.

The bathroom entrance, opposite the front door to the apartment, led to a petite space with the basic amenities—a tub, a toilet and a sink. When he came into the hallway, Cashe found Kia looking through the cabinets in the kitchen.

"Look, there's a door in the kitchen!" said Kia with seemingly revelatory enthusiasm.

He unlocked it and walked outside onto the bottom flight of a fire escape. There really wasn't much to see, except for an extension of the same cement wall they had viewed from the living room window. The kitchen was very spacious and seemed to be about the same size as the studio. There would be more than enough room to put the dining room table and chairs.

"Cool," he said. "Mr. Reddy, you said this is available immediately?"

"Yes," answered Reddy.

"Well, what do you think, Kia?" Cashe asked as he stood next to her, putting his arm around her shoulder. "I like it."

"I think we should look around a little more before we give him an answer."

"But we aren't going to find another apartment in this area for $520 a month," he whispered. "We're right in the middle of Squirrel Hill, we're less than a half a mile away from your father's house, and everything is within walking distance."

"That is true," she said, stepping away from him. She looked at Reddy and responded with an odd choice of words. "Okay, let's do it."

"You want it?" he asked again, giving them the opportunity to be sure.

In unison, they both answered, "Yes."

They followed Reddy and the sound of his flip flopping sandals back to his home in Building B, which also turned out to be the rental office. After they climbed the three flights of stairs again, Reddy invited them inside.

"Please, take your shoes off," he said to them both, then disappeared into a back room cordoned off with hanging beads.

Cashe bent down to untie his shoes. Kia easily slipped out of her clogs. Reddy's place didn't seem as if it belonged in the same complex. The floor was decked with a white fluffy carpet that covered the living room, the dining room and a spiral staircase that swirled up from the middle of the apartment to an upstairs level. There were white statues of various Hindu gods and goddesses inside display cases in each corner, and a painting of Ganesha above a lamp near the window. The couches were also white, and at first glance the room appeared perfect until, upon closer inspection, he began to see insignificant, yet noticeable cracks in the vase of its façade. While the armrests on the couch were a bit worn-out and threadbare patches in the carpet randomly adorned inconspicuous spots on the floor, these discrepancies did not diminish the effect of the room's décor.

They came prepared to sign a lease. Both he and Kia had stopped by PNC Bank and withdrew $600 each to cover a deposit, first month's rent and any fees. While they waited, they continued to stare around the room, peeking every now and then down at their rings, until Reddy's return. Cashe picked up Kia's hand and kissed it in an act of affectionate boredom.

Reddy came back with the lease and took a moment to make tiny X's next to the signature lines in the contract.

"Please sign here and here," he said, flipping through the pages, "and here and here."

"Will both of our names to be on this lease?" Cashe asked before signing. He saw his name but didn't see Kia's.

"No, just your name," said Reddy.

"Could you also add her name to it, please? We want both of our names on the lease," he asked, scooting around in his seat, trying to stay comfortable. He almost felt as if he offended Reddy by asking him to make the correction.

"Okay," he said before snatching the lease out of Cashe's hand. He exited the living room and once again went back to his office.

"Did you see the way he grabbed the lease out of my hand?" he whispered to Kia.

"Calm down, Cashe," she said, still looking around the place. "He's an old man."

Reddy re-entered the living room a second time sooner than expected, and like a gust of wind, they both signed, paid the $1040 that included the deposit and the first month's rent, tested the keys to the apartment, shook the landlord's hand in appreciation, then left.

Transition

OVER THE NEXT FEW DAYS, Cashe and Kia spent all their free time moving their belongings from Florida Avenue in Mount Lebanon to the new place on Shady Avenue in Squirrel Hill. After cleaning the old apartment, handing in the keys and returning the U-Haul, the two sat down to rest at the kitchen table in their disorganized new pad, and began to talk business. Cashe brought out a couple of cans of lemonade and an unopened bag of tortillas.

"So, I don't know anything about marriage," he said while munching on a chip. "I never got the chance to ask Mom and Dad how they did it."

"What do you mean?"

"Finances for one thing." He watched her contemplate his statement.

"Why can't we just do what we've been doing?"

Even though Cashe had a basic understanding of what it meant to be married, he had never really thought out the details of exactly what a union between and man and woman entailed. He watched movies and read books that showed the importance of family ties and how social standing influenced decisions on who to marry; he examined the ideas of beauty and age, of power and influence. But, as he reflected upon the simplicity of what he and Kia had just done, all those grandiose concepts seemed so far away.

"Well, now that we're married, what's mine is yours, and what's yours is mine," he said, "Right?"

"That's easy for you to say, you don't have shit."

The truthfulness of her comment stung, and he found himself momentarily tongue-tied. She giggled, probably just to make him feel better, and it did. When Cashe's parents died suddenly, they left him with nothing. Neither of them had much life insurance, nor money saved up in CD's or investment accounts. What little the companies paid out all went toward the funerals.

"I mean, I don't have much either. My dad has money, but it's not mine, you know that."

"In that case, I have more than you, because you still haven't found a job. I don't want to argue, I'm just wondering what you were thinking about as far as how to handle this."

In his heart, he did want to combine everything they owned, at least as a symbolic gesture of starting a new life together. He believed that they should share all things, from their bodies to the marriage license and bank accounts, but found out his philosophy would only go so far.

"So, you're saying that if my dad gives me money," she went on, "I automatically have to give you half?"

"No, I'm just saying I want to know what I should pay."

Already, the conversation was beginning to give him a headache. Kia complained of wanting her own money to spend as she pleased, to buy things exclusively for her, like tampons, fingernail polish and clothes. And, she protested, what if his truck broke down—should she have to pay for that? Or, if her father needed something, should he contribute? In the end, they compromised and decided to split the things they shared down the middle. They'd have one joint bank account used to deposit money for all the general household expenses like rent, utilities, insurance and food. What was left over in their stash of petty cash at the end of the month could be spent as they individually pleased. That sounded like a good plan as any, and he felt no need to explore the topic of finances anymore.

"I'll have money for my half of things until I find something," she reassured. "Don't worry about that."

"All right then, I have another question for you," said Cashe.

"Go ahead."

"Do you want a tree? Christmas is in two weeks."

"That's totally up to you," she said. "You're the one who believes that."

"Believes what?"

"In Christmas trees."

"I don't agree with summing up an entire faith in a Christmas tree, there's a lot more to it than that."

"It's whatever, Cashe. I'll respect it if that's what you want to do."

"Honestly, I don't care anymore."

What Cashe thought as a more important subject than money and putting up a Christmas tree for the holiday was getting himself together. He wanted to start making some decisions that would eventually lead him to his *purpose* in life, whatever that might be. The best choice he'd made—it transitioned so flawlessly; for some reason, God *really* steered him clear on this one—was quitting his job at Coccelli's. Since he and Kia had once again moved back to the east side of Pittsburgh, it made sense to find employment a little closer to home. A secret in the pizza delivery business, he quickly realized, was the extremely high demand for drivers. It turned out to be one of the most pleasant surprises Cashe had experienced in a very long time when he got hired twice in the same day, driving for a shop called Perfect Papa Pizza on Centre Avenue and another, named Angelina's Pizzeria on Highland.

Christmas and New Year's passed uneventfully, and during his first summer of marriage, he spent more and more time trying to think of practical ways to be a great husband for his new wife. It was a competitive thing, the athlete in him coming out to fight. The random trips to the bar for an occasional drink and smoke would stop. He bought a new road bike, scheduled-in exercising at the downtown YMCA on a regular basis—like he used to do while in school—and even started praying and reading the Bible, something he hadn't done seriously in years. He sensed a new obligation to prepare for what might happen in the future—buying a house or having kids. And as a result, even early on, his life began to change, in a good way.

That was, before he began having the nightmares.

Azazel

IN THE PREDAWN, early hours of the morning, Cashe's eyes suddenly opened. It took a long time to register where he actually was as he stared at the foreign ceiling above. He still hadn't totally adjusted to living on Shady Avenue. Right away, he realized that Kia lay next to him. He sat up lazily, took his cell phone off the windowsill and read the glowing numbers on the display. Exactly *3:00 A.M.* He laid back down, tossed to his stomach, then blindly examined the floor next to the bed, wondering *why* he had awakened so abruptly. Cognizant of his surroundings and of himself, he scanned the room. His dreamy eyes moved across the hardwood below, the terraced molding, the legs of the table in the corner and the triangular edge of the rug. He looked from the closet door to the desk against the wall, back to the covers on the futon and then again to Kia's body next to him. The room was dim and blurred his periphery, and light from the window projected a soft, oblong box of moonlight that bent against the wall.

Something fluttered through the beam. His mind thought bird or a bat, *again;* its shadow startled him enough to pique his interest, so he turned his head. When he saw that nothing was happening there, he returned his attention once more to the floor, and just as he began to close his eyes, to forget about all the imaginary activity of the room and drift off to sleep, he heard what sounded like the weight of a foot creaking the floorboards in the hallway near the front door.

As he squinted through the darkness, an intense, airy fear seeped into his nostrils while he watched a shadowy presence move forward towards him to the living room studio. It was the kind of horror that came with the certainty and assurance that without a doubt, his mind wasn't playing tricks on him, with all his senses affirming this fact in agreement.

Someone's here in the apartment.

With the question no longer being about *if* someone was there, but rather what to do now, Cashe listened to a second squeak from the floor. In his hesitation, he watched the stranger slowly raise an arm up against the side of the wall. *And was that fur on the hand?* The form in the hallway came into view through his dream eyes, a glittery black mass centered among the cloaked murkiness of the room. He lay paralyzed as he saw, of all things on earth, a large goat's head, with arching horns and a long, bushy beard underneath its grinning mouth appear, followed by the rest of its body standing firm and erect in the doorway, covered in a sparkling purple robe. When Cashe tried to move, nothing happened. His body was lifeless as a quadriplegic.

He observed the creature as if he were watching an image on a screen, not knowing whether he was asleep or awake. Its rigid, rectangular face, and its yellow eyes, staring ahead, had a mystical and unnatural glint. For some unexplained reason, Cashe did something that was totally out of character for him in real life, but absolutely rational in a dream. He spoke, using some strange type of mental telepathy, not understanding how he said it, as if someone else had asked the question through him.

"Who are you?"

When the thing answered back, that too, seemed presupposed. Like Cashe should already have known.

I am Azazel, it giggled.

Cashe jumped out of the dream with a scream and a shiver and instinctively reached for Kia to make sure it was all finally over. That he was back.

"What's wrong? What happened?" she had asked, untangling herself from the blanket.

"I was having a nightmare," he said, turning over, pressing his head back into the pillow, breathing deeply.

"So was I," said Kia. "I was dreaming that there was someone in the hallway trying to come into the bedroom."

His heart dropped. The deep, poignant dread returned as the realization of this apparent coincidence completely befuddled him. He felt the paralysis again and couldn't move. It was still a dream.

"What did they look like?" he asked, in that airy telepathy, experiencing a rush of emotions, a mix of fear and wonderment.

"The same way he always looks," she said in the dream, just as he woke up a second time, again with his wife lying asleep in bed next to him, knowing that she had never said anything at all. In the silence of the room, the words of the prophet had finally come to pass as Cashe had his first nightmare of Azazel, the beast, the goat-man.

And he was terrified.

He got out of bed and went to the bathroom. The potency of the vision still lingered, and on one hand, he wanted to splash water on his face and totally pull out of it. Yet at the same time, there was something within him that desired to hold on to what he had just dreamt. He remembered flashes of its details. The goat's head was alive, not some Halloween mask or taxidermic recreation made from roadkill. The thing spoke and wore a shiny purple gown. *As a matter of fact, the same kind of material the little angel boy was dressed in that dream a few months ago.*

Now wide awake, he left the bathroom and went into the kitchen. From the absence of light behind the Venetian blinds, he knew the sun hadn't risen. After digging through the cupboards, trying to find something that could match his sudden craving for food, he finally settled upon tea. While boiling the water in the teapot and pouring just the right amount of sugar and whole milk into a coffee mug, Cashe noticed Kia's laptop computer on the dining room table. That's when another memory came to him. Before the move, he had promised himself to look up this goat-creature online, but for some reason had gotten distracted by something. *What was it?*

As he caught the teapot before it whistled, so not to disturb Kia, he poured the scalding hot water into his cup and then remembered. *Ah, yes. It was the phone call from that guy Adam.*

Cashe stirred his tea, took a sip and then sat down at the table. He opened the computer, hit the power button, waited a few moments, signed on and then clicked the browser's icon. Google's website popped-up showing an intricate artwork design where they changed the "G" of their logo into the head of a goat for the celebration of the zodiac sign Capricorn, and it scared him beyond belief. His life suddenly felt fake and uncontrollable, as if he had somehow reentered his nightmare. The creature, it seemed, had now taken over the Internet.

With a heaving chest, he continued on in this mindless fantasy world and typed the word a-z-e-z-e-l into the search engine box. The results came up as follows:

> About 3,890,000 results (0.59 seconds)
> Showing results for ***azazel***
> Search instead for ***azezel***

When he clicked on the first option, he sat confounded as the world of Azazel opened up. He began reading commentaries, perusing photographs and symbols and exploring comic book drawings of a fictionalized super villain he had previously never known to exist. The most relevant information came in the form of excerpts from ancient texts:

> *For other uses, see Azazel (disambiguation).*
> *Not to be confused with Azrael.*
> **Azazel** (/əˈzeɪzəl/), also spelled **Azazael** (Hebrew: עֲזָאזֵל, translit. Azazel; Arabic: عزازيل, translit. Azāzīl), appears in the Bible in association with the scapegoat rite. In some traditions of Judaism and Christianity, it is the name for a fallen angel. In Rabbinic Judaism, it is not a name of an entity but rather means literally "for the complete removal", i.e., designating the goat to be cast out into the wilderness as opposed to the goat sacrificed "for YHWH".

And there was this one:

> Aaron shall offer the bull as a sin offering for himself and shall make atonement for himself and for his house. Then he shall take the two goats and set them before the Lord at the entrance of the tent of meeting. And Aaron shall cast lots over the two goats, one lot for the Lord and the other lot for Azazel. And Aaron shall present the goat on which the lot fell for the Lord and use it as a sin offering, but the goat on which the lot fell for Azazel shall be presented alive before the Lord to make atonement over it, that it may be sent away into the wilderness to Azazel.
>
> —*English Standard Version, Leviticus 16:8–10*

Yes, the prophet in the park had said something about the lots, he remembered. It went on:

> According to the Book of Enoch (a book of the Apocrypha), Azazel (here spelled 'ăzā'zyēl) was one of the chief Grigori, a group of fallen angels who married women. This same story (without any mention of Azazel) is told in the book of Genesis 6:2–4: "That the sons of God saw the daughters of men that they were fair; and they took them wives of all which they chose. [...] There were giants in the earth in those days; and also afterward, when the sons of God came in unto the daughters of men, and they bore children to them, the same became mighty men which were of old, men of renown." Enoch portrays Azazel as responsible for teaching people to make weapons and cosmetics, for which he was cast out of heaven. The Book of Enoch 8:1–3a reads, "And Azazel taught men to make swords and knives and shields and breastplates; and made known to them the metals [of the earth] and the art of working them; and bracelets and ornaments; and the use of antimony and the beautifying of the eyelids; and all kinds of costly stones and all colouring tinctures. And there arose much godlessness, and they committed fornication, and they were led astray and became corrupt in all their ways."

The information was too much for Cashe to take in. He rose from the table, walked through the hallway and stared at Kia lying underneath the comforter on the futon, a mound of warmth unaffected by his recent revelations.

What the fuck is going on? What's happening to me?

Kia's body appeared to jump and switch positions at his gaze, and he imagined himself having laser eyes or x-ray vision into her soul. She suddenly turned toward him, squinting, as he, hovering in the doorway, gave a face that exuded confusion.

"What the hell are you doing?" she asked.

"I can't sleep."

She quickly shoveled back under the covers, giving him her rear.

"Turn off that light in the kitchen. It's too bright."

If Kia's words hadn't been so harsh, Cashe might have climbed back into bed and attempted to confide in her about the dreams and the new information he found concerning this cannibalistic beast named Azazel. Instead, he decided to wait until a more opportune time, after his thoughts and feelings were more subdued.

His eyes had been opened, and he knew, *he sensed*, that he was in the midst of some type of life-changing experience. It wasn't just recovering from his parent's death—if that were possible—the murder, getting married or the dreams. All of them combined acted as a catalyst that propelled him toward something—or someplace— he just wasn't sure what or where.

He had never experienced a double dream before, and with great difficulty, he tried to conceptualize and describe what happened to himself in his own mind. *Was it that he fell deeper into a dream state? Had he stumbled upon a door in his unconsciousness that opened up a dream-to-dream portal?* Yet more than that, it seemed to be some sort of a strange mode of communication, as if the Azazel thing traveled there and *wanted* something from him. Even before he discovered that it was knocking on the door to his castle in the sky, others knew. The prophet knew.

Cashe eventually shut down the computer, got back into bed and fell asleep. In the morning, when he and Kia awoke, he shared the dream.

"I think you're taking all this a bit too far," she responded. "The devil isn't out to get you."

"Perhaps he's got his eye on me."

"What makes you so unique?"

"I don't know," said Cashe. "Maybe I did something to piss him off."

"Like what?"

That question threw him off guard, and he fell silent because he knew she had hit upon something.

"Maybe he's mad because I married you."

Kia too had nothing more to say. She pursed her lips, rolled her eyes and said, "*Whatever.*"

Days after the dream, he still perceived a connection to a supernatural wavelength which more than frightened him; it scared the bejesus out of him. Yet, it too, had a positive effect. It made him get serious about his faith and having a prayer life. It changed his behavior, as if a part of him had died and something from within had been birthed. He supplemented his normal daily activities with idiosyncratic rituals like crossing his chest before leaving the apartment, or when performing common decisions such as pulling into traffic when driving his truck. It made him designate a "special" place to go and meditate outside in his new neighborhood before he left for the YMCA on his workout days, a hidden spot on the steps of a synagogue a block away, underneath the ancient stars of David that decorated the side of the building. He'd walk there in the mornings before work, or in the evenings after dinner as the sun went down, when the traffic on Shady Avenue ebbed to a few stragglers, and spend time there talking to God.

Despite Kia's seemingly lax practice of Islam, when he told her how he thought that the dream was demonic, he knew she would understand and believe him up to a certain point. There were many legends about jinn and the parallel world of spirits in the Qur'an, but it frustrated him to know that they differed in opinion as to how they should be handled. Perhaps it was his inner desire for some pastor to come by, Bible in hand, and cast that cursed goat-thing to the depths of hell in the name of Jesus. He might have been wrong, but as far as he knew, Muslims didn't perform exorcisms. And if he expected Kia to partake in such a ritual, he would only be fooling himself. Not that she didn't talk to the Lord or that they didn't pray together; it was just done in a different way.

Before dinner, after he'd say grace, she always added *Subhaana alah humma wa bihamdika*—Glory to you Allah, yours is the praise—on top of his prayer, as if his supplication to God wasn't enough. On the inside, he knew her intent was far from demeaning, but rather an *attempt*, a try at approaching God together. Yes, at times, their individual beliefs clashed, but during many other instances it overlapped. She used a prayer rug. He stooped to his knees. When Cashe came home after paying a random visit to some church on a Sunday, he always succumbed to an irresistible desire to talk about the message he had just heard. Kia would sit and listen, but then give her unchanging, scripted response to Jesus: *We believe in Jesus, peace be upon Him, but not in the way you do. Muhammad was the final prophet. He came to set everything straight.*

Yousef

ON AN UNUSUALLY MILD, late Sunday afternoon in the fall, Cashe left Perfect Papa after a day of slow business, feeling hungry. Today, there were no freebies at work, but that didn't matter; Kia had made lasagna and peas the night before. As he neared the apartment, he got excited just thinking about eating leftovers, lying in bed for a while and maybe watching a movie. He parked behind Kia's truck, in his usual spot next to the young maple tree, waited for the traffic to pass, and started toward the crooked steps which led up to the courtyard. As he approached Building A, he saw her coming out of the entrance. The sight both surprised and pleased him, but then immediately his spirit dampened. He looked forward to her being around and thought they might spend the evening together.

"Where are *you* off to?" he asked as they met underneath a tree like two trains nearing the same track. She looked up from the sidewalk, holding back a smile.

"To my dad's," she said. "I'm going to clean his kitchen. You should have seen it yesterday, it was a mess."

"Oh. They let me off early. Business was slow."

"It's so warm today."

"I know, but it's supposed to snow tomorrow. This crazy Pittsburgh weather is weird."

"Do you want to come with me?"

At first, he wasn't sure he heard her correctly. He had even started walking away toward the apartment. Visiting her father had been the last thing on his mind.

"Huh? Do I—yeah, I'll go," he said. "I'll drive."

All of a sudden, he got nervous and started thinking about things which five minutes before getting the invitation weren't important. Was he wearing the right clothes? Should he brush his teeth?

"Give me a second to change my clothes."

She followed him back inside and waited, and then the two went down the steps toward the street, together. They paused for the traffic to clear, and then got into his truck. Kia rambled on about her efforts with trying to find a new job, how she had just finished cleaning their apartment, and her unsuccessful attempts at buying a new purse while shopping at Target. As they drove through Schenley Park, Cashe noticed several joggers on the sidewalk and an old man riding a bicycle on the road, causing the cars to swerve around him.

"That guy needs get out of the street," he said. "It's too dangerous during this time of the day."

Kia didn't respond, and instead looked away at the trees in the park, put her elbow on the armrest and rested her cheek into her palm. Her diamond ring was pointed directly at him, sparkling like a thousand pieces of shattered rainbows. He wanted to ask if her father had seen the ring, and if so, had he said anything about it to her, but remained quiet. The topic was still too sensitive.

Cashe parked at the laundromat across the street from the row homes on the Boulevard of the Allies. A muscular black man in a yellow jacket and blue jeans passed by them, speaking only to Kia after they stepped out of the truck and neared the sidewalk. It made Cashe feel uneasy and jealous, and as a result, he momentarily separated himself from her. The nervousness about meeting her father for the first time overshadowed what could have been the start of an argument as he saw Yousef perched at the top of the steps in a chair, cane in hand, watching them cross. Cashe's stomach began to turn.

"His name is Yousef, right?" he whispered.

"Yes," she said. "Yousef Alawi."

"Well, what should I call him?" asked Cashe when they reached the other side of the street. "Yousef, Mr. Alawi or Dad?"

"Call him whatever you want to call him," said Kia as she went ahead of him giggling, then climbed the steps up to the porch. Her backside swayed to and fro to an unheard rhythm. He didn't totally fall into its hypnotic draw as he might have done if they were at home by themselves, but rather paid careful attention to his feet as he inclined the steep concrete stairway.

Yousef greeted Kia and they spoke to one another in Arabic. Cashe watched as her father's eyes went down to her hand and the ring, but then he pretended to look around the porch before the old man caught him staring. There were two empty folding chairs and several planks of wood in the corner. A thick curtain hung on the other side of the window behind where Yousef was sitting. The front door was painted the same color green as the porch and was partially hidden by a glassed-in screen.

Kia looked like a female version of her father, except for his gray hair and tawny complexion. They both had very dark pupils, thick eyebrows and prominent noses.

"Baba, this is Cashe. Cashe this is my dad," said Kia and Cashe instinctively stuck out a straight arm, offering his hand.

"A salaam—" Yousef began, but Kia interjected by laughing out loud.

"Baba, speak English to him," she said at the precise moment he lifted his hand. "He doesn't speak Arabic."

"You look Egyptian," said Yousef with smirk that made a mutual grin rise on Cashe's face and they quickly shook hands. "Really. One hundred percent."

"Seriously?" said Cashe, still smiling at the old man, holding on with a firm grip.

"Yes," said Yousef, scooting a little forward into his chair. "Okay. Kia, get him something to drink. I have tea, Coca-Cola, Sunny Delight—"

"I'll have tea," said Cashe, and in that instant he felt so comfortable that he leaned against the brick pillar holding up the roof over the porch.

Kia left the two alone by themselves and went into the house. Yousef began to stare off into the distance again, like Cashe had seen him do so many times when he had passed by this stretch of the Boulevard.

This is definitely the guy.

He looked over his own shoulder, across the street, following the direction of Yousef's gaze and saw dark clouds bubbling over the trees. They seemed to be sneaking up on them, trying to surprise Oakland with unexpected rain. The air was balmy and electric, and the unusually humid 70-degree September breeze found its way into the loose spaces in his shirt, making his sleeves flap. He didn't want to leave this time and place and all the while kept thinking of the deep, echoing statement Yousef had made about him looking *one hundred percent Egyptian,* over and over again in his head.

A young couple, two of Yousef's tenants, came out of the house next door and onto the shared porch. He watched and listened as they said something in Arabic to Yousef and then departed down the steps. Cashe glanced at himself in the reflection of glass in the door they had just come out of.

He's right. We all do look alike.

It was like Yousef had awakened him from a dream. Cashe wished that he too could speak Arabic, as he flicked his wedding ring with his thumb.

"*So,* what kind of work do you do?" asked Yousef in his slight, Middle Eastern accent, breaking into Cashe's daydreaming. The *so* in his question sounded elevated, like it had been at the top of a mountain, or riding on a cloud.

"I work for a couple of pizza shops. I deliver pizza," he said.

"Pizza? Hmm…" said Yousef, shifting his cane from his right to his left hand, smiling. "There used to be a guy from Syria who lived in the apartment next door. He would come home with $300 every night."

"Wow, how many hours did he work?" Cashe asked. "He must have driven all day and night to pull in that kind of money."

"Open to close," said Yousef, switching hands again.

He thought about delving further into the details of the business by asking how many drivers they had or how much in sales they averaged, but he kept silent.

"You know, why you don't open your own pizza shop?" asked Yousef.

Cashe had never really entertained the idea. But now, especially because he was married, he thought it might be something worth considering. Before he could answer, Kia came back to the porch and looked at her father with squinting, inquisitive eyes.

"The tea is done, Baba," she said, then spoke something in Arabic again. "Why don't you both come inside? It's going to rain."

"Okay," said Yousef, and he struggled a bit to stand up, even with the support of his cane.

He wanted to grab Yousef's hand and help him out of his chair, but resisted. The old man's maneuver consisted of a slide to the left, a quick forward lean, and a push off with his legs. Once on his feet, he hurriedly shuffled through the door and into his home. Cashe followed, thinking how Yousef appeared to be in great shape for a sixty-eight-year-old man, but more than that, he couldn't believe he was actually getting the opportunity to enter Kia's father's home. It almost seemed like destiny; he somehow knew one day he might get the chance to go inside.

The living room was dim. Only a small lamp in the corner and the remnant of evening light glowing through the curtains in the window illuminated the room. Worn out Turkish rugs covered the floor. Ancient Egyptian hieroglyphs with animal headed gods and golden busts of pharaohs adorned the walls. Intricate patterns of Arabic writing in the form of shiny golden onion shapes hung behind the television set. In the back, the door to a bedroom was half opened.

"What does that say?" Cashe asked, pointing to one on the wall, just as Yousef sat on a broken-in recliner positioned directly in front of the TV, grabbed the remote control from the armrest and turned on Al-Jazeera.

"That says 'Allah is one,'" he answered.

Cashe caught himself standing alone while Kia was in the other room and her father occupied himself with the program. He couldn't figure out where to sit, but finally decided on the nearest piece of furniture—a dark blue sofa positioned up against the opposite wall. When he sat down, his butt sank into it a little further than expected, and his back bent at such an obtuse angle that his feet barely touched the ground. Out of the corner of his eye, Cashe could see Kia in the kitchen pouring hot water into coffee mugs.

From the stories she told him about her father, he had lived in this house for almost forty years, and oddly enough, it showed. It was like Yousef *belonged* here. The earthy tones in the décor of the interior of the home matched Yousef's skin and clothes and gave the appearance that he was an extension of his chair and the room.

"Cashe, can you come here for a minute?" asked Kia.

He pushed himself out of the sofa with a trace of excitement in his chest. Curiosity about the rest of the house was getting the best of him. The kitchen was much like the living room, and similar to the glimpse of Yousef's bedroom that he saw, was decoratively cluttered. Clean dishes were stacked in a plastic dish rack next to the sink, still drip-drying from when Kia had rinsed them. On a shelf near a dining table were jars of what seemed to be every kind of spice imaginable. Several rows of the containers were filled with herbs he didn't recognize. A tablecloth with yellow, brown and orange flowers covered a second kitchen table upon which lay piles of coupons and advertisements from the Sunday paper.

"I don't know how much sugar you want in your tea," said Kia, "You have to put it in yourself."

Above the sink were three different vessels of sugar—one with heavy brown raw granules, the other two with bleached white. Cashe grabbed the white sugar and poured, covering the bottom of the cup. He had a sweet tooth, so he eyed it and stopped when it looked like enough.

"Do you have any milk?" he asked.

"It's in the refrigerator."

As he opened the door, the feeling of déjà vu came over him with such force it made him lose his balance. He saw an image of himself stopping outside this very house at the red light—a fuzzy picture of Yousef on the front porch, cane in hand, and the foreboding stare on his face as he looked across the street and beyond the horizon.

The realization of what was actually happening stunned him. A strong sense of *predestination* and purpose overcame him as he opened Yousef's refrigerator and searched for the milk.

Never in a million, trillion years would I ever have imagined that I would be digging through Kia's father's food.

But here he was, pouring two percent milk into a cup of tea and carrying it back into the living room with Kia following.

She sat next to Cashe on the sofa as they watched television. Three women in jeans, T-shirts, long hair and glossy lipstick gossiped about something he couldn't understand.

"What are they talking about?" asked Cashe.

"This is a Saudi program," she said. "They're talking about how the styles of dress have changed with this newer, younger generation."

Cashe took a swallow of his tea and looked up at Yousef, who raised the cup to his lips and carefully sipped the hot liquid before changing the channel to a sports station. An Iranian soccer team had been practicing, and again, Cashe wanted to know what was being said, but decided not to bother Kia so much with decoding the commentary. The three sat in the living room watching the television, and for the most part, he let them do the talking. Occasionally, Kia would say something to her father and he would translate, or he would speak and she would interpret. Then Yousef came back to the same conversation they were having on the porch. He wanted to know what Cashe planned to do with his life. Surprisingly, he brought up the subject of pizza again and asked why Cashe didn't want to open a shop of his own.

"I just don't have the money to open my own store. I'd have to take out a loan. Maybe five years from now I might consider it," he said, then changed the subject and began to inquire about Egypt.

"So, Kia tells me you have been in the United States for forty years now?"

Yousef's eyes lit up. "I left Cairo when I was twenty-years-old and attended school at Pitt," he said, his voice dropping several octaves as he spoke. "I was married to Kia's mother and she wanted to go back to Egypt after she finished school. But I didn't want to go, I wanted to stay here and work."

His voice, now heavily accentuated, was magical, drawing him in with every word. Yousef paused and stared at a framed photograph on top of the television. It was Kia's college graduation picture. She stood between her parents wearing a red cap and gown, with one arm around her father and the other around her mother. She and her father were smiling, but her mother just stared blankly at the camera.

"So, she left, and I bought these two houses for $15,000. Now they are worth together about $300,000."

"Talk about a good investment," said Cashe.

"Yes, that is precisely what I am trying to say. You are young. You have your whole life ahead of you, and there are many decisions a young man must, no, will, make."

Kia got up and went back into the kitchen as if she had heard this speech from her father a thousand times. Cashe could see her putting away everything she had taken out for the tea.

"Yes, it is very important for a young man not only to invest his money wisely into this business or that business—" said Yousef, waving his left hand and then his right. Cashe couldn't quite see where the conversation might be going, but patiently continued to listen.

"But a young man must also strive to live his life before Allah knowing the things he does will come back upon him," he said.

Cashe looked the old man in the eye and saw sincerity. What he was saying was true, but didn't sound the same as when he had heard it in the past.

"In other words, you're basically saying that *you reap what you sow?*" he asked, reconfiguring his statement into the biblical terminology he had been accustomed to hearing all of his life.

"What is this *reap what you sow?*" asked Yousef with a puzzled look on his face. Cashe couldn't tell if he were being solemn or theatrical.

"It's a proverb, you know, a wise saying," said Cashe. "When you plant or sow a seed into the ground and it grows, um, and like an apple tree, you reap the fruit. Apples. So, like you said, if we do good or bad before God, then it is like planting a seed. Everything good or bad you do before God will grow and come back to you."

"Yes," said Yousef.

Cashe thought about taking the next step and bringing Jesus into the conversation. At first he hesitated, but then thought, *Why not?*

"The one who said that statement about reaping and sowing was Jesus," said Cashe.

The old man didn't budge. He didn't twitch, he didn't blink.

"I'm a Christian, and we believe that He was the God who came here to earth in the form of a man, healed the sick, raised the dead, preached the Kingdom of God, was killed, and made alive again by the Father in heaven. So if anyone—"

Yousef scooted forward in his chair and cut Cashe off mid-sentence.

"There is no other God but Allah," said Yousef, holding up an ancient, wrinkled index finger. "*We believe in Jesus,* peace be upon Him, but not in the same way as you."

"I know," said Cashe, also moving to the tip of his seat, beginning to feel a little dizzy from the tea. "You believe that He was just a prophet."

"Yes, *we believe in Jesus,*" said Yousef, repeating the statement.

The phrase turned over and over in Cashe's head. *We believe, we believe, we believe…*

"But was he God? No," he said definitively.

"Well that's the difference between Christianity and Islam."

"But Jesus was not just any prophet," he said, switching the cane from his right hand back to his left again. "Do you know that there is a tree in Egypt, with a sign that reads, *'Jesus as a boy sat under this tree'*?"

"What?!" asked Cashe in absolute wonderment. He had never in his life heard of such a thing.

Yousef giggled.

"Yes, really," he said. "Can you believe, Jesus as *a boy*, sat under that very tree? Look it up, I tell you the truth."

"I'd love to go there," said Cashe.

His eyes had been diverted to Yousef's feet. For some reason, he had been attracted to a big toe that had been sticking out of his brown sandal. Cashe watched it wiggle. Yousef raised his foot and stamped the ground as if squashing a bug.

Kia came back from the kitchen, took the empty coffee mugs from Yousef and Cashe, and stood next to him.

"Are you ready to go, Cashe?" she asked.

The truth was that he wasn't. He wanted to stay. He wanted to finish the conversation he was having with the old man. But he knew, the way things were going, they could be up into the late hours of the night talking about the mysteries of ancient religious history.

"Yeah, Kia let's go," said Cashe getting up from the sofa. He wanted to shake Yousef's hand again but restrained himself.

"It was really nice meeting you, Yousef, thanks for the tea," he said.

"Yes, it was nice meeting you, come back anytime."

Kia spoke to her father in Arabic one last time before they made their way to the truck, hurrying in the rain, side by side, trying to stay dry.

Once inside, Cashe couldn't stop staring at himself in the rearview mirror. During every traffic-free instance and at all the red lights from the Boulevard of the Allies to Murray Avenue, he tilted the mirror and looked at his face as if he'd never seen it before.

"What are you *doing*?" asked Kia.

"I can't believe how much I look like an Egyptian."

At the bottom of Shady Avenue, after turning the mirror to see himself *again* (for the fifth time) it broke off from the inside of the windshield, and he held it in his hand, feeling like a little kid who had just wet his pants. Kia erupted in laughter.

"Shit," said Cashe, embarrassed.

He altered their course, waiting for a salt truck spraying pebbles onto the road to pass, and made a stop at Rite Aid to pick up the strongest super glue he could find. Kia watched as he tried to replace it back as close to its original position as possible. When it appeared to stick permanently after the 15 minute-wait recommended on the box, he gave a sigh of relief and drove off.

"You are such a goofball," she said, and Cashe saw an expression on her face which he could only describe as motherly. "Come here."

Kia reached over and began French kissing him until the car behind them started honking. As they neared the apartment, his desire for his wife reached an unbearable peak. They arrived home and quickly performed their bedtime rituals before snuggling underneath the comforter on the futon. Like two ravenous people searching through the cabinets for food when hungry, they reached for one another and Cashe made love with his wife.

Chapter Six

SHE IS MINE CASHEMENTE.

Darkness. A cursive fluorescent aurora feathered over a sheet of pure black wound its way through the nothingness. It was kind of like those pictures of the Northern Lights he had seen a long time ago in some National Geographic magazine. Cashe knew it had been Azazel again, and the only proof of his presence was the lingering purple trail. Inexplicably, he wished that everything hidden in the deep partition of empty space before him would come back and re-reveal itself. But he also wanted to be awake. The feeling of being stuck was frightening. He wrestled with himself, trying to *will* his mind to spark movement in his body, to come up and out of the deep, murky waters of abeyance. Even though it seemed like the connection had been lost, he refused to drown.

He imagined the thick, violet neon squiggles as lifelines, wires that somehow attached his brain to his body, but couldn't get away from the truth of what they really were—traces left behind from that *creature*. Something wasn't right. Instead of having a complete circuit of mind, body and spirit, each separate entity seemed strangely dislocated, and all he could do was lie in bed, paralyzed.

Memory of last night's events dripped awareness from above, rippling through him like drops of liquid falling into a puddle. They fell from an unreachable sky far over his head, and with every splash, new information about his identity and location cleared the fogginess and blackness away. He desired so much to break free, but couldn't.

He remembered the visit to Yousef's house and sleeping with Kia in his arms. And he also had a picture of the goat-man in his mind, his chortles and declarations coming from the dream.

The lot has been cast, Cashemente. She is mine.

Now, he wasn't sure if he and Kia were even in the same room. That fearful indignation stunned him, and he worked madly to dispel the barrenness, to pull in the reigns of his brain, to become unfrozen and to see.

Again and again, he commanded his limp members on the bed to take action as he began to gain strength, to return to clear mindfulness, to rise to the surface. With all his heart he knew he wasn't dead. He *believed* his body was right there on the bed where he had fallen asleep.

Move. Arms, move. Sit up, Cashe. Break this thing. Get up.

His eyes opened, and with all his might he lifted up out of semi-catalepsy and untangled himself from the comforter. The hold of the invisible binding that encased him like a cocoon gradually began to loosen. He struggled to fill his lungs but was relieved to be able to breathe again. Next to him, Kia rolled over into a fetal position, her backside a round ball under the blanket, nudging him away. Finally, he forced himself to sit all the way up.

Now that he no longer felt suffocated, he knew that what he just experienced was another episode of sleep apnea, a disorder a doctor had diagnosed last year. He learned the word *apnea* meant "without breath" in Greek, and people who had the condition stopped breathing for a minute or longer during the final stages of sleep. As a result, the brain made frantic attempts to communicate with the body in order to inhale and exhale again. Medically, the diagnosis sounded legitimate, but he no doubt knew that other forces were also at work.

The encounters became so frequent that he had memorized the sequence of events. First, he would dream of Azazel. Then, the paralysis set in and he'd find himself in that God forsaken purgatory, neither asleep nor awake, lost inside the *spirit's playground*. And finally, he'd wake up with proof, certain that the episode was real.

In the past, it had worked the other way around. He'd see or experience an object, person, or sound during his waking hours, and then it would return to him in his dreams. But after the words of the prophet came to pass and the nightmares began, his dreams now bled into his waking life. Without a doubt, he knew that purple would be the color of the day, somehow left behind by the goat-man as a sign that these *visitations* weren't just his imagination.

From the windowsill, he reached for his cell phone and checked the time. 10:00 A.M. Last night he had forgotten to set the alarm and overslept. He quickly jumped out of bed and rushed into the bathroom. After flipping the light switch, he shut the door and stopped at the sink. Both of the naked bulbs over the mirror lit up his face, making it shine for several seconds, revealing every crease and crevice, every pimple and pink spot, until his eyes adjusted and he stopped glowing. Up close, he saw an infinite number of microscopic black hairs breaking through the surface of his skin around his mouth and cheeks. After showering and shaving, he hastily threw on his uniform, covered it in a Perfect Papa hoodie and headed to the kitchen. From the refrigerator, he grabbed a banana, tore away at the yellow husk, chomped on it like a fat stogie, and stuffed an apple into his pouch pocket. He returned to the bedroom, softly kissed Kia on the cheek and left the apartment, locking the door behind him, chewing on the banana as he made his way down the hallway. He had totally forgotten about his dream until he noticed a purple lid from a bottle of juice right in the middle of the checkered floor, evidently placed there as a reminder, specifically for him.

But he didn't want to see it. Not today. He wasn't in the mood and had no desire to think about how it got there, whether it was an intentional set up or a random coincidence. With his foot, he punted the metal cap, making it skip across the tiles the way a flat rock glides across the smooth surface of tranquil pond water. It bounced off the double-doors and fell to the ground.

Thick drifts of snow twirled out of the sky like confetti, creating miniscule tornadoes in the courtyard. One flake seemed to peep into the door's glass for a moment, and then floated off to rejoin the millions of others. He was glad to see that the snow hadn't stuck to the ground and the temperature wasn't quite cold enough for ice to form and make the roads slick. As he walked down the pathway toward Shady Avenue, he continued to see more of the ever-present reminders of Azazel. Three vehicles parked on the street formed a triangle around his pickup. A mini-van at the far end of the block, a small hatchback parked a few feet behind his truck and a four-door SUV on the apartment side of the street. All three of them painted *Azazel's* purple. Not the most common color for vehicles, but there they were. Despite the fact that it was Kia's favorite hue, he was beginning to nest a deep hatred for it. Though it had started in his dream, it now seemed to be growing into some sort of abstract, cohering conglomeration in the real world that had to be more than just mere happenstance. And would Kia believe him if he tried to explain what he was seeing? Probably not. She would most likely recommend a psychiatric visit. A brief thought came to take out his phone and snap a picture, but for some reason he didn't. He needed to get to work.

Cashe waited for the traffic on Shady Avenue to clear, standing motionless in his hooded sweatshirt like an advertisement for Perfect Papa Pizza. When a break between two cars opened, he jogged across the street and hugged up as close as he possibly could to the dirty pickup, without getting his clothes soiled from the grit and salt and leaf particles which had been splashed from the traffic and now stuck to the driver's side door. Silently, he crossed his chest and prayed that the approaching semi or school bus following wouldn't bounce him all the way down to the synagogue lawn a block away. After they went by without harm, he carefully climbed in, started the ignition, and turned the heat all the way up, waiting for the truck to get warm. He sat shivering, blowing hot air into his cold hands and looked at the clock. 10:51 A.M.

When he threw the transmission into neutral, the truck rolled a few feet forward before he pressed the clutch and shifted into first gear. He turned right on Douglass Avenue and passed an old woman in a purple coat and hat on the left.

Damn, they all must somehow know. But how?

On Murray Avenue, two girls with long, curly black hair strolled through the crosswalk. One wore a black coat; her friend's was purple. At the next light, he stared at a chrome emblem on the back of a Dodge pickup truck. To everyone else, it was just the head of a male ram, but to Cashe, he was once again face-to-face with Azazel. He wanted desperately to lose the thing, to get away from it, but for some reason its current flooded the landscape and he knew that wouldn't happen today.

Perfect Papa

WHEN CASHE FIRST STARTED working at Perfect Papa, he quickly found out that there were only two possible scenarios on any given day. It was either completely calm and clean or entirely filthy and chaotic. Today, after parking and coming through the transparent, double-doored entrance, he noticed that the store appeared abnormally spotless. Cardboard pizza boxes were stacked neatly in sets of ten under the cut table. The stainless-steel countertop shone. Fresh, sky blue dishwater and hot, crystal clear rinse water were ready for use. White steam swirled above both sinks, awaiting dirty dishes.

The floor had been swept, and the room seemed oddly empty. It was almost as if he was back in the Marine Corps when everyone arrived at the cafeteria before sunrise, the barracks during inspection, or like toting a polished gun to the firing range.

Parallel lines and perpendiculars were everywhere, from the Perfect Papa posters on the walls advertising this month's specials, to the glowing red insignia displayed outside on the storefront and on the face of the counter. Even the employees stood up straight, everyone waiting for something to happen.

Jeff Mitchell, one of the store managers, a skinny, forty-something orange haired man with a thick French mustache, was talking on the phone behind monitor one, finishing up an order. From what Cashe knew about him, he had been working on and off with the company for over five years. Every now and then he'd quit because of some conflict with upper management, but always came back. It was rumored that he was gay and had an affinity for short men—specifically, the squat and who some also saw as effeminate, district manager of Perfect Papa, a man named Buck Alvarez.

Next to him, and also on the phone with a customer, was Antonio Smith, a driver and part-time assistant manager who everyone called Cleveland. He, of course, hailed from that city, was a huge Browns fan and an honors student at the Art Institute of Pittsburgh, oftentimes bringing in stacks of drawing paper to sketch cartoon characters on when business slowed down. Obsessed with one day locking down a job with EA Sports to design video games, he constantly talked about his high priority of maintaining a perfect GPA and was Cashe's only true acquaintance.

Sam Thomas, the general manager, was behind the cut-table snatching boxes and lifting pizzas out of the oven. He expertly cut each pie and then slid them skillfully into the open boxes, stuffing each order with the correct amenities of special seasoning packets, pepperoncinis, and sauce cups. Cashe couldn't look at him without laughing on the inside. The top of his bald head was covered with less than a dozen strands of hair. He wore glasses that did a poor job of hiding his stray left eye, which wandered aimlessly whenever he stopped to talk. The white apron tied around his neck barely covered his huge belly. Ripped calf muscles held up the rest of his body and it looked like each piece of his stocky frame didn't belong with the rest. He was like the living incarnation of Mr. Potato Head. As if God had stuck together his many parts from different people and collectively created Sam. His kind voice had been the hardest thing in the world to resist, and Cashe often found himself raptured by his words.

"There he is," said Sam, placing a pizza atop the heat rack.

"S'up, Sam," answered Cashe as he typed a username and password into the antiquated computer system.

The DOS text on the screen was green and most often than not, no matter how many times he entered the correct information, something always went wrong. Words would just randomly disappear, like the system was haunted. Today everything worked on the first try. When finished, he moved toward the check-in, check-out terminals, then went further to the back of the store and grabbed a Perfect Papa car topper. Some drivers didn't like to use them, but he always took one, if for no other reason than to dissuade the police from pulling him over.

On the way out to his truck, he stopped at the driver's table. It was the area where everyone congregated when business was slow, and the place some of the drivers left the little trinkets they all needed like pens, rubber bands, or extra pieces of uniform, such as a cap or a shirt. Today, he saw a newspaper there. On the front page of the *Pittsburgh Post Gazette*, the headline read:

Mayor Dreams Up New Proposal for Turnpike Renovation

The young Mayor, a man named Luke Ravenstahl, a rookie politician who had taken over after the sudden death of the more experienced Bob O'Conner, wore a strange smile as he looked into the lens of the camera. What really made Cashe cringe, the one *surprise* detail that jumped from the photo, temporarily disorienting him, was what the Mayor had gripped in his hand. With a balled-up fist, he held a silk tie that hung between the lapels on his his navy sportscoat. It was purple. The color of Azazel.

Cashe went out to his truck with the feeling that Kris Williams was around somewhere. He was learning in life that everyone didn't want to be his friend, and no other person in the Perfect Papa shop did a better job of exemplifying that than Kris. It was as if his purpose in life was to stand in direct opposition to everything he did. The second Cashe had been hired, Kris took on the role of his nemesis and rival.

And who else would have left the front page of the paper right there in the open, but him?

From the stories he heard, Kris had been the one driver who worked for Perfect Papa the longest time. Eight long years. He was a stout, thirty-something black man with a shaved bald head who didn't have any qualms about exhibiting his strange mannerisms. To Cashe, his behavior was border-line abnormal to just plain bizarre. Even the way he talked was weird. It was all part of the *magic*, the only word Cashe could think to describe it, that surrounded this fellow.

One of the most obvious and irritating things he'd do was leave random objects around the store for no apparent reason. Once, he brought in a shoe and left it on the middle of the driver's table during an entire shift. No one complained or said anything about it, which seemed just as peculiar, but when Cashe finally spoke up and asked, the other guys only said it belonged to Kris.

From the very beginning—and he knew it was a crazy thing to think about someone—Cashe made up his mind that, without a doubt, Kris had superhuman powers. He swore, though he never told anyone when it happened, that once or twice Kris had even read his mind. Throughout Cashe's life, he was unaware people could do such things. Yet, he began to understand after careful consideration, that in times past, as far as the Bible was concerned, they probably categorized these practices as witchcraft, sorcery, or seeing. *What else could it be?* He never imagined himself working so closely with someone who had these *abilities*, and especially not in a *pizza shop* of all places. And he had a hunch that Kris wasn't alone in this, either. There were others. Later, these suspicions would be proven true.

Cashe went outside into the brisk air and stuck the car topper to the roof of his truck with a loud "thump," then quickly re-entered the store.

"I need a bank," he said to Jeff, who had now turned his back to the registers, and started twirling and tossing a large pizza dough above his head. Cashe watched as he set the stretched-out disk on top of a black metal screen. Jeff approached the register, pressed a secret combination of buttons and the drawer popped open. He was relieved to be handed a wad of ten ones and a five. It frustrated him whenever the store was short on dollar bills because that made it impossible make change on deliveries. It was like trying to drive with flat tires. But even a $15 bank wasn't always enough. Depending on the roll of the dice, someone might drop a $50 bill on a $10 order on his first run. He'd have to use his personal money, return to the store for more ones, or even worse, tell the customer he didn't have enough change, which he hated doing. Usually, it took about three or four cash exchanges to build up a nice register in his pocket.

He checked to make sure he had all the right tools in his possession before leaving for his delivery. First, he needed pens, preferably two or three. Going through a cheap twenty pack of Bics from CVS in two weeks' time proved to be an easy task. When business was up and labor was low, and he was often expected to take up to five orders on each run, they seemed to go missing all the time.

On those hectic days, he always forgot to make sure that one was neatly folded inside the customer's credit card receipt so they could sign, failed to count each and every dollar given to him, and didn't remember to smile when addressing customers.

But he loved when everything did work perfectly, just as the store's slogan proclaimed—*Perfect Ingredients, Perfect Pizza, Perfect Papa*. Often, he thought they should have added in *Perfect Deliveries* to the tagline to help him out a bit. But drivers got no help. It was great on those few infrequent occasions when he *did* actually arrive at his destination on schedule, could find a parking space in the crowded side streets of Pittsburgh, somewhere near the apartment buildings or businesses and not ridiculously far down the street, and locate a doorbell or buzzer at an entrance which actually worked. Unfortunately, that rarely happened.

After snapping a fresh rubber band around his money, he went back to the computer monitor to find out where fate would lead him today. His first delivery was to 4774 Sciota Street. Cashe stuffed a hot-bag with the pizza, exited the shop, then jumped into his truck, tuning the radio to Carnegie Mellon University's station, WRCT. He cranked the volume as a new song, one he hadn't heard, began to play. A few blocks away on the corner of Centre and South Millvale Avenues, a baby in the arms of his mother wiggled its feet. The child wore purple Converse low-tops caked with gold glitter. Again, it reminded him of the front page of the paper, and then of his dream earlier that morning. He tried to repress these thoughts as he drove into a space across the street from 4774. For some odd reason, he checked the receipt to see if the customer was male or female. Her name was Heather.

He hopped up three steps to the porch, rang the buzzer, and also knocked, just in case the bell didn't work. A few seconds later, a silhouette formed behind the white curtains hanging in the window of the door. A young woman in cut-off shorts and a T-shirt answered with a smile. He immediately noticed she wasn't wearing a bra, then quickly reviewed the ticket once again, attempting to find the price of the order. At the bottom of the receipt, he saw the amount. *$14.76.*

"Hi," Cashe said, quickly returning a smile because of her breasts. He earnestly tried to concentrate and stare only into her blue eyes. "Your total is $14.76."

"Oh," she replied, as if surprised, and held out both a ten and a five-dollar bill. "Hold on one second, I'll see if I can find some *ones* for a tip."

Before he could give her the food, she stepped away, and a giant, square-headed guy appeared in the doorway. He seemed to be approximately the same age as the girl who had first answered—only much larger—built like he might be one of the new freshmen on Pitt's football team. She returned and tried to hand the chap several dollar bills.

Cashe was all-too familiar with this scheme. She wanted him to pay for the bra-less peepshow by having to deal with her boyfriend during the transaction, a purchase he really didn't want to make; it was something subtly forced upon to unsuspecting victims. It seemed to be the common move of a woman, a puzzle he couldn't quite understand. They desired to show the goods, but only with protection nearby. Girls, he thought, liked *seeing* the chicken dance of fear.

"You can go back upstairs," said the lineman, pushing her to one side, "I have a few bucks in my wallet."

He handed five dollars to Cashe.

"Thank you very, very much," Cashe said without the slightest hesitation or annoyance, and took the five, crisp one-dollar bills. He quickly joined them to the others inside the rubber band in his pocket, and then bounced back down the steps to his truck.

Chapter Seven

LATER THAT EVENING when Cashe returned to the shop, he saw Cleveland holding on to the cut table so he wouldn't fall over from laughing so hard. All the guy's eyes were slightly bloodshot. The faint smell of marijuana in the air meant that they had just finished smoking pot in the back parking lot, and as usual, they talked race and politics. Both Sam and Jeff had finished their day shifts and gone home, so the coast was clear. Brian Guy, a gentle, jolly giant of a man who drove for Perfect Papa when he wasn't in a classroom teaching junior high school students music, unknowingly stared with a befuddled look on his face as Cashe approached the driver's station.

"Hey, Cashe, let's see that $100 bill!" he said, brightening up.

He had showed it to him before, but for whatever reason, every time Brian looked at it, it always seemed brand new. Cashe took it out from a hidden compartment in his wallet and handed it to him.

"Damn, you can still see the blood on it," said Brian looking it over, holding it up to the light. "That shit's unbelievable."

"This hundred-dollar bill could have been a bullet in my ass. I'm just glad to be alive."

"I think that it's cool you're keeping as a personal memento," said Brian. "It's almost like a medal or something. I'm telling you, we go to war in this business, man."

Cleveland had stopped laughing and moved to the oven and grabbed the peel. He slid a pizza into an open box, cut it into eight slices and put the finished product under the heat rack in what appeared to be one motion. Occasionally, he peered inside the oven to judge when the next pie would be coming through on the conveyer belt. Kris was near the registers placing stickers, which gave all the pertinent details of each order—the customer's address, telephone number, type of pizza, and list of toppings—on the side of the boxes. Cashe's heart jumped when he noticed that Kris had a purple towel thrown over his left shoulder. Among all of the other quirky characteristics Kris exhibited, (and there were many the sweaty, mind reading bastard held), the one which annoyed Cashe the most was what he would describe as a canny ability to get close, way too close, without actually *touching*. It made him feel a whole hell of a lot of uneasiness. For example, and again, as crazy as it might sound—and though he didn't quite understand it—he *knew* without a doubt that Kris had some type of connection to Azazel and his dreams. The towel was *right* there. Only he had no way to prove it. He was also absolutely convinced that Kris was using some type of Voodoo to conjure up his personal purple information—he was positive of it—but Cashe just wasn't quite sure how he, or anyone could accomplish such a thing.

"Listen, you have to be the stupidest person on earth if you think a *real* black man will ever be President of the United States of America," said Kris, finally speaking up. As he switched the violet towel from his left shoulder to his right, he glanced over in Cashe's direction, as if to say, *me and my buddy Azazel have got you my yellow friend. Don't try to run.*

"What are you talking about, Kris?" said Brian. "Obama's black."

"No, he ain't black," answered Kris, slamming one of the stickered boxes in front of Cleveland. "He ain't nothin' but a mixed breed."

"How about I think you're gay," said Cleveland, who was now slapping out a medium ball of dough. "And you're just using your wife as a decoy. You and your gay purple towel."

The comment made Brian chortle.

"Cleveland, if you were a few shades darker, you might understand," said Kris. "And that's precisely the problem. There are so many outsiders coming into this country that the plight of the black man has been forgotten."

As the discussion began to turn toward the topic of border patrol, out of nowhere, Kris suddenly spoke to Cashe.

"And what are you? A Puerto Rican?"

"Who, me? No, I'm an American," Cashe shot back, more curious about how Kris would respond than anything else.

"Well, where are your parents from?" he asked.

"They're from America."

"Anyone who has ever come into this country has come from somewhere else," Kris said to everybody, nudging Brian on the arm. "That is, unless you're one of the leftovers who happened to escape the slaughter of the American Indians. What, do you think I'm going to call ICE on you or something?"

"Now hold up buddy," said Cleveland. "I'm bi-racial and you're starting to offend me."

"Isn't it obvious what I am?" asked Cashe.

"No," he said, turning his back to check the oven. "Cashe, you ain't white and you ain't black. Honestly, I don't know what you is."

Kris mumbled something under his breath, barely audible, a phrase that sounded like, *I got your bitch you fucking tin.*

"What did you call me?" asked Cashe.

"Nothing man, nothing."

Kris hardly ever talked to him. Only if it directly related to work, like relaying directions to a delivery. And even then, it was an uncomfortable confrontation. That's what had been so shocking about all of this, that he had finally come out and spoken.

The simple truth was that Cashe didn't like him. He considered him a racist, apart from everything else. All Kris ever complained about had to do with race and ethnicity, and more than anything, it drove Cashe nuts listening to him openly, yet inconspicuously talk about white people. He called them pigs and white supremacists. All of them were members of the Ku Klux Klan and their kids were skinheads. And if he wasn't talking about what he termed "the white race," he ranted about every foreign folk under the sun. The dirty Mexicans. The stinky Indians. He made fun of Italian accents and mocked the eyes of Asian people. He called them "Japs."

"Let me ask a question," said Cashe, kind of throwing it out into the air to no one in particular. "Why is it that people in almost every country in the world have the same race and nationality, except in America?"

"What?" asked Cleveland, who up until this point only seemed to be listening.

"Like, Kris is an African American, but I'd venture to say that he's never been to that continent," said Cashe. "So, why isn't Kris just an American?"

"Because he's black," said Cleveland with a chuckle.

"But that doesn't make any sense," said Cashe. "White people aren't European Americans. They're just white Americans."

Brian silently nodded, rubbing his stubble.

"I'm like a combination of eight different races," said Cashe. "I don't see myself fitting into any of those categorizations I always see on applications, and that's why I wish they just had an American box to check."

"You're right," said Cleveland. "They don't do that shit any-where else except in America."

"It's because of the history, man, the history," Kris said, oddly turning back again to Cashe, starting to speak proper English.

"America is such a young country in the whole scheme of things, if you think about it. What, we're like 250 years old?"

"Well, technically, the United States is 239 years old this year," said Brian, butting back into the conversation.

"Back then, everybody wanted to relate to their original homeland, that's all," said Kris. "But slaves didn't have shit. Them niggas wasn't even considered citizens."

"Yeah, I understand that, but now it's different," said Cashe. "It seems that everyone in this country has to form some type of coalition or join a society to prove that their national identity is anything in the world other than American. So what I'm saying to everyone standing here is this—I'm an American. I don't need to be a part of any special *separate* community under a different name."

"Especially if you're born here," said Cleveland.

"He does have a point," Brian said with the biggest grin on the planet, high from the weed and the conversation. Cashe could see every tooth in his mouth. "Americans…we like categorizing categories or something. I don't know how else to say it."

"It's true," said Cashe. "Think about it, why does America have to have the whole world within its gates? It gets confusing."

"Yeah, I think I know what you're getting at," said Cleveland. "It's kind of like Christianity. You're a Christian Cashe, aren't you?"

"No, I'm really a Muslim pissed off at the shaven-face policy here. You know that they just don't want me to grow my beard because I might look too much like a terrorist, right?"

Everyone went silent.

"I'm just joking," said Cashe. "Yes. I am a Christian."

"How many fucking—I'm sorry, I don't mean to offend you, Cashe—but how many *fucking* denominations are there anyway? You have Baptists, Lutherans, Catholics—" he said, counting them all finger by finger on his right hand as he emphasized his point.

"That's *exactly* what I'm saying. There comes a time," said Cashe, staring at the computer monitor to check how many orders were on the screen, "when people must be called infidels. And that is America's problem, in my opinion. Either you're in or you're out. There is way too much separatism, and honestly, I'm tired of it all."

Cashe thought Kris, for some reason, had gotten upset at the comment. He watched how he walked away from the small circle and began organizing the pizza screens into the cool-down slots near the side of the cut table. One by one, he placed them into the metal rack.

"Oh damn," he said looking down at his hands, with an overly dramatic homosexual intonation. "I didn't want to get this *black shit* all over my hands."

All of a sudden, the phones began ringing out of control. Brian answered the first call. While he was on the phone, another came in. Within less than a minute, everyone but Cashe and Cleveland had taken a call. Cashe used this opportunity to sneak away to the bathroom in the back of the store. He tried to lock the door behind him, but it was broken.

About a month ago, as the story went, Kris had been inside taking a dump late on a Friday night near closing time. And as usual, they were all high from smoking pot. As a prank, Cleveland and Brian slid a double stack of dough trays nine feet high, and probably filled with 800 pounds of bloated, over-yeasted dough in front of the bathroom door, then leaned up against the towers so Kris couldn't get out. What they didn't know was that Kris was extremely claustrophobic. When he finished using the bathroom, he tried to open the door but it wouldn't budge. He tried again, but it wouldn't move, no matter how many times he clicked the button lock open and turned the latch. He had kicked the door and even thrown his shoulder into it, but it stayed shut. Cleveland and Brian almost started crying with jubilation when Kris screamed at the top his lungs for help. When they finally moved the dough trays out of the way, Kris lunged so hard into the door that the frame blew off the wall.

Cashe stood over the urine-stained toilet, counting the pubic hairs on the rim of the bowl as he pissed. They were all different colors. It seemed that everyone in the store had left a few behind. That sight and the bitter smell of urine put a sour taste in his mouth, and he knew he wouldn't be eating any pizza until the thought totally disappeared from his brain.

He buckled his pants and noticed how someone had brought the front page from the newspaper into the bathroom. It had been placed face-up on top of a broken computer monitor stored directly across from the toilet. Cashe looked at the headline once more, and at the tie gripped in the right hand of the mayor. Again, he began to think back to the ubiquitous purple and his dreams.

When he came out, he found Cleveland posted against the driver's table. There were four deliveries "In Progress," and he knew that it would be another fifteen minutes before they were ready.

"Hey, Cashe," said Cleveland softly, giving him a small backhand smack on his shoulder. "I know Kris talks a lot of shit, but I wouldn't let it get to you."

"Well, that's easier said than done," said Cashe. "He has a big mouth, and people with big mouths will one day answer for the things they say."

"He just thinks he's all big and bad because he belongs to their secret club—" whispered Cleveland.

"Huh?" asked Cashe. *"A secret club?"*

"Oh, you don't know?" he asked with a slight smirk on his face. "There are a few guys working here who are members."

"Are you?" asked Cashe, looking Cleveland in the eye.

"Hell, no, I don't want to be a part of that stupid shit," he said. "Besides, I don't have the time. I have too much schoolwork to do."

"So, what, do you have to be invited or something?" he asked, shifting his weight from one foot to the other, exploring the topic since Cleveland had brought it up. "What do they do?"

"Let's step outside," he said.

Cashe followed Cleveland past Kris, who was working the oven, out into the street and faced the traffic on Centre Avenue. They both tucked their hands into their pockets like twins to keep warm.

"This shit is kind of crazy," he said, looking around as if someone might overhear what he was saying. "Before Sam hired you, Kris, Brian, and this guy Rich Levine, who doesn't work here anymore, started acting *really* strange. They always huddled together in the back of the store folding boxes or outside in the parking lot, smoking weed amongst themselves. If I walked over while they were gathered together, they would suddenly change the subject.

"So, one day I just came up and asked Kris what the fuck was going on, and he said they were planning to have this once-a-year initiation ceremony at some undisclosed location for an organization they were joining."

The door to the shop opened behind Cashe and Cleveland, and when they turned around they saw that it was Kris.

"Hey, Cleveland," Kris said, looking at them both as if they were two pieces of warm dog poop on the sidewalk. "You're up. You have a delivery."

After Kris went back inside the store, Cleveland looked around at the cars passing by, and at students strolling near the funeral parlor directly across the street, on their way home from evening classes. He kind of looked fidgety, as if he had something on his mind.

"I have to take this delivery, but listen," he said. "You want to go shoot a game of pool somewhere tonight so I can finish telling you about *what happened?*"

The offer seemed abruptly imposing to Cashe. It was like when salespeople at the mall tried to get him to open a credit card he didn't want. He was never interested, but stuck around and listened to the pitch anyway. Immediately, he sensed something amiss, and thought that Cleveland might be part of this gang, acting as their recruiter, trying to get him in on the action. But at the same time, there was a sincere concern in Cleveland's voice, as if he had a burden to set down.

His choice of words, *about what happened*, had hooked him. Initially, he presumed the conversation was only going down the road of giving general information. But Cleveland was saying that something actually *occurred*. The two worked well together and always got along, but Cashe seldom talked to him outside of Perfect Papa. He had always been the type of worker who gave people their space. Shooting a game of pool with Cleveland was definitely out of the ordinary, but could also be a welcomed first.

"Yeah, sure," said Cashe. "How about Uncle Jimmy's? It's over on Semple Street a few doors up from the beer distributor."

"Yeah, I know where that is," said Cleveland.

"We can shoot a game of pool and you can finish telling me about *what happened*," said Cashe, carefully testing out those two words.

When all was said and done, he told himself that his curiosity had only gotten the best of him, and even as awkward as the moment was, he had made up his mind to go, at least only for camaraderie's sake.

The New Mafia

CASHE WALKED UP TO the bar at Uncle Jimmy's, ordered a Sprite, and then went to the rear of the room. Round tables with cheap folding chairs lined the wooden walls, though the place didn't serve food—only beer, alcohol, and light snacks like thin potato chips and pretzel rods. He sat in an empty seat next to a pool table and watched a couple as they shot a game of eight ball.

Uncle Jimmy's was the kind of place, like many others in the area, where students in the Oakland community and residents of nearby places like the Hill District, Soho and Greenfield came just to get drunk, smoke cigarettes and watch sports. Two television sets hung from the ceiling over the bar, and an antique juke box filled up space near the entrance to the bathrooms, but the main attraction was the billiards. A professional, full-length pool table took up half of the floor on one side of the cramped room. Just behind it was another, though a bit smaller in size. It cost a dollar fifty to play on the "big" table, and 75 cents to play on the "little" one.

If someone wanted to shoot a game, all they had to do was put up stack of quarters and wait their turn. From playing here during his collegiate years, Cashe had learned that people were pretty decent about being fair to newcomers. Mainly, because of a much-loved rule that allowed the winner to stay on as long as they could win. Only incoming challengers had to pay.

The place wasn't dirty, but like the Tavern in Mount Lebanon, seemed to be littered with a little bit of everything. All the major beer companies, like Budweiser, Michelob and Yuengling adorned every inch of territory on the walls. An array of liquor bottles reflected in the mirror behind the bartender, giving the illusion of having double the amount in stock. Hunchbacked old men on stools drank glasses of draft poured from the tap and stared at ESPN. A group of women next to them wearing too much makeup cackled out loud while being served Cosmopolitans and Strawberry Daiquiris.

As Cashe watched a pony-tailed brunette concentrate on hitting the two-ball in the side pocket, Cleveland appeared from around the corner and slid into the seat across from him.

"Sorry I'm late," he apologized, smiling. "On my last delivery to Chatham, I forgot the customer's Coke. I had to go all the way back to the shop, get the drink, return to the dorm, give it to her, drive back to the shop, cash out, and then come here."

"I hate when that happens," Cashe said, glancing over at the pool table, watching the woman sink another shot. "But don't worry about it, I haven't been waiting long. I've been anticipating hearing your story about Kris and this secret club."

"Yeah, this is some crazy shit," said Cleveland. He smiled again, scooted up in his chair a bit and jumped right into it.

"Okay, like I was saying, one day last year I noticed that Kris and some of the other guys were starting to act all secretive and what not. I could tell that something weird was up. So, when they went out back to smoke, I walked over and asked what was going on. At first, no one said anything, but then Brian spilled the beans."

"We're getting ready for initiation night, is what Brian had said," said Cleveland. "Rich told him to shut the fuck up, but it was too late."

"An initiation?"

"Yup," said Cleveland. "But no one would say anything else about it, so I was like, *whatever*, and walked away."

A week later, Cleveland said he had totally forgotten about it. While doing the dishes near closing time, he overheard Kris, Brian and Rich planning on going down to Club Utopia on East Carson Street on the South Side. They talked about *something* being there. *Something*, not someone. He said he kept hearing them say, *It's going to show up tonight, watch, I'm telling you.* Cleveland told Cashe the way they were talking didn't make sense and that they were getting all excited like little kids. And though no one explicitly said it, he put two and two together and figured that they were talking about the initiation.

"That's when I got really got suspicious," said Cleveland.

Cashe thought briefly of how Kris constantly used abstract lingo and imagined him saying a phrase *exactly* like *It's going to show up*, then glanced at the pool table to the left again. The chick smacked the six-ball into the corner pocket with a pop. Her boyfriend leaned silently on his cue in the corner, scowling. The guy's hat was low over his eyes, and he almost looked depressed watching his girlfriend give him a first-class ass whipping.

"I don't know why I did this, I guess I was just feeling up to it that night, but I said to myself, 'I'm going to follow them to see where they're going and find out what the heck they're talking about.'"

Cashe squirmed in his seat a bit and put both of his elbows on the table.

"But Cashe, let me say this first before I go on," said Cleveland holding up his right his hand. "I've never told anyone this, but I don't know, it's weird, *something* told me to tell you what I'm about to say. I think it's God. I've really been needing to get it off my chest for a while."

Cashe sensed that beneath the surface, something truly was bothering Cleveland. He even seemed a little choked up.

"Sure, I'm here to listen to you, man," said Cashe.

"Thanks. But I'm warning you dude, this is some crazy shit."

"Don't worry, I've heard a lot in my lifetime."

"Alright, you asked for it," he said.

After work that night, Cleveland said he pretended like he was going home, but instead drove around the block a few times before finally parking in the Pep Boys lot on South Millvale Avenue to wait for the crew to close the store. When he saw them hit the lights, lock the doors and get into their cars, he kept a safe distance and followed them to the South Side to Club Utopia.

"When I get there, I roll a joint and hit it a few times while I'm in the car," he said. "I figured I'd wait about a half hour or so after they went inside, because I didn't want them to know that I was spying. So, I pay the ten-dollar cover and the place is *jam-packed* with people. I mean, I couldn't believe how crowded it was."

Out the corner of his eye, Cashe watched the girl hit the ten-ball softly into the side pocket, setting herself up for the win. Her boyfriend still hadn't said a word.

"But this is the amazing part," said Cleveland, with a sparkle in his eye and a hidden smirk on his lips. "Guess who was there?"

"Who?" asked Cashe.

"Half the Pittsburgh Steelers starting lineup, star players from the Penguins, the Pirates, even the fucking mayor was there. And the girls, oh my God, Cashe, the girls! I had never seen so many hot women in my entire life."

"A celebrity extravaganza, huh?"

"Yes, but hold on," said Cleveland. "It gets even *crazier*. So, I'm looking around the room trying to recognize faces, when all of a sudden, I notice Brian and Kris standing near this red door in the back. I tried my best to remain low key as possible, waiting to see what they would do until I saw them go through."

Cashe imagined Kris and Brian standing inconspicuously on either side of a hidden door at the back of a club. In his vision, they both had on sunglasses. He tried to hold back a chuckle and wondered if Cleveland could see the grin on his face.

"You're right," said Cashe, still processing it all. "That is kind of weird. I know what you're going to say. You followed them."

"Exactamundo. I go through the door and on the other side there's a stairway, also painted red, leading down to a lower floor. It's dark. Music is blasting, and there are strobe lights flashing everywhere, lighting up the ceiling and the steps. But something wasn't right. It's kind of hard to explain how I felt. Like my mind had warped or something. I almost thought I was going to pass out."

"It was the weed," said Cashe.

"No, believe me, it wasn't," said Cleveland. "I barely smoked one little joint and wasn't all that high. That's why I'm positive about what I saw."

Here he was again, giving out the information before it was time. *He saw something.*

"Now Cashe, you might think I'm—", he paused, but went on. "You know what, I really don't care at this point. Yeah, you might think that I've lost it, but I'm going to say it anyway. It's just the truth and there is no other way around it."

"If you don't just tell me what happened, I swear Cleveland, I'm going to get up and leave. This is driving me insane!"

"When I get downstairs, it's *really* dark except for the strobe lights flashing on and off, and I couldn't get a real good look around because it was so crowded. But in the middle of the room, there was this tight group of people encircling something. At first, I thought it was some showoff dancing and everybody was watching."

The girl finally beat her boyfriend with a smooth, clean shot to the eight ball in the corner pocket. She raised both hands in victory and yelled out *Yay!* When she tried to kiss her boyfriend, he pushed her away, but she just laughed. They both placed their sticks on a rack hanging on the back wall and left.

"Hey, Cleveland," said Cashe. "Do you want to shoot a game of pool? I don't mean to interrupt, but this table's open and if we're going to play, we better do it now before someone else comes."

"Yeah, that's cool," he said.

Cashe dug in his pocket, pulled out three quarters, and put them in the coin slot on the side of the "little" table. Cleveland chose a cue. After the balls fell out at the far end with a loud rumble, he placed them in order from one to fifteen inside the triangle, the way he always did when he shot pool. It made a perfect rainbow. He racked the balls, chose a stick and rolled it on the surface of the table to make sure it wasn't bent.

"So, you're at this rave inside Utopia, and there's a crowd in the dark basement surrounding something," said Cashe, holding the cue ball in his hand.

"Yeah. So, I try to push my way a little closer. You know how it is. I'm squeezing through people, rubbing up against them trying to get to the middle. When I finally arrive, I stop for a minute and just stare at what the fuck's going on," said Cleveland. "I couldn't believe it."

"What did you see?"

"You're going to think I'm lying."

"That's *exactly* what *I* said before I told you guys about that murder I saw, remember?"

"Yeah, but the only difference is, you showed us the hundred-dollar bill with the bloody fingerprint, and the person who killed that guy was on the news," said Cleveland. "I couldn't bring back any proof."

"Proof? Proof of what?" asked Cashe.

"When I get to the middle of the crowd, everybody's hootin' and hollerin' and shit. Then I see this really low table, almost like a bed, on the floor with this girl lying on top, spread eagle. I mean butt fucking naked. There were four guys around it, two holding her arms and two holding her legs. Dude, they were running a train on her," said Cleveland.

"A what?" asked Cashe. He placed the cue ball opposite the rainbow triangle on the table. "You break."

"You've never heard of running a train on a girl?"

"No."

"It's when a group of guys line up and take turns banging one chic."

"And that's what they were doing? At a club on the South Side?"

"Yup, and Kris was one of them. And Brian. And Rich," whispered Cleveland, with big bug eyes.

"What?!" asked Cashe in a piercing falsetto, cocking his head back in disbelief.

They both smiled. It was both hilarious and also *odd* thinking about them participating in such an uncouth act. Cleveland told him that his dizziness turned into a state of vertigo. How he felt possessed and started looking around the room, scanning everything in sight as his mind became intoxicated by the DJ's music. He said the people's faces all of a sudden started turning into ghastly demons, like in some depiction of Dante's Inferno. Flashes from the strobe light seemed to take photographs of the scene as if it were an invisible paparazzi. Images of the table-bed and a girl lying on top of a white star inside a circle blinked repetitively before his eyes. He said it was the same Satanic pentagram symbol he'd always see on black "burnout" cars loaded down with dozens of bumper stickers while driving through the city. In the back of the room, Cleveland said there were a disguised group of men wearing dark cloaks draped with hoods lined up against the far wall, their faces hidden.

Cashe listened to Cleveland as he spoke, slowly making his way to the head of the table.

"I don't know why, but I happened to look over at this spot near the guys with the hoods and there was this *thing* there. At first, I didn't know what I was looking at, and then I realized what it had to be…"

Cleveland positioned himself behind the cue ball and began to aim. He hit it hard, and the sound of the crack rang throughout the bar. Then he looked up at Cashe and held his gaze.

"Dude, I saw the devil."

Cashe thought about what Cleveland had just said and waited for all the balls to fall into place on the table before he spoke. He watched the eight-ball inch toward the side pocket so slowly it seemed as if it would stop short of the hole. But it fell in. The game was over. Cleveland had won.

"*The* devil or *a* devil?"

"I think it was Satan himself," said Cleveland. "It had to be."

"What was he doing?"

"He was just standing there."

"Well, what did he look like?"

"This thing looked like an Egyptian god, have you ever seen them in hieroglyphics?"

"As a matter of fact, I have," said Cashe. He suddenly thought that Cleveland was starting to *get too close* with his words, like Kris had done with the purple towel.

"We studied them in this mythology class I took. It had the head of a sheep, or a goat, I'm not sure, and stood straight up like a person. But his legs weren't human legs. They had fur and his feet had hooves—like a *satyr*. Have you ever heard of a satyr?"

Yes, he's getting too close.

"No."

"They're half man, half goat. But they have human upper bodies with goat legs," said Cleveland, all *excited*, it seemed.

"And as soon as I saw that thing, I got the fuck out of there," he said. "It scared the shit out of me."

Cleveland didn't mention the win, but with shortness of breath and his hands now shaking, Cashe put quarters in the slot to retrieve the eight ball and gathered the rest of the billiards back into the triangle. At first, Cashe was unsure of it all. Maybe he was making up this cockamamie story just to screw with his head. Cashe had a brief flash of distrust, and he thought Cleveland somehow secretly had some unexplainable access to his personal life, like Kris and the towel or the mayor in the newspaper gripping the tie all over again. But then, his story gradually started to make sense, and he *believed* that Cleveland was telling the truth. His description *was* the exact depiction of the creature in his dreams. He envisioned the goat's head coming into his room and the distant wind of its whisper. *I am Azazel,* the thing had said. He felt his heart beating in his chest. It was impossible for Cleveland to know such precise details, and his words, like pinpointing darts, made him even more uneasy. As soon as he began to recall his dream about the angel, Cleveland spoke.

"Cashe, do you believe in demons and angels?"

"Yeah," he said, thinking Cleveland *possibly* might have just read his mind. "I do. But let me ask you something before you go on. Were you the only one who saw the devil? Or was everyone okay with him chillin' in the club, passing a joint around like a normal human being?"

Cleveland burst out loud with laughter.

"You know, I didn't even consider that until now."

Cashe laughed too, but not so hard. He couldn't.

"I know what I saw, and afterwards I just assumed that everyone else saw it too. But, at the same time, I wanted to believe it was all in my head, you know, that I was imagining it. And that's one of the frightening things about all of this. I really don't know who knows and who doesn't. Maybe no one saw what I did."

"Well, Cleveland, since you are being honest with me, I think I need to be honest with you about something," said Cashe. Now was the perfect time for him to speak about his dreams. It was now or never.

Cashe looked Cleveland in the eye.

"Under normal circumstances, I might think you were a little loony. But recently I've been having dreams about that goat-faced thing you're telling me about. Just dreams, though. I wouldn't know what to do if I saw something like that in real life. Probably run as fast as I could to get away from it, like you did."

He paused and thought again about that constant stream of ubiquitous purple he often saw, and how he *couldn't* escape it, wondering if that was similar to seeing a demon.

"I'm not just jumping on the bandwagon about this either," said Cashe. "But recently, I've been having some horrible nightmares about angels and demons. Ever since I saw that murder. There's other stuff too, but I'm not quite sure how to say it."

"Hmm," grunted Cleveland, rubbing his chin. "I don't know what's happening, but something fucking creepy is going on."

Cleveland stared at the floor for minute. He looked like someone had come and stolen a thought he had just been working with.

"Yeah, definitely. Something *real* creepy is going on," said Cashe.

He listened to the clutter of conversations over at the bar, and the tings of glass cups as the bartender filled them with ice and liquor. The women with too much makeup on began blathering like a coterie of witches.

"So, has Kris or any of the other guys you saw that night at the club ever confronted you, or said *anything* to you?"

"Nope. I don't even think they knew I was there," he said. "But I'll tell you what did happen. The next time I saw them at the shop, they all were wearing these huge, ruby *Superbowl* looking rings, flaunting them around like they were the shit or something."

Cashe thought about the glossy catalogue of class rings they sent him the semester before his graduation from Pitt. He envisioned the others wearing them around the store like they all had just earned degrees.

"What else do you know about this club or secret society, or whatever it is?" asked Cashe. "Does it have a name?"

Cleveland took his stick from the wall and walked to the head of the table. He pointed it at the cue ball and shot. The billiards bounced and knocked against one another, but nothing fell in this time.

"From what I heard, they have two names. One is like their stupid gang name, *The New Mafia*," he said. "The other more official one is the Order of Azel—or Azazel, I can't remember what he said."

A wave of disorientation hit Cashe, and he began to feel his heart beating harder through his shirt. The name *Azazel* echoed through his mind like a loud bell. His dreams, once again, had somehow resurfaced. Usually, it had only been the colors. The constant stream of purples, and sometimes reds and yellows, that appeared on cars, people's clothing or garbage left in the street. But now, for the first time ever, a word, a name even, had come through the magic door. He shook his head, stepped away from the pool table and sat down.

"No," said Cashe. "No fucking way, that's impossible."

"What is it?" asked Cleveland, not quite sure about what was going on. "Did I lay too much on you?"

"Too much?" asked Cashe, sounding as if he were a thousand miles away, because he was.

"I'm sorry," said Cleveland. "I know it's a lot, but I'm telling you the truth, man. I just couldn't hold it in any longer. I know you probably think I'm weird or something, but I had to talk to someone about it."

Cashe turned his gaze from the table and looked at Cleveland again.

"Don't apologize. Now I know for a fact that it had to be God Himself who told you to tell me what you said tonight," he said with a blank stare. "I believe everything you said, Cleveland. I swear I do."

Cleveland walked over and sat in the empty chair across from him.

"Oh, you had me worried for a second."

"If you think what you told me is crazy, then listen to this," said Cashe shaking his head. "I think I have this sleep disorder or something. It's called sleep apnea. Sometimes, when I'm really tired and try to take a nap, I have a hard time waking up. It's like my mind will wake up, but my body won't move."

"Hmm, that's odd," said Cleveland.

"Yeah, but the strange part is that it only happens when I have this recurring nightmare that's been haunting me for a while now."

Cleveland folded his arms and leaned back in his chair.

"But I don't know if I'm dreaming or if I'm awake until I actually wake up, if that makes sense. And there's that creature, or that thing, that always comes into the room I was telling you about. Only I can't move when I see it. It's like I'm paralyzed when it happens, and I think it looks exactly like the goat-devil you described in the basement of that club."

"Did it have long curved horns on its head?" asked Cleveland putting up both hands on either side of his face.

"Yeah. But listen, this is the part that really scares the shit out of me. Once, I had a dream and it spoke to me. And it said its name…"

He paused.

"It said, its name was Azazel," said Cashe.

They both looked at one another with stunned expressions, smiling with uncontrollable alien grins. The kind people try to hold in when they are thinking the same thing, but don't want to express the joy of connecting thoughts.

"What the fuck?!" asked Cleveland shaking his head. "What the fuck?!"

"Alright," said Cashe. "Since you kind of put yourself out there by telling me about this New Mafia thing, there's something else I want to share with you too. Google *Azazel*."

Cleveland whipped out his phone.

"How do you spell it?" he asked.

"Just like it sounds. A-z-a-z-e-l."

Cleveland thumbed through the Internet browser on his phone in awe.

"I can't believe the amount of stuff they have online about this. A fallen angel? A comic book character? Jewish mythology?"

"Read the Bible verses and the passages from the Book of Enoch when you get a chance," said Cashe. "It's interesting."

Cashe told him the story about the prophet and his dogs in the park, then they sat in silence while Cleveland continued to read the information on his phone. Cashe's mind wandered from the image of the goat-head in his dreams, to the bat flying around the apartment in Mount Lebanon, to the boy angel blowing out the fire, to the hieroglyphics on Yousef's wall, then back to himself sitting at a table in Uncle Jimmy's.

"Cleveland, there's something else I want to ask you," he finally blurted out after the extended silence.

"Sure."

"Are you positive that Kris or any of the other guys never said anything else about this secret organization?" he asked. "*Anything?*"

"No, what I told you is basically it," he said, putting his hand up to his chin, pulling on the little hairs of his scrawny beard. "I already said how they hold initiations every year. I'm almost positive there's another one coming up soon."

Then it dawned on Cleveland. He opened his mouth and waved his finger in the air.

"Oh, I forgot. There *is* something else. You know how Kris is always talking that political mumbo jumbo?"

"Yeah."

"Well, once he tried to explain some biblical conspiracy theory shit to me about the New Mafia, and until that night at Utopia's, I thought he was joking."

"I was wondering about that. If you belong to an organization, you have to have some type of goal or mission. What is it that they believe?"

"To tell you the truth, I'm not sure. I think he said they have links to some secret government program working on trying to bring fulfillment to the end of the world, or something to that effect. He was saying that every baby born in the United States from the year 1976 onward has a very tiny computer chip placed under their skin, and that all the doctors in the hospitals know about it."

"Wait a minute, I knew that he liked to talk about politics and the government, but wow, he really is one of *those* fanatics," said Cashe shifting in his seat.

"He is," Cleveland agreed. "And it gets better. Evidently, they believe in the Bible, in heaven and hell and all that stuff, but in a backwards, strange kind of way. Like, he was saying that all American citizens will have a choice, once in their lifetime, to join the New Mafia or be damned forever. He called it the *Inescapable Consequence*—"

"That's just nuts," said Cashe, smiling. "Who do they have, Jesus as their leader?"

"Well, according to Kris," said Cleveland returning the grin, "the reasoning behind such a *tremendous* statement is that he says we've entered this new post millennium era where everything on earth is under the control of a single governing entity called the 'One World Order'. He said now, people have to make a choice— to join those who are for the advancements of mankind that this organization espouses, or find themselves all alone in the world. And those who are for it will one day have access to some "new technology". Of course, he didn't say exactly what it was, only that once the decision is made, eventually they'll have power over those who refused the offer. He said the day is coming, and as a matter of fact, has already begun, when they will go around turning people into moonstruck lunatics, you know, like those crazy bums who are always talking to themselves downtown. But he said they are going to do it en mass, like some holocaust type shit by using the same scientific know-how used to make radio waves, TV's, cell phones and all other wireless devices. He said somehow, they will be able to make a connection to that microchip and fuck with your brain."

"What?"

"Yup, Kris said they're doing it now," said Cleveland. "But if you join, they'll remove the chip so that you will be *untouchable,* in a sense."

"So, if that's true, both you and I have a chip somewhere under our skin?"

"If you believe what he says."

His brain seemed frozen in "processing mode" as he considered Cleveland's words. It all made sense in a weird kind of way. He thought about the prophet and his dogs. *Maybe that's what happened to him.* But what did all of this have to do with his dreams of Azazel? They were just as real as Cleveland sitting across from him and couldn't be denied. And if an organization had that much power, what was all the secrecy about?

Yeah, he thought. *It really could be the end of the world.*

"You almost sound like *you're* a member," said Cashe squinting with a hint of inquisitiveness. He felt the sudden urge to turn the tables.

"No," said Cleveland, shaking his head and giggling again. "Not me."

His youthfulness and naiveté suddenly seemed to glow. In the back of Cashe's mind, there was still this doubt that Cleveland was just saying all this to test him. Maybe to find out if *he* knew something. But he couldn't settle on that.

No, there's no way. He's not one of them. Not Cleveland.

Chapter Eight

YMCA

IN A DREAM, CASHE waited peacefully in what seemed like a crowded restaurant. Yes, people, if they could be called *people*, sat across from each other at tables and booths. But there was no food before them. And, yes, the murmur of conversation filled the air, but the patrons were *stationary*. No mouths moved, no hands waved, no heads bobbled or turned. The occupants only took up space, like fleshly mannequins, complimenting the rest of the inanimate plants and partitions in the room. The walls looked as if they were made of black velvet, mixed with oily rainbow swirls, the kind found in parking lot puddles of water next to leaky automobiles. The tie-dyed colors splashed every detail of space—even the air. Prismatic butterflies fluttered in all directions like sparrows do when startled from their secret hiding places inside prickly bushes. He heard a chimerical, hypnotic, hip-hop instrumental beat accompanied by the strings of an orchestra grow more and more pronounced, over-shadowing the disconnected chatter. A drum pounded out a lethargic downbeat, and a deep vibration reverberated through his chest. The music intoxicated him with all his being—never in his life had ever he wanted to stay seated in one place so badly. He couldn't move. There was no sense of urgency, there was no place he had to be, there was no time.

The bellowing voice of a man speaking in the tone of casual conversation began to pervade the music surrounding him. It sounded as if he were reciting poetry. His words mingled with the rising and decrescendo of the strings.

The first falling of snow in season, or the first kiss of an admirer is what I feel for you Kia, it truly is…

Cashe's eyes focused straight ahead, and he suddenly noticed sitting across from him at the table, decked in a shiny purple robe with crossed furry legs and a black hoof sticking out the left side of the hem, the goat-man, Azazel. On top of its head, spiraled horns wound behind attentive ears and curled forward. Each tip formed the hissing mouth of a living snake. The goat's head tilted slightly to the left, then licked its nose with a long pink tongue. Its half human, half animal torso had been mostly covered, except for its hairy neck and hands. Cashe fell backwards out of his seat.

He woke up, rising out of unconsciousness with a startling shiver, into the hidden place in-between his dream and reality, and tried to move. His body strained to pull himself further up and out, until finally his eyes opened. Lazily, he stared at the ceiling and then looked down to his right, trying to figure out where he might be. The tables from the restaurant had disappeared and were replaced with two large closet doors. The floors reflected the dull blue light that shone from his cell phone on the windowsill. He remembered setting the alarm for 5:15 A.M. last night before bed. When he picked up the phone to check the time it read 5:14 A.M.

As the digits changed to a quarter after, the phone buzzed in his hand and the alarm sounded. He tapped the screen to stop the ringing, placed it back on the sill, reclined on the futon and looked at the ceiling again. The feeling from the dream still lingered in his chest. He recalled the sensation of the balmy, dim, velvety room and the draw of the creature's voice. *What* Azazel had said to him fit perfectly into the mystic vision, and was as perplexing as the goat-man himself. The words stuck to him, making it impossible not to carry them back into his waking life.

The first kiss of an admirer is what I feel for you Kia, it truly is…

Another thought came to Cashe, though it was more of an observation than anything else. It was how effeminate the creature was, sitting at the table like somebody's mother. That made the whole thing even more bizarre because animals or creatures weren't supposed to have LGBTQ-identity issues, *and* if the thing was a homosexual goat-man, why would he be sending flirtatious messages to Kia through *his* dreams?

As much as the heaviness of sleep held his body down, as if he were a block of cold steel and the bed a gigantic magnet, he did what his body didn't want to do. He sat up and slid his feet into his sandals. After standing, he stretched both arms toward the ceiling above like a cat, rising all the way up on the tips of his toes, thinking how it had been a few weeks since his last dream. He glanced over at Kia, still asleep under the mound of covers, and tried to decide whether or not to give her the message from Azazel.

Maybe later on, when the time is right.

Today his schedule was a full one. 6:00 A.M., prayer. Workout at the downtown YMCA at 7:00 A.M. Drive for Angelina's at 10:00 A.M., then for Perfect Papa at 5:00 P.M., and somehow in all the back and forth he had to eat.

He took off his pajama bottoms and began to gear-up in a pair of silver basketball shorts, a white Nike T-shirt, a pair of socks, thick, dark blue sweatpants, a matching sweatshirt, gloves and running shoes. From his closet, he checked his backpack to make sure it had all the equipment he needed for his morning trip—basketball shoes, a folded pair of swim trunks, flip flops, goggles, a swim cap, a bike lock, two extra inner tubes and a handheld tire pump. Last, he placed a bike helmet on top of his head and snapped the strap underneath his chin.

Cashe patted his sides to make sure he had his keys and then moved his road bike (a nifty Gary Fisher that took a year's worth of saving to buy) from the studio to the hallway. In the kitchen, he stuffed a banana into his mouth and took three huge gulps of orange juice straight from the gallon jug in the refrigerator before kissing Kia on the cheek and walking the bike out the front door.

The street was empty, which made for a quick ride to the light blue arches of the old beige and green Poale Zedeck synagogue on the corner of Shady and Phillips Avenues. He laid his bike down, sat at the top of the second flight of steps and bowed his head in prayer.

Dear Lord Jesus, I thank you for waking me up this morning and for giving me another day to live life and to live it more abundantly before you in a way that is pleasing to you…

Cashe loved this place; the predominantly Jewish neighborhood whose men periodically passed by in black suits, pressed white shirts, straight-brimmed hats and beards which hung down to the middle of their chests. He had a sincere admiration of how the menorahs and stars of David decorated the facade of the building and lent the place a certain *biblical* air. It made him feel as if he were tapping into some ancient door to the lost Jewish-Christian connection he had so often read about in the scriptures. He prayed for Kia, his co-workers, even for the guys he would be playing basketball with in less than an hour at the YMCA. These cold steps had become his special secret place to communicate with God since he moved into the neighborhood.

After he finished, he stood up, feeling refreshed. It was as if he had just taken a shower, but on the inside. The change, so profoundly different from when he had first sat down, made him stop momentarily. He looked up toward the tops of the trees across the street, then at the sky above, desiring to see some type of visual confirmation of where the switch had come from—something he could put in his hand and observe.

He climbed onto his bike and began coasting down Shady Avenue. The decline in the road caused him to pick up speed with little effort. As he hit the valley, exactly the opposite happened when he reached the halfway point and struggled to climb up the next hill toward Lilac Street. Droplets of perspiration began to surface on his forehead. One seemed to drip to his face at every downward rotation. The heat underneath his sweat clothes warmed his chest.

Some people labeled Cashe a "workout fanatic" in the past— and it was partly true. Growing up, he had always been an active child, constantly exploring in the woods, playing tackle football in the park with friends, and of course, riding his bicycle around the neighborhood. He excelled in high school sports and even dressed at Pitt on the football and basketball team for a year. His coaches called him a "natural" athlete. Competing came easy to him. And thank God, apart from his off-season straying during drinking parties or just for fun, cigarettes, beer and marijuana had never been able to enslave him like he had seen them do to so many others.

A right turn past the Giant Eagle brought him to Greenfield Avenue and he coasted down the hill towards the all too familiar Magee Playground. He peered up at the sign where the parks and recreation crew had painted MAGEE GREENFIELD PARK in humongous white letters at the top of the grandstand over the football field. Working the pedals around the bend, he prepared himself for the dangerously steep dive down to Second Avenue. As he went over the peak, wind blew past his face effortlessly, and he gripped the handlebars to keep control, respecting how fast he was really going. Cashe tried not to think about what might happen if he made one wrong move to the left or right, or what a car or truck coming up the hill too far in the wrong lane might do to him if they collided. The raw freedom and the feeling of flight overshadowed the risk he was taking, and he wished that he had wings to unfold from his back to lift him high into the cool, morning sky.

Near the bottom of Greenfield Avenue, he began to rhythmically squeeze the brakes to not slow down too fast. He leaned to the right, through a narrow passageway separated by medians that blocked the Second Avenue traffic, and up into a parking lot. Instinctively, from years of riding this path, he hit the smooth spots where the concrete squares met, and tried his best to avoid the sharp, jagged protrusions to keep his tires full of air. A defunct railroad track surrounded by giant steel mills once connected this four-mile stretch to the center of the city, but now the old thoroughfare had been made into a smooth, paved trail that many bikers, runners and rollerbladers used for a quick and easy, traffic-free commute from Greenfield to downtown Pittsburgh. It had appropriately been named the Eliza Furnace Trail.

Two vehicles were side by side in the lot, making the fenced-in area look more spacious than usual. From the empty bike racks attached to the trunks of a minivan and sedan, Cashe knew that whoever had parked there was now already far ahead of him down the path.

In the distance just over the trees, the beginnings of daybreak blushed above the horizon. Across the river, on the South Side of town, streetlights twinkled like distant orange suns along the mountainside, miniature spheres filling the hills with electric constellations. Rising from the seat, he pushed all his weight forward and down onto the pedals of the bike, thrusting ahead, clicking the gears into the hardest resistance. As fast as he was going, he still felt as if he were traveling in slow motion after the fast, downhill ride, his thighs and calf muscles burning at every cycle.

Baby rabbits darted from underneath the thick brush that lined the right side of the trail and crossed before him, playing a game of life or death, coming incredibly close to being run over by the front tire of his Gary Fisher. It was too dark to admire the multiple layers of graffiti art along the high cement wall that ran underneath the overpass of Interstate 376—whose course was parallel to the river and the path—but he could still make out their lettered mosaics. As his course wound beneath the highway, the sound of tractor trailers thundered above, echoing inside the cavernous tunnel, creating the illusion of jets passing overhead. He cruised underneath the second overpass of the Birmingham Bridge, and reached the halfway point of his trip. Just ahead, the four buildings of the Allegheny County Jail complex loomed in the distance. During afternoon rides, he could hear the skidding and squeaks of the inmates' shoes as they played games of basketball inside. But this morning, the path was unusually peaceful as he raced by security guards, clad in all black, approaching from the opposite direction on the trail, arriving for their morning shifts. At the end of the path, he entered the city like he had landed through some magical portal into another world. The titanic, metallic skyscrapers of downtown Pittsburgh suddenly towered above him, not shrinking his accomplishment, but rather serving as a fitting accompaniment. He eased to a stop and waited for the red light to turn green at the Grant Street intersection, then coasted down Fort Pitt Boulevard to the back entrance of the YMCA building.

Next to a thick steel fence, he locked his bike, removed his helmet, and passed through the glass double doors. Heat rose up his neck and more trickles of sweat dripped from his eyebrows as he made his way toward the security desk. A petite brunette with onyx eyes and a nametag that read "Kate" smiled as he approached.

"Good morning," she said enthusiastically, as if checking people into the Y was her favorite thing in the whole wide world to do.

He held out the barcode attached to his key ring and allowed her to scan him in, then grabbed one of the warm towels stacked to the right of the counter. As he went through the stairwell door, he tried to clear his mind, despite all the rubber bands, crushed potato chips and empty energy drink cans randomly littered on what seemed to be every other flight of steps leading up to the fifth-floor gymnasium.

When he entered the basketball court, he saw two teams sprinting from one end of the floor to the other through the hallway window. The games started at 7:00 A.M., and he knew he was late. Just out of bounds, Tony Jackson, a six-foot five dread-head, tied his shoes. Jimmy Rizzo read the morning issue of the *USA Today* next to Rich Douglass, who sat on the floor with his back up against the wall.

"Here comes Cashe! These young guys I tell ya—look at him glowing!" said Tony, extending his arms behind his back in a stretch, eying the black helmet in Cashe's hand. "Still riding that bike in, huh?"

"You know it," Cashe shot back, finding an empty space to undress next to the wall. After he stripped off his top layer of sweat clothes and folded them neatly next to his helmet, he switched shoes and tucked his T-shirt into the waistband of his basketball shorts. He was the thirteenth man to arrive, and as he tightened his laces, two others, Dave May and Chris Holloway, came into the gym, completing the next team.

On the court, Cliff Pataski shot and made a three-point jumper over Danny Corbo, and with a hint of swagger in his step, sprinted back up the court and yelled out the score.

"Six to four!"

The games were to seven and each basket was worth one point. Shots made from three-point range counted as two. If Cliff's team scored again, it would be Cashe's turn to play. While stretching, his mind drifted to the random thoughts that often came during these morning workouts. He noticed the petty details of the men on the court and began to read them like hieroglyphic symbols. Three wore black tennis shoes. Less than half had facial hair, the rest were clean-shaven. Four wore white T-shirts. All the guys had on red, gray, or blue shorts. He observed how the majority of the men on the court were over the age of forty. Some carried middle-aged weight around the waistline, yet somehow managed to be in great cardiovascular shape.

Cliff sunk the winning shot, another jumper, and ended the game. Cashe and the other four waiting men left their spots against the wall and instinctively gathered together under the nearest basket, taking jump shots and layups whenever a ball bounced their way. The team who won caught their breath around the solitary water cooler in the hallway, gulping cold mouthfuls out of cone-shaped paper cups, while a few from the losing squad forlornly meandered toward the gymnasium wall.

The men weren't speaking to one another this morning. Only one or two blurted out quick comments about too much pushing and put the blame on one another for shooting the ball at the wrong time. The five winners silently made their way out of the hallway and back onto the court, matching up with their new opponents and occasionally taking random shots.

Then "it" happened—a strange phenomenon which always seemed to rear its head almost every time Cashe played basketball at the downtown YMCA, one that took many forms, and as far as he was concerned, its origins were unknown. Sometimes he expected it, but more often than not it was forgotten, only to show up as a very unpleasant surprise.

A ball bounced off the top of the rim in Cashe's direction and rolled behind him. As he turned around to go after it, a basketball smacked him dead center in the back of his head.

Some of the men snickered, others remained silent. Everyone saw it happen, but no one said anything. Cashe didn't know what to think. His first thought wasn't that a stray ball had bounced inadvertently in his direction and accidentally hit him, but that someone had intentionally taken a cheap shot. He turned around and scanned the faces of the men. A few of the guys wore stupid smirks. The rest stood expressionless, appearing to ignore what had happened.

"Who hit me with the ball?" Cashe came out and said, half serious and half joking.

No one answered. As he scanned the faces of the men, trying to find an answer, one man seemed to stand out among the rest, a guy they all called "Johnny Brown." Obviously, he was the shortest man on the court, standing at a measly five feet, five inches tall, and the only one, he suddenly noticed, in the gym wearing a purple tank top. *Azazel's color.* Cashe sensed that he was the cause behind what had just went down, for several reasons. John Brown had been known not only for his deadly three-point jump shot, but also for throwing elbows, pulling shirts and stepping on players toes. Most of the time, everyone let him get away with it, because of his height. But there had been times when his antics started fights.

John Brown turned away and made a playful punch at Cliff, trying to knock away the basketball he was holding under his arm.

"Don't you touch my ball!" said Cliff, lifting it over his head and out of his reach.

"What are you going to do about it?" John Brown said to Cliff (and it seemed, also to Cashe) with a revealing grin, as if trying to hold back a laugh.

Cashe wanted to react and respond. He wanted to run over, push John Brown to the ground, and punch him in the face. But he had no proof, no evidence that he had thrown the ball. An indirect comment and a devious smirk wouldn't be enough to justify his actions, so he had no choice but to drop it.

"Let's go," said Buzz Orney, a white-haired man in his late fifties, "Ballgame! Let's get this one started."

Jimmy checked up the ball at the top of the key. For a quick moment, Cashe studied the emblem on the front of his gray Nike T-shirt; a shoe with angel's wings.

"Let's get 'em, Cashe!" said Jimmy, passing him the ball.

Cashe dribbled to the top of key and sunk a three-pointer. As he jogged backwards to get on defense, out the corner of his eye he saw that John Brown had tripped over his own feet. "It" wasn't over. It almost looked like an invisible person had snuck up from behind and pushed him, causing his head to smack face first onto the hard, wooden gym floor. He groaned, and then slowly rolled onto his back, holding both hands over his face. Cashe bit his lip, trying to prevent the alien grin from rising up.

A few of the guys surrounded John Brown for several minutes until he pushed himself off the ground, covering his mouth with one hand. In the place where he was sitting, a smudge of bloody fingerprints left three crimson lines on the floor. The gym fell silent. Before walking away, he bent over and picked up the remains of a broken tooth.

Everyone waited and watched to see what he might do next. John Brown took his time off the court, occasionally sopping up the blood pouring from his mouth with his T-shirt as he steadily approached the bathroom in the hallway. Danny from the losing team replaced him. Tony opened up the janitor's door, grabbed a mop, and did a once-over to the spot where John had fallen. The gymnasium felt empty as the players made their way back to the court, but after the game resumed, the momentum picked up, and soon everyone began balling again as if nothing had happened. After a quick, punctual win, Cashe and his teammates complimented each other on a good game, then listened to the losers complain. No one mentioned Johnny Brown.

"See what happens when you leave a man open," said Cliff.

"Well, if you play lax defense, it gets ugly," Danny shot back.

It was an amazing morning. Following the team's fifth consecutive win, Cashe called it quits. He took up his folded sweat clothes in one hand and his bike helmet in the other, went down the stairwell to the fourth-floor weight room and headed straight to his favorite fountain. Frigid water made an arch on top of the machine, and he moaned out loud in raw pleasure as he took hearty gulps.

After doing his usual routine—the bench press, pull-up bar, dumbbell curls and sit-ups—he left the weight room, now in a zone, and went down two more flights to the second-floor locker room. On the other side of the door, the wrinkled backside of a naked, old man caught him by surprise. He too undressed, swapping a sweat-soaked T-shirt and shorts for a towel, a dry pair of swim trunks and flip flops. It was 8:15 A.M. and he only had a half an hour to swim, and another forty minutes to mount his bike and complete the treacherous workout ride home to get ready for work. Rushing, he quickly went to the showers toward the back of the carpeted locker room, washed all the sweat from his body, and then waited for the wet elevator to take him to the basement floor pool. When the doors slid open, an elderly, crippled black woman in a red bathing suit, sitting on top of a Hoveround power chair, ordered him inside.

"Come on in, baby, there's plenty of room," she said, sounding more like she was giving a command than offering a welcome.

He silently entered with a smile and listened while the old woman spoke to her younger helper about how she hoped the temperature of the pool wouldn't give her goose pimples. As the elevator doors opened, he noticed that two out of the five lanes were occupied. One of the regulars, a woman who had once introduced herself to him as Gertrude Morris, was clad in scuba gear down in lane one (also known as the *old people's* lane). Only her head stuck out of the water. She stared in their direction through her huge goggles like the unofficial pool monitor, probably waiting to see who would swim where, or maybe just *looking* around. The old woman in the scooter headed for lane one to join Gertrude. The old people's lane was just a bit wider in size than the others and had the handicapped mechanical lift she needed to put her down into the water.

Cashe went to a shelf near the middle of the wall that contained folded towels, swimming accessories and several floatable objects of different shapes, sizes and colors, grabbed a pair of blue shoe fins, wiggled his feet inside, and then stepped up to lane three. He wrapped his goggles around his head, and then totally submerged himself into the water feet first, allowing his body time to adjust to the temperature before resurfacing. With a deep inhale, he dropped back underwater, pushed off the wall and began to swim.

Because of the extra boost the shoe fins gave him, the black cross painted at the far end of the lane arrived sooner than expected. On the return backstroke, he watched the stripes of gold on the ceiling and the red walls of the catwalk just above the pool gradually pass by. People poked their heads into the windows overhead every now and then to observe the swimmers down below.

After ten laps, he climbed out the pool, dried off, and then returned to the locker room. Some of the basketball players from the gym were there talking about the Pittsburgh Steelers, assessing how good their performance had been so far this season. While he dressed, Cliff and Danny walked by.

"See you on Thursday, Cashe," they both said, one after the other, not really looking into his direction.

"Yeah, see you then," said Cashe.

He finished lacing his shoes and stringing up his pants, left the locker room, taking double steps down the stairway, and rushed past the receptionist's counter.

"Have a nice day," he sang as he rounded the corner.

Through the windows of the back door he saw his locked bike, now covered with a light layer of snow. Three pigeons bobbed their heads, pecking at an uncovered patch of ground underneath a tree on the side of the building. The combination on the bike lock released with ease and in a matter of seconds he was able to unzip his bag, put the lock inside, climb on and cycle to Smithfield Street.

At the intersection, he waited for an opening in the traffic between a gold PAT bus and a black Saab to widen a little further, hit the gap, and shot off. He wove in and out of the standstill traffic until he reached a red light at the Boulevard of the Allies. There, he squeezed beside an illegally parked truck unloading merchandise to his right and stand-still traffic on his left. The driver of the truck carried boxes down to a sublevel storage area in the middle of the sidewalk that looked more like a tornado storm shelter than an entrance to a basement. When the light turned green, he hung two quick rights, coasted to the entrance of the Eliza Furnace Trail, pushed his gears into high speed and cruised the even path, eying the muddy Monongahela River. Every now and then, he glanced at the vehicles zipping by on the other side of a wire fence that separated the trail and the highway, considering the fragility of life.

When he arrived back at the apartment, the digital clock on top of the yellow cupboard next to the refrigerator read 9:25 A.M. He hurriedly set his bike up against the studio wall, knowing he had less than 15 minutes to shower and dress, and five minutes to eat. After tossing his workout clothes into his mesh laundry bag in the closet, and taking a three-minute shower, he put on his clothes, stuffed an apple into his jacket pocket, gave Kia—who was still sound asleep under the covers—another quick kiss goodbye and rushed out to the truck. As he drove down Shady Avenue toward Angelina's Pizzeria, he felt incredibly fresh and rejuvenated, recollecting why he so much enjoyed these morning workouts.

Chapter Nine

Angelina's

WHILE STOPPED AT the traffic light in front of Angelina's Pizzeria, Cashe searched for a place to park. Cars lined both sides of the street, except for one empty opening close to the intersection. Parking in the East End of Pittsburgh was a never-ending problem; all the drivers agreed it equaled borderline insanity. It was hard enough for the residents of Shadyside, let alone any random person who needed a temporary slot. Everyone seemed set up for failure.

Most mornings, no parking spaces were available, and on both sides of all the streets, green and white signs stated the rules:

**2 Hour Parking Monday Thru Saturday,
9AM to 6PM, Except Sunday**

There were no meters on this block, however, the parking authority routinely made rounds throughout the neighborhood. The only legitimate place ever open was in a small, gravel lot on the side of the pizzeria that offered enough room for five vehicles. But the usual people always had their cars there—the two managers working that day and the first few drivers who arrived the earliest. Cashe saw trouble brewing from the very beginning—how many

of the workers had taken unofficial ownership of certain spaces—
and decided immediately after he was hired to use public parking
on the street rather than get involved in the politics of the pizzeria lot. He didn't want to steal someone's spot, nor did he want to
suffer the embarrassment of one the managers telling him to move
because, *So and so has always parked there.* If nothing on the street was
open when he arrived for work, he'd park in the Highland Avenue
Laundromat lot, a few buildings down the pot-holed Greenbrier
Way alley which ran behind the storefronts. The rationale of all this
was that the closer a driver could park to the shop, the less distance
he had to carry orders to his car. So, the laundromat lot was a viable
alternative, but always a last option.

A huge symbol and reminder of the severity of the seriousness of the situation manifested itself in the form of a silver Toyota
Solara that had been sitting on the side of Angelina's for over two
months. Tacked to its flat front tire was a mammoth, yellow metal
boot. More than ten pink and white parking tickets were tucked
underneath the left windshield wiper. As Cashe walked toward the
shop, he stopped for a minute, peeped through its tinted window
and gazed in awe at a pile of tickets overflowing from the middle
console onto the passenger seat.

Angelina's occupied the first-floor of a 100-year-old, three-
story house on the corner of Alder Street and Highland Avenue.
The building was owned by a man named Bruno Luciano, a short,
mustached Italian, whose once firm chest muscles now sagged like
breast-fed tits. He often showed up with a cigar in his mouth, just to
hang around and check up on things, always announcing the best
places to buy the cheapest coffee in town.

When Cashe crossed the street and walked through the
entrance, the usual thought crossed his mind—how dirty the place
looked. Unlike the spacious Perfect Papa Pizza, with all the latest amenities and brand-new equipment, (they had an oven that
cooked a pizza in less than four minutes), Angelina's was old,

worn out and run down. It didn't have the smooth, clean cut tables, slick make lines and heat racks. Instead, its machinery was used and antiquated, and its tightly cramped space offered little room to move around in. But all that meant nothing. State-of-the-art equipment only amounted to a hill of beans as far as the owners were concerned. Angelina's served the best pizza in the metro area according to the *Pittsburgh City Paper*, the town's most respected restaurant critic.

The mornings, on no matter what day, always consisted of the same routine. When Cashe crossed the red line between customer and employee and walked behind the counter to the back of the shop for his apron and to check in, he already knew what to expect. As he came around the corner, he saw Ingrid, the wife of Miyad Burek, the Russian manager and co-owner of the shop, stacking napkins near the two computer monitors at the driver's station, blocking him from clocking in. She always seemed to meet him at the entrance to the kitchen, or at the door when he arrived, con-stantly, but not purposely getting in his way. She turned her head, and for the briefest of moments, he stared into her clear blue eyes. He scanned her ruffled blonde hair and noticed the evidence of age in her face. There was beauty masked behind her distinguished wrinkles and creases, and for some reason, he saw her as appealing, even *sexy*. She always dressed comfortably. Sweats and a zip-up hoodie. Socks and clogs. Little, if any jewelry. He felt like he wanted to say "good morning"—it jumped to the tip of his tongue—but instead he resisted the urge and stepped to the monitor on the other side of her.

Marcus Tolman stood in the rear of the kitchen, wearing a white apron covered with flour, and used a docker to flatten out round balls of extra-large dough on a stainless-steel table. He stacked them, one on top of the other, like humongous flapjacks. His face was chiseled with a cornered chin, high cheekbones, and tight lips that at first sight made him look frightening, as if he should be slaughtering hogs instead of making pizzas. Cold eyes were hidden behind square wire frame glasses, and his forearms bulged from his daily dose of smoothing out the chilled balls of dough. Marcus looked as though he lived a hard life; it was like he had endured a long series of life-threatening mishaps. Cashe thought that maybe he had been dropped several times as a toddler by his mother, fallen out of a tree, or survived multiple automobile accidents. Other than the uppermost part of his arms, nothing else appeared attractive about him. He stood in white, clunky, size 14 sneakers, and the measure of his hands matched his feet. On his head was a mesh baseball cap that said "Kick'n Ass" on the front.

From the stories Cashe heard about Marcus, he had been with Angelina's for seven years and seemed to know the most about what happened around the shop. He knew when all the trucks arrived for the deliveries of bread, vegetables, meats and sodas, what measurements to use during prep time, and the correct toppings to put on every pizza and sandwich on the menu. All the regular customers he spoke to on a first-name basis and had memorized the usual tip amounts they gave on deliveries. Marcus took pleasure in being on top of all the goings-on in the store, and off the record, had been given the authority to do so by Miyad himself.

Next to Marcus was Keith Odenga, a 24-year-old Kenyan who looked more like 40. With a cigarette perched at the top of his right ear, he silently took up the stacks of flattened dough Marcus had made, slapped them back and forth in each hand, threw the discs into a dusty flour cloud above his head, and then stretched them out onto round metal screens.

Sarvar Salih, a 22-year-old Uzbek, came in right behind Cashe, hurriedly clocked in at the computer, rushed to the back of the shop, stripped off his jacket and replaced it with the same kind of white apron that Marcus and Keith already had neatly tied around their necks and waists.

Ingrid had set up the usual revolving duties to perform for those, like Cashe and Sarvar, who always showed up late in the morning. Three large colanders, each individually piled with spaghetti, fettuccini noodles and shelled shrimp waited to be measured and portioned, while sliced-in-half tubs of blue cheese, Tzatziki sauce and Italian dressing had been placed on the cut table near the microwave to be poured into plastic cups. Cashe made the decision to perform the task of what everyone there called "doing the sauce," instead of working with the noodles. He set up an area on the hoagie line with rows of the tiny containers, matching lids and a wet cloth to wipe up any unplanned spills.

Seconds later, Jihad Muhammad Peterson, whose name curiously sounded almost identical to *Miyad* and meant exactly what Cashe thought it meant, "holy war," (Cashe had personally asked just to make sure) and Trent Blake, the only African Americans, scrambled through the kitchen to hang up their coats. Jihad returned in an apron and began dressing the dough-topped screens that Keith had prepared with marinara sauce and mozzarella cheese. When finished, he slid them into a rack up against the wall behind him. Both of Jihad's names, *Jihad* and his nickname, *Muhammad*, fit the character of the shop. Unlike Perfect Papa, where most of the employees were either default American Christians or didn't profess to believe in anything at all, the majority of the people who worked at Angelina's were of the Muslim faith.

Jihad's body was thick and wide, his head, large and square. A curved, eagle-like nose protruded from his face, and his bulging back took up most of the space at the pizza line. People always asked if he were Ethiopian or Sudanese, though he had been born and raised partly in Yonkers, New York and then later Richmond, Virginia. In another cosmic time and place, he might have been a professional wrestler or cage fighter, and his only visible handicap was a rotund, obtruded belly.

A tinier Trent returned without an apron and made his way to the hoagie line. He turned on the fryer, chopped up celery and sliced open rolls of bread. Both he and Frank Lindsay, who moments before had arrived into the kitchen and mounted up in front of the spaghetti and fettuccini noodles, were the same height. Trent wore a *Steelers* hat similar to Marcus' cap, a T-shirt and blue jeans. Frank had the appearance of a much smaller and shorter version of the potbellied Jihad, except for his beige skin, salt and pepper hair and beard, and dark slanted eyes.

As usual, everything started off quiet and careful, as if instead of making pizzas and pasta, they all had the duty of handling new-born babies. It wasn't until forty-five minutes into the shift that someone sparked up a conversation, and that someone was Marcus.

"Hey Trent," he said in a perfectly graveled, raspy Pittsburgh accent, one which matched his rugged appearance. It was a voice that demanded attention. "How bout dem fuckin' Pittsburgh Steelers?"

"Yeah man," Trent responded, expertly slicing open another roll of bread, "Did you see that catch by Heinz Ward last night? Oh…my…God!"

"They're definitely beginning to look like a Super Bowl caliber team," said Marcus.

Marcus continued to shoot out individual player and team statistics as if he had the sports section of the Sunday's paper programmed into his head. He talked about the details of the game, from how many sacks the defense had to the number of passes thrown by the quarterback.

"Ben Roethlisberger threw for 216 yards, had 17 completions and two touchdown passes," Marcus proudly said with a slight grin on his face. "I think they're headed in the right direction."

"Yeah, but we still have to play the Giants next week," said Trent, looking up at Marcus, who stood about a foot taller than himself.

Cashe tried not to pay too much attention to their conversation, not only because he really wasn't interested in football that much anymore—it had sort of died away with his parents' passing—but because of something else which always seemed to spoil his mood and therefore his involvement in 'kitchen talk' time. As if on cue, Miyad, made his way down the steps like a preacher suddenly appearing from behind the pulpit after a worship service, or like the President swiftly coming out to the podium at a press conference to give remarks on the latest national crisis. Like Jihad, Miyad looked as if he also could have been a gladiator in his heyday. He had a hulking frame, sky blue eyes and a pointy nose. His gorilla-like arms and hands were hairy and thick skinned, and his belly stuck out like a medicine ball. The air of peace and contentment Cashe had been enjoying while he slowly and meticulously filled the clear plastic cups with sauce immediately slipped away.

Out of the corner of his eye, he noticed Miyad roaming around, checking on the guys grinding out dough while they talked sports in the far corner, and on Frank bagging up the 12-ounce bags of noodles. Finally, he came and stood at Cashe's side. He stayed in the same spot over his shoulder in what seemed to be an extra-long pause, looking at who knows what, until he did the thing Cashe hated most; he snatched the container of Tzatziki sauce out of his hand.

"You put too much sauce in da cups!" Miyad said in his thick Russian accent. "Only fill dem up haf way, like dis."

Miyad took an empty sauce cup, filled it up three-quarters of the way with the sauce, and set it down on the thick plastic cut pad. No matter how perfectly Cashe performed his job at Angelina's, it appeared as though someone, especially Miyad, loved to correct his work. Cashe learned to expect these types of interruptions, as they had happened many times before and would surely happen again. Those unnecessary comments were the primary reason as to why he kept his distance from both management and all the other followers of Miyad's antics, (namely, Marcus). Over time, he learned to *watch them* all instead of becoming emotionally involved. Keeping a safe distance did help to ease the pain of this unpredictable manager-employee relationship, but the recurring hits had done nothing but build a hard shell around him.

"Right Miyad," Cashe threw back, knowing his bubble had already been popped long before he arrived. He thought of the old cowboy movies he used to watch as a child at his grandpa's house. If they had been in some saloon in the Wild West a century earlier, Cashe thought Miyad may have been shot a long time ago by an itchy trigger finger.

With a slightly shaky hand from the sudden disturbance—he couldn't say that he was entirely unaffected—Cashe finished filling *da sauce cups*, stored them in the cooler underneath the make-line, and then took the wet cloth and wiped down the cut pad. When that task was complete, he went up the steps to the very back of the shop, where another work area had been set up between two walk-in coolers. There, Benyamin Dini, a short, thin man with impeccable grooming, and crisp, ironed clothing under his apron stood chopping up lettuce for salads with a butcher knife and placing all of it into a purple plastic tub. Next to him was Hakan Selim, a tall, slender fellow with black, feathered hair, carving up a bulky chunk of turkey on the slice machine. They both spoke what sounded like Turkish slang to one another, snickering every now and then, and stopping just as often with a piece of meat or lettuce in hand to emphasize a point.

"Cashe is here!" Hakan said as he entered the space between them, lifting an unopened package of Styrofoam salad containers from a top shelf in front of them.

"S'up Benyamin. G'morning Hakan," Cashe said as he lined up six of the containers side by side and began putting monster handfuls of lettuce from the tub into each one.

"Hello, Cashe," said Benyamin.

"Hakan, how much in tips did you make last night?" asked Cashe.

"I didn't work last night, only daytime," he said in broken English. "I made, maybe eighty…ninety dollar."

"Liar!" Cashe said smiling. He looked at Hakan's face, examining the slip of a grin on his lips and bright eyes. He knew Hakan didn't like to talk about the *exact* amount in tips he made. For some reason, someone put it into his head that the IRS might be doing surveillance at Angelina's because he didn't report earnings on his taxes.

The three went silent for a while, and Cashe began to savor the peace this time offered, as it always seemed to do during mornings in the back room. He wanted to believe that it was a result of his morning prayer, or exercise, but over the course of his employment at Angelina's, he began to think otherwise, that perhaps it had something to do with Hakan and Benyamin. They too seemed to enjoy the same quietness of spirit and serenity during morning prep-time, away from the hustle and bustle amongst the rest of the crew in the kitchen. These two didn't show the same enthusiasm for all the gritty sports talk or ogling over pornographic pictures that the others often had. In the tranquility of the cramped space in the back of the shop at the cut table, their work took on an almost sacred atmosphere. Even the simplest duties, like cutting lettuce, somehow had greater significance.

"Done already!" said Benyamin after finishing the last head of lettuce, clapping his hands together as if he had just won a hundred dollars at a slot machine.

Cashe picked up ten salads, carefully balancing five in each hand, strolled past the walk-in cooler, down six steps back through the kitchen, and out to the lobby to put them in the refrigerated display case. Ingrid stood with her back to him near the doors of the cooler, again blocking him with empty animus, perfectly timed, standing cross-armed and staring out the window onto South

Highland Avenue as if she were deciphering a secret code. Cashe hoped that she might sense him coming and move, but it didn't happen.

"Excuse me," said Cashe, setting the salads on top of the counter, "I'm sorry."

"Sure," Ingrid offered, slightly startled, then moved her soft buttocks to the left.

After he finished placing the last of the salads inside, he felt a presence behind him. When he turned his head, Miyad was over his shoulder again, eying the display case, checking out his work.

"Where are da new salads?" Miyad asked, holding out both of his palms.

"All the old salads are on the left, in the first two rows there," said Cashe, beginning to feel the uneasiness of Miyad standing so close beside him. It was like a stranger had opened up the passenger door of his truck, come inside, and started eating a sandwich. "The new ones are on the right."

"You haf to keep dem *separate.* Here, put dem in like dis," he explained and began rearranging them, switching all the new salads to the left side instead of the right. It was an insane spectacle, but it was classic Miyad. Cashe looked at Ingrid, but she only shrugged her shoulders. Though he had put them inside exactly the way Miyad told him last week, he kept silent, didn't argue and just watched.

"My fault, Miyad, I'm sorry," he said mordantly, then went to the back for the rest of the salads. Miyad rolled his eyes.

After the cooler was stocked, he tried to find more work to do, and saw that the sink in the corner had been ignored. To Cashe, all the piled-up frying pans, empty plastic containers and metal trays were like a hidden treasure. For some reason, the other guys hated doing dishes. They'd sit at the top of the steps and smoke cigarettes all afternoon before lifting one finger to wash them.

The shop increasingly became busier and busier as telephone calls kept coming in and the computer screens lined up with orders. He opened the hot faucet and filled the sink, stirring in blue heavy-duty dish detergent until the water turned the color of a postcard tropical ocean. Jihad rushed specialty pizzas from the make line to the oven as Trent loaded it up with hoagies and pasta. Sarvar wrapped and bagged the heated food at the end of the line. Hakan took the pizzas out of the oven, cut and boxed them, while Cashe scrubbed the cooked grease off the steak trays.

"Ahh…," observed Keith as he continued to slap out and toss the dough, making his thin frame shake back and forth in a strange, comical dance, "Cashe is doing dishes!"

Cashe couldn't tell if he were asking a question or making a statement. Keith never really talked to anyone directly when they were busy, but instead threw statements into the air over the commotion of the shop, singing in his heavy English-Kenyan accent while everyone moved to the music of the lunch hour rush. He was like a teddy bear stuffed with an automated voice box in a toy store. Whenever someone pushed its stomach, it spoke.

Hurry Frank! Don't forget plates and napkins! Shoot right here! Oh my God, Cashe is back! What are you guys doing?

Miyad moved from the dispatch screen, to the hoagie line, to the pizza oven cut table, then back to the computer, bringing in the tickets for new orders and checking to make sure the correct food was boxed together. He had created a provisional system where only he had the power to assign deliveries. It enabled him to control the flow of incoming orders and eliminated the problem of greedy drivers taking more than they were supposed to. Anyone who even had the appearance of touching the order screen would be met with swift resistance, and if questions about unfairness arose, they were immediately told to "talk to Miyad about it."

"Who's the next driver?" yelled Miyad over Keith's cadence.

"I think Benyamin," said Hakan sliding another pizza into a large box.

"Somebody call Benny from the back!" Miyad said as he made his way toward the dispatch to assign the deliveries Benyamin would take. Hakan ran up the steps and called for him.

Within seconds, Benyamin suddenly and solemnly, made an appearance from the rear of the kitchen—similar to the way Miyad had done earlier—bagged up his orders, and then disappeared out the front door. In less than ten minutes, Cashe heard his name called.

"Don't worry about the dishes Cashe, let's go!" said Miyad looking over the boxed-up orders that were placed on a metal rack near the side of the oven.

"Take these three, but numba five goes first, cause it's a timed order for eleven thirty, you know."

Cashe looked over the long printouts of each receipt, then fetched cups, plastic forks, knives and spoons for each one from a bottom shelf stock under the computer monitors. Because of the amount of food for each delivery, he knew the bags would be heavy, and that he would have to be very cautious handling them. He also knew that the absolute worst fate to befall a pizza delivery driver was to drop the food. Neatly loading up each order into several raggedy hot-bags, he set them on the ground next to the salad cooler, and then paused, trying to figure out how he would carry them outside. Instead of picking up everything at once, he decided to make two trips to the truck. After handing him $15 in ones from the register, Ingrid watched as he lifted the first set of bags and made an exit through the door—an eyewitness to any mishaps that might occur—seemingly curious as to just how he might pull this one off. Keith recanted his song in the background.

Hurry Cashe! Don't be late! Hurry!

Once the second trip was made and everything had been loaded into the passenger side, Cashe took the receipts, re-read the totals, the addresses and room numbers, and steered into the Highland Avenue morning traffic. He kept the radio off, wanting a little peace and quiet to concentrate. The racket of the shop, Miyad's constant interruptions, and listening to the loud chants of Keith made his truck seem like a library.

The first delivery was to Hamburg Hall. Of all the schools and hospitals he often visited, he enjoyed going to Carnegie Mellon University's campus the most. Maybe it was because the magic of walking through these castle-like institutions offered a placid flip side to the grimy kitchen. Places like the University of Pittsburgh, Carlow College and UPMC (The University of Pittsburgh Medical Center) really seemed to have *it*, whatever *it* was. There was something soothing about the calm, elaborate vestibules, the carpeted, winding hallways and the mazes of connecting catwalks. All the drivers wanted to go to these locations for those very reasons, and of course, because of the generous tips.

After parking in the turnaround at Hamburg Hall on Forbes Avenue, he took the pizzas and sodas out of the passenger seat and set them into the bed of the truck. At Angelina's, there were no car toppers, so he had to be quick. He rechecked the building's name, the room number and total again, making sure all the information was correct. The thick black numbers, **4800**, beamed from the glass window above the gold revolving doors. Students from all over the world entered and exited Hamburg Hall, some wearing backpacks, others dressed in suits, as if it were their special day to give presentations. Cashe laid the three 2-liters that belonged with the order side by side on top of the two hot-bags, grabbed the handles, and lifted everything up and out of the bed of the truck.

Outside the entrance, a brunette student with an oatmeal complexion—perhaps she was Tunisian or Turkish or maybe Palestinian—leaned against the wall like a sculpture. As he went up the steps, she watched, exhaling white smoke from her nostrils. She seemed far too pretty to be holding a cigarette; smoking was an act for hard, rugged, masculine men, he thought, not meant for delicate beauty. Nevertheless, while the glance she gave him through her mascara made his penis involuntarily jump to the left, he held onto the hot-bags with a firm grip and kept straight to the side door, knowing he had to pay attention to the job at hand. One mistake might easily cause him to spill the order right there in front of everyone, and he wasn't trying to trade a sexy gaze for humiliation and laughter. Nor did he want to provide the opportunity for Miyad to do what he loved to do most by exerting his managerial authority over his error.

To the right of the revolving doors, a separate entry led to the foyer. Once inside, he cautiously climbed the steps to the first floor, and made a right down the hallway, passing a group of students who could have been Indian and Japanese or maybe Iranians and Koreans—he wasn't sure—gathered near the classroom number on the receipt. As he entered 1100A, he saw people scattered in small circles around the room. Several girls, all the cheerleading type— long ponytails and tight-fitting pants—surrounded the professor. He was a bearded man, almost seven feet tall in height and had been taking papers out of a soft denim briefcase.

"Here comes the food!" said the giant teacher, and for an instant, Cashe thought *he* was the food.

"Hi, how are you? Where would you like me to put this?" Cashe asked, looking around for the ideal place.

"Just put it there behind you," said the professor, pointing past Cashe's shoulder to a long table that ran the length of the room, only breaking for the aisle. Behind it were several chairs which formed the continuous desk of the first row in the amphitheater-style classroom.

Cashe neatly unloaded the order, set the five pizzas one on top of the other, and put the cups and 2-liters beside them. He took out a black pen from his side pocket, and then handed it and the receipt to the professor. A brown-haired, freckled student stood cross-legged near the fore, listening to him explain the details of their class syllabus. The jeans she wore were so tight, Cashe's eyes strained as he tried not to stare at the sharp, round fold underneath her right buttocks.

The professor swiftly scribbled on the receipt and gave it back to him. In dark ink, Cashe saw $20 drawn into the tip line, and as habit trained him to do, he pretended not to notice. It wasn't professional to gawk at the numbers in front of the customers. He said "thank you" to the professor, stuffed the receipt into the center of his rubber-banded one-dollar bills, scooped up the empty hot-bags and exited the lecture hall.

Done already, as Benyamin would say. *Mission complete. Two more to go.*

Still feeling good from prayer and the morning workout, he pulled up to his next delivery at the hospice on South Negley Avenue. There, he saw three black women on the other side of the glassed, automatic sliding doors of the clinic. One of them, the receptionist, sat behind a raised counter, relaxing. On a sofa to the right, an elderly lady watched as he entered the lobby. To her left, reclining on a couch opposite the receptionist's desk, a hip, young woman with red braided hair and pink Reeboks stared lazily at her painted fingernails. His delivery sixth sense made him guess that she was probably the one who had ordered. They all ignored him, as if they just hadn't seen a deliveryman walk into the lobby carrying a large bag of food.

He double checked his side of things before speaking, to make sure all the information was correct, and that he was in the right place. After a fleeting look at the three women before him, and with the instinct of delivering food what might now have been over a thousand times, he stepped up to the receptionist's counter.

"How's it going?" he said sharply, not really wanting an answer, only using the tart introduction to get her attention. She didn't acknowledge him. None of them did. Not even with a turn of a head.

Finally, the receptionist looked up, but still didn't speak.

"I have a delivery here for Desiree," said Cashe trying to stay as personable as possible, sensing the unfriendliness in the lobby.

"Desiree?" the woman behind the counter asked with an annoyingly cute smirk. "That ain't for no Desiree."

They both paused momentarily and he looked at the receipt again. The name was right there at the top of the ticket, but before he could make a decision about how to respond, the receptionist shot first. Her tone tasted like gasoline fumes.

"Turn around!" she ordered.

He froze, not *wanting* to obey, only struck by those two unpleasantly curt words. From the instant he walked in, he knew *something* wasn't right and didn't feel obliged to go along with whatever it was that she was trying to do. It felt like he had been set up, and he thought that if the three women would have been men, they probably would have robbed him. In his mind, he wanted to drop the food, reach across the counter and strangle her with a two-handed chokehold. But he considered where he was, and what he was doing.

Cashe, you are at work, you have a job to do. Just deliver the food. Turn around.

With everything inside him telling him to do the opposite, he made an about-face toward the woman sitting on the sofa in front of the receptionist counter. Before he could breathe in the air to ask if her name was Desiree, he was once again attacked.

"What's in the bag?" she asked firmly, taking control of the way she wanted the delivery to go, instead of staying in line with his modus operandi. Determined to keep some hint of dignity, he glanced through the window behind her, just to mentally get away from it all. He watched a blue and white shuttle bus filled with elderly, handicapped people park near his truck. *These bitches must be handicapped.*

"Are you Desiree?" he asked, returning his gaze to the woman, thinking that perhaps the information placed into the computer when the order was first taken might not have been updated. Someone named Desiree could have ordered from this same address in the past.

"No, my name is Toiya," she said, and the old woman sitting at her side laughed out loud. All of a sudden, *Toiya* began to have a separate conversation with her while he attempted to complete the delivery.

"What is that?" the elderly spectator asked her.

"I think it's a man delivering food," the young woman answered, as if Cashe's five o'clock shadow and bags of food weren't enough proof of his masculinity and profession.

But he understood clearly what was going on. They were talking about his race. He had heard the script too many times before. His beige skin and sabel hair always seemed to confuse black and white American customers alike.

"How much is it, Rico Suave?" she asked, smiling.

Through gritted teeth, he read the total and finally she handed him the money, which included a two-dollar tip. He gave her the food, offered a "Have a nice day," that got no reply, and then walked through the automatic sliding doors, back to the truck, perturbed.

The weather took a slightly warmer turn and the sky had begun to sputter drops of rain as he started the ignition and prepared for his last delivery. The humidity made the fabric on the seats feel damp and the inside of the truck smell like a mixture of mildew and stale food. He considered a trip to the car wash while mapping out the fastest route to the VA Hospital in his head. Cashe's tires skidded as he hurriedly sped ahead of the shuttle before the bus driver began to block the turnaround by lowering patients down the handicapped lift.

From the valley of Negley Run Road, Highland Drive wound up a tangled mountainside to a plateau where the VA Hospital conglomerate had been built in the 1950's. It was a gigantic military style, gated community of buildings numbered from one to twenty-five, settled next to two other high security facilities—The Shuman Center, (a prison for delinquent youths), and a Job Corps of Army Engineers base. Like most of the neglected streets in the Greater Pittsburgh area, it too looked as if mini-bombs had been dropped from toy airplanes, creating numerous craters in the middle of the road. When making runs there, he always worried about blowing a tire, breaking an axle, or inflicting some other type of damage to his vehicle. He imagined that this was probably what it was like driving on the moon. Highland Drive still looked like the old country thoroughfare it once was, but without the farm at the end. Its steep incline and dense foliage created the illusion that it wasn't really centered in the middle of a major city.

At the fork near the peak of the hill, he bore to the left and passed the Veterans Administration, the only building outside the confines of the larger campus. A flock of wild turkeys had flown from a grassy knoll near the fence separating the VA compound from Shuman Center and into the branches of a sycamore. The sight awed him so much that he almost veered off onto the lawn, amazed at how such obese birds could actually land in trees.

Just before the entrance of the complex were two signs on either side of the road which read:

Unmanned Security Checkpoint and **Keep Right**

Near the intersection, a color-coded map showed the quadrants for each numbered building on site. Behind it, a marble statue of a bald eagle spread its wings. A white arrow pointed to the left for Building One, and he followed the road until he came close to the entrance.

Three black men waited at a bus stop on the corner. Two of them smoked cigarettes, and when he slowed down at the stop sign, he sensed them staring. After taking a quick glance in their direction, he turned into the parking lot beside the hospital, where hundreds of cars seemed to take up every inch of asphalt. The only open spots were marked with signs that read:

VAH Emergency Vehicles Only and **Handicapped Parking Only**

Weaving in and out of the narrow drive between cars on the right and left of him, he circled the lot until he finally decided to settle in one of the reserved VAH spaces. A bearded white man wearing a turquoise baseball cap and a wool jacket looked up from a newspaper inside his unmarked van, and then glanced in Cashe's direction. As Cashe got out of the truck and began preparing for the delivery, the man suddenly stepped out, obviously pissed off, and stood inside the opened driver's side door.

"You can't park there!" he screamed, moving the folded paper to his right hand, resting it on his hip. The man's body had begun to shake like he had a nervous condition.

"I'm just going to—" Cashe had begun to say, but then threw the hot-bags back into the passenger side seat. "Okay, you know what? Never mind!"

He really wasn't in the mood for arguing with some fake VAH cop over an illegal parking job. After the merry-go-round with the ladies at the hospice on Negley Avenue, he didn't trust himself and needed to get far, far away before he did or said something that he might regret later.

"You can park over there by the—" Cashe heard the man say before slamming the door and throwing the truck into reverse.

Without thinking, he noticed a small patch of grass close to the first row of cars, a place that really wasn't a space at all. Dried tire marks left in the hard mud were evidence that someone else had probably encountered a similar dilemma, possibly with the same bearded man, and made their own parking spot here as a temporary solution. In one motion, he drove atop the grass, walked around to the passenger side, grabbed the order and strode to the double doors of the VA Hospital Building without looking back.

As he approached the foyer, he noticed how everyone coming in and out seemed a little "off" and a bit strange. They all chain smoked, had glazed eyeballs, and wore mismatched clothing—red pants and green jackets, or yellow high-waters and black loafers. Like sick zombies, or the results of heinous medical research experiments gone awry, they walked around sluggish and clueless. He tried his damnedest to not stare, to stay focused, and to avoid becoming distracted by what was going on around him. There was a task at hand, an order to deliver.

He scurried past a congested area that had a sign which read:

VA Highland Police Headquarters

A one-armed security guard ignored him as he went by. The route was familiar, and instinctively he traversed the hallway, following behind two healthier looking men in military fatigues ahead of him. Their last names had been sown onto the back of their caps in bold letters. SMITH and MORRIS.

At the first set of elevators, he pushed the "Up" button and immediately a bell somewhere near the ceiling rang. An empty, silver car slid open. Inside, he noticed how the floor numbers were double-horizontally placed near the handrail instead of vertically like in most elevators. This, he reasoned, must have been designed for people in wheelchairs. He hit the *three* button, the doors closed, and he felt a quick jerk as the car began its ascent. Seconds later, after another equally abrupt jolt, the elevator stopped. The same bell rang above his head, and the doors parted in separate directions.

The delivery was to room 3113. The first two offices in the empty hallway were listed as 3001 and 3003. With a bag of tuna salads in one hand and five hoagies in the other, Cashe continued down the glossy corridor, reading the rectangular room numbers in chronological order.

The door to 3113 was opened and the light was on. As he came inside, the first thing that caught his attention was the color green. At a desk on the other side of the door, his eyes focused on nearly a hundred different images of frogs. There were miniature statues of frogs, folded origami frogs that looked like they were ready to pounce off the desk at any moment, glass sculptures of frogs, posters of frogs hanging on the wall, the word "FROGS" carved out of single blocks of wood, and a giant Kermit the Frog stuffed animal in the corner with his arm around a lipstick-wearing female version of himself.

With a smile on her face, a small, curly haired woman slowly rose from underneath the desk, as if she had been searching for something that had fallen to the floor.

"The food!" she exclaimed. She got up from her seat and came around to where he was standing.

Cashe thought he should comment about all the frogs in the room, maybe say something like, *damn, you've got a lot of frogs*, as if it were an issue that must be resolved or a problem which required medical attention, but he held his tongue. He didn't want to be the one to bring it up. It seemed to be her personal taboo—like commenting on someone's really bad acne, or an overly obese person's weight—so he stuck to the business at hand. He wasn't there to offend anybody.

"Hi, it's $41.50," he said, involuntarily looking down and checking over his receipt.

"Set the food on the table," she said, rather rudely, as if she had somehow switched and become the evil version of herself, and then began digging through a purse on the desk.

Usually, the customer pulled out the money and paid first, but when this woman changed and began to give him bad vibes like the receptionist had done at the hospice, he dropped delivery procedures. Wanting to get this encounter over with as quickly as possible, he opened both hot-bags and set the salads and hoagies on the table across from her desk.

"I'm going to check and see if everything is here first," she said lazily, "If you don't mind—"

She slammed the money that was in her hand on top of the table instead of handing it to him, and then methodically thumbed through one of the sandwiches, slowly unwrapping the aluminum foil from around it. He watched her chubby arms wiggle and jiggle as she peeked inside. Cashe began to notice that she carried the scent of body odor, and the more he stared at her, the more she began to look like—a human frog. Overcome by repugnancy, and without really thinking about what he was saying, he blurted out a response to the woman's inspection.

"Ma'am, I really don't have time to stand here while you check each and every sandwich," he said. He sensed a nervous tremor in his hands coming on. "If you have any problems, please call back to the shop and they'll take care of you."

"Oh," had been her only reply. Giggling, as if all of this had been some fun game just to annoy him, she pushed her glasses to the top of her nose. He thought that she had probably practiced this move on other delivery drivers and mastered it. She pointed to the three twenty-dollar bills on the table.

"You can keep the change."

Without staying a moment longer, he thanked the woman, and then left the office. As he rode the elevators to the ground floor, he started to worry about his truck again, hoping the bearded man hadn't reported him to the police, or wasn't hanging out in the parking lot waiting for his return. He exited the stuffy hospital, burst into the open air outside, and with a sigh of relief, saw that no one was there.

Chapter Ten

CASHE RETURNED FROM HIS final delivery, parked, then walked through the entrance of Angelina's. The atmosphere had changed. The lunch hour circus was over, and now everyone relaxed. Marcus leaned over the salad cooler, resting his chin on his folded forearms. He gazed out the window at two women behind baby strollers standing on the corner, waiting for the crosswalk signal to change.

"Ain't nothing goin' on. It's dead," he said as Cashe passed by.

Cashe neatly placed the hot-bags on the bottom shelf of the steel racks next to the computer terminal, looked up at the screen and saw that Marcus was right. There were no more orders. It was 1:30 P.M. and almost time to "cash out" for the end his shift. Before he could put his hand in his pocket to check over his money and credit slips, Miyad appeared from behind the other side of the hoagie line.

"Let's go Cashe. I'm gonna cash you out," said Miyad.

"Okay, give me one second," he answered, holding up his receipts.

After Cashe adjusted the tip totals into the credit card machine, he met Miyad at the registers and paid him the money he owed the shop. He waited until Miyad finished double-checking the amount, thumbed through the sixty dollars in fives and ones he had made that morning, clocked out, and left without saying goodbye.

His second shift at Perfect Papa started at five, and he had to decide what he was going to eat for lunch. Ordering something out of the shop would probably have been the easiest thing to do, but he hated buying food from Angelina's while on the job. No one ever got freebees there, and it always seemed as if it was a big deal to ask one of the guys to make him a sandwich or pizza. He didn't quite trust his fellow employees at either joint and wouldn't put it past one of them to do 'who knows what' to his food. It was more of a mental game than anything else, but right now he didn't feel like being bothered—especially after how the day had gone. So, for peace of mind's sake, he ignored the fifty percent employee discount and instead opted to buy something from Giant Eagle and eat a simple lunch at home, possibly with Kia, if she was around.

Due to the constant, never ending problems with customers on deliveries and the confrontations from Miyad, he almost always left at the end of his shift on a sour note. No matter how sincerely he prayed to God in the morning or how hard he exercised at the gym before work, by 2:00 P.M., every bit of calm and contentment was consistently and thoroughly flushed from his system.

The light at the top of the street didn't seem to turn green fast enough, and while waiting, he studied a girl at the bus stop on the corner of College and Fifth Avenue, taking in her miscellaneous details: brown leather knee-high boots over blue jeans, dark sunglasses, a Cashmere sweater and red scarf kept her warm in the brisk, fall air. He observed how she shifted all the weight of her body to the left side.

Traveling these neighborhoods gave him the privilege of viewing the viridity of young fashionistas, but also the opportunity to see those queer, everyday oddities others might not pay that much attention to. Unfortunately, they always reminded him of his dreams and hardly ever made sense. After he had begun to notice the curious streams of color flowing through the streets, he often found himself searching for it, even when it wasn't there. Yet, many times it *was* there, and he just wasn't looking hard enough or in the right places.

For whatever reason, the girl suddenly stopped facing Fifth Avenue, as it would have been appropriate to do, and instead, turned her back to the traffic. She peered into a row of bushes. He tried to think of every possible reason as to *why* she was facing a bush and not the street, but couldn't come up with an idea that made any sense.

Maybe she doesn't want to be eyeballed by people like me driving by. Or, perhaps there's something in the bush—a sparrow or a bug crawling on a stem.

The light turned green and when he made a left and continued up the road, he noticed that she wasn't alone. At all the bus stops along Fifth Avenue, every female student followed the same unspoken order, their backs turned away from the traffic. At first, he believed he was out of the loop, figuring that it must be the latest trend. But then he realized it wasn't that at all and thought he understood.

The flow of color had somehow morphed into turned backs.

He wasn't exactly sure *why*, but the women made Cashe think of his wife. When he dialed Kia's number, after the second ring she picked up. He forced himself to return to normal considerations as quickly as possible before his mind wandered off any further.

"Where are you?" he asked.

"I'm with my dad at Sam's Club," she answered, rather pleasantly. Even though it was her father, he became jealous. It was an irrational emotion, he knew, yet there was no mistaking it, that's what he had in his gut.

"Oh," said Cashe. "I thought you would be home. I'm heading there now for lunch and was hoping you might join me."

"Aw, I'm sorry sweetie." Sometimes, she had a way of making him feel like a 10-year-old. Maybe Yousef's age was rubbing off on her. He listened while she spoke Arabic to her father in the background. "Dad says hi," she said when she finished, and that made things a little better.

"Well, I don't want to hold you two up," said Cashe. "I only have a couple of hours before I start my next shift, so I'll talk to you tonight." They told one another that they loved each other, and he continued on toward the grocery store.

The parking lot at the Squirrel Hill Giant Eagle was packed. It was an awkwardly compact lot built on top of a weird slant—because of all the hills, there were many *weird* slants in Pittsburgh—closed in on four sides by three buildings and a row of Evergreen trees. He turned inside, and circled a few times, trying to find a space. Finally, he saw the profile of a man with a long beard and black brimmed hat backing out an old Honda Accord. When the car drove away, Cashe pulled in, got out of the truck and walked towards the entrance. A store employee with a pink clean-shaven face and wearing glasses so thick that they made his eyes seem twice their normal size, locked up with a long stack of grocery carts. Struggling, but clearly handling the load, he pushed it in the direction of the automatic doors. They almost met at precisely the same time, but Cashe had picked up his pace a bit, hurrying past to beat him to the sidewalk so he wouldn't be held up.

In the produce department, he grabbed a black shopping basket and surveyed a row of lime-yellow bananas. Red vine-ripe tomatoes, cucumbers and fresh lettuce soaked moisture from the automatic misting machines. He wanted to eat everything he laid his eyes on but remembered that he had a specific list of items on the menu for lunch—a six pack of various Top Ramen Noodles flavors, sliced wheat bread, Jif crunchy peanut butter, Smucker's strawberry jam (on sale 2 for $5) and a gallon of orange juice.

Fortunately, the registers weren't crowded, and only one person was ahead of him at the express checkout line. The cashier, a stocky transvestite with a Giant Eagle smock tied around his neck and waist, gave a lackadaisical hello. Cashe couldn't help staring at his getup. He wore several styles of rings, combinations of silver and gold on all eight fingers and thumbs. His thin lips were covered with dull crimson gloss. On his head, a long ponytail extended from a balding hairline, revealing hints of gray at the roots. Blue eyeliner surrounded his inquiring eyes. The guy was big, even for a man, but on the inside, a meek, gentle spirit seeped through his pores. It emanated from his voice.

"That'll be $7.95, please," the cashier said softly.

Cashe handed him a ten—the man smiled and touched the palm of his hand when he gave back the change—then waited for the plump, Down Syndromed bagger to complete the loading of his groceries into plastic bags at the end of the conveyor belt.

"Hab a nice daaaaaay!" said the bagger with a curt seriousness, and gave Cashe the impression that as physically and mentally incapable he might be, there was something about life which he perceived that the rest of them weren't privy to. Right then and there, Cashe believed the two were probably the nicest Giant Eagle employees on the planet.

"Thank you and do the same."

After he arrived home and finished two peanut butter and jelly sandwiches and a bowl of chicken flavored Ramen Noodles, he washed the dishes. With his stomach warm from slowing sipping every ounce of the broth, he went to the bedroom and lay in bed. From his pocket, he took out his cell phone, set the alarm for 4:30 P.M., placed it on the windowsill and stared at the ceiling. His body still ached from his workout earlier, and he knew he could probably sleep until midnight. Not really wanting to fall asleep—because an hour of rest was never enough—he closed his eyes anyway. When he opened them again, he grabbed the phone and checked the time, thinking he had overslept. It was 4:29 P.M. Basking in the lethargic waters of drowsiness, the alarm sounded in his hand.

Fuck Buck

AS SOON AS CASHE arrived at Perfect Papa, he saw Buck Alvarez's shiny, crimson Hummer parked on Centre Avenue. During the time Cashe had worked there, he noticed how no one ever had anything good to say about the district manager. Whenever Buck paid a surprise visit, everyone straightened their backs and the entire complexion of the store seemed to transform. The covering of dust under the cut table disappeared, and all the loose pieces of trash usually left on the floor outside the garbage cans were correctly placed inside the bins. Kris' newspapers and other miscellaneous objects, normally strewn across the cut table, or on top of the boxes of unopened pizza sauce, were neatly folded and stored away.

Inside, Buck spoke into the air, dominating the conversation between he and Sam, who never stopped to look at Buck as he spoke, but kept working, nervously wiping down a heat rack that didn't need cleaning.

"We have to make sure all the dough is properly stored away in the trays near the back of the shop…Hi Cashe…and don't keep them, like, near the front of the store by the registers," he said as he slapped out a large ball of dough. Even the higher-ups like Buck performed shop work, like topping or boxing up pizzas.

"I agree," said Sam, scrubbing harder.

Cashe stepped up to the computer screen, clocked in, and gave Cleveland, who was on the phone with a customer at the register next to him, a nudge. Cleveland rolled his eyes at Buck, who had his back turned spreading the thinned-out dough over a screen, then gave a look of disapproval to Cashe.

Even though no one at Perfect Papa seemed to like Buck, Cashe never had any problems with him. In a strange, yet comforting kind of way, Buck reminded him of a shorter version of his father. It was his straight hair, tanned, bronze skin and goatee. But to the rest of the employees, he represented law enforcement. When Buck wasn't around, everyone, even Sam, didn't hesitate to vocalize their discontent.

"I hate Buck," Sam once said, after a surprise hour inspection of the store during a slow evening of business a month earlier.

"Why?" Cashe had asked, looking straight into his one, normal functioning eye.

"Becaaaause," responded Sam, "He's just so damn irritating. Nothing is ever right with him. He's just one of those people who knows how to get under your skin. Like last week. We cleaned this store in the morning because we *knew* he was coming in. I mean you could fucking eat off the floor. And you know what he says?"

"What?"

"*Scrub the walls*. I could have choked him."

The disease of animosity seemed as contagious as chicken pox, and Cashe started to hear people like Brian and Cleveland follow suit.

"What's your manager passcode?" asked Cashe after Cleveland had hung up the phone. "I need to clock in."

"It's, uh, hold on—"

Cleveland looked over his shoulder at Buck, who had walked to the back of the store, then slowly leaned toward Cashe and whispered, "It's FUCKBUCK."

"Fuck Buck?" he asked again silently, just to make sure. "Is that two words with a space or all one word?"

"It's one word in all caps," he whispered.

"You're crazy," said Cashe, punching in the code, chuckling under his breath.

"I know," responded Cleveland with a grin the size of Texas.

On the surface, he knew Cleveland really had no reason to hate Buck and felt sorry for him because he had succumbed to the obvious influence of peer pressure. He seemed too young and naïve to really hate someone. Of all the employees at Perfect Papa, Cleveland had been the only one, besides Brian, who seemed normal, and it was partly because of his age. Cashe assumed an instinctive, natural inclination to protect him from all the crap that circled around, especially coming from Kris, who had just parked behind his truck.

When Cleveland walked away from the register, the door opened, and Kris came inside. Cashe switched to "on-guard mode," and could literally perceive the mood change in the room. It was because Kris enjoyed starting trouble; it always seemed that at any moment he might do something unexpected, like fly into an uncontrollable rage. Kris went past him to the back of the store without waving or saying hello, and before Cashe could finish the thought about what kind of rude or racist comment would come out of his mouth today, Kris beat him to the punch.

"Anybody hungry?" asked Kris out loud to the entire store. "I really don't like Mexicans, but I feel like eating a chicken quesadilla!"

Cashe watched as he put his arm around Cleveland, mocking him from across the room, knowing Cashe didn't like seeing them two together.

"What's going on man?" asked Kris to Cleveland. "I heard you got your car fixed."

"Yeah, but check this out, you're not going to believe what happened," Cleveland said. "Hey Cashe, come here for a second."

Cashe walked over to the two and stood opposite Kris.

"What's up?"

He couldn't forget the conversation they had at Uncle Jimmy's. It was hard for him to blot out the images Cleveland had created of the dark club, specifically of Kris and the others waiting in line to run a train on some chic with the devil in the room. While Cleveland talked, Cashe finally got the chance to take a glimpse at the ring he said the members of the New Mafia wore as a sign of their loyalty. The ruby revealed itself briefly, then disappeared again as Kris tucked his hand into his pocket, as if he knew Cashe wanted to see it.

"Come outside, I want to show you guys something," said Cleveland.

They went out the door, made a left down the sidewalk to the parking lot, and Cashe watched Cleveland pop and prop the hood of his burgundy Toyota Corolla.

"I just got back from BFT Auto Repair today, and look at this shit," he said.

There were loose hoses and the battery had been sloppily thrown off its tray. It tilted off kilter next to the fuse box. On the other side of the engine, it looked like someone had placed a half-eaten piece of chicken breast next to the windshield washing fluid container.

"What is a piece of chicken doing under your hood, Cleveland?" asked Cashe.

"That's my whole point," he said. "I didn't put it there, the mechanics did!"

"Hold-up. Wait-a-minute," sang Kris. "What did you say was wrong with your car?"

"I needed a new starter."

"Did they put a new one in?" asked Cashe.

"Yeah, they fixed it, but they obviously did some other things too!"

"What?!" exclaimed Kris. "Didn't you tell me your dad is like one of the VP's at BFT?"

"He is, but what does that have to with them trashing my car?"

"Your dad must have made some serious enemies along the way at that company," said Kris. "I mean, he must have done something to someone."

Kris caught Cashe looking at his ring again, and finally spoke up.

"Looking at something?"

"I was just checking out your ring," he said. "Where did you get it?"

He saw Cleveland squirm a little out of the corner of his eye. Cleveland hadn't said anything to Cashe about keeping quiet, nor had he sworn him to secrecy.

"From this club I belong to," said Kris and held out his hand like a newlywed bride showing off a diamond.

The golden ring was shiny, set with an octagonal ruby. Just as he had imagined, it looked like the type of class ring students bought after graduation, but the designs at its sides didn't have a school name or a year. There were intricate patterns and crisscrossing lines leading up to the gem.

"I'm going to get back inside," said Kris, taking his hand away abruptly, before any further questions could be asked.

"Cool," said Cashe.

"Mmm, hmm" hummed Kris as he took one last look at the piece of chicken under the hood before making his way back into the store, sounding like he had just taken a bite of a delicious sandwich, "That shit's crazy."

"I've *never* seen anything like this before in my life," said Cashe, as Cleveland grabbed the scrap of chicken, threw it into the parking lot and lowered the hood of his car.

"Neither have I," he said, looking down at his feet.

"Well, what are you going to do now? Take your car back and demand some answers?"

He knew this was a defining question, and Cleveland's response would say volumes about what he *really* thought about the situation.

"Nah, fuck 'em. I'm just going to put the battery back, reconnected the hoses and let bygones be bygones."

"But Cleveland, you paid money to have them perform a service for you," said Cashe, still thinking the problem through. "Yes, they did the work, but they—they vandalized your car! I think you should go back and complain."

"Nah, I just need to let it go," said Cleveland.

"Can you imagine," Cashe continued, "If we cut zigzags into someone's pizza and then delivered it? They'd come back ready to kill somebody."

Cleveland's demeanor switched and his tone changed from serious to joking as they walked together along the side of the store.

"Yeah Cashe, I say let's go buy a couple of Glocks and some ski masks, then roll up to BFT and say, 'You know what happens to motherfuckers who put chicken under people's hoods? Huh? Huh?'"

Once before, they had talked about each of their short-lived four-year enlistments spent in the Marine Corps after high school, the guns they had learned to shoot and the exhilaration of firing off rounds during target practice. Though Cleveland seemed to be just playing about buying guns, Cashe wondered if there wasn't a little truth mixed into his mockery.

He shook his head while Cleveland laughed at himself, and wondered whether or not he fully comprehended how *bad* some people could be. Signing up to fight a war on foreign soil was one thing—but this type of cruelty happening at home somehow seemed *worse*.

Cashe took a car topper, went back outside to his truck, placed it on the roof and re-entered the store. The buzzer sounded, signaling that customers were placing online orders. At the computer terminal, the screen suddenly filled up. In less than 20 minutes Cashe had bagged up two deliveries and was off. One was going to the Hampton Inn, the other to an apartment building on Liberty Avenue.

After placing both orders into the passenger side of the cab, he slowly backed up, being careful not to tap the car parked behind him, nor sideswipe the one in front. When he looked over his shoulder into the road, what he saw surprised him. Another truck, the exact make, model and color of his, waved him on. The only difference between his truck and the other guy's was that he had a Perfect

Papa topper on top. The truck letting him out advertised a sign that said "Total Landscaping" on its door, and two chrome toolboxes lined either side of the bed. Cashe acknowledged his truck's doppelganger, accepted the kind gesture and drove into the early evening Centre Avenue traffic.

A block ahead, a mixture of Pitt and Carnegie Mellon students walked past, avoiding the drunks loitering outside the bars on Neville and Craig streets. Groups of "Jitney Drivers," members of the unofficial underground cab system in Pittsburgh, solicited business from atop the low, wooden fence surrounding the Giant Eagle parking lot across the street from the busy Centre Avenue Cleaners. This was his favorite time to drive, when the neighborhoods were filled with the mellow buzz of the end of the day traffic, and all the pressures of the late afternoon seemed to wane with the setting of the sun.

A left on Craig Street took him through North Oakland, a more upscale area of town, as he approached the university halls, libraries and coffee shops near campus. The majority of people traversing either side of the road no longer wore bright mismatching colors like the blacks loitering the storefronts or cruising down Centre Avenue on bicycles, but instead dressed as if they had shopped out of J. Crew and Abercrombie & Fitch catalogues. Girls modeled every corner, showing off tight corduroys, turtleneck sweaters and neck scarves over sculpted curves. He adjusted the heat in the truck to just the right temperature, one that allowed him to stay warm but at the same time kept the steam of the hot pizzas from fogging up the windows.

Cashe turned onto Schenley Drive, taking a shortcut through the park in an attempt to avoid the tight traffic on Forbes Avenue. Visually, the comforting scenes of dog-walkers and couples lovingly holding hands contrasted the gridlock of Oakland and soaked into his car like the soothing smell of seasoned firewood.

As he approached the Boulevard of the Allies by the empty swimming pool and brightly lit playground, with its slides and monkey bars decorated in a dinosaur motif, the red sign of the Hampton Inn appeared in the foreground of the horizon. When he stopped at the intersection of Bates Street, he glanced over into Kia's father's porch and saw Yousef sitting outside alone. His thick, furrowed brows hid his dark eyes and he seemed to be staring at something on the other side of the street. They briefly shifted down to the boulevard, and not wanting to match his gaze, Cashe concentrated on the traffic before him. At the green light, he drove onward toward the hotel.

There were no parking spaces available in the parking lot of the Hampton Inn, so he took a handicapped space. The unspoken rule, that it was okay for delivery drivers to park wherever they wanted—just as long as the vehicle had a sign and four-way flashers blinking—for the most part was respected by the police and local businesses. But, even with this silent law in effect, every now and then he encountered problems.

Several months ago, he had parked in the driveway at the hotel's entrance, directly under the awning, even putting his hazard lights on as an extra precaution. But as soon as he went inside the lobby, a shuttle driver pulled up behind, followed him inside and made a big stink about the exit being blocked. Cashe told him that he would only be a few minutes, but the hotel receptionists embarrassed him, siding with the other driver before an audience of spectators sitting in the lounge. Ever since then, the Hampton Inn's staff seemed overly rude and curt when he made deliveries to the hotel. Fortunately, his longevity outlasted their tenure as hotel clerks. A couple of months later, the guys who gave him problems that day no longer worked there, and everything went back to normal.

At the front desk were two concierges. A dark-skinned black man with a beard, and a white guy with a shaven face. Both wore jackets, collared shirts and ties, held phones up to their ears and watched Cashe as he settled into a spot on the other side of the counter. In his mind, he gambled and guessed which would respond to his presence first.

I think the black guy.

His guess was wrong. The other receptionist hung up his phone.

"Where ya going?" he asked.

"I have a delivery for a Harry DeVose in room 610," said Cashe, reading over the receipt.

"One second please," he said, swiftly picking up the phone again, dialing the room number. Cashe shifted the pizza and two liter of Coca-Cola into his other arm to give his right side a rest.

"Hi, Mr. DeVose? Your food is here in the lobby. Do you want me to send him up? Okay…All right…Bye," he said, and after dropping the phone on the handset, gave a thumbs up.

Cashe loved when things went as smoothly as they were going tonight. He was so happy he had to suppress the urge to skip to the golden elevators at the end of the lobby. Out of the corner of his eye, he noticed a woman with bouncing cleavage and a short gait trying to catch the car. When he hit the "Up" button, it lit up, the bell sounded and the double doors slid open.

He smiled at the woman, and using his work manners, motioned for her to enter the elevator first, catching a quick glimpse of her shapely figure and curly, shoulder length hair before she turned around. As the doors closed, they took spots at opposite ends. After pushing the *six* button, he realized that she hadn't selected a number and presumed they were going to the same floor. A strong impulse that wanted to put an arm around her and kiss her on the cheek came over him.

Instead, he stared above while the numbered lights at the top of the door illuminated as they passed each floor. She shifted her weight from one foot to the other, moving closer to him, and he began to fantasize about the conversation they might have, if things had gone another way:

The woman would turn away from the lit-up number six and face him.

"You having a busy night?" she'd ask.

"It's been a little busy, but nothing to complain about," he'd answer, surprised by his own smooth response.

She'd turn her whole body towards him and lean up against one side of the elevator wall.

"That pizza smells good, I think I want some Perfect Papa," she'd say, seductively smiling. He'd look her straight in the face, zeroing in on her white teeth, and soft lips.

"Do you want a menu?" Cashe would ask, zeroing in for a kiss, again, not believing how fast of an answer had come to him.

"Yeah, I do. Bring it to room 6—"

The bell sounded, the doors opened on the sixth floor, and Cashe snapped out of his daydream, watching, as the woman walked away like he didn't exist, as if they didn't just ride an entire six floors on the elevator together.

He held up the receipt and checked the numbers again. Room 610. When he reached the "T" at the end of the hallway, he saw signs posted on either side of the wall with large numbers written in black lettering. Rooms 601 to 612 were to the left side. Rooms 613 to 624 were to the right, the hall where the woman on the elevator had gone down. He made a left, staring at the intricate designs under his feet, thinking the carpet was much too elegant to be on the floor of the Hampton Inn. Room 610 was near the end of the corridor, and when he knocked on the door next to the peephole, a large, hairy, beer belly materialized out of the darkness from behind the swung open door. When he looked up from the stomach, an equally scruffy face and disheveled head stared down at him.

"Put the pizza on the table," was the only thing the man said before Cashe could breathe a word, pointing to the wooden desk behind him.

One of the rules of pizza delivery, both mentioned in the Perfect Papa handbook and known by all drivers in general, was that it is not required to enter the home, or hotel room of a customer. This activity was strictly frowned upon by management. However, he knew that every now and then, it was something that just *happened*, and realistically, drivers were often forced to make a decision in the moment, to react upon impulse. If an old woman asked him to come in to keep the flies out, most likely he'd go.

It wasn't until he tentatively put the pizza and drink on the table, and the door to the hotel room slammed behind him, that Cashe began to think that he really shouldn't have come inside. When he turned around, he swore he heard the door lock and saw the man blocking his only way out. In the room, the curtains were shut, clothes were spread on the bed and the television blinked in the reflection of the mirror hanging over the headboard. All of a sudden, he found himself in a situation where his right to leave without confrontation or obstacle had become immediately and instantly revoked. Depending on the sanity and intentions of this person, he knew that it had the possibility of turning into a caged death match. Surveying the room, he mentally turned furniture into weapons. He could grab the lamp to smash the guy's head in, or throw the comforter over his head and beat him with the clothes iron. Cashe wanted to punch himself for also breaking the other important rule—giving the food away before getting the money. Nevertheless, the pizza was on the table next to him, and with the receipt still in his hand, he read the total.

"It's $19.25," said Cashe, looking at the half naked orangutan, still standing by the door.

The time in-between his comment and the answer seemed like an eternity, but like magic, the awkwardness of the predicament changed to his favor. The beefy man began to look like a child as he searched for the money to pay him.

"I'm sorry," he said, and brushed past Cashe to the bed, digging through the pockets of a pair of pants lying on top of the comforter. "I can't remember where I put my wallet…"

Following a long minute or two of observing him rummaging through the pockets of the pants on the bed, then inside his suitcase, the customer finally sighed in an act of complete triumph.

"Whew, I got scared there for a minute," he said holding up a crumpled wad of bills. He singled out a twenty and a five and handed them to Cashe. "Keep the change."

"Thank you," Cashe said, quickly leaving the room, relieved. "Have a good night."

Timing

THE GLASS DOORS AT the ground entrance of the Liberty Avenue apartment building were locked when Cashed arrived to his next delivery. After checking the receipt, he found out that there was no apartment number, so he couldn't ring one of the buzzers outside the doorway. He raised his hand, putting it to the window as if giving a salute, then peered through to see if he could locate the name *Gaines* on a mailbox, or find some other clue verifying that he might be in the right place. After dialing the telephone number and listening to an endless barrage of rings, the answering service finally picked up. Not wanting to leave a message, but rather speak to someone in person, he ended the call prematurely and tried to call again. After a second and third attempt, he still got no answer.

Giving up on the order, he placed the warm hot-bag inside the truck and started the ignition. As he made his way back to Perfect Papa, he thought about how the address really wasn't all that far away, and it how it wouldn't be that big of a deal if they had decided to call back. Sure enough, at the exact moment he returned to the shop, his cell phone rang.

"Hello?"

"Did you just call my phone?" the woman on the other end of the line asked, ignorantly.

"Did you place an order with Perfect Papa?"

"Yeah, I did," she said lazily. "Are you downstairs?"

"No, I'm, not," said Cashe, "I was there about ten minutes ago, but no one picked up."

"I'm sorry, my husband had the phone in the other room—" she started to explain.

Though she was already beginning to annoy him, he reassured her that he would return and call from downstairs when he arrived. Ten minutes later, he slid into the same parking space as before, took the pizza out of the passenger seat, strode to the entrance of the apartment building and redialed the number. Again, there was no answer. Ready to call it quits, though this delivery didn't seem to be a prank call, he once more made his way back to the truck. There, his cell phone rang again.

"I'm sorry," the woman apologized. "This is the person you just called."

He considered hanging up, but forced himself to talk.

"Yes, ma'am, are you at home now?" he asked, trying to take the authoritative role, understanding that he was the one receiving all the blows in this fight to deliver her food.

"Are you downstairs?" she asked again, and the absurdity of the statement almost made it impossible not to hang up.

No, I'm on the fucking moon.

"Yes, I am," he said.

"Okay, I'm coming."

Beside him, two pigeons stumbled by, bobbing their heads, picking at random crumbs on the sidewalk. He imagined kicking the bird to the left, and then snapping in half a branch from one of the young trees planted alongside the street. The customers tonight were turning him into a violent person. A man passed by wearing an untucked blue shirt that perfectly matched his uniform, but without the Perfect Papa logo. Even their khaki pants were identical. They looked like twins. As he considered this, a Domino's Pizza delivery driver arrived and parked behind him. The driver grabbed a hot-bag out of the passenger seat of his car and approached his side. Cashe thought he was looking into a huge living mirror, without the glass, and wondered what kind of color monster this could be.

The door at the entrance of the apartment building finally opened. Across from him stood a chubby black man wearing a yellow T-shirt and white sneakers. Simultaneously, he observed both Cashe and the other driver.

"Did *dis* woman order from Perfect Papa or Dominoes?" he said, switching his head back and forth between the two. "I *thank* she said Perfect Papa…"

"The receipt I have says *Gaines*," said Cashe, speaking up.

"Oh, that's us. Hold on one second—I need to go out to the car," the man said, giggling. "My wife left her purse in the back seat."

Cashe couldn't believe how these people had such a high degree of unpreparedness. He whispered a prayer to God.

Lord, help me please.

He watched the fat man wobble to the car, search through the pockets of his dirty jeans until he found his keys, and then climb inside. Five minutes later, he closed and locked all the doors, walked back up to the entrance and handed him a twenty and a five-dollar bill.

"Keep the change," he said, and after leaving, Cashe wondered if he had ever worked so hard for a tip.

Do Not Touch

WHEN HE ARRIVED BACK at Perfect Papa, he found Kris sitting on the hood of Cleveland's car, speaking like he was giving a dissertation from atop a podium at a lecture hall, while Cleveland posted on the side of the building, listening to him talk. They both held wrapped sandwiches in their hands from the Sub Station hoagie shop a few doors down from the store. He couldn't help to not consider how Cleveland tolerated Kris so easily, apathetically allowing him to turn his car into a makeshift bench. Obviously, it didn't bother him as much as it did Cashe.

If I ever saw you sitting on the hood of my truck, I think I'd punch you...

Cashe kept quiet as he went by, only giving a nod to Cleveland as he passed. Kris jumped off the car, and they both followed him inside the store. He heard Cleveland ranting about how he might respond to Buck's strictness if he had Sam's job.

"Oh really, is that what you'd do?" Kris said to Cleveland out loud, and Cashe thought it odd how his words jumped over Cleveland's head and spoke directly to his notion about punching him. He had read Cashe's mind again.

They both set their sandwiches on the driver's table; Cleveland stepped to the other side of the heat rack to catch a sausage pizza coming out of the oven, while Cashe silently clocked back in from his two deliveries. Kris looked down at the table with the two sandwiches and examined them. He took Cleveland's food and began unwrapping it, loosening the sticker that held the paper together. Then he opened the bread roll, spreading it out before him.

And if I ever caught you touching my food, I might...

As Kris lifted a piece of chicken from the melted cheese, Cleveland screamed from the cut table.

"Hey fuckoff, that's my sandwich!" he said, coming out from behind the heat rack, bumping Kris to the side, then rolling it back inside the paper.

Kris walked away, laughing. "He hates it when I do that shit!"

What he said flew high into the air, and the duality of his comment seemed to let Cashe know that he wasn't just talking about Cleveland, but also about him.

You're right Kristopher, I hate it with everything that is in me…

The intensity of his frustration, a build up from the hotel room at the Hampton Inn, the delivery on Liberty Avenue and now what was happening in the shop, gave Cashe the urge to go to the back of the store and check to see if there was any in-house work to do. He found the broom and began sweeping the floor, then soaked a white cloth in the sanitizer sink and wiped down the cut table. When he was finished with those tasks, he opened a stack of fifty 14-inch boxes and began folding and stacking them into neat piles of ten.

It didn't take long before the incoming online order buzzer sounded and the computer screen over the make line began filling up with the specifics of what customers wanted on their pizzas. The phones rang incessantly. Sam stopped slapping out a large dough, set it aside, and answered one of the calls. Buck hung up his cell phone, seeing how they were beginning to get slammed, and approached one of the computers near the front to help.

"Hey Cashe," said Buck, trying to log on to a locked computer screen. "Whose user I.D. is this?"

He pointed to a highlighted series of numbers that Cashe immediately knew belonged Cleveland.

"I think that's Cleveland's I.D."

"Hey, Cleveland! What's your password?" Buck yelled out loud. "I need to get into this computer!"

Cleveland stopped slicing the pizza he was prepping, looked up from the cut table and saw Buck trying to log on to the terminal with his user I.D. He turned his head to Cashe and silently mouthed the word "shit."

"Um, let me think," said Cleveland pretending that he had forgotten. "What *is* my password?"

"It's FU, uh, CKB, um, UC…K," trying his best to scramble the syntax.

Buck only frowned, scrunching up the right side of his face in an awkward grimace, and after tapping in the code he answered one of the phones.

"Thank you for calling Perfect Papa Pizza," said Buck, holding the phone to his ear, "How may I help you?"

Cashe looked at Cleveland, who wiped imaginary drops of sweat from his forehead, then back at Buck, and for the very first time, perceived something about the district manager he had never noticed before. Like Kris, he wore a ruby ring on his finger that sparkled from the overhead lights and reflected down over the glistening countertop.

PART TWO

The Angels

Chapter Eleven

WITH THE SWEET STINK of the previous night's intimacies stuck to his body, Cashe rolled out of bed, trying to keep quiet as possible, climbed over Kia and stepped into his sandals. He walked naked into the bathroom, turned on the faucet in the shower and tested his hand underneath the water. As he got in and began scrubbing his body and lathering his inch-long hair with shampoo, he thought of how well many aspects of his life were going as of late. They all were peaking at pinnacles, like several little mountain top experiences. His marriage appeared to be going in the right direction. At work, tip money had been more than rewarding. All his bills were paid. He was healthy and in shape. The logical next step, the way he saw it, was having a child.

Underneath the blue sponge hanging over the showerhead, he rinsed his face, arms, stomach, and feet, then turned around to run the water down his back, basking in the warmth of the spray until he couldn't take another second of it, knowing he had to go.

In his mind, he planned for this morning's workout to be a rigorous one. Monday was always the most important day of the week, he believed, and if he could start it off right, the rest of the days would practically take care of themselves. He dressed and packed his bag, checking and double checking, making sure there was nothing missing. The time on the alarm clock read 6:05 A.M.

Just before removing his bike from the wall in the living room and strapping on his helmet, he leaned over Kia, carefully uncovering the comforter from her head, and gently touched his lips to her soft cheek.

"Goodbye, baby," he said. "See you later."

Second Accident

THERE WAS A STRANGE, eerie silence as he led his bike into the empty, lifeless street. Not a single bird chirped, and no purring car engines passed by as they normally would, disappearing into the darkness of first light. For some reason, everything on Shady Avenue seemed—*fake*. Both the natural and inanimate outdoor decor had the look of being overly pronounced and set up, like props for a *Midsummer Night's Dream* play he'd seen at the theater as a child. Stagnant telephone poles and their wires made a giant fence between the robust trees and boxed homes across the street, and the late September grass blanketed the patched, tiny lawns like a stage.

He climbed onto his bike and shifted into the highest gear, picking up enough speed to carry him quickly to the bottom of the hill, pedaling hard and fast until there was no more resistance. In that brief instance, it felt as if he was floating on air.

As he came to the corner of the synagogue, just before the traffic light midway down Shady Avenue, he remembered that he had forgotten to stop and pray. With all his might, he gripped the brakes with both hands in an attempt to slow down, and at the same time saw what he thought to be the high beams of an approaching car from behind suddenly paint the road beneath him. The fast, white light somehow *hit* him with the sound of a loud, audible *clap*, and the force of the impact turned him to the left. Desperately, he tried to regain control of his handlebars, but couldn't. Toppling over the skewed frame of his bike, he crashed.

The disorientation of the painless fall confused him, and he didn't know if he had collapsed in the middle of the street or somewhere near the sidewalk. Squeezing his eyes closed, he lay motionless, reluctant to move, wanting to know what kind of damage had been done to his body. When he reopened them, he looked into the sky above—though something seemed different about it—then sat up and waited for an overwhelming tinge of pain that never came.

Gradually, he rose to his feet and searched for the gnarled handlebars and bent rims of his bike, and for the car that had caused his fall. But as he turned in every direction, his recognition strained, not conceiving or comprehending what his eyes were taking in. He had the peculiar sensation of being elevated, and when he finally stood all the way up, he realized that, indeed, he was high up in the air. After twirling in a complete circle, he understood that he could only look out into the distance. Orange and white globes of light lined the streets on the slopes of the surrounding hills and plateaus. When he saw the rim of pink and purple coloring the horizon and the rivers below separating land from land, he immediately recognized that he was in the clouds, directly over downtown Pittsburgh.

Oh my God, I'm dead. I just died.

Tulpehocken

A TRANQUIL SERENITY SETTLED him, alongside a fear of uncertainty which almost brought him to tears, as he saw that there were no longer any houses or buildings towering above. Under his feet, a smooth, polished marble disc supported him. It was suspended in midair and composed of the same mix of colors as the sky above and the pending sunrise in the distance. He was standing in the exact center of the disc and judged there to be about twenty feet to its edge. There were no walls on the platform and nothing preventing him from falling off. He took a few steps towards the periphery, stretching his neck over the side as far as it would go until he thought he might faint. From his height, it was as if he were looking out of the window of an airplane. The "Y" shaped connection of the Monongahela, Ohio and the Allegheny rivers and the buildings of downtown were visible below. He eyed the grids of streets and alleys crisscrossing between each skyscraper before finally pulling himself away. As he backpedaled to the center of the circle, the voice of a child called his name.

"Cashemente!"

What struck him more than hearing the words of a boy, or that someone was actually speaking to him wherever it was he might be, was that his full, proper name had been spoken. No one ever called him by that name, except his parents. Hearing it startled him, yet at the same time contained the natural, intrinsic quality to relax and comfort him. It was as if he recognized the voice, like the person speaking was a member of his family, maybe a little brother, if he'd ever had one.

When he did an about face, he instantly became aware that the name came from the angel in his dreams. The child stood straight and erect, arms hanging at his side; his black wings, shiny and raven-like, pulsated and adjusted themselves behind him. His clothes were layers of a bronze metallic cloth which stopped at his wrists and ankles. Cashe remembered him blowing away the flames of the burning building with his breath.

"Cashemente," the angel said again, speaking in the tone of an early adolescent, but with the confidence and authority of an old man, "I'm going to do two, no, three things—open your eyes, open your ears, and also open your mind. You must see the spirits, hear the spirits and feel the spirits. It is to strengthen you."

What?

Cashe considered the angel's statement, and a wave of what he could only think of to be *peace* overcame him so powerfully that he sat on the ground, wrapping his arms around his knees. The angel took three steps forward.

"You have been chosen Cashemente," said the angel, with watery eyes and they too shone like his clothes and wings. The boy moistened his lips with his tongue.

"I am Tulpehocken, messenger from the Overseers of the Great Beloved, and I have been sent to tell you that there was, and is, even now, a war raging over the mind, the body and soul of your wife, Kia."

What do you mean a war?

He was beginning to feel warm and intoxicated, as if he had just taken a sip of very strong liquor. The angel, once again, interpreted his thought and answered his question as if the words had been written in plain view.

"The Father has heard your prayers Cashemente, and it is time. From now on, you must be very careful to remain pure and holy before God. Until now, everything has come to pass in your life for this very reason, and you are the only one who may be able to turn her away from the hand of Azazel. Even now, right now, her desire is set on destroying you," said Tulpehocken, his teary, glowing eyes almost overflowing to his cheeks, and Cashe sensed a deep, excruciating sadness around him.

But, we were just together.

"Azazel has been working very hard to take her away, but there is still hope. He is one of the fallen Watchers, the seducer of the men of old, released in this last day for judgment on earth."

The angel took another few steps toward him on the glossy marble, coming so close that Cashe could see the clinquant material of the angel's robe and the strands of a golden cord tied around his waist. As Tulpehocken came closer, Cashe allowed himself to relax and welcomed him.

Tulpehocken lifted his right arm and opened his hand, like a blooming flower. Spread on the middle of his palm and on his fingers was what looked like Vaseline, or some sort of shiny gel, made of bright red sparks that jumped and danced erratically in every direction.

The angel reached out toward his face and Cashe closed his eyes. Tulpehocken touched the side of his temple with four fingers and with his thumb rubbed the substance from his hand over Cashe's left eye. A balmy, tingling sensation came over him, like the perfect temperature of hot, steamy bathwater, and after the process was repeated on his other side, he opened his eyes.

"Now, you will see," said Tulpehocken.

Cashe's vision went blurry as a cloud passed over their place in the sky, and when the thick fog cleared away, several other angels came into view. The white mist vanished in waves, breaking here and there, revealing details of the other angelic beings. Six of them, who all seemed to be the same age and size as Tulpehocken were in front of him, and when he turned his head over his shoulder, he saw six more behind. They surrounded the two, floating in the air slightly beyond the sphere of the marble disc, forming a circle. Their clothing, identical to the metallic, glistening material that Tulpehocken wore, stopped short of their hands and feet, but were of different colors. Sky blue. Emerald green. Yellow. Orange. Red. Silver. Black. They each seemed to belong to a distinct ethnicity, if he had to guess—a blonde haired, blue eyed Swede, an olive skinned Italian, a Chinese girl with fair skin, a Jewish angel with thick woolly hair, a red-headed Irish boy, a bronze skinned Iranian.

Their wings were also different than Tulpehocken's. One had white wings. Another speckled. Yet another had blue-gray feathers splotched with verdant ends. They all stared at him, but he wasn't afraid, nor had he been moved. A slow, burning feeling first stirred and then rose within, like a simmering anticipation, and he watched the scene change before him.

The sky, which had been the brightening tone of twilight fading, a dark violet with splashes of rosy pinks and orange cream from the arriving sun, had now turned clear crimson, accenting the twinkling of the stars and the half-moon above.

Tulpehocken slightly bowed over Cashe, this time opening both hands. Flames flickered in the middle of each palm, and with the tips of his thumbs and index fingers, the angel touched his earlobes. Suddenly, Cashe's ears went cold, as if someone had put ice cubes on the sides of his head.

"Now you will hear," said Tulpehocken, and in an instant, the angel's flapping wings opened and closed twice, first pulling the boy up into the air, and then backwards to another place on the circle of marble.

More clouds of dense fog passed, and he now heard the voices of the twelve angels conversing with each other. Like Tulpehocken, their speech was young and joyful, but they, too, spoke with the seriousness of the aged. Some asked questions. Others seemed to be giving directions. One used familiar streets like Centre Avenue, Fifth Avenue and even Shady Avenue, the street where Cashe lived. Then he heard Kia's name, and his heart jumped.

He desired to stand up, so he pushed off the ground, feeling the cold of the stone on his hands. When he got to his feet, he noticed how small and childlike Tulpehocken seemed in size and stature, as they stood opposite each other.

"Now you will feel," said the angel, and a glow, the same intensity of the sun at noonday strength, began to slowly and evenly expand from the middle of the chests of all the angels, as if someone had turned the knob of a switch, steadily increasing the light. It made him squint, and the strong peace he experienced when he first sat down, drowned him again. A faint smell of nectar hit his nostrils in the breeze. The aura that was beginning to radiate from the angels also lit Cashe from within, and when he looked down at his hands and arms, he saw how the light made his body transparent. All the tendons and snake-like curves of his veins were revealed. He had become a living lamp.

One by one, each angel left their position in the ring and flew away. Some lifted up into the air then dropped down out of sight beneath the marble disc. Others disappeared into the horizon of the hills in the distance. As each angel departed, so did their voice, until the heavy, potent serenity that filled him gradually waned, the light faded away, and he began to feel cold and empty again.

Behind Tulpehocken, what seemed to be an innumerable flock of black, drunken birds, dotted the red sky, steadily coming nearer. He recognized the choppy flight pattern and the cut edges of their wings and knew they weren't birds at all, but what might be giant bats. Tulpehocken broke away from his duties and turned his head. For the first time in what seemed like forever, Cashe sensed a foreign, unfamiliar and forgotten sensation—*fear*. The shrieks of laughter coming from the advancing crowd disoriented him, and suddenly he knew he was stuck with nowhere to go. He turned around and looked behind him, seeing an equal number of the creatures coming from the other direction. Then he heard their voices. They began to describe what had just transpired.

Bat demons:

There were thirteen of them surrounding a man! Ha! On the disc! Woo! Ha! Ha! He was sitting on the ground by Tulpehocken!

The angel spread his wings and lifted himself into the sky again, his legs dangling and his hands balled up into fists.

He has fear and can now see! Ha! His feet waver and his hands and fingers fail! Woo! Look around son of man!

"It is time to leave here, Cashemente," Tulpehocken said, "The enemy has smelled the gathering. Speak to Yousef, he will tell you what to do next. Go now, the Beloved is with you."

Tulpehocken flapped his wings, hovering high in the air over the marble disc, and before Cashe could respond, the angel suddenly flew *into* him with a loud *clap* and a blinding blur of white light.

Auras

WHEN CASHE OPENED HIS EYES, the system of branches and leaves in the trees above him on Shady Avenue hid the iridescent glow of the rising sun. He sat up, unscathed, and saw his bike at his side, leaning on the top of the curb in the same condition it was in when he removed it from the wall in the living room. A woman in a green minivan slowly crept up next to him, and her automatic window disappeared down into the middle of the driver's side door.

"Are you okay?" she asked, making Cashe feel a tinge of embarrassment, realizing that a second before, he must have looked silly on his back, splayed out on the side of the road in a respectable neighborhood.

"Uh, yeah, I think I'm alright," he said, brushing away small pebbles that had been indented into the palms of his hands.

"Do you need me to call an ambulance?" asked the woman with motherly concern. "Are you hurt?"

He stood to his feet and lifted the bike off the ground.

"No, really, I'm okay."

When she saw him moving around, her countenance changed.

"All right, honey. You be careful riding that bike," she cautioned, then rolled up the window and drove down the hill. Ahead, he could still see her, like she had turned the light on inside her van. As Cashe watched her drive away, he saw that it wasn't an overhead lamp at all. The woman was glowing.

Cashe removed his backpack from his shoulders and dug into the bag, searching for his cell phone. He wanted to make sure it hadn't been crushed. When he pressed one of its buttons, the time lit up on the display. 6:10 A.M. Maybe two minutes had elapsed since he left the apartment, had been taken up into the air by the angel, and returned to the sidewalk on Shady Avenue. He debated whether or not he should go back home or take the entire day off and tell Kia about his encounter and past visions of Tulpehocken. But another urge, a stronger impulse, told him to continue on with his day. Everything was just as it was before, like nothing had happened, as if it all had been a dream. But it was no dream.

Why not go on? I'm not hurt.

Cashe climbed onto his bike and carefully coasted down the street on the right side of the road. He thought about how the angel had said Kia was against him, not quite understanding what that meant. Perhaps he *wasn't* ready to talk to her just yet.

The traffic light in front of the synagogue changed just as he came to the intersection. He sped to the bottom of the right lane, pedaling harder and harder, swimming in an unexpected rush of excitement further down the decline and around the corner. Part of him remained in that other dimension, and now he carried the weight of *knowing*.

"Wooooooooo! Yes!" he screamed into the air with an explosive charge of energy that broke his restraint. It was all he could do to express the uncontrollable exuberance, the disorientation and wonder, and the simple normality of his experience. "Oh, yeah!"

The auras were everywhere. Cashe watched as a cyclist a few blocks ahead disappeared behind the bend underneath the Interstate 376 overpass. She shone like a florescent necklace, similar to one he had once bought for Kia during a date-night at Kennywood Amusement Park. Many of the kids had worn them on their wrists; some held glow sticks, which they waved in zigzags and figure eight patterns.

At the end of the Eliza Furnace Trail near Grant Street, he stopped a block away from the YMCA, and waited for a PAT bus filled with people arriving into the city to pass, then turned into the alleyway behind the building. Through the windows of the bus, he noticed the light from yellow auras surrounding some of the passengers. He saw it shining on those driving by in cars, and on pedestrians crossing at the intersection. But not everyone shared the radiant glare. There was another presence exuding from some without it. A dark, black, smoke-cloud engulfed them, and like the aureole of the auras, it stuck close, as if they had been swallowed by gigantic jellyfish. Instead of empowering, it seemed to suck the life from them. Then there were the others, people who had nothing at all, neither the darkness nor the light.

After locking his bike to the back gate, he went through the doors of the YMCA and paused at the desk so the clerk could scan his ID card.

"Good morning," Kate said with a smile, and he couldn't help staring at her aura.

"What?" she asked, digging her fingers into her head, "Do I have something in my hair?"

"Oh, no," said Cashe, "You just look different today. That's all."

He grabbed a towel from the folded stack on the counter and went through the doorway leading to the stairwell. As he climbed the steps to the fifth floor, he thought of how he would have to be careful about not gaping too hard at what he could now see. When he reached the top of the steps and entered the hallway outside the gymnasium, he saw Tony Jackson getting off the elevator, carrying a gym bag, with nothing surrounding him. A white towel was slung over his right shoulder.

"Uh, oh, Cashe is here," he said. "Look at you, glowing. What are you so happy about?"

"Really? I'm glowing? I look happy?" asked Cashe naively. "I don't know. Just glad to be here, I guess."

When they entered the gym, Andy Rinski shouted from the court.

"Tony's ten. Cashe you're number eleven. Let's go Tony, we've been waiting."

"Okay, okay, I'm coming," he said.

Tony slid down his sweatpants, revealing his red and white basketball shorts, and unzipped his hoodie. After a quick stretch, he walked to the basket where the rest of the guys had been shooting around.

While waiting for the next game, Cashe had time to undress and see what in the world might happen today at the gym in what was turning out to be the most interesting morning of his life.

At first, nothing seemed different. None of the guys glowed or had the black, smoky shadows around them, until Timmy Burrell, who everybody called "Coach" started yelling at Dave Foster.

"Quit hooking me!" he screamed after interrupting the game by holding the ball. "That's a foul and it's the third time you did it!"

When Coach got in Dave's face, acting as if he might throw a punch, Cashe's eyes opened up in the spirit. A round, lime-green, fluorescent orb the size of a tennis ball fell out of Dave's stomach, and after a few bounces, rolled several feet across the floor, stopping near the black out-of-bounds line. Dave seemed confused and unsettled and bent down to re-tie a loose shoestring.

"Well, call a foul, and shut the fuck up!" Dave said, after standing up and walking away from him to the other side of the court.

"Fuck you!" said Coach. "Quit hookin' me!"

The impending fight influenced the atmosphere in the gym, and Cashe sensed a flame spark in his chest. It had been like an alarm going off, warning him that something was wrong. *It* was about to happen again.

Black steam rose from the shoulders of half of the players on the court. Their faces morphed into conniving, evil smirks, covered by a thin veil of gray film, making it look like they had on masks. The shadowy cloud that enveloped Coach intensified more than the smoke around the others, and then lifted from him all together, transforming into the shape of one of the large bats he had seen while on the marble disc high in the air above downtown. With a deep bellow, the obscure form spread its wings and let out a hoarse laugh into the air. It swooped down to the glowing ball, lifted it off the ground with one wing hand, and then flew back *into* Coach.

Cashe stopped shooting at a bent side basket rim and posted up against the wall at the far end of the court, wanting to take some type of action and respond to what his eyes were seeing. Jimmy, the latest newcomer, walked through the gym door and sat on the floor against the wall.

"Just check the fucking ball, and shut the fuck up," yelled Coach again, throwing the basketball to one of the players on the other team.

"I can't believe what I'm looking at," said Jimmy, tying his shoes, a gold cross hanging from his hairy neck. "It's way too early in the morning for this fighting stuff."

"Yeah, I don't know what's going on," said Cashe, appreciating how his words perfectly fit into the peculiar spiritual world that his eyes now had access to.

Danny Corbo, one of the more athletic and talented players, received a pass after the ball had been checked up, and made a shot from five feet outside the three-point line over Tony. Everyone on his team ignited in cheers.

"Aww, come on!" said Coach, "Tony, you gotta play some defense!"

At the top of the gymnasium ceiling, near the metal rafters, two of the angels Cashe had seen earlier materialized through the walls in each corner up at the opposite end of the room, and he could hear the loud smacking from the in unison flapping of their wings. It sounded as if groups of people had been shaking out giant bed sheets. One wore silver layered clothing, the other gold, and their clothes seemed to wave in an invisible wind, though no breeze could be felt in the gym. He clearly saw their eyes shining, how a deer, or a raccoon's reflect light in the middle of the night when caught in the high beams of a car, and the anticipation of an impending tragedy overcame him.

At his end of the gym, two more young, celestial beings dropped through the corners of the ceiling and hung in mid-air. One wore purple and crossed his arms; the other was in blue, squatting on nothing and watching the teams beneath pass and dribble the ball. A fifth angel, in all white, dropped from the middle of the ceiling and circled the gym on a circuit, searching the court.

"Where is it!" the angel in white yelled in a loud voice, stopping momentarily over each player covered in the black mist. The players continued on, attempting to make shots, running up and down the floor, oblivious to what was happening invisibly overhead.

Coach had taken the basketball and slowly dribbled up the court as point-guard, with Dave playing defense against him.

"You want it?" he said to Dave, speaking with the voice of the demon, his throat sounding raspy and filled with phlegm. "You want some?"

The shadowy figure rose out of Coach and up into the air again, but this time four bat-like forms followed, coming out of the other possessed players, slowly exiting their hosts. The demon that flew out of Coach was the largest of the five and had the green orb in its hand.

"If you want it Xio," it said, tauntingly. "Come and get it."

The angel wearing the glittering gold clothing left his position from the corner of the gymnasium ceiling and dropped down toward the creature with the glowing orb like a bird gliding to the ground from the highest limb of a tree. After a turn and a twist, the angel tackled the demon with such force that the orb was knocked out of its hand and into the air. One of the dark creatures flapped its wings in choppy, drunken flight, caught the orb, and flew to another part of the gym. The scene repeated itself with the angel in silver falling from his position, tackling the demon and knocking the orb to the floor.

Cashe watched as two separate games were played before him, both in the air and on the ground. When angels gained control of the sphere, he thought it all would be over, until they too in turn were hit by one of the bat creatures who knocked the orb loose.

After several minutes of this back and forth action, the angel in all white finally gained possession, and a thought had come to Cashe that he hadn't yet considered.

Pray for Dave.

It made perfect sense, and he didn't understand why he hadn't thought of it before.

Father, please help Dave and strengthen the angels above.

When he whispered the prayer to himself, immediately the angel with red hair and golden clothing performed a maneuver that consisted of a backward fall away from a chasing demon, a quick turn to the right, and an upside-down flight pattern toward Dave, placing the glowing orb back into his chest.

"Nooooooo!" cried the largest demon of them all, and the instant the orb returned to Dave, Coach fell to the ground after blindly running into a solid Danny, who stood firm, giving a pick, and freeing up Dave for a clean layup to win the game.

At once, all five of the angels departed from the gym, one after the other, in a curved line through the ceiling. The bats dispersed in several different directions; two flew into the gym floor, and another went through the wall at the opposite end of the court. The largest demon glided directly toward Cashe, stopped inches in front of his face, and let out a threatening growl before flying toward the stair-well and through the opened door of the gymnasium. Everyone on Dave's team cheered and exchanged high-fives.

Chapter Twelve

Third Accident

THE TRUCK RIDE FROM the apartment to Angelina's was uneventful, but pleasant. Today, Cashe sensed more than the warm, post workout calm, the welcome soreness in his body, and the freshness of scouring all the sweat and dirt off his body in the shower. It was an indescribable feeling and he actually thought he could possibly take flight from the road and soar to his job on Highland Avenue, if only he knew *how*. The sensation, like a burst of exhilaration or a piercing high, was *new*. He gripped the steering wheel and tried to mentally make the wheels leave the ground, but it didn't work. His mind seemed on fire with revelatory thoughts.

Angelina's—My Lord Jesus, I even work at the place!

He wanted to talk about everything with Kia. Earlier, she had been gone when he arrived home to drop off his gym bag, and he almost called to see where she went off to so early in the morning, but thought otherwise after remembering the warning Tulpehocken gave him. The wiser decision would be to take the safe approach and wait for whatever might happen to happen, instead of forcing the issue.

When he reached the bottom of Shady Avenue, he made a left turn on Alder Street. At the light he saw Miyad come from around

232

the corner of the shop and enter through the front door. He couldn't see the auras anymore. For some reason, they had decided to disappear after the angels and bat demons left the gym. In an open space on the side of the building, he parked and checked the time on his phone. 9:45 A.M. When he went into the shop, Miyad was nowhere in sight, and figured he had most likely retreated to the office in the back to do paperwork.

Ingrid busied herself, rinsing the fettuccini noodles that would be weighed and bagged for individual orders of pasta in the sink. Marcus stood in his usual position, slapping and docking out large-sized dough balls next to Keith. Trent worked in silence, chopping up boneless chicken. Cashe thought about washing the dishes but decided to wait until more piled up. He walked up the flight of six steps to the rear of the shop and started to fold boxes until Hakan called him over.

"Cashe, we need help with da salads," he said in his heavy Turkish accent.

"Yes, Cashe," repeated Benyamin, peeling a curved cucumber that resembled a large, erect penis, "We need like forty."

Cashe pushed the thought about the phallic vegetable away and drifted into the simple pleasure of placing handfuls of cold lettuce from the purple tub into the Styrofoam salad containers. He put four cherry tomatoes in each corner, four cucumber slices in the middle, and topped it all off with mache greens. Benyamin made small salads, which only got two cherry tomatoes and two cucumber slices. Hakan, in full deli decorum—a white apron tied securely around his waist and neck, and plastic gloves on each hand—piled slices of Italian hoagie lunch meat in-between sheets of wax paper.

"Cashe, why you so quiet today?" Hakan asked, pulling off two slices of salami, in a thick, guttural tone. "Like you an *angel* or some ting. Why you little angel today?"

The comment made all three of them laugh. Benyamin said something in Turkish to Hakan, and a wave of uncertainty came over him. For a split second, he actually *believed* they knew about what had happened earlier that morning, but he dismissed it as coincidence and went along with the flow of the conversation.

How could they know?

"Benyamin say it's quiet back here, like baby sleeping," said Hakan, interpreting.

"I don't know what you guys are talking about Hakan," said Cashe. "The both of you are just as quiet as I am. Why are you blaming me?"

"I just joke with you," said Hakan holding up a white piece of wax paper in his gloved right hand, looking Cashe in the eye. "It is nothing. Just joke."

Miyad opened the door of the office behind them, and began scowling at the work the three of them were doing.

"Hakan, don't make so much. Iss too much," said Miyad. He reached over his shoulder, picked up a piece of lunch meat from the pile, and threw it back into the three-pound bag of ham slices.

"Okay, okay," said Hakan and started putting away the food.

After the salads were done, Cashe posted at the top of the steps and tried to decide what to do next. Remembering that there were large boxes that still needed folding, he walked to the narrow storage area opposite Miyad's office, lifted an unopened package and carried them out near the coolers.

Both the hoagie and pizza make-lines were uneventful. Jihad and Keith whispered to one another about a girl in a club they both had seen, something about getting a telephone number and how ugly the girl had been. Marcus opened up cans of sauce, poured them into the mixer and listened to their conversation with a grin, commenting every now and then with a smart remark, and giving advice on how to deal with women. Trent prepared hoagie buns for an upcoming order. Miyad and Ingrid stood silent, like a pair of lifeless ghosts near the computer screens, waiting for the afternoon rush of telephone calls and watching over the activities of their employees. Cashe had been grateful that neither Miyad nor his wife had found an opportunity to use their managerial authority to pick with him as of yet, but it was still early.

After folding the entire stack of fifty boxes, he neatly placed them on a top shelf beside the cooler in groups of ten, then searched the shop for any work that might have been left undone. In plain eye's view, he noticed something he had either overlooked, or previously never paid attention to. Above the top of the hoagie line was a plastic container filled with orange powder among a row of other seasonings and spices. On its face in black letters were written the words **ANGEL WING DUST**. He ignored the label, moved from the steps to the sink, and studied the pile of dirty containers and cooking utensils. When he started the hot water, Trent began to speak.

"Oh yeah, that's what I wanted to ask you guys—" he said, waving a sharp butcher knife into the air. "Did you hear about what happened downtown this morning?"

Keith and Jihad stopped giggling and took a few steps closer to where Cashe and Marcus were standing.

"What? Somebody got shot?" said Jihad.

"No, but check this out, this is some *crazy* shit—" he said and everyone in the room turned their head, except Cashe.

"You guys know where they're constructing that new building on the corner of Fifth and Market downtown?" he asked, crossing his arms in the air, drawing street intersections with his hands.

"Yeah, yeah," said Marcus, in his heavy accent, "Right on the other side of Market Square, where there are like a *thaasand* pigeons flying *raand* cause they always throw bread and shit on the *graand*. Where all dem homeless people hang *aat*, I know where yur talkin' bout."

Cashe's attention began to wander, as certain words in their conversation burnt impressions into his thought process. *Downtown. Pigeons flying. Something happening.* It was as if every remark that related to his encounter with Tulpehocken rang a bell. His heart began to pound, and he felt like the verbal police were breaking down the door of his mind with their words, searching for illegal substances hidden in his brain. He knew what they are looking for. They wanted his *information.*

"There were *thirteen* construction workers way up in the air, like walking on those beams," said Trent, his voice starting to quiver and rise a few octaves. "Apparently, a crane broke, crashed into the building and knocked them off. They fell down, like two hundred feet and all of them died."

"What?" said Marcus, "No, I didn't hear bout that!"

"Look, I'm going to pull it up on my phone," said Trent taking it out of his pocket. "This shit will be on the national news tonight."

Cashe turned away from the circle of men, his heart racing faster and his brain searing. *Thirteen. Falling out of the sky.* There seemed to be a connection between the accident and his encounter on the disc. When the sink filled up to the perfect level, he turned off the faucet, pumped several squirts of blue dishwashing detergent into the water and began stacking stainless steel frying pans caked with steak gristle into the sink.

"But that's not even the craziest part," said Trent. "I made a mistake…there was *one* guy who survived. It was like a freak accident on top of freak accident. He fell into a dumpster filled with some type of insulation or foam, and it broke his fall."

"What?" said Jihad laughing. "No he didn't."

"I swear to God, they caught the whole thing on tape," said Trent with a giggle, and the group surrounded him trying to get a peek of the video footage on his phone. Cashe, glanced over his shoulder, watching them gather around, but stayed near the sink, trying to scrub the thoughts of this morning's lingo out of his head.

"Wait a minute. It gets better," said Trent playing the video clip of the footage, listening to the voice of the reporter. "Watch this."

Teresa Witowski:

"After falling over two hundred feet from the top of the BTC con-struction site into a dumpster filled with unused insulation from a sep-arate building project next door to the old G.C. Murphy building down-town, welder Stephen Avaloni miraculously survived with only a broken arm. His account of the incident has some questioning how much of his story is actually true or as a result of traumatic shock. He claims to have seen what he described as large bat-like creatures that attacked the crane holding the steel beam which crashed into the structure, knocking twelve workers to their death. Avaloni says an angel caught him in mid-air just before landing into the dumpster. Earlier this morning he was released from Mercy Hospital, and is now being evaluated at Western Psychiatric Hospital for further testing. Reporting live from Market Square, this is Teresa Witowski…"

Trent let out a chuckle, put the phone in his pocket and strut-ted back to the hoagie line.

"Do you believe that shit?" he asked, slicing open another hoagie bun. "He said an *angel* caught his ass and carried him to a dumpster. I think that motherfucker's crazy as hell."

"Well, just hold on," said Marcus, leaning over a bag of flour. He pushed his glasses from the tip of his nose closer to his face and tugged the brim of his cap over his forehead. "There have been certain cases where people who were in terrible accidents survived, and then later claimed that some type of a supernatural being saved them."

"Dude, after they put that cast on his arm and released him from the hospital, what did they do?" asked Trent. "They took his ass straight to the nut house! A giant bat-like creature? Come on man!"

"He said the nut house!" said Keith, repeating Trent's words, and he too started laughing.

"I believe in angels," Jihad said, after taking an extra-large pizza float off the rack. "There could be an angel standing right there in the corner protecting us now, but we don't see it."

"People who go through traumatic experiences hallucinate, and see things that aren't there," said Trent pointing his knife into the air, emphasizing his point.

To Cashe it sounded as if he were beginning to get angry.

"The only reason that *one* guy survived was because of pure luck, nothing else. You are *never* going to hear me say, an angel really saved his ass."

Cashe felt a tap on his back. When he turned around, he saw Marcus standing next to him.

"You believe in angels Cashe?" he asked.

He looked around at all the other guys. Every single one of them had their head turned towards him, waiting for his answer.

"Yeah, I believe in angels, sure."

"See, even Cashe believes in angels," Marcus said, pointing a finger back at Trent. "Looks like you're the one outnumbered!"

Ubiquitous

BY THE TIME THE MORNING rush hit, Cashe had finished the dishes, the phone continued to ring uncontrollably, and Miyad started checking the orders brought to the make line. All the major prep duties had been completed; the sauce was made, the boxes were folded and placed in their correct slots on the shelves, and the salads were done. Cashe dried his hands, took a stroll to the back of the shop and saw that Benyamin was in the middle of cutting up green peppers.

"Somebody call Benny from the back!" Miyad screamed from the oven behind him. "His order is ready!"

Benyamin put down his knife and looked at his hands, which were covered in green pepper juice. He wiped them with the white cloth that lay on top of the cut table and hurried to the front of the store. Hakan, still in the same place as before, but now slicing tomatoes, turned toward Cashe and smiled.

"Ahhhh, the angel is back," he said.

Cashe brushed off the comment with a smack of his lips, picked up the knife and started on the green peppers.

The angel comments won't leave. I wonder if this will go on all day?

"Hakan," yelled Miyad from the other side of the shop again, "Let's go!"

After watching Hakan perform the same routine of taking off his apron and throwing his plastic gloves into the garbage, he hurried off to the front of the store. A few minutes later, Miyad called again.

"Cashe, hurry, you have a delivery!"

The sudden urge to rush came over him, and he checked himself over. He threw the knife he used to cut the green peppers on the cut table, and wiped his hands with the towel. There was no need to do too much cleaning, Benyamin would soon return and finish.

Miyad stood near the oven waiting for Cashe, as if he had stopped working, awaiting the moment for him to arrive. Something inside made Cashe brace himself for a smart remark about what took him so long to come to the fore of the shop, but Miyad said nothing.

"Cashe," said Miyad softly with a gentle smile, and pointed to the table next to the mixer. It was an enormous order, stacked with ten pizzas, five on each side. Two rows of the number *thirteen* were written in black marker down the front of each box.

"Isa a twelve o'clock order, you hab plenty of time. Remembur," Miyad said rolling his *r's,* "Plates, napkins forks…it's all business."

The clock over the computers read 11:15 A.M. He took the receipt and read it over.

Order #13, 12:00 P.M. Timed order, For Gabriella, Western Psychiatric Hospital, Main lobby.

Here it was again, the angels calling.

For Gabriella, like the angel Gabriel.

For some reason, he knew he *had* to make a delivery to Western Psychiatric Hospital, it was destiny. Cashe also could see that he was being sent. He was stepping into fate, and everything this morning was falling into place for what needed to be done. Today, he would meet Stephen Avaloni.

Cashe recalled the words of Tulpehocken, *Now, you will see. Now you will hear. Now you will feel.* He remembered the sparks that jumped inside the Vaseline in the angel's hand. He thought about the strange string of visual and auditory *cues* this morning and was amazed by the way they mimicked the scene earlier in the sky above the city. The auras hadn't come back, but on another level, the constant reminders of Tulpehocken wouldn't cease. Maybe they were coming from the angel himself.

A need within tugged so strongly at his inner core to *speak* about seeing the angels, but he had to be cautious. The guys might think he was a lunatic. They might try to send *him* to an insane asylum filled with crazies and the mentally disturbed.

But he also had a sense of purpose; a gentle, confirming notion that he was on the right track came over him. As he bagged up the pizzas he became more and more confident. *To strengthen you,* Tulpehocken had said.

After carrying his order to the area near the computers, he stuffed the extra-large pizzas into two giant, hot-bags made especially for deliveries such as these and started out to the truck, realizing that it wasn't too difficult for him to carry all the pizzas at once.

"Be careful," said Miyad as he watched Cashe walk by.

Any other day, the comment would have annoyed him, being the perfect opportunity for his usual commanding interference. But today, the statement seemed endearing and sincere. Like he cared. Miyad *really* told him to be careful.

Once the order had been loaded into the back of the truck, he sat for a minute in the driver's seat, and took out his phone. After searching for the article about the man falling from the building, a picture of Stephen Avaloni's face came up.

He cranked the ignition, and while driving down Alder Street, tried to envision a mental map of the quickest, least congested way to the Psychiatric Hospital. Centre Avenue would no doubt slow him down by at least twenty minutes, being one of the most well-frequented roads in Pittsburgh. It was a straight shot to Craig Street, which lead directly into Oakland. Most people coming from other parts of the city didn't know of any other way, but he had learned several lunch hour shortcuts. A right on Highland Avenue would bring him to Fifth Avenue, which was always clear up until Neville Street. From there, the winding road would lead him through the valley below CMU and take him to Bouquet Street, up the hill, and directly to the entrance of the hospital.

At the top of Highland, a student in jeans and a jacket with an angel's wings design on back waited at the bus stop. He talked to his friend, who had his right arm raised, pointing down Fifth Avenue, unknowingly guiding Cashe in the correct direction.

Avaloni

CASHE FOUND AN OPEN space near the entrance of the building, in one of the places reserved for deliveries. After parking, he walked around to the other side of his truck, slung the bags over his shoulders, and went up a set of steps through the main doors of the Western Psychiatric Hospital. In the lobby, a security guard sat behind an L-shaped counter, watching social workers flash their ID cards as they came in the building, and then stroll to the elevators a little further down the hallway. Doctors wearing starched white jackets and stethoscopes draped around their necks talked softly, smiling to one another as they passed by in groups.

After setting down the bags and standing like a soldier on duty across from the security desk for several minutes, he smiled, listening to the employees of the hospital blurt out questions and statements to him, but not really wanting answers.

Is that pizza for me? Wow, that food smells good. Mmmm…pizza!

He gave up trying to look for Gabriella and decided to give her a call. When he dialed the number on the receipt, the telephone behind the security counter rang. He watched as the guard, a black man with a rough face filled with razor bumps, answered the phone. After they both made eye contact with one another, he ended the call, and walked over.

"Who ya looking for?" the guard asked, putting a right hand on top of the smooth stone countertop.

"I have a delivery for a Gabriella," said Cashe looking down at the receipt.

"What floor?"

"I'm not sure, but it says here—"

"Oh, I think I know who it's for," he said, raising his eyebrows. "Take those elevators to the fifth floor and someone there should be able to help you."

"Thanks," said Cashe, then lugged the ten pizzas down the hall.

When he pressed the "Up" button, the ding of the bell sounded, the door opened and he stepped inside. All alone, he studied the interior of the car—the lights, the side paneling, the metal guard rails. Over in the corner, something caught his eye. Underneath the numbered buttons was a small sticker of two white cartoon wings on the floor. With his foot, he tried scraping it up with his shoe, but it wouldn't budge. The elevator bell rang once again and the doors slid open.

When he arrived on the fifth floor, he found himself in a narrow corridor. To his left, he saw that a heavy wooden door with a square glass window had just closed shut. On both sides of the door were windows, and he watched the woman who had gone through disappear down the hallway. He tried to open it, but it was locked. After putting his face to the glass, he peered through and saw a slice of an office, and inside, a desk with scattered papers where the woman had sat down. Though he couldn't see her face, only part of her shoulder and arm, he tapped on the pane to get her attention, but got no response.

Cashe saw that the hallway was symmetrical. Behind him was an identical door which also had a square glass window. He tried the handle, but it too was locked. Not knowing what to do, he turned toward the elevators and thought about going back to the first floor when out of the corner of his eye, to his horror, he saw something appear in the window to the right of the first door.

On the other side of the glass, a black swarm, which at first glance seemed to be smoke made up of thousands upon thousands of tiny flying insects, formed the shape of what looked like a person. The bugs, which were similar to flies or giant gnats, swirled and twirled around one another, creating a haze. One of them left the frenzy and landed on the opposite side of the window. He put his face close to the glass, right where the likeness of the head was, confident of the barrier separating he and it, knowing they couldn't possibly get through to him, except maybe by sneaking under the door.

The tiny creature was of a species unlike anything he had ever seen before in his life, and as a matter of fact, he wasn't sure if it were an insect or an animal. It had a face similar to that of a horse. A tiny mane ran down the nape of its neck. Miniature horns extended out and upward from the top of its head. The body, a wiggling maggot larvae, was dark green and covered with a glaze of translucent polychromatic film. Clear, heart shaped wings protruded from its back. Two pairs of legs were on each side of the front of the torso, and a third pair, large grasshopper hinds, a lighter shade of green, made a triangle at its rear.

He caught himself staring, lost in wonder, examining its details. When his mind refocused, he once again saw the swarm, forgetting that it had been in the form of a person. The entire mass flew away, leaving a black, smoky trail behind that evaporated like an approaching mirage. His body jerked and shivered, and he took a step backwards.

The door next to the window opened and a woman wearing a black buttoned-down shirt, thick amber-colored glasses and glossy lip balm came into plain view. In her hand she held a manila folder.

"Hi, are you from Angelina's?" she asked, excited to see him.

"Uh…yeah," said Cashe looking to the left where the bugs had flown away.

"Come on in. You can put the pizzas in the kitchen," she said, waving the folder in the direction he should go, inviting him. As he lifted the food from the floor, the woman held the door open with her hand, revealing a ring studded with a giant, shiny, onyx stone surrounded by diamonds on her hand. Now, like a curse, he couldn't keep his eyes off rings.

He followed her down the corridor, the heaviness of the bags weighing on his arms, yet all the while watching the curve of her back, thin waist and the way her large buttocks rhythmically danced to the click of her heels. Then he saw it again. The swarm briefly showed itself at the end of the hallway; it suspended in mid-air, peeking its head around the corner before disappearing again.

They went by several doors that looked like hospital rooms converted into tiny studio apartments. Each had been furnished with a small bed, a chair, and a television. Most were empty, but some had patients in them. Then, they passed a nurse's station on the left where four women in a circle talked about Stephen Avaloni.

"So, then he says," said one of the nurses in a hifalutin tone with a Southern accent, "Right before he hit the ground, the angel caught him, dropped him in the dumpster, then flew away around the corner!"

"What?" asked the nurse next to her. "That sounds a little…I don't know."

"Yeah," the first nurse answered, "But I'm not sure, he doesn't seem like he's lying though."

He continued to follow the woman as she turned left into a well-lit room equipped with a table and compact kitchen.

"You can sit them there," she said. "On the counter."

With all the craziness going on around him, he tried his best to stick with the normal protocol of a delivery.

"Can you please sign this?" he asked, giving her a pen and the receipt.

The woman took it, turned to the kitchen counter and began scribbling away while he set up the pizzas in two neat stacks. After folding the hot-bags under his arm, he waited as she checked the receipt over and then handed it back.

"Thank you," said Cashe.

"No, thank you," said the woman.

When he came out of the kitchen, a wave of disorientation hit him, almost knocking him off balance. His directional bearing was thrown off, and it seemed as if the hallway had flipped. Everything that had been on the right was now on the left, and vice versa. Even the woman seemed to notice his confusion.

"Are you alright?" she asked.

"Yes, I just forgot which way I came in."

"Just make a left down the hallway, pass the nurse's station and you will see the exit on your left," she ordered, pointing down the hall again.

"But didn't we come from the other way?" he asked.

"Excuse me?"

"Uh—never mind."

He made a left down the corridor and walked past the empty nurse's station that was now on his left. A red exit sign glowed over the door at the far end of the hallway, and the closer he came to it, the more he wanted to leave.

"Hey buddy," he heard someone call from behind, and when he turned around, he saw a man standing in the doorway of one of the studio-rooms. His bent arm was wrapped in a cast up to his armpit. Across the hall, in the opposite room, someone screamed. Two nurses suddenly appeared a few doors down and began coming towards them.

"Ahhhhhh!," the patient yelled again, sounding as if he were whining. "They're back! Oh my God they're back!"

The swarm of bugs flew out of the room from where the commotion had come, leaving a smoky black trail in its wake, like the exhaust from an airplane. The mist hit Cashe square in the nose this time, smelling like a rotting carcass on the shoulder of a road in the middle of July.

He immediately recognized the man with the cast. It was Stephen Avaloni. The picture on his phone from the news clip made him look older. He wore faded jeans, a T-shirt, had dark hair and a five o'clock shadow.

"You saw them, didn't you?" he asked. "Please, tell me you saw them."

"Yes, I saw them," Cashe said, looking him over, and then quickly continued down the hallway toward the exit, and into the elevator lobby.

Hospice

WHEN CASHE RETURNED to Angelina's and noticed all the activity in the shop, he knew it wouldn't be long before he'd be back out on another delivery. He threw the empty hot-bags on the shelf next to the checkout station and waited for his next orders. In a matter of seconds, Miyad came around the corner with several boxes of pizzas and bags filled with salads and appetizers.

"Cashe," Miyad said, looking at him with clear, serious blue eyes. "You hab two. You gonna go to South Negley Avenue, and you gonna go to the VA Hospital."

Cashe recognized the addresses and figured it would be a quick run. Repeating his routine, he neatly placed each order inside a hot-bag, made sure they all had plates, napkins and forks, slid the receipts into the clear, plastic slots on top and carried them out to his truck.

As he approached the turnaround in front of the Hospice on South Negley, a shuttle bus positioned at the main entrance prevented him from moving any further ahead, so he parked to the side. The elderly driver helped what seemed to be an equally geriatric man in a wheelchair down the lift, then pushed him to the double doors of the clinic. He couldn't help but stare at an old man wheeling an old man.

With the order in hand, he followed them to the automatic doors and waited while the two slowly went ahead. The patient in the wheelchair appeared to be in a coma. His skin was beige, splotches of brown spots speckled his hands and face, and his bald head, which at one time probably overflowed with hair, now only had about a dozen strands combed across his pate. The shuttle driver commentated their arrival.

"We're gonna go right through this door and look for Nurse Sarah," he said, going through the door, searching for the nurse.

The usual receptionist lifted her head, nodded to the man behind the wheelchair, glanced at Cashe for a moment, then dropped her eyes back to the magazine on the desk before her.

"Mr. Todd," she said, suddenly standing up from her seat, "Are you looking for Nurse Sarah?"

"Yes, ma'am, I am."

"Hold on one second, I'm going to page her now."

Cashe posted near the two couches before the counter and waited for her to finish the phone call. Directly to the left and behind the desk were a set of double doors, which swung open every few moments as hospital employees and patients entered and exited the foyer. Outside, an ambulance with its siren lights blazing turned into the drive behind his truck. For a minute, he thought he might have been blocking its path, but was relieved when he saw that the ambulance had enough room pass and park behind the shuttle. Its lights shut off the very moment Nurse Sarah showed up to meet the old man in the wheelchair.

"Ya'll have a nice day," said the driver, "Time for me to go."

While in the lobby, Cashe searched for the spirits to reveal themselves, but they were nowhere in sight. The receptionist surprised him; she showed up out of nowhere with an outstretched arm, holding a hand full of dollar bills, robbing him of his greeting before he could dictate his spiel about the price. But he gave it to her anyway, stealing it back.

"Oh. Hi. I'm sorry," he said, off balance. "I didn't know that this order was for you. It's $18.47."

Frogs

FROM SOUTH NEGLEY, Cashe made a left onto Fifth Avenue until it turned into Washington Boulevard. After traveling a few miles, he came to the traffic light across from the police station, made a right, then drove up the steep rise on Highland Drive to the VA Hospital. At the top of the plateau, a parking space seemed to have his name written on it near the entrance in Building One's lot. He grabbed the hot-bag, making his way through the automatic doors, past the one-armed man sitting behind the podium, rushed by several soldiers in full uniform, and followed another who had THOMAS written on the back of his cap to the elevators. For some reason, he thought of the disciple in the Bible who didn't believe.

Cashe checked the receipt for the room number and tried to remember who had placed the order. He knew that there had only been two customers who he delivered to on the third floor; a group of researchers in a lab and woman who worked in an office. Once on the elevator, he pushed the silver button, making the number *three* light up. After a short ride, the bell rang, and he made a right down the glossy floor of the silent, empty hall.

In the middle of the corridor, where a separate hallway tapered off to the left, he saw something on the ground. As he came closer, he noticed that it was covered with patchy brown and green patterns, and smooth, lustrous skin. A frog. It jumped about a foot ahead of him. A childish instinct, one that told him to *catch it*, almost made him put down the hot-bag and chase it down the hall, until it hopped *through* the wall on the right. He realized it was a spirit. Four doors down, a group of them were gathered in front of room 3113, as if they had just been dumped out of a bag onto the floor.

"Get out of here!" he heard a woman's voice scream from the room, and it sounded as if she was speaking to *him*, like he might have been invading the privacy of her bedroom at home, though a small part of him knew she was really speaking to the frogs. "Get out!"

He sensed fear, where he wasn't the catalyst; it was an external sensation, like feeling an increase in temperature. As he came near the door to the office, the frogs scattered, leaping in different directions; under her desk, into a file cabinet and through the walls.

"Get out!" the woman screamed again. "This is *my* office!"

A plethora of visual imagery exposed itself, accompanied by the woman's high-pitched yelps, and he recognized the room. She was the lady with the frogs all over the place, but now, dozens of animated spiritual amphibians had invaded, jumping and moving around. They poked out their heads from shelves on a bookcase, and some lay frozen next to her collection of statues and effigies of frogs on top of her desk. Others had even defied gravity and stuck to the walls and ceiling. Three of them covered the face on the poster of a Warner Brothers cartoon frog who stood on his feet, wearing a black top hat, leaning on a cane. Cashe stood paralyzed.

Oh. My. God. Father, help me.

The woman wore a dark green dress and swatted at a *real* horsefly, about the diameter of a quarter in size, buzzing around the room. In the corner, next to the stuffed, life sized Kermit, a giant spirit frog as big as a German Shepherd made a deep croaking sound that immediately caught Cashe's attention. It jumped behind her desk, then through the opposite wall.

One of the thirteen angels from the downtown circle, a Japanese girl with two long, woven braids over her shoulders dropped feet first from the ceiling with a flap of her black, shiny wings. She hung in the air for a second, staring down at Cashe, her eyes two flames, then flew through the same wall the frog had leaped into seconds earlier. The horsefly stopped buzzing, and also landed on the same wall.

"These damn flies!" said the woman, finally pausing in her efforts to rid it from the room, "Ugh!"

"Yup, and that's a big one."

Cashe held his ground in front of the desk, surprisingly composed, only moderately affected by what he was witnessing before him. Most of the fear he sensed when first coming to this floor of the building had seeped out of his chest, and he began to relax.

"How much do I owe you?" the woman asked, wiggling her head in frustration, pushing her glasses closer to her face.

"It's $21.67."

"Here."

She handed him a twenty and a ten, almost sounding upset. He took the food out of the bag, and gave it to her, immediately feeling the urge to *leave*.

Chapter Thirteen

Fairies

CASHE FINISHED HIS SHIFT at Angelina's and returned to the apartment for lunch. To his relief, the barrage of signs and symbols depicting angel's wings or some derivative of the word ANGEL written on license plates, baseball caps and on the back of jackets, and the sudden appearance of diverse types of baby cherubim in the architecture throughout the city's neighborhoods—especially on top of buildings or as décor on the lawns of elegant homes—had finally ended.

He unlocked the front door, and the silence inside told him Kia wasn't there. When he went into the kitchen to search for the jelly in the refrigerator and the peanut butter in the cupboard, he saw that the place had been cleaned. Though he was now at home making a sandwich and boiling the water for tea and Ramen Noodles, the dreamy feeling of the spirit realm hadn't left from earlier that morning, and all he could think of over and over again were the words of Tulpehocken.

Now, you will see. Now, you will hear. Now, you will feel.

He scooped out the thick, crunchy peanut butter with a butter knife and almost tore the bread trying to spread it. After the sandwich was made, he set the table for himself with a coffee mug filled with hot Lipton Tea, a bowl of creamy chicken Ramen Noodle soup, a plate with the peanut butter and jelly sandwich and a napkin. The steam from the soup made the room smell like flavored salt.

Even now, right now, her mind is set on destroying you.

Although he had just woken up next to Kia that morning, it seemed like an eternity since they had really spoken to each other. The feeling of pending danger lingered at the thought of the angel's words and he desperately needed the surprise to be over with. He didn't want to imagine his new wife preparing to do anything other than making a family and staying with him for the rest of his life, but Tulpehocken was very clear. She was planning to do something *to him.* It didn't make sense, but as he again recalled his dreams, the prophet and visions of Azazel, he could see that no doubt, there was a connection to all of this, if only a loose one. He blew into the bowl cooling the soup, then tasted.

But why would Kia premeditate something against me?

The timing of the dreams and the encounter with the boy angel seemed unbelievable at times, and if it had been anyone else other than an angel from God, or maybe a real *prophet* who had given him the news, he would have brushed them off as insane.

This is insane.

His teeth crunched the kernels of peanuts in his mouth, and he took sips of the hot, milky tea, washing down the thick, pasty sandwich. With his fork, he twirled the noodles in his bowl, breathing in the savory vapor. The rimmed circle on top of the blue coffee mug, the matching bowl and round wooden table at which he was seated reminded him of the marble disc in the sky.

Speak to Kia's father. He will tell you what to do next.

Yes, there had been something else the angel had instructed him to do. He said to pay Kia's father a visit.

But, what could Yousef have to say about all of this?

The thought made him chew his sandwich faster, take bigger gulps of tea and suck down the noodles with more urgency. He looked at the digital clock on the shelf next to the cabinets. 2:15 P.M. His shift at Perfect Papa didn't start until six, and Kia's father lived less than five minutes away.

Even though he had never visited Yousef alone, the idea of stopping by fit flawlessly into his schedule today. He finished the sandwich, sipped the last bit of broth from the bowl, and then cleaned his dishes. As a general rule for himself, one he also tried to set for the house, no dishes were to be left in the sink nor clothes on the bed or on the floor. They were old military habits, but good ones.

"We should tidy up the apartment before we leave the house," he had always preached to Kia, often to no avail. For the most part, she did a good job here in the new place, but there *were* times when he came home and found things astray. Instead of getting angry, he used them as reminders that no one, including himself, was perfect.

He flirted with calling Yousef, but then became aware of an entirely new set of problems he hadn't considered, particularly, information concerning the old man he didn't need before, but could use now.

What was his telephone number and his address? Did he go out at all, or was he stuck in the house? What does a sixty-eight-year-old man do all day long? Does he drive?

The best and only way to follow the instructions given by Tulpehocken would be just to show up and let whatever might happen, happen. He didn't have to try to meet Stephen Avaloni, and presumed that the reasons behind visiting Yousef would reveal themselves in a similar fashion. His job simply required obedience; to go and knock on the door.

On the way to Yousef's, everything outside seemed peaceful and normal. As usual, young mothers pushed their baby strollers, and young men and women jogged or walked their dogs up and down Hobart Street and the Boulevard of the Allies. Children explored the playground in the park across from the now empty and closed, waterless swimming pool like a crew of munchkins working on a construction project.

On the side of Yousef's house in the gravel parking lot, a white Chevy Celebrity was parked to the far right. Cashe decided to pull in next to it, perpendicular to a telephone pole lying on the ground that had been sawn into three sections and used as parking blocks. From his viewpoint, he could see behind Yousef's house into the back yard. A patch of grass that looked as if it hadn't been cut in a couple of years grew up to a height that matched the level of the top step to his raggedy back porch. The alley and the rear of all the houses that lined the adjacent Bates Street could be seen from where he put his truck. The homes had mounds of junk stored beside them, making their connecting yards look like a giant flea market. There was an assortment of old boards, broken gutters, bottles, lawn mowers, doors no longer on their hinges, and hoarded tires stacked up against brick walls and inside fenced-in plots. Bizarre, random items, like plastic big wheels and mud flaps marked with the sil-houettes of naked women were scattered amid heaps of colossal refuse. Even cars half covered by tarps, with their stripped parts hanging out like intestines, sat in many of the back-alley driveways. But what really caught his attention was a Little Caesar's cut-out caricature of a grubby Roman, chomping mouthfuls of pepperoni pizza. It leaned inconspicuously against a neighbor's step, and kind of reminded Cashe of a cartoon version of Yousef. He wondered if Kia had ever seen it.

He made his way around to the front of the house, walking along the sidewalk on the Boulevard, not knowing what to expect. The first thing he noticed was that the door to Yousef's basement was ajar. Inside were unopened, rusty cans of paint stacked next to one another on the floor, car batteries and tons of assorted, greasy items. Doubt came over him, and he thought about whether or not to climb the steps and ring the bell at the porch door or just to enter the basement without an invitation.

Worn out, and heavily faded green cement steps led upstairs to the porch at the left of the opened door, the place where they had first met. Two chairs and a table were still there, and the glass panel above the entrance bore the address in large black and gold letters—3507.

He started to climb the steps, but then thought otherwise. The confidence to go inside had suddenly come out of nowhere, and he no longer cared about his intrusion. The words of Tulpehocken echoed in his mind, and that was enough.

Speak to Kia's father. He will tell you what to do next.

After backing away from the porch, he went through the dark entrance. What looked like dead, amber-colored scarabs lying on their backs dotted the floor on the other side of the doorway, making him hesitate before going any further. As he moved forward, trying his best not to crush one of them underfoot, all at once, the lifeless exoskeletons spread their wings and flipped to their feet, zig-zagged in different directions and disappeared *through* the cinderblock walls. He kept on, unmoved by what his eyes had just seen; he was beginning to get used to having vision in the spirit, like children who quickly become bored in the aquarium at the zoo. It isn't long before the exotic fish seem less fascinating, and the kids are ready to move on to the more exciting creatures, like giraffes and hippopotamuses.

"Yousef!" he shouted, cupping his hand against his mouth.

He got no answer in return, only the rustling sound of paper coming from the end of the room. He yelled Yousef's name again, taking cautious steps ahead, going deeper and deeper into the dimly lit sub-level of the rowhouse. Every object imaginable seemed to be placed on the ground or stored on several shelves lined all the way to the far wall of the basement. A lamp could be seen glowing through a shelf in the very back, one that had been made into a makeshift wall, and he sensed that someone was on the other side. As he neared the light, the objects in the cellar became more and more visible. Furniture of all kinds was strewn through-out the room—wooden chairs, tables, some assembled, others in pieces, their legs detached, wrapped with clear plastic in groups of four. Books and tools were stored in cardboard boxes. There were wrenches and pliers, Phillips and flathead screwdrivers of all different colors, shapes and sizes. Dish sets of plates, bowls, cups, and containers of forks and knives were caked with dust. Mirrors, sinks, bathtubs, paintings, posters and statues of various forms and designs cluttered every portion of once empty space. Kia had said that as a result of Yousef's thirty years in the landlord business, the one problem he couldn't avoid were tenants who always left things behind, and it was true.

"Whatever you need," she once had said, "my father has in his basement."

A wooden staircase went up to a closed door on the left side of the room. Strings of cobwebs and scraps of tiny, miscellaneous objects adorned the cracked boards and hidden crevasses like junk jewels, and on each step, loose washers, nuts, pieces of copper wire and snippets of paper seemed fossilized under a layer of sticky crud. The door at the top squeaked open, and someone began to come down the unlit stairwell.

A short man, who at first glance Cashe thought to be a fif-ty-something version of his grandfather approached, holding on to the guard rails attached to the walls on each side. He wore blue Dickies pants and a short-sleeved button-down shirt. Above his lip was a thick, neatly trimmed mustache. When he reached the last step at the bottom, he stopped for a moment as if to suck up the pain he had just experienced from his brief downward journey. Slowly, he raised his head, and looked Cashe in the eye. The smell of alcohol and cigarettes from the man's breath hit his nostrils.

"Where's Yousef?" asked Cashe.

"Huh?" asked the man, then smacked his lips. He dug into his pockets and pulled out a handful of quarters.

"You have dolla for quata?" he asked with a rumbling, baritone voice. He sounded as if he could call Tulpehocken and all twelve of the angels into the room by the resonance of his words.

"Yeah," said Cashe, immediately understanding why the man had asked.

A few weeks before, Cashe had been doing laundry by himself across the street. He had put too many dollar bills through the coin machine, and while waiting for his clothes to dry, he tried to figure out what to do with all the extra quarters. Just as he thought about walking up the street to the Mini-Mart to buy a snack or a soda, this very man had come to him, out of nowhere it seemed, with a handful of one-dollar bills, asking for them. The timing of it all seemed weird, but Cashe gave them to him, hesitantly at first, wondering why he didn't just use the change machine. After the exchange, he understood that the wrinkled bills the man had would never have made it through the slot.

Cashe opened up his wallet in the stale basement, took out two crisp dollar bills and gave them to him in exchange for eight quarters.

"Ahhh," the man said, as if he had just connected this moment to the same memory at the laundromat a few weeks before, or perhaps to signify that he understood that Cashe also needed help remembering.

"Yousef-abib!" the man yelled with his booming voice toward the far end of the room. Cashe thought that the sound waves might knock something from the shelves. In the back where the light was on, he heard Yousef answer back in Arabic. The man waddled to the rear of the basement like every step hurt, and Cashe followed.

On the other side of the wall, Yousef sat in a chair, digging through a large cardboard box. Next to him on the floor by his foot was a solid gold statue of an angel, wings spread, cheeks puffed out, blowing into a long, one-piece trumpet. And beside that, was a piece of scroll depicting a colorful Egyptian god who had the head of a goat. Above it was written the name KHNUM.

When they arrived, Yousef stopped searching through the box, turned slightly to the left and paused like he too had just retrieved some distant recollection, or as if someone just whispered softly into his ear. He squinted his eyes and looked over Cashe and the man standing next to him, as if he had never seen either of them before in his entire life. When he bent over to take the gold statue from the ground, his body strained as he reached for it. With a slight hint of urgency, he rose from his chair, pushing off from his cane. After he got to his feet, he went to the man, stood in front of him and began speaking in Arabic again, staring him in the eye and waving the statue in his face. Cashe couldn't understand a word he was saying, and only watched Yousef's dark eyes and furrowed brows as he relayed information that seemed much too serious and important to be conveyed in the cavern of a dingy basement. While they talked to one another, Cashe's ears opened with a *pop,* as if a bubble in his head had burst.

He thought he heard the word *nigger;* it sounded more like *niggah,* but he wasn't sure. Then, *Tulpehocken*…followed by more Arabic…*has come and given a message…*and more words he couldn't understand. He didn't know how it could be happening, but he heard English words rising out of their conversation, bit by bit, piece by piece. After Yousef was done speaking, he naturally turned to Cashe with a smile.

"Please excuse the place," he said with a face of reason and with the same sincerity that he had used when speaking to the man from the laundromat, "And I apologize for the cockroaches. It is almost impossible to keep them out, you understand?"

"Oh," Cashe answered, not really having a response.

The man spoke back to Yousef in Arabic, then began walking away before Yousef stopped him.

"This is Abbas al-Masoud. He lives upstairs and helps with the houses. He's from Iraq."

"Nice to meet you Abbas," said Cashe holding out his hand.

Abbas turned, took it, and smiled, revealing a mouthful of crooked and missing teeth.

"Nice to meet you, brudda," he said with his booming voice, then left the two alone.

Yousef placed the gold statue of the angel on the ground, sat down in the chair once again and began sifting through the contents of the box. Cashe wanted to ask him why he had taken the statue out in the first place and what it was he might be looking for down here in the basement. Instead he kept silent, wondering what to do next, beginning to feel a bit awkward.

"Have you had anything to eat today?" asked Yousef, finally pressing all the contents of the box down with his hand, and kicking it to the side with his foot.

"Well, yes, but I—"

"Come," he said, standing up from his chair impressively quick for his age. He wobbled past, and then up the staircase. Cashe watched him for a second, then tagged along.

"I have Sunny Delight, apple juice, milk, tea—" Yousef shot off while climbing each step. "Do you want tea?"

"Uh," moaned Cashe, still feeling discomfited, not knowing what to do or say.

He waited for a sign as to which direction to take, believing that the purpose for this visit would soon be revealed. They went into the kitchen and he stood behind a chair at the dining room table.

"Please, sit," said the old man, and Cashe sat down, looking over the flower patterns in the thick plastic tablecloth. Yousef opened the refrigerator, hunched inside, and pulled out every container of liquid he laid his hands on.

"I'll have some Sunny Delight," said Cashe.

He sat in silence while the old man moved from the refrigerator, to the kitchen sink, to the stove, setting the table before him with brown and yellow dishes, silver forks, cups and containers from the fridge. Though he had just eaten, the soup and peanut butter and jelly sandwich hadn't filled him up all the way, and there was still room for more.

"Do you like olives?" he asked opening a jar. He poured some on the plate in front of Cashe before he could answer, then did the same thing with other kinds of foods, adding hummus, pita, and a mixture of what looked like diced tomatoes, corn, and relish to the table. The heat from a boiling pot of water began to warm up the kitchen. Yousef poured two glasses of the juice, and when the teapot whistled, he turned off the range and made tea.

After all the preparation was complete, Cashe found himself looking at a feast before him, with Yousef sitting across the table. They ate in silence for several minutes, both seemingly waiting for the other person to make conversation about why he had shown up uninvited. And that's when Cashe noticed his ring.

It was the exact same style that Kris had worn at Perfect Papa, except the stone was a different color—a blue sapphire instead of a ruby—but the gold patterns on either side seemed identical. The evidence of this Azazel, and the New Mafia mess he found himself becoming immersed in was *unimaginably* more extensive and far-reaching than he originally thought. Cashe didn't want to question Yousef about the ring yet, so he diverted to the next best topic.

"So, what were you doing with that statue of the angel downstairs?" asked Cashe, chewing an olive.

"It was given to me as a gift, a long time ago," he said. "Do you want it? You can have it if you like."

"No, no," said Cashe. "That's not why I asked."

Yousef looked up from his plate at Cashe like something had rung a bell inside his head.

"Oh," said Yousef.

The urge to spill the beans about *everything* began to boil over, and he could no longer hold it in. He desperately needed to talk to someone about his meeting with Tulpehocken earlier that morning. It was impossible to contain. *Irresistible.*

"Yousef, I have something to tell you," he said, putting his fork down on the plate.

His emotions had gone haywire, and he now felt as if he were going to cry. He wasn't sure how Yousef would take the news of the angel's visitation, and in a way, really didn't care. Surely, Kia's father would think he had lost his marbles, but he knew it was time. There was a deadly truth-serum in the air, and he had been infected. Cashe took a deep breath, then, slowly and clearly, spoke.

"This morning I was visited by an angel named Tulpehocken. He told me to come and talk to you, and he said you would tell me what to do."

He looked at Yousef, whose head was still bowed down over his plate, and absorbed the anxiety of an unanswered response. The old man wiped his mouth, held a white napkin to his lips with a long pause, and then dropped it on his plate. After whispering something in Arabic to himself that sounded like a complaint, he rose from his chair, walked to the sink, and put his dishes inside in silence.

"I know it sounds crazy. I haven't told anyone else but you…"

Yousef turned around from the sink.

"Are you finished?" he asked.

"Am I finished?" he questioned back, now confused. "Finished with what?"

"Are you done eating? I will take your plate."

"Oh, yes," he answered, and handed it to him.

For some reason, Yousef didn't respond to the news. Cashe couldn't tell if his silence was an attempt to cover the embarrassment he had brought upon himself, or if Kia's father was thinking about what he said, carefully considering a reply.

The atmosphere in the room began to change. Cashe's mind suddenly lit up as if it were on fire; a burning blaze flickered inside his head and chest. It made him high, and he forgot about Yousef's silence. The tip of his nose began to itch. He felt a sneeze coming on and snatched one of the napkins from the table just in time to catch it. When he opened his eyes he saw hundreds of bright swirling dots. At first, he thought it was just his blurred vision, and that in a few seconds they would fade away as his sight returned, but they didn't. The tiny, white sparks fluttered around each other like gnats on a hot summer day, until they finally dispersed, one landing on every object in the kitchen. Glowing wings sprouted from the tangled patterns in the tablecloth and the designs on the wallpaper, as the forms of shimmery fairies and pixies revealed themselves from all the places the flying dots had rested. Their slender bodies grew, even from the mist rising out of the hot water in the sink, budding from the blurry shapes of flowers, vines and steam, into colorful, luminous, living creatures.

He thought of Peter Pan; pixie dust now sprinkled the ether in Yousef's kitchen, and it looked as though the stars in space had somehow descended out of the sky into the room. Incandescent light emanated through the fairies, uncovering the nakedness of their legs and arms. He noticed how tiny, lace-like material of various shades of the spectrum clothed both their groins and upper body if they were female, but only below the waist if they were male. They transmitted messages to one another in high-pitched gibberish and giggles. It was impossible for him to speak to Yousef about what he saw because he didn't *want* to talk. Yousef turned around from the sink and waved one of the fairies away as if it were a common housefly.

"What time do you work today?" Yousef asked, putting his right hand on top of the kitchen table, totally ignoring his statement about the angels, and staying quiet about what was now going on in the kitchen. Cashe figured that he too would keep mum about the matter and play along with Yousef's game. Besides, he wasn't absolutely sure that Yousef could see the spirits in the first place, and if that *was* the case, any further talk about it might set himself up for another trip to Western Psych to be roommates with Steven Avaloni.

He dug into his pocket and took out his cell phone. It was only 3:30 P.M., but it seemed like he had been at Yousef's all day.

"I have to work at six," Cashe said, straining to breath out the words.

"Ahh. Six," said Yousef. "Come. I have to drop off something to a friend. We will take your truck and I will pay you ten dollars for gas."

"You don't have to pay me," said Cashe, beginning to rise from his chair and follow Yousef through the glittering air and undulating stars into the living room. He stopped for a brief second and tried to look at a pixy with crossed eyes as it flew to the tip of his nose. The tiny fairy spoke in a diminutive voice, pointing to the back of Yousef's head.

Not in here! In there! In there!

"I just need my jacket and we will go," said Yousef.

The pixy flew away, and Cashe went into the living room just as Yousef lifted a dark blue jacket from the sofa and slung it around his shoulders. His arms blindly searched for the holes to the sleeves. All of a sudden, this scene seemed hilarious to Cashe and he fought the urge to laugh. He didn't understand what was so funny about an old man putting on his coat, but it was. Perhaps the pixy dust had gotten the best of him. Yousef grabbed his cane, his keys and a tiny wooden box from the coffee table in the living room.

"Let's go," he said.

He had no clue of where they were off to, but was comfortable knowing he had at least made it to *his* destination. It was happening. He didn't need to ask too many questions. Ever since his encounter with Tulpehocken, it seemed as if he weren't really in control anymore anyway, like he had been riding in the back of a huge limousine, staring through a tinted window. Now, he desired to do nothing else but continue with it all and go along for the ride—even if it meant pretending that what he was seeing didn't exist.

Fourth Accident

AS THEY WALKED THROUGH the living room and out to the porch, he could still sense the presence of the fairies flying around in the room behind him. After Yousef had locked the door, he turned and saw that none of them had gotten out.

On the way down the steps to his truck, Cashe looked into the sky and saw what he thought at first to be a helicopter flying unusually close to the tops of the trees across the street. The shadowy, gray object hardly moved—it hovered above like a hot air balloon, coming out of what looked like a swirling black hole in the daytime sky. A tear in the blue canopy among the clouds had opened, revealing the dark star-studded space in the heavens. Two red eyes inside glowed as bright as the traffic signals on the Boulevard in the direction of Cashe and Yousef from the gateway. He saw that they were attached to the body of a deeper blackness.

Cashe kept focusing until the entity had completely transported itself from the portal. His spiritual sight now clearly saw what was before him. The gray shape in the sky was no helicopter at all, but an angel. The crimson eyes belonged to a hideous creature, an assortment of several different animals in one. It had the head of a moose, the body of a bear, the muscular, hairy arms of a gorilla, and the glistening, scaly tail fin of a fish. Both forms had been so enormous that, at first glance, his brain couldn't register them as anything else but some type of aircraft. The huge wings of the angel in sky flapped one gigantic time, propelling it forward, in the direction of the other creature.

The mega-beast continued to look down with its crimson stare, until a fearful chill erupted through Cashe's inner parts at the realization that the monster *really was* focused upon them. It held its ground in the clouds as if it were standing guard in front of the heavenly gate to the dimension it had just come from.

"Cashe, is something the matter…?" Yousef started to ask after he turned around at the bottom of the steps, seeing that Cashe hadn't been following him.

"Yousef, look!" said Cashe.

The angel let out a scream, removed a flaming sword from a sheath at its side, and swung it into the creature before him. Like a smashed centipede, the demon disintegrated into thousands of pieces, then immediately reformed seconds later, back into its original monstrous form. It backed out of the hole and away from the angel and the doorway, who had now replaced the creature's former position at the gate of the portal.

In that same instant on the Boulevard of the Allies, directly in front of Yousef's home, a truck hauling a load of brand new cars straight from the factory went through the red light at the intersection of Bates Street, and slammed into an empty Carnegie Mellon shuttle bus making a left turn. The bus attached itself to the grille of the semi with a loud crash that had coincided with the angels' shout, and both vehicles were driven into a yard across the street from the laundromat. The trailer behind the truck tilted, and then fell. The cars underneath buckled and crunched on top of each other into the street. When Cashe looked into the sky, he saw that the angel and the creature were no longer there. The clouds above had formed a distorted, bubbled image of what the angel *looked like* slicing into the beast, an obscure snapshot of the event which had just taken place seconds before.

"Oh, my God," said Yousef, looking into the street, then said something again in what may have been Arabic. It sounded like he said, *Annunaki*. He pointed one hand into the air, box in hand, at the clouds, and the other toward the accident. "I cannot *believe*!"

Again, Cashe wasn't totally sure if Yousef had seen the angel and the creature too, or if he was only talking about what took place in the street.

"That truck ran the red light!" said Cashe meeting him on the sidewalk at the bottom of the steps.

Both the driver of the tractor trailer and the shuttle bus stepped out of their vehicles unharmed and assessed the damage. People came outside from their homes and exited the laundromat into the street, gawking at the accident site. Some wore auras of light, others had cloaks of smoky darkness, and there were those with nothing at all.

He knew something obviously happened in the spirit, and that there was a connection between what the angel had done in the sky and the crash, just as there had been a correlation with the meeting of the angels on the marble disc and the construction accident downtown.

Cashe and Yousef quickly realized there was nothing more to do but watch, so they made their way to the lot on the side of the house.

"We should hurry before we get stuck in the traffic," warned Cashe.

They got inside the truck and carefully backed up into the street just as the police and fire department could be heard in the distance. As the cars stopped near the accident site, creating a jam, Cashe noticed the auras of light and fogs of darkness surrounding drivers that came through the Bates Street intersection. Yousef put on a pair reading glasses, dug into the breast pocket of his shirt and read over a slip of paper he had hidden there, balancing the small wooden box on his lap.

"We need to go to the Liberty Tunnels," he said. "Do you know how to get there?"

Cashe could hardly pay attention to the road, let alone listen to the directions Yousef began to give him. There was too much to take in, and he anticipated more of the unpredictable to happen.

"Yes," said Cashe over his directions, "I know how to get to the tunnels."

As he drove down the Boulevard of the Allies, he searched the landscape, trying his best not to miss anything that the spirit world might be revealing. The Monongahela below glistened and sparkled and momentarily the river didn't seem brown. He searched the clouds over the buildings in the downtown skyline, the sides of the highway, and even around the beams and cables holding up the yellow bridges that led to the South Side, but there was nothing. No spiritual monsters surfaced out of the river or dropped out of the air; he could only see the glow of the auras and the mists of blackness inside the cars and trucks ahead, or passing by in the opposite lane. Like Kia, Yousef hadn't been encompassed by an aura, but in a way, Cashe wished he had. The uncertainty of what he was dealing with made him crave for more information, but for now, he remained content with the instructions Tulpehocken had given him.

Talk to Kia's father. He will tell you what to do...

As they neared downtown, he bore to the right around the bend on the ramp to the Liberty Bridge exit and was halted by traffic. Again, he couldn't think of what to say to Yousef, so they both remained speechless as the congestion loosened and they steadily crept toward the tunnels that led through the mountain on the opposite side of the bridge. Though together, the two seemed to exist in separate worlds.

Mt. Washington loomed before them like a sleeping giant, and as they came close to the tunnel, Cashe saw what he had been searching for. Sitting above the entrance, where a retaining wall had been built to hold back rocks from falling off the side of the mountain down onto the road, a goliath angel, whose legs dangled above the traffic, inspected each and every vehicle that drove through. He had never paid attention to the form of this structure in his life, how the wall was like a massive cement chair, though he had been across this bridge an uncountable number of times.

At the red light just before the entry, Cashe caught a close up look at the angel's face and body. Its clothing was of the same fashion as that of Tulpehocken and the group of twelve, only larger in scale. On top of his enormous, square head, his hair seemed as if it had been neatly cut and his face appeared clean shaven, though the beginning of a five o'clock shadow peeked through his cheeks. The color of his raiment, a mixture of blacks, lime greens, blues and whites covered his body from neck to wrist to ankle. Every square inch of the pattern matched perfectly with the scheme of his wings, which hung on each side like colossal curtains in a window. Silver sandals adorned his humungous feet, and the massive angel glowed from within. His blazing eyes, as bright as unshaded lamp bulbs, pierced into each passing car, making the fogs of blackness flutter off many of the drivers below.

Yousef didn't appear to be the least bit phased by the presence of the angel, and Cashe still couldn't tell if he was practicing his composure or if he could see anything at all. Maybe he too had gotten used to them. He wished Yousef would just come out and say something, but instead of talking, he only clutched the small wooden box in his hand and gazed off into the distance, perhaps somewhere beyond the river or up into the trees. The light turned green and they went through the dimly lit tunnel as yellow, then white dashes from the lighting lit the inside of the passageway underneath the mountain.

"What's in the box you have there?" asked Cashe.

"It's a gift. When we get to the other side, make a left on Pioneer Avenue. Go up the hill, and there will be apartments on the left. Turn in there," Yousef said abruptly derailing the line of questioning, using his hands.

The old man's directions had been precise, as if he had given them a hundred times. Once through the tunnel, the streets were exactly as Yousef had said. He made a left at the second light to Pioneer Avenue, then at the top of the hill turned into an apartment complex.

"Park here," said Yousef, and Cashe drove into an empty space in the street.

Yousef got out of the truck in a hurry, with the small box in one hand, tapping the cane on the paved sidewalk with the other, and made his way to the front door of the building. Cashe checked to make sure the truck was locked and that he had his keys before catching up. At the door, Yousef rang a buzzer. A man's voice came through the intercom, speaking Arabic.

"A salaam—" Yousef answered and the two were buzzed in.

He went up a flight of stairs, following behind Yousef, and watched the old man patiently rise, one foot after the other, and wondered if he would be able to climb steps like that in his years to come.

When they reached the top, someone wearing brown slacks and an untucked, beige button-down short sleeved shirt stood in the doorway of an apartment, grinning. Yousef immediately handed him the wooden box and the men greeted one another, clasping hands, and kissing each other on both cheeks as if they hadn't been together in years. Yousef entered, and when Cashe came to the door, the man shook his hand and smiled.

"A salaam—" he said.

"Hello," said Cashe, then went inside.

Sami

IN THE LIVING ROOM, two women in black abayas reclined on a sofa, speaking softly to each other. They were covered from head to toe; the only visible parts of their body were their hands and a slit of skin just below the eyebrows and above the nose that exposed their eyes. In chorus, they glanced over at Cashe with looks that made a shiver run down his back, laughed out loud in a womanly way, and then returned to one another, continuing their conversation.

The man who answered the door wore no shoes, his mustache was thick, and his face looked grubby, as if he hadn't shaved in three days. Cashe mimicked Yousef and left his shoes on a mat near the entrance, and they were led into the kitchen to a small, square table. Once seated, the man began speaking Arabic to Cashe, until Yousef stopped him and told him that he only spoke English.

"I'm sorry, I wasn't sure," he said extending his hand, leaning over the table, "My name is Sami Asim."

"Hi, I'm Cashe Alvin," he said, taking his hand again.

After the introduction, Yousef spoke to Sami. The sound of his voice sounded different, like he had raised it up a few octaves, and Cashe could tell that whatever he was saying was of the utmost importance. Sami listened while Cashe looked around the room. He noticed the earthly colors of the Persian rug and how the vases on the counter had been covered with intricate, symmetrical designs. The apartment was warm and smelled of spice; it made him hungry again though he had just eaten twice in the past three hours. It took him back to a time in his childhood when he used to visit the home of his friend Shamoon, whose family had come from Pakistan. There, he could almost taste the food in the air.

He listened to the two men, and it wasn't long before his mind *popped* and began to wander upwards. English words poked out through the Arabic now and then in choppy, yet understandable sequences: *Tulpehocken…Kia…angels…help…my daughter.*

Heat in his chest began to rise in temperature as the spirit world came alive around him. A small, dog-like creature appeared over the right shoulder of Sami. It sat on its hind legs in the middle of the air, opened its mouth, and exposed abnormal double rows of sharp teeth; a pink tongue hung out over its jowls all the way to the floor as if it were panting. Shortly after it became visible, Yousef raised his hand and pointed at the mongrel in the middle of his sentence, as if to say with his index finger, *Go that way! Get out of here!* The hound flew backwards with a yelp and disappeared somewhere behind the cabinets.

Then, on top of Yousef's head, a blue sphere steadily appeared, pulsating with miniature electric lightning flashes as it increased in size. With one wave of his hand, Sami made the plasmic globe vanish. This back and forth went on for most of the conversation, and though Cashe couldn't understand what the two men were saying, the visual effects that had come around the table made the discourse very interesting. Yousef and Sami didn't just expel the spirits that showed themselves, but in a sense were like crossing guards, directing spiritual traffic.

Something that looked like a wall made of windows of square mirrors, each having a ghastly face trapped inside, formed to the left of the kitchen table. With one emphatic statement in Arabic—it had almost seemed as if Yousef had gotten upset—he raised both his hands in the direction of the wall of faces and threw it *inside* of Sami. Again, Cashe couldn't tell whether or not the two men could see what he saw, but their movements had been more than enough proof that they either knowingly or inadvertently reacted to what was happening around them. Sami leaned back in his chair and took a deep sigh, as if he had *felt* the wall of mirrors come into his chest.

They continued to battle on with their words and with their hands; Sami made a zigzag motion with his pointer finger, and in the spirit, threw a red light on the right side of Yousef. The old man's cane, which had rested against his side a moment earlier, fell to the floor. Apologetically, Sami rose from his chair to get it.

"I am sorry," said Sami, "I didn't mean to say that."

"I can reach for it myself," Yousef spoke back in English. "Sit down."

As if his eyes had been suddenly opened wider, Cashe noticed an obvious detail he had somehow overlooked. Like Yousef, Sami also wore a blue ring.

My God, how many people are involved in this thing?

At the end of the conversation, Yousef finally sat the small box on the table and slid it to Sami.

"Cashe, would you like some tea?" asked Sami, rising from his chair with a strange sadness. He went to the cabinets and pulled out a green chest that looked like it might contain chess pieces, or the ivory chips to a backgammon game. On the top, something had been written in structured, gold Arabic lettering. Sami opened it and rainbow-colored balls of light floated out and around the room. Inside were light brown delicacies, covered in what appeared to be a sweet, clear glaze.

"Here, try one," said Sami. "They are from Saudi Arabia."

"Okay," said Cashe. "I'll have one, but no thanks, I don't want any tea."

It tasted like a mix between cookies and candy, and after Cashe chewed and swallowed, he wished he hadn't just taken one. A hot, burning sensation flowed over his body, and he heard the women in the other room laughing again. Whatever he had just eaten made him slightly drunk.

He took out his cell phone from his pocket and checked the time. 4:45 P.M. As if Yousef had just read his mind, he got up from the table.

"Let's go now," he said. "It is done."

Chapter Fourteen

THE SPACE NEXT TO the young tree across the street from the apartment complex was empty when Cashe arrived home a little past midnight following his shift at Perfect Papa. An old man wrapped in a scarf, knit cap and slacks gradually making his way down the hill with a cane reminded him of Yousef. The thought took him back to the basement and he also remembered Abbas al-Masoud.

Almost twenty-four hours had passed from the time when he had last seen his wife, and a part of him couldn't wait to be with her again. So much happened since the night before, when they enjoyed such a peaceful evening together and then made love before falling asleep in each other's arms. He wanted to talk with her and give the details about all these extraordinary, recent events which had occurred. It was the craziest, most interesting day of his life, and though he worked both jobs and spent the entire afternoon with Yousef, there was no one to share it with, at least not in the way he desired. Considering how so much could be going on around him, and yet at the end of the evening still feel so alone, he stepped out of the truck.

He stared at the bright headlights of a stray car coming up Shady Avenue and waited for it to pass before crossing the empty street. On the other side, near the flight of steps leading to the courtyard, he saw Kia's truck. The sight of it usually comforted him. It was a familiar symbol that confirmed the presence of his only love in the whole wide world, but tonight it loomed forebodingly along the side of the road like a bad omen. The sign of her being home frightened him and made him nervous, much in the same way it did when they had gone on their first date; he didn't know what he might find behind her made-up pretty face, beaded necklaces, gold earrings, bracelets and tight jeans. He had no idea what her true intentions might reveal.

After coming inside, he saw that she was in the bathroom with the door shut. Standing outside in the hallway, he listened to the sound of the faucet running and smelled the fragrances of the body lotion and soap she had been using to prep herself before bed. He imagined slowly opening the door and surprising her in her possible nakedness. Maybe he'd push her wet hair away, kiss the nape of her neck and tell her how much he missed her. Instead, he restrained himself and went to the bedroom.

As he undressed in the warmth of the room, snapshots of the encounter earlier that morning flashed in his head; images of Tulpehocken standing on the marble disc; his young, concerned face and watery eyes; his layered clothing that somehow clung to him; those immense wings which drew him backwards and up into the air; the deep sadness he felt from the news of a war raging over Kia's soul. Cashe contemplated how it was even possible for her to be so far out of his reach, way beyond his grasp.

Even now, right now, her mind is set on destroying you.

He wanted everything to be normal, but with the additional knowledge of an unseen spiritual link affecting their every action, and the assurance that *some otherworldly* thing was occurring on the outskirts of their lives, he knew he was forced to deal with her with some degree of falseness. Unless, that was, he decided to be totally honest about everything.

But what could he say?

Kia, this morning I was visited by a group of angels who told me that both your life and soul are in danger. I have been seeing and hearing and feeling in the spiritual realm all day. I didn't know how to tell you…

Right then and there, he decided that he couldn't tell her the truth. Not yet. He would have to use some level of wisdom in this situation. She had always been the type of woman to overreact, and if he came out and told her tonight, she might take him for a lunatic. He also knew how she had a tendency to be trigger happy when it came to calling the authorities, so it was definitely a real possibility that if he said something, he may not make it to bed for a good night's sleep. Though he did trust her more now than before, he also knew that a hidden part of her unpredictability still remained, somewhere deep within.

Yes, he concluded, *it would be too much of a risk.*

After he stripped down to his underwear and T-shirt, he heard the bathroom door open. The sound of Kia's house shoes flip-flopping against the bottom of her feet in the hallway brought her into the bedroom and he held back a gasp.

"Hi," she simply said, then turned toward the dresser. Thin, loose fitting pajama bottoms sunk into the middle of her buttocks, and a tank top revealed the birthmark on the back of her left shoulder. She opened the top drawer and dug through all the miscellaneous items she kept there until she took out a comb. Wet, black curls stuck to the nape of her neck, just as he had imaged. Though she was turned away from him, he watched her comb her hair in the mirror. Bobby pins hung from her mouth like unlit cigarettes, and every so often she'd place one of them into her hair.

Instead of succumbing to the urge to talk about today's events, he rested in his choice to remain silent—even about his surprise visit to her father's house. He figured he should pray and ask God to tell him when to speak about it, and then allow it to happen on its own. It was a proven method that always seemed to be the best answer to all his qualms about which direction to take and what to do in life. And that was precisely how the situation with Yousef had turned out, in its own way. Don't ask questions. Obey the command, and then let the chips fall where they may.

Cashe rose from the bed, snuck up behind his wife and acted out the scene he imagined earlier in his mind. Standing behind her, he forced himself to follow through with actions of intimacy as he carefully squeezed her waist and kissed her on the shoulder. He lifted his eyes; in the reflection, he saw her smile.

"How was your day?" he asked, gently. "It seems like I haven't seen you in such a long time."

"It was okay. I got up early and ran some errands. We needed some stuff from the store. Toilet paper. Dish detergent. Sugar—"

"Well, if you need some extra cash, let me know."

"Yes, I *do* need some extra *Cashe* mister," she said, turning around and kissing him on the mouth.

"Whatever. You know the deal. I'm not falling for that," he said, returning the affection.

"Don't worry about it. Next time you buy."

He went to the bathroom feeling sticky and dirty and then thoroughly bathed, looking forward to a clean pair of boxers and a T-shirt. When he returned to the bedroom, Kia was under the comforter reading an Elle magazine with Kim Kardashian on the cover, flipping through its glossy pages, probing the pictures of women standing in various poses, modeling chic clothing, expensive fragrances and other dazzling merchandise. She had lain on the near side of the bed, so he had to climb over her to reach the other side. He put his cell phone on the windowsill, slipped under the comforter, fatigued, and stared at the ceiling before finally closing his eyes. In the room, he could hear nothing but the sound of her turning the pages, until she finally folded up the magazine and threw it on the coffee table. The bed squeaked as she got up, turned out the light, then bounced again when she returned. When she lay on her side, facing him, he felt her hand slide to the middle of his chest, directly above his heart.

"Cashe?" whispered Kia from her pillow.

He put his hand on top of hers.

"What's up?"

She said nothing in return. He listened to the buzzing refrigerator in the kitchen, waiting for her to respond.

"Kia?" he asked. "Is everything alright?"

"No," he barely heard her say. It almost sounded as if it hurt for her to speak.

"What's wrong? Did something happen today?" he asked again, testing the water and trying not to sound too condescending, already convinced that whatever she might have to say would be directly linked to *what happened.*

"No, nothing happened. I don't know what I'm trying to say," she said and took her hand away. She turned around for a third time, giving him her derriere. He scooted closer, spooning her backside.

"What's wrong, Kia?"

"Cashe, I don't know if like being married."

The comment stabbed him in the chest. Of all the things she could have said to him, he never would have guessed it to be that. Though he foresaw some variety of disappointment, he didn't expect her riposte to be so piercing. Now, he was the one left speechless. His natural inclination was to take it personally and contemplate his own actions, to wonder if it was because he had done or said something wrong. But at the same time, like a cool breeze blowing the pain in his heart away, the words of Tulpehocken came to him like a sweet lullaby.

There is a war waging over the soul of your wife Kia.

His trust in what the angel said put everything back into perspective, somewhat eased the sting, and instead of taking Kia's words as a direct insult, he began to think about their relationship on a grander scale.

"Maybe it's because you're not working. I know you help your father out a lot, but is that really giving you satisfaction?"

"No, that's not it."

"Is it something I've done?" he asked.

"Never mind, just forget it."

"But, Kia, I don't get it."

"Just forget what I said."

"That's a hard thing to forget, you know—your wife telling you that she is unhappily married."

She sighed. "Please, just drop it."

Though he knew that there were spiritual reasons behind her statement, a part of him still wanted to understand, but couldn't. His emotions rose again, swirling like violent chemical reactions in the test tube of a mad scientist. For a split second, he wondered if he would be able to handle what might occur in the days to come. Exhausted, he closed his eyes and tried to clear his mind. He tried to forget the angels and the demons and the visit to Yousef's house. What he wanted more than anything in the world was to rest.

Threesome

IN A DREAM, he stood face to face with a long row of shiny black-beaded strings which hung from the top of a doorway to the floor. He felt hot and inebriated. Anxious and curious. Light music adorned the air; the repetitive plucks of an oud sounded far away, yet clear, as if someone had been strumming from behind the wall in another room. Following his urge to enter, with both hands he parted the beads and moved forward. They made a harmonic tinkle as they crashed against one another, falling fluidly over his arms. Before him were two women, sitting on a red leather couch.

Directly in the center, an ebony coffee table in the shape of a wavy rectangle was filled with different kinds of sweet delicacies. Some Cashe recognized—the ma'amoul, cashew baklava and sticky deblah—others he didn't.

The two women behind the table laughed into the air. Only their eyes could be seen. Their heads, faces and bodies were covered in the long, black cloth of the abaya, much like the pair he would later remember seeing at Sami's house. Perhaps, it was them. They called out to him, winking and slowly writhing, holding out their arms, beckoning for him to come closer with their hands. Though he heard a language not his own, their movements spoke volumes.

Come to us Cashemente, come!

Smiling, he approached the couch and sat in-between them. Their legs touched his and he rested each hand on a soft thigh on either side of him. They wrapped their arms around him, giggling and crooning, giving delicate kisses, bringing him closer. The smell of potent, yet faint perfume on their clothes and hair touched his nose as they rubbed his head and chest; he sensed an erection arising and wanted to undress them.

The sound of the beads at the entrance ahead made him look up, and a third woman, dressed identically as the two on the ruby-colored sofa, came into the room walking straight-backed and stiff-shouldered. What was odd was how she didn't push the beads out of the way as he had done; she walked *through* them. They ran the length of her body from the front, went over her head and sides, then fell down her back. An intense erotic wave hit him as she stopped short of the table before him.

Leaning forward, he put his hand to a bowl that was filled with what looked like the square, glazed sweets Kia had called Turkish delights. Taking just one, he chewed it, and then sucked the powder off his fingers. When he sat back, both women began to undress. He turned to the one on his right and watched her take back her head covering. Long black hair fell on either side of her creamy, tanned face. Dark eyes blinked at him, and he saw that her lips were painted the color of blood. On his left, the woman did the same. She tied her equally obsidian hair into a ponytail with a band from her wrist. Their abayas dropped to the floor, uncovering the nakedness of their circled nipples, belly buttons, trimmed vaginas and feet.

They interlocked him with their bare legs around his, pecking his neck, grabbing his groin. Just as he began to *really* enjoy their advances, now wanting to take off his own clothes, he realized that he couldn't move. He tried to shift his position by nudging the woman on his right away, but she only fought back; she pressed his arm to the couch, wrapped her legs tighter around his and pinned him down. The woman on the other side followed suit.

Now constrained, he looked at the person standing on the other side of the table, and though he couldn't see her face, he realized it was Kia. She laughed at him, throwing back her head. It changed into a harsh cackle, then into the hollow, rapid-firing call of a goat. He felt the heat in the room suddenly increase as sweat dripped over his brows, until the high, brute noise coming from her bowels finally died down. Underneath her clothing he witnessed— still held by his two lovers—how Kia's body bulged and bubbled in uncustomary places. It was as if a rabid groundhog underneath her skin was frantically crawling around her arms, stomach and legs. Her head began to grow upward and outward until curved horns and an equine face protruded forward, tearing through her head covering. Hair grew around her eyes. Her legs, thick and furry, came into view; her feet burst into hooves. Azazel's head cocked slightly to the right side as he looked at Cashe with one hollow animal eye.

She is mine, Cashemente. Kia is mine! it said, hysterically cawing with an insane guffaw, a pink tongue swinging from its wet mouth.

"Get...off...of...me!" Cashe grunted, trying with all his might to lift both women up at the same time. They dug their nails into his arms, and aggressively shoved him harder into the couch. To his horror, he saw how their shiny, oily skin had turned gray, wrinkled and waterlogged, as if they had been soaking in a bathtub for years; their faces were three-holed bags of deteriorated roadkill. The room, which moments ago had the aroma of food, now smelled like sizzling feces and he thought he might vomit. He screamed, strained and pushed with all his might until he regained consciousness and found himself shoving his giggling wife away.

"Cashe, what in the world were you dreaming about?" she asked, her eyes stretching wide to take in as much moonlight as they could possibly absorb while she glared at him through the darkness. "You kept pushing me away from you while you were sleeping."

He brought his face close to hers, checking to see if it was really her or if this was just another extension of his dream. Reaching over, he touched her tank top to validate its authenticity, then rolled to his back and stared at the ceiling.

"I was having a nightmare," he said. "It was about you."

"What was going on? You woke up screaming."

"Promise you won't get mad."

"I won't," she said. "It's only a dream."

He told her in detail, down to what the women on the couch were wearing, the food, and how she had transformed into Azazel.

"What do you think it means?" she asked, setting up the perfect opportunity for him to talk about all of the dreams he ever had about the goat beast and his encounter with Tulpehocken.

"I think it's a message about you Kia. I think it might be warning you about something," he said, stopping short, only speaking in figurative terms, not wanting to totally come out and tell her everything.

"Warning me about what?" she asked.

Cashe kept silent, wanting to go further, but his intuition demanded otherwise.

"I don't know, but whatever that bum in the park said to me is coming true. I think I'll be able to understand it better later," he said. "All I know is that I'm tired."

Tableaux

THOUGH IT WAS HIS DAY off from work, the alarm sounded at 6:00 A.M. He hit one of the buttons to quiet the ringing, then reluctantly climbed over Kia and out of bed. After walking into the kitchen in a lethargic daze, he turned on the lamp and surveyed the contents of the fridge for a snack. When he couldn't decide what to eat, trying to be as silent as possible, he tip-toed back into the bedroom, careful not to make the hardwood floors creak, and reached into the closet for his Bible. With just as much caution, he reentered the kitchen and sat down at the table. In his mind, he had begun to prepare for a morning at the gym, then work, but sleepily, he reminded himself that he didn't have to. Cashe considered getting back into bed, but too many issues and concerns were flooding his brain. He needed prayer, answers and direction. As he stared at the worn book, contemplating where he had been over the past day or so—naturally, spiritually, in dreams and visions—he suddenly became wide awake. It was as if someone had poured a bucket of cold water over his head. Reverently, he closed his eyes, bowed his head and prayed.

Lord Jesus, I need your help now more than I ever have in my entire life. Show me what to do. Help me. Strengthen me…

He prayed for Kia, for help when he traveled in the spirit realm and for the guys at work. When finished, he opened the Bible; it had been one of those times when God, for whatever reason, decided to answer immediately and precisely. There, on the page was the book of Ephesians, chapter six. His eyes fell directly on verse twelve:

...For we do not wrestle against flesh and blood, but against principalities, against powers, against the rulers of the darkness of this age, against the spiritual hosts of wickedness in the heavenly places...

What he read made him sit back in his seat, virtually paralyzed and out of breath. He had heard the verse before, but this morning, the passage seemed so alive, so real. Retrospectively, he thought about the "hosts" of demonic bat creatures in the sky yelling and screaming when Tulpehocken rushed him from the spirit realm back to the sidewalk on Shady Avenue, and how the angels fought *against* them in the gymnasium at the YMCA.

Before his musings could delve any further into meditation, he was interrupted by the sound of shuffling sheets and the creaks and squeaks of the mattress in the studio. Seconds later, like another answer to his prayers, Kia appeared, standing in the doorway, looking disheveled and cute as ever. Her left hand was raised and dug into her curly hair. She scratched her head as if she didn't know what else to do, looking innocently apologetic for the brief, but damaging protest against their marriage hours before.

"Good morning, Cashe."

"Morning, babe."

"I can't sleep," she said, scoping the kitchen, as if it might give her some clues about her problem. "What are you up to?"

"I was just praying and doing a little studying."

She walked past the table, went to the cabinet, found the teapot and filled it with water. He watched her put it on the stove and light the gas burner. Blue flames spurted up until a full circle formed and the bottom of the metal pot crackled. When finished, she sat in the chair opposite him.

"So, what are you studying?" she asked.

"Do you really want to know? I thought..."

He caught himself before going into some long exposition about *why* she might be asking questions concerning his faith, when it was *she* who had insisted over and over again in the past that *she* didn't believe it. But the fact of the matter was that he didn't know what her intentions might be this morning, and he figured instead of pushing her away, as if he had her and everything else in the world figured out, he should simply answer the question.

"I was sitting here after I prayed and when I opened up the Bible, here was this verse about spiritual warfare staring back at me. Christians, as you already know, really believe in demons and angels. God basically tells us about it here and says that all the problems we encounter in life as believers are related to what goes on in the spirit world."

He pointed to the verse, then Kia took the Bible from him and began reading.

"Interesting," had been her only response, and after she gave the book back, she returned to the cupboard, took out two coffee mugs, and then went to the sink to rinse them out.

"Do you want tea?" she asked.

"Yeah, I'll have some."

Kia prepared the tea, breaking only to ask how much sugar and milk he wanted, brought the two cups to the table, and sat back down in the chair. He sipped his drink, thinking to himself that times like these were the kind of occasions which he would never forget.

Cashe closed the Bible, then changed the subject and began discussing the domestic issues of the household. He talked about what bills were due and how much they had been spending over the past month. He acknowledged that he hadn't splurged in a while and joked, though it was partly true, that all of his extra money seemed to have gone to putting gas in the truck and purchasing an occasional Coca-Cola while at work. Kia's side of their expenses had gone to the same kind of necessities, and by the end of the conversation, they both agreed they were long overdue for some type of entertainment.

"I'm off tonight, do want to go out to get something to eat and maybe see a movie?" asked Cashe.

"Well, I have to go to Baba's house this afternoon, but after that I don't have anything else to do," she said, sipping her tea.

"Okay, when you're done give me a call. I'll drive."

After they finished their tea, Kia made breakfast and was the first to head to the bathroom to dress for the day. When she left for Yousef's house, he washed the dishes and made the bed, trying to think of what he could do to pass the time until later that evening. It had been such a long while since he could actually sit down, relax and do nothing, so he just hung out in the kitchen for a while. He stared at the tabletop until the lines of the wood grain morphed into patterns that started to look like ghostly faces. The colors of the cabinets, painted a dull yellow, seemed foreign, as if he had never seen them before. On the ceiling, he noticed cracks that had spread and extended like tree branches; they began in the corners and made their way to the gold light fixture centered in the middle. In the windows, he observed how the blinds had faded and were no longer brand new and white.

When he heard a limb fall from the top of one of the tall trees rooted on the other side of the cement wall outside the window, an idea came to him; to leave the apartment for the afternoon and take a walk. Cashe climbed into a pair of jeans and a T-shirt, threw on his coat, laced up his boots and left the building with a bit of excitement. He made his way past the courtyard and down the steps to Shady Avenue, taking in the crisp, cool air.

The plan was to make a complete circle, beginning his route at the business district near Hobart; he'd stay on the left up Murray until he reached Forbes, cross over, then return the way he came, only on the other side of the street.

As he passed the synagogue, he strained trying to think about the difference between what he had gone through yesterday, compared to the way the day seemed to be starting off so far. All the extreme emotional highs, the extraordinary angels and demons he saw, and the sounds he heard seemed inexplicably far away. Today was so normal, so regular, so ordinary. It was almost hard to even recollect how it had been before. Now, he sensed nothing but a peace which drifted in the light breeze of the early afternoon, both inside and outside his being. But Cashe knew something else too. If the spirit world had any connections to the colors he saw, the calm he was experiencing would only be a temporary condition. It wouldn't last.

A bearded father across the street from the Giant Eagle parking lot, wearing khakis, black bifocals and a blue button-down shirt, watched his son ride a tricycle up the path toward the porch of their home. He glanced at Cashe and gave a simple smile.

When he reached the corner of Hobart and Murray, he noticed that the tea shop across the intersection, conveniently named *The Te' Café,* was filled with customers. Though the windows were covered with patchy steam, he could still make out the crowd. He waited for the crossing signal and considered whether or not to stay his course, or stop in for a drink. The idea just wouldn't leave, and he decided another cup of something hot would certainly hit the spot.

After making a brief stop at an ATM, he crossed the street and walked through the entrance of the café, making the cluster of bells tied near the top jingle. Although the shop was packed with customers, there was no one in line, so he made his way directly to the register. There, he was met by a red-headed barista with a glittering lime green scarf tied around her neck. She grinned up at him.

"How may I help you?" she asked.

"Give me a second," he said, reading over the variety of teas and other drinks on the menu written in pink, light blue and purple pastel chalks on three blackboards that hung from the ceiling like floating picture frames.

"I'll just have an apple cider," he said, it being the only beverage that seemed desirable, and not wanting to spend too much time on trying to figure out what to drink. He paid and she said she'd bring it out to him. From a news rack near the counter, he grabbed a copy of the *Pittsburgh City Paper* and looked for a place to sit.

He took the only open seat in the corner near the window, spread the paper on top of the table, and began examining the photos and reading the headlines. Out of all of them, there was only one that caught his attention:

Sculptured Bat Exhibit Creeps Viewers

A close-up photo of what appeared to be a tall, life-sized bat, standing upright, wings spread, revealing its sharp teeth and a snout nose had been placed under the caption. Cashe almost wanted to laugh at the picture, but then thought how the flock of them hadn't been so humorous when he had been with the young angel on the disc yesterday morning.

The barista brought out his apple cider delightfully and placed it on an empty spot on the table in front of him. He thanked her, took a sip and looked around the room, checking out the types of hairstyles the women wore, the clothing of the men, and some of the artwork that decorated the room. In the opposing corner, in a tiny square space in the storefront window, someone had created what seemed to be an overly embellished miniature version of the seating in the café out of just two chairs and a table.

The tablecloth had studded, plastic replicas of diverse colored precious stones and metals. One of the chairs was painted white, and the other on the opposite side had been painted black. Above half of the table, hanging on individual pieces of yarn from the ceiling were paper cut-outs of black birds; on the other half were little angels. And *that's* when it hit him.

His eyes suddenly opened and he made the connection. What was in the storefront window was a representation of his meeting with Tulpehocken on the marble disc in the air. It was as if a drape had been pulled away; he could feel his eyes expanding as he absorbed more of its details. A bike leaning along the wall on the left. A circle of marble on the floor. One of the paper cut-out angels' faces had been painted brown; it was Tulpehocken. Cashe turned back to the story in the City Paper about the bat sculpture.

A glitch in the comfortable, *easy going* vibe that he had been enjoying since he left the apartment from the start of the day skewed his reticence, and he perceived the impending presence of a gateway to the spirit world beginning to raise its curtain right there in the café. A couple of college students at a table in front of him out of nowhere began talking about Stephen Avaloni and the construction accident as if on cue.

"Dude, did you hear about that guy who fell from the construction site downtown across from the G.C. Murphy building after that crane broke?" asked the one.

"Yeah, man. I heard about it, how the survivor said he had been saved by an angel," said the other.

"That's pretty freakin cool," said the first, more or less and unknowingly describing the nuts and bolts of a scene Cashe experienced in the spirit firsthand, "Like a bunch of angels and demons fighting over Pittsburgh trying to save one life…"

On top of being unaware of the vividly specific images they discussed of the very subject in Cashe's mind, they both giggled as if it were funny. But to Cashe, it all seemed a bit too strange. He no longer wanted to be in the Te Café as the familiar fear of that unusual, abstract presence seeped into his gut. Instinctively, he wanted to leave right then and there, but another force within urged him to wait around for just a bit. Maybe more of the creatures would manifest themselves today. Trying to ignore what the students at the table near him were saying, he instead examined the display in the storefront window, taking in as much information as possible. The more he studied its details, the more of what transpired yesterday came into clearer focus and the more he recalled. Each adornment on the tablecloth had been the exact same color of the garment of each angel. Even the bronze, metallic color Tulpehocken had worn was painted onto the brown-faced paper cut-out. It was becoming too frightening for Cashe, as he squirmed in his seat, too unbelievable; the feeling was too unbearable, its minutia absurdly too accurate.

What in the hell is that? This has to be some type of trap.

He couldn't move, yet wanted to escape; his strength and confidence slowly leaked out of him like liquid from a pin-holed water balloon. It seemed as if the decorative model in the window was sucking the life from his very spirit. He could no longer bear it, and knew he had to retreat and leave. Even Tulpehocken had sent him back to the street when the demons were on the way. Something was wrong; pain was God's natural indicator of that—it was time to go.

After finishing the last bit of his cider, he returned the newspaper to the stall, placed a dollar in the tip jar and went back outside. Looking for *something*, some sign that there was more to come, he searched his immediate surroundings on the corner of Hobart and Murray. Across the street, a young couple held hands, waiting for the traffic light to change. To his right, a group of teenage girls with ponytails, tight jeans and overlapping boots strutted down the hill. When he turned to his left, he noticed an old woman dressed in thick, mismatched layers of clothing crossing the street, carrying several plastic bags, and seemingly on a direct track towards him. Even from a distance, he could see her thick blue eyeliner and bright red lipstick. The deep wrinkles in her face made it resemble a Halloween mask. He recognized that she was the same bag lady who asked him for money downtown several months ago.

"What are you doing?" she screamed, stopping in front of him, blocking him from moving forward with her bags.

He took a step backwards but couldn't escape her clear gray eyes. They were empty and cold.

"What are you doing?" she asked, yelling again.

Cashe ignored her, moved to the side and crossed the street.

Astral Projection

AS HE MADE HIS WAY up Murray Avenue, miraculously, the feeling steadily faded until it finally dissipated altogether, and he almost felt normal again. He tucked his hands into his pockets, going further up the street away from the woman, noticing how the business district today was overly crowded. All the demonic interference he had experienced in the café must have been coming directly from the bag lady, he was sure of it, though he couldn't see her aura. As he neared Giant Eagle, he listened to a street musician playing the violin outside the store, right next to an outdoor fruit and vegetable stand. Elderly couples in matching black coats and slacks strolled in unison. High school students, who had probably skipped school, wearing baggy pants and sloppy tennis shoes with fat laces, rolled by on skateboards. Yet, even in the apparent ease of his afternoon walk through Squirrel Hill, his mind still couldn't get away from what he'd seen in the café and its irritating redolence lingered. All the objects in there had pointed him back to that crucial moment, back to the sky over downtown Pittsburgh. Back to the angels.

But how did they know?

At the corner of the Murray and Forbes Avenue intersection, he came behind a crowd of people who had just gotten off the bus near the Rite Aid Pharmacy and congregated on the corner, waiting for the light to change. When the crossing walk signal sounded, the hordes shifted, and he moved with them. On the other side of the street was the Squirrel Hill Branch of the Carnegie Public Library, and as he came closer, his intuition told him to stop. Up against a wall, just outside the automatic door, the place where people often paused to smoke cigarettes, was Tulpehocken.

It was *him*, but yet it wasn't. The angel he saw on the disc in the morning shone with an inner light, his clothes glittered, and his eyes were on fire. This little boy had no wings. He wore blue jeans and a black jacket with the name Rocawear written with bronze letters across his chest. They both had the same spongy hair and shared identical facial features and height. The boy's hands rested inside his pockets as he lazily stared at the people walking past.

Instead of speaking to him and risking the embarrassment of being wrong—though it had to be him—he took a place next to this apparent *copy* on the wall and pretended to watch the crowds of passersby. Cashe didn't quite understand what it was, but he knew there was *something* going on spiritually around this place, just like the table and chairs display in the store window at the café, only without the suppressing feeling of being mentally closed-in on. Just when he was beginning to relax and have a greater sense of ease as he stood there, all that changed. His eyes opened.

First, he saw a flying insect. A crane fly with long legs hanging from its skinny body fluttered away, as if it had just finished hitching a ride on his coat. Next, a white butterfly flew by from the opposite direction, and when he looked up into the air over the Rite Aid, he saw a black raven hovering in erratic circles, surveying something below. A jumbo jet thundered across the sky over the bird. Each image followed one after the other so that he naturally expected to see an angel next. But instead of seeing one, he heard its voice. Tulpehocken's voice.

Cashemente, you must learn to walk in the spirit, see in the spirit, hear in the spirit, taste in the spirit and feel in the spirit…

His first response had been to peek to the right, at Tulpehocken's look-alike. The angel must have finally decided to come out and reveal who he really was, but in a very peculiar way. When he looked over to respond, the little boy had his back turned.

You must be very careful Cashemente…Azazel and his workers will do anything to stop the Father's will.

Cashe didn't speak, but only thought in his mind.

Cashe:

What do you mean they will do anything to stop the Father's will?

Tulpehocken:

Even now, Cashemente, they war to prevent you from spending time with your wife.

Cashe:

Why do I sometimes feel so weak? And what happened at the café? What was that thing in the window?

Before he could receive an answer, he saw the bag lady again. Rushing, as if she were late for an appointment, she barged up the sidewalk towards them. She made a straight line to a spot near a trash can positioned directly in front of him and the boy, brushing past onlookers walking by with her bags as if no one else was around. She haphazardly dropped all her belongings sloppily to the ground, and Cashe could hear the crunch of the contents inside, knocking against each other. After an interlude of bending over and digging through one of the plastic bags, she finally stopped and stood up. From her sacks of clutter, she had found a tiny porcelain statue of an angel. Carefully, she placed the chubby, winged figurine on the lid atop the trash can. He thought of Yousef and the golden angel statue in his basement.

In her other hand, she held a puppet-like action figure of a man. The bag lady bent its arms and legs, manipulating its joints, then balanced it next to the angel so that they were standing right next to one another—just like he and Tulpehocken on the outside wall of the library. A puff of irritation hit Cashe in his chest, below his breastplate, a little above his stomach. His legs began to go numb, and he thought he might fall over on the sidewalk as he saw how the action figure had been an identical representation of himself, like a tiny little Voodoo doll. They wore the same blue jeans, boots and jacket; even the head on the toy had been painted over with a tan face and black hair. The woman seemed be sending them a message, as if saying, "I know what's was going on over there against that wall; you can't fool me, and you can't fool Azazel!"

Cashe:

What is that? It's like the table and chairs in the window of the café. It makes me feel horrible.

Tulpehocken:

Azazel and his workers use sorcery and witchcraft to steal your spirit.

Cashe:

But it's so strong.

Tulpehocken:

They need to show you as inferior.

Cashe:

What can I do?

Tulpehocken:

Cashe, you must always be aware in the spirit. The enemy loves to show their evil thoughts. You must not only be a hearer in the Spirit, but you must also see in the Spirit. Father, open his eyes, and reveal the truth.

Satisfied by the tableau she had just created, the bag lady sat down on the right side of the trash can, Indian style, and rocked back and forth as if listening to a hypnotic chant.

Sorcery and witchcraft. So that's what she was doing with the figurines. He heard a crack of thunder overhead, though the sky had been blue and only scattered with lines of sinewy cirrus clouds. He could see in the spirit. Golden rays of light shined through some of the people passing by the old woman and the trash can; others wore dark, hazy cloaks behind them like backpacks. A few had nothing. The bag lady was suddenly encompassed in a thick cloud of smoke, as if the sidewalk underneath her was on fire. Even the trash can seemed to be burning.

A long billow of the black exhaust poured out from under Cashe's clothing. He looked down at himself to see where it might be coming from. Tiny wisps leaked from the sleeves of his coat, and when he tugged the collar of his shirt, he could feel heat rising up the nape of his neck. Instead of the glowing aura of light emanating from him, for some reason, dark vapor bled from his body as if he had been mortally wounded.

His vision blacked out. He thought he had gone blind until just as abruptly as his sight left, perception gradually spread out before him again, and he could almost see clearly. When his eyes came back into focus, he knew that he was no longer on Forbes Avenue, but outside the entrance to his apartment building. His normal eyesight had only partially returned. Now, he viewed his surroundings through fuzzy tunnel vision. It was as if he were looking through a long periscope or tube with his peripheral crescent blurred. He had somehow separated from himself and been detached; he was *removed* from his body. At the library, he was physically present, but his mind had dislocated and traveled to the courtyard on Shady Avenue; he was nothing but a floating head, it seemed.

On the inside of the double glass doors of his building, Tulpehocken the *angel* stood wearing a bronze robe in the left window with his back turned, staring over his right wing as if waiting for Cashe to come through. In front of him, the door to the basement, which was usually locked, had been propped wide open. Tulpehocken turned away and levitated down the steps.

Not knowing if his *spiritual* body would operate in the same way as his physical body, Cashe tested and *willed* himself forward. His movement wasn't a walk and it wasn't flying, but rather a *roll* ahead toward the entrance, up the steps and *through* the windows of the unopened doors, as if he were riding on a giant hoverboard.

Mentally, he controlled his course, like playing a real-life video game. He again willed himself to one side, then the other, lower to the floor and then higher into the air. The black smoke that had spewed from underneath his T-shirt now made trails through the hallway and in all the places he had been, like a smoky marker. He rolled straight through the wall at the end of the corridor and into his own kitchen, hovering somewhere over the refrigerator.

Next, when he moved up higher through the ceiling and into the upstairs apartment, he found himself in a bathroom. The woman who lived upstairs sat on the toilet, staring straight through him as if he weren't there.

He had almost forgotten that Tulpehocken had summoned him downstairs, so he made himself descend through the floor, into the hallway and then backwards toward the entrance of the basement door slowly, beginning to master his movements. As he awkwardly floated down the steps, his spirit body passed halfway inside the stairwell and halfway through the blackness of one side of the wall.

The basement was unlit, and he could barely see the locked storage bins and naked pipes running overhead. At the far end near a set of washers and dryers, Tulpehocken waited, his head turned to one side again, looking over his right wing again. Cashe went straight ahead until the rest of the room came into view and stopped near the washer. Then the angel spoke, without moving his lips.

Tulpehocken:

Look, Cashe. The workers of Azazel show the heart of whatever you do to steal your strength.

Next to the washer on a table was a montage of images, each a symbolic depiction of some aspect of his life. A lime green Muslim prayer rug with a knit image of the Kaaba had been spread out like a tablecloth. It was his marriage to Kia. On top of the rug was a thick, hardcover KJV Bible—his relationship to God. Next to the Bible was an empty pizza box—his job. Next to the pizza box was a deflated basketball—his exercise.

Another blackout.

His vision gradually came back, though the entire time it seemed as if he had never closed his eyes. It reminded him of a game he used to play as a child. The Mexican boys in the neighborhood called it *knockout*. While standing up against a wall, they would tell him to take ten deep breaths, then on the last, to hold air in his lungs. Another kid would then press on his chest until he

295

passed out, only to wake up a few seconds later, not knowing what had just taken place.

It was like that now. He had dozed off after experiencing the very lucid spirit-trip with Tulpehocken to the apartment. He awakened back on Forbes Avenue, leaning on the wall behind the bag lady, who still sat on the sidewalk simmering in a cloud of smoke, not understanding how he got there. She continued to methodically sway her body to and fro, sitting crossed legged on the ground like a child riding a toy horse. Cashe opened his hands and saw them trembling. His entire body seemed jittery.

He looked to his left to seek answers from the boy Tulpehocken, only to find his spot against the wall now empty. The old woman and the smoke and the figurines kept bothering him, and he wanted to move, to quench the flames and extinguish the fire, to halt his inward irritation and shaking. With Tulpehocken gone, there was now no reason to be there all alone.

Half delirious and uncomfortable, as if he had just wet his pants, he hoped that the invisible smoke would somehow fall away. He left his position outside the library and joined the crowds of people in the street, walking up Forbes Avenue, pushed out of his place by the spiritual entity which surrounded the bag woman and her sorcerous charms.

It had been true. The farther away he separated from her spiritual stench, the better he began to feel. The auras encompassing the people walking up the street and driving by in their cars had also waned, and by the time he reached the corner of Forbes and Shady, the black smoke coming from underneath his shirt had totally dispersed.

Beginning to feel normal again—he was truly amazed at how fast it all went away—he entertained the idea of continuing on with his original plan to tour the business district in Squirrel Hill on the other side of the avenue, but instead he kept a straight pace.

He couldn't wait to check the basement and see for himself if his dreamy voyage was true.

Nothing about the apartment courtyard or the building or the entrance was different when he arrived. There were no signs of angel's wings on the ground, or strange messages written in the thin layer of dust covering the glass doors. Everything had been exactly the same as in the vision. Even the door to the basement was propped open.

Cashe retraced his former path and descended down the steps, holding onto the guardrail. When he reached the bottom, he saw that just as in the dream trip, the lights had been shut off, except for one at the end of the long basement near the washer and dryer. He went toward the far end of the room, peering into the tenant's wooden storage bins, touching the silver and gold padlocks hanging from the doors as he passed through, confident that what he wanted to see would be waiting for him.

Finally, he arrived at the washer and dryer and the table at their side. It was precisely as he had envisioned it—a lime green prayer rug lay on top like a place mat. On top was the basketball, an empty pizza box and the Bible.

He shook his head, puzzled at how something so obviously strange could have been set up right underneath his nose. If it hadn't been for the out of body experience given to him by Tulpehocken, he might never have noticed—and there had been no reason to. Whenever laundry needed to be done, he and Kia always used the laundromat across the street from her father's house. As he examined what was there, he began to feel angry and violated. Someone was secretly monitoring him. He needed to act and wanted to do something in response to what he saw.

Who put this shit here? How do they know about my life?

Without a second thought, in an uncontrollable rage, he threw everything on the table into a garbage can next to the dryer and walked upstairs.

Chapter Fifteen

CASHE'S CELL PHONE VIBRATED at his hip as he lay on the futon in the living room, recuperating and deep in thought about how the rest of the evening might transpire. He was up against something, but what? *His wife? Azazel? The devil? Really?* It hurt to think of his wife as an enemy, but the message from Tulpehocken had been clear.

Even now, right now, her mind is set on destroying you.
It just didn't make sense. What could she do?

"Destroy" was such a harsh word. His phone vibrated again, and when he checked it, the text on the display flashed her name. He hesitated, not wanting to answer because he hadn't quite come to any conclusions about how to handle them meeting tonight. In his chest, he could feel the burning pressure. Ultimately, he knew he needed to try and counteract the devastation, however it might come, with love.

"Hello?"

"Hey, I'm going to be leaving Baba's house in about fifteen minutes," she said. "Did you still want to hang out tonight?"

"Yeah," he answered, though something sounded different about her tone, almost as if going out had suddenly become an issue.

"*What* exactly did you want to do again?" she asked.

Here it was. He thought she might back out. Reflections of how she had, at the drop of dime, decided that she no longer wanted him living at the apartment in Mount Lebanon arrived like a torrent of rushing water. The way she called the cops. His night in the freezing, cold truck. And all of it out of the blue it seemed, for no reason.

"Like I said, I thought we might go grab something to eat and catch a movie. Is there a problem? You kind of sound like you might be having second thoughts."

"No, it's not that," said Kia. "I'm just tired of dealing with Baba. Listen, I'll see you soon."

Cashe hung up, and then opened the Internet Explorer on his phone to look up the word "destroy."

> **de-stroy** pron. [di-stroi] —verb 1. to reduce an object to useless fragments, a useless form, or remains as by rending, burning, or dissolving; injure beyond repair or renewal; demolish; ruin; annihilate. 2. to put an end to; extinguish. 3. to kill; slay. 4. to render ineffective or useless; nullify; neutralize; invalidate. 5. to defeat completely.

Yes, it was a pretty heavy word, he knew, but for some reason the enormity of the angel's message wasn't registering. Yet, as tough as it was to believe, in a way he still did. He understood what Kia was capable of. But for now, the only immediate defense he had against any such attack was to know that it was on the way. Kia would be arriving in less than fifteen minutes.

He went to the bathroom, washed his face, combed his hair, brushed his teeth, then sat at the kitchen table, nervously wanting her to speed up the process. Finally, the door opened, and she entered the apartment in what almost seemed like a gust of wind, like more than one person had come through the door.

Her arms were full. A purse was slung over her shoulder, tucked under her arm. In both hands, she carried a long golden lamp that curved like a cane at the top. A white glass shade covered the bulb. He watched as she turned it at just the right angle so it wouldn't hit the doorframe or bump the wall.

"More stuff from your father's basement, I presume?" he asked from the kitchen.

"I'm replacing the lamp in the hallway," said Kia. "Isn't it so cute?"

"It's okay," he said. "What's wrong with the one we have?"

Kia swapped them, putting the old one somewhere in the studio, and then reappeared in the doorway of the kitchen.

"Nothing, I just want a new one," she said. "Are you ready?"

He looked at his wife, savoring a glimpse of the plain, innate, innocence emanating through the complexion of her face and in her clothes. She was surely a woman, but a hint of a little girl slipped through the expressions of her facade. Cashe continued to pause, searching for answers to unasked questions, considering the soft black scarf wrapped around her neck. Her wool coat. The way she wore her hair down. She gazed back, meeting him with a fearless, penetrating look, and in the thought filled silence, they peered through the windows of each other souls.

"I am," he said. "Let's go."

Enough

CASHE WARMED UP THE TRUCK, pressing on the gas and revving the engine, while Kia sat quietly in the passenger seat, thumbing through her cell phone. He had been drawn to her side, wondering what she might be doing *over there*, but kept to himself. Normally, he would have all day to think about the details of where they could eat and which movie theater to attend, but this day hadn't been *normal* at all. He was still coming down from spirit traveling with Tulpehocken, which left him with too much to contemplate and feel through; his mind had been stretched to places he didn't think it could go.

"So, do you have a taste for anything in particular?" he asked, fishing for some direction or new idea. Currently, he had none.

"I really don't care," she said abruptly, "Right now, I feel like I could eat anything."

There was an eerie emphasis in the way she said *I could eat anything.* He thought she might be talking about more than just food, but wasn't sure what. Her answer didn't help either; the way all the decisions and choices of the evening had been delegated to him only added to his overall worries and concerns. The easiest and most convenient place to both eat and watch a movie, he thought to himself, would be in the Waterfront District, less than three miles away on the other side of the Homestead Gray's Bridge. Everything anyone could ever need was there—gas stations, grocery stores, banks, clothing boutiques, restaurants, movie theaters and even a post office.

As he turned into the Shady Avenue traffic, partially retracing his morning cycle route to the YMCA, he drove by the synagogue, past the place he had fallen during his angelic encounter, and down the hill towards Murray Avenue. Everything seemed crisp, clear and magnified, from the crescent moon hanging lopsidedly in the sky, to the streetlights, the storefront businesses and golden parallel lines dividing traffic down the middle of the street. Even the music on the radio sounded more intense than usual.

He turned down the volume, stretched over to Kia, and kissed her on the cheek.

"You know I love you, don't you?" he asked, trying his best not to remember the words of discontent she had spoken last night in bed.

"That's what you say, but sometimes you don't act like it," she responded. "Watch out before you run off the road and hit one of those parked cars!"

He backed away from her, ignoring the comment, and placed both hands on the steering wheel. As they crossed the bridge, he looked down at the overabundance of lights illuminating the parking lots of the Home Depot, Giant Eagle, and the Lowes Movie Theater complex.

"How does Fridays sound?" he asked, making his way down what seemed like an endless row of restaurants and shops.

"That's fine."

One empty space had been left open directly in front of the entrance, as if it had been waiting for them. He parked, they got out, and were met by the hostess once inside. The girl was a young, chubby brunette wearing thick tortoiseshell glasses and a bob haircut. She totally ignored Cashe's presence, turned her head, and spoke only to Kia.

"Would you like a table or a booth?" she asked her.

"A booth," said Cashe, abruptly interrupting.

He had dealt with that type of behavior from hostesses on other occasions when he and Kia had gone out together, and his response had always been the same—disgusting disapproval.

"I hate when they do that," he whispered as they followed her to a booth near a window.

"When they do what?" Kia asked, as if she didn't have the slightest clue about what had just taken place.

"They aren't supposed to talk to the woman whenever a couple is standing together," he said. "It's correct to speak to the man."

"I don't know what planet you're from," said Kia, "but it is *not* like that on earth."

He suddenly sensed his hunger. They slid into their seats, and after the waitress put menus and silverware wrapped in white napkins on the table, he scanned the specials for something big and hearty. Tonight, he wanted to be full. An appetizer of Buffalo wings, an entree of steak fajitas and a Coke with free refills would do the trick. Because he hadn't eaten all day, he knew there would be plenty of room for popcorn at the theater.

Dinner started off perfectly. A waitress with a nametag that read "Tiffany" had been friendly, and the food was hot.

"The next round of movies begins at nine, so we have a little time to decide what we want to see," he said, checking the showtimes on his phone.

Kia prompted a nice conversation about her father and how much trouble he was starting to become because of his age, until Cashe accidentally spilled the beans.

"I think he's getting a little senile," she said chopping on a French fry.

"He's not that bad," said Cashe. "I actually think he's kind of sharp for an old man."

"You don't know him."

"I stopped by his house yesterday, and we talked for a while."

The comment slipped out. He didn't mean to say it; it kind of just happened, and after he realized what he had done, he didn't try to cover it up or lie about it. He only continued on.

"You did what?"

Cashe knew he had gotten caught with his hand in the cookie jar, and immediately saw that he was in trouble.

"Please don't be upset with me."

"You went over there behind my back?"

"Yeah, but I wouldn't call it behind your back. I mean—what's the problem?"

"I told you that he doesn't like guys coming to the house! What the fuck is wrong with you?"

At that point, he could no longer speak. And after the *way* she had spoken to him, he no longer wanted to. He thought about just ending the entire night, but somehow made a vain attempt to continue anyway.

When they almost finished emptying their plates, Tiffany came back with a smile and tilt of the head and placed a plastic tray with the bill on Kia's side of the table.

"There they go again," he said after she walked away.

"You know what? I'm getting a little tired of your chauvinistic remarks."

He reached over and took the receipt from the other side of the table, opened his wallet and placed his bank card in the center of the tray. A few minutes later the same waitress returned, asked how their dinner had been, then left to process the payment.

"Listen, I'm not just some guy, I'm your husband. And the only reason I went over there in the first place was because something strange happened—"

Before he could say another word, Tiffany returned and stood at the center of the table.

"I'm sorry, but your card has been declined," she said, tilting her head to one side again.

He thought the evening couldn't get any worse, but it was.

"What? That's impossible," said Cashe, glancing across the table at Kia.

He guessed she had been staring at him the entire time and hadn't heard a word the waitress said. She was eyeing him with almost the same blank expression she had given when he was sitting at the kitchen table; but this look was a bit different. She was holding something back. Fury. Maybe rage. At any random trigger, he thought she might jump over to his side of the booth and tear his heart out.

"I just checked the account, so the money's in there," he said reaching for his wallet again. "But who knows? Maybe the system's down."

He pulled out another credit card and handed it to the waitress.

"Try this one," he said, and Tiffany shot down the aisle.

"Kia, I don't know what's going on. I just checked the account this morning. Maybe the waitress is pissed off or something."

She ignored his words, turned her head and stared out the window into the parking lot. A few seconds later, she looked back at him, sat up straight—about as solid as a statue—and spoke.

"I am *so* glad I didn't trust you with my money," she said gritting her teeth and shaking her head, making her hair fall out of place onto her forehead. "You are *so* fucking careless and irresponsible!"

"Wait a minute, Kia," he said with a whisper, giving her a sign with his hand for her to lower her voice. "Didn't you hear me just say that I checked the bank account this morning?"

Kia turned and spoke to the window.

"Well, obviously you did something wrong or else we wouldn't have to sit here hoping that your credit card goes through. And I'm not just talking about your account!"

The waitress returned, repeating the same condolence.

"I'm sorry, sir, but your credit card has been declined again," she said.

Cashe sat in the booth, stunned and motionless.

"Give us one second please," he said, holding up a finger to the waitress.

"Sure," she said, smiling at Kia.

Finally, *it* happened.

"I'm so tired of this shit!" she yelled, breaking from the table. The volume of noise chatter at the bar decreased to almost a silence and the people at the surrounding booths stopped to watch a scene in the making.

Kia snatched her coat and scarf, ignoring the bewildering stares from the patrons and walked away towards the exit. She had shoved the empty dishes on her side of the table with such force that they slammed into Cashe's plates. One of them fell to the ground and broke in two. A half empty glass of water tipped over, spilling into his lap. Tiffany hesitantly returned, looking bewildered.

"I think I'm going to need some napkins," said Cashe, frozen in his seat, feeling the cold water soaking into his groin. The waitress quickly left and returned with a roll of paper towels.

"Is everything okay?" she asked, picking up the broken pieces of the plate from the floor and sopping up the drips of water with a towel.

"I don't know what's going on with my credit cards," said Cashe, getting up from his seat. A dark, wet spot stained the front of his pants. "And I don't know what's going on with her. I need to find a bank machine or something."

"Um, I think I need to get my manager," she said. "Can you please just wait here for a second before you go?"

She piled as many of the dishes she could hold into a plastic tub and Cashe sat back down on the edge of his seat. The people in his corner of the restaurant began to speak again, but it didn't matter. He was both upset and embarrassed by all the commotion. A silent busboy rolled up with a cart and began cleaning the remaining mess.

A tall man in black dress pants and a red and white striped shirt briskly walked down the aisle with Tiffany at his side, then stopped at his table. He indignantly looked the area over, obviously irritated by what Kia had done.

"Hi, I'm Simon Wertheim, the manager here at Fridays. Tiffany says that you were having problems with your credit card?" he asked, digging both hands into his pockets.

"Yeah, I don't understand what's wrong," said Cashe. "I just checked the balances this morning and everything was fine. Will it be a problem if I go to an ATM?"

"Not a problem sir," said Wertheim firmly, holding his stance. "But just to let you know, we also have our own ATM machine right here in the restaurant. It happens all the time. If, for some reason that doesn't work and you need to leave and come back, what I'll need to do is get some information from you. And I'm not saying this is going to be the situation, but if you don't return, I won't hesitate to call the police."

Just in case his cards didn't work at the ATM in the restaurant, he decided to give Wertheim what he asked for—his name, a phone number, his address and even his driver's license information. As expected, none of them worked, so he left Fridays, unsure of how everything might pan out. It was true. The waitresses *weren't* just screwing with him. Outside, he examined his truck, still parked in the space nearest to the door. He peeked through the window, but Kia was nowhere in sight. It seemed hopeless; she could have disappeared into any store.

Instead of wasting time trying to guess where she might have gone, he decided to take care of the most pressing issue at hand, which was paying the restaurant what he owed. He drove straight to the Giant Eagle lot, knowing that on the other side of the customer service department inside was a PNC Bank ATM machine. He parked in a spot next to the cart return and followed a mother and her young daughter through the automatic double doors into the grocery store.

His mind, as he considered what had happened, was puzzled by Kia's capricious behavior, but at the same time, partially comforted by the forewarning of Tulpehocken, knowing this wasn't his first rendezvous with her totally flipping the script. As he made his way past the cases of soda and bags of chips set up in the vestibule, then through the fruit and vegetable aisle, he saw Kia coming from the other direction.

"Kia, what are you doing?" he asked, trying to reconnect with her, attempting to gain some piece of rational understanding from her point of view.

Instead of speaking, she threw money in his face. Twenty-dollar bills floated in the air, rolling off his shirt and onto the ground. She stepped aside, ignoring him, and he watched her leave the same way he had just come in.

"Kia!" he said, calling after her while picking up the money from off the floor.

He followed her into the parking lot. On the sidewalk outside, he grabbed her arm and turned her around.

"What is your *fucking* problem?" he asked, now angry, staring into her eyes, gripping her soft bicep.

She spit into his face and snatched herself away.

"Fuck you!" she said and started across the parking lot. "I can't wait until all this shit is over and done with Cashe—you are such a fucking loser!"

"What do you mean when this is over and done with?" he questioned again, following after.

"Oh, don't you worry," she said, increasing her pace away from him. "You'll find out soon enough. Yeah, my friend. You're going to find out."

He wiped the wet saliva off his face, tempted to run up to her from behind and tackle her onto the cold parking lot pavement. As soon as he denied the impulse to act out, an unnatural peace hit him in his chest, forcing him to regain his composure. For no reason at all, he suddenly felt sorry for her as she disappeared through the lot.

Kia had thrown sixty dollars at him in the store. He returned to Fridays and paid the bill, including the tip. It had only amounted to forty dollars, and the only thing he could think about was returning the remaining twenty to her. At least it would give him an excuse for them to speak again. He desperately wanted to patch things up, to fix it all. Somehow, someway, he thought, there might be an avenue to change her mind, to convince her otherwise. But he knew there wasn't. Kia was gone physically, but more so, she was gone mentally. Something had taken her away. Or someone.

Perhaps Azazel.

He hoped that Kia might be waiting for him by the truck in the parking lot of Fridays, but again, she was nowhere to be found.

Instead of spending his time performing futile surveillance of the Waterfront complex to locate her, he gave up, thinking that she most likely had decided to take the bus home or call a cab.

He drove up the ramp to the Homestead Gray's Bridge, being the first vehicle in line at the light. Again, he reminded himself of the angel's words, knowing *something* would happen, but not in a million, trillion years could he ever have guessed that it would go down like this. Over and over again, he sensed the humiliation of the scene Kia had created in the restaurant, the tingling of spit running down his face, and the soft impact that the bills of money made against his chest. The dinner he anticipated had been ruined, and there would be no movie tonight.

On the hood of his truck, he noticed that the glow of the traffic light turned from red to green and he thought of the auras. If only he had been able to see the spirit realm at Fridays, he thought. He gradually began to piece together everything that occurred, from his meeting with Cleveland and his revelations about this so-called "New Mafia," to his visit with Yousef, searching for meaning and a possible connection.

It was absolutely preposterous to not assume that tonight's episode at the restaurant was nothing other than a direct hit, personally aimed at him. Tulpehocken said that the objective of the enemy had been to separate he and his wife, and that was precisely the outcome. He would have bet his last dollar that the manager and the waitress and many of the other workers wore black shadows stuck to their backs in the spirit. More than anything, he wished Kia's aura was visible. He wanted to know what kind of spirits he was dealing with, yet had nothing but Tulpehocken's words to go on.

Under the rows of yellow streetlights, he weaved in and out of vehicles on the bridge trying to figure out what could have gone wrong with his bank and credit cards. He had been unexpectedly knocked out of his comfort zone, and now drove indifferently to no particular destination, unsure if he should return to the apartment or continue to search for his wife. In a way, he felt the same as he had while driving Yousef to Sami's place: clueless. Just like a helpless child strapped into the back of a car seat, unaware of the enormity of the world out there, never fully grasping the true meaning of even the simple things, *like traffic signs,* along the way. Kia's behavior was a perfect example of this; he knew she was angry but didn't know why. He couldn't understand how to read the situation and had no way to comprehend it. What he needed was a *revelation.*

At the other end of the bridge, he saw her walking along a worn-out path that wove its way through the tall, dead weeds alongside the road. It had been the only substitute for the lack of a paved sidewalk, and was the common thoroughfare used by people who didn't drive or couldn't take the bus. He hit the brakes, reached across the passenger side seat and rolled down the window.

"Kia, I don't know why you're walking," he said, inconveniencing the few cars behind him. "Why don't you just stop all this and get in? You have no reason to be this upset!"

She ignored him, keeping a steady stride, gripped her purse and fervently hiked up the hill. The cars behind him began to honk wildly, so he acquiesced to her wishes. If she wanted to unnecessarily make a three mile walk home, if that was where she was headed, then so be it.

He passed her, not wanting to go back home and wait for her to return, believing another confrontation was sure to happen. Every bit of the seemingly impenetrable and protected comfort zone they used to share had been blown to bits. The strong connection between a man and his wife was something he never really thought about until now; so many aspects of the relationship were contingent upon the stability of the union. It made him sad. Marriage was the stamp of approval of two people joining lives together, but as soon as one side disconnected, there was nothing.

He thought about the few things they *did* have left. Supposedly, they loved each other and had a marriage license to prove it; on a less significant note, there *was* the lease to the apartment. Other than those two things, they had little else invested in each other except what was only proving to be a very fragile bond that now might be irreparably broken.

Cashe took the long way home, slowly driving along Beechwood Boulevard through the park. He didn't have anywhere else to go and couldn't comprehend how fast and easily his world had shrunk by an unexpected reversal of commitment. Just because Kia was having issues didn't mean that he had to leave and no longer show his face at home—even though that was exactly how it seemed. He had every right to be there; now, legally. Calling the police wouldn't work this time around either, he assured himself.

Thank God we don't have any children.

Instead of wandering off any further, unnecessarily burning gas while cogitating about what to do next, he decided to return to the apartment. He parked in an open space near the courtyard steps and went inside. After shutting the door behind him, he stood in the darkness for a moment, absorbing the ambient silence. When he flicked the switch on the wall next to the door, the lamp that Kia had brought from her father's house dimly lit the hallway. Three arched passageways were before him—the bedroom, the kitchen and the bathroom. Cashe felt *stuck* next to the light, not knowing exactly what to do next.

He entered the bedroom, hung up his coat and undressed. Tonight, he decided, was officially over with. Though he didn't *feel* like it, he put on a pair of pajama bottoms, slid into his house shoes, and brushed his teeth. The futon unfolded effortlessly, and after reaching for the comforter at the top of Kia's closet, he spread it and lay underneath.

Over an hour had passed before he heard the sound of keys on the other side of the door, the rotation of the knob and the footsteps of his wife coming inside. He turned his back to the rest of the room and curled into a fetal position before she had the chance to turn on the light. His plan had been to ignore her, to allow her to complete her evening routine uninterrupted, without any interference on his behalf.

Underneath the blanket, he played possum, waiting for what might befall him next. He wasn't sure what to expect—the smack of a frying pan to the head, a glass of cold water dumped on his covered body, a punch to the back. Even with his eyes closed tight, it had been impossible to fall asleep. But being sleepy wasn't in this equation. Before that could happen, he needed some type of assurance that all the drama of the evening had simmered down.

When the bumps and creaks of the floorboards from Kia's slumbering footsteps throughout the room had stopped, and the opening and shutting of the bathroom and closet doors had ceased, he heard the click of the light being cut off and the chilly presence of her climbing into bed next to him. Her frigid arm touched his back, and he could tell that her body temperature had dropped considerably from the three-mile uphill march.

"Will you please scoot over?" was all that she asked before taking her half of the comforter.

"Kia, will you stop this?" pleaded Cashe. "You're going in the wrong direction. If you don't stop, the devil's going to take you away from me."

"Good," she answered. "I'm ready."

These simple words had been enough to put him at ease, yet in the quiet of the room, he yearned for more, for any expression of affection. He waited for the time when she might turn around and reach for him, but it never came. With their backs to one another, they both fell asleep.

Chapter Sixteen

THE ROOM ON THE OTHER SIDE of the singular square window in Cashe's dream had been painted blood red. He was neither outside nor inside, but rather in a place in-between, where there was no light from the sun, moon or stars, only a crimson glow shining through the pane. It was as if he were hiding in the warmth of a dark closet, like he had done when he was just a child, the door shut behind him, tucked among the protection of several layers of his parent's winter coats. On the other side of the glass was Kia, sitting in a black wooden chair, her back up against the wall at the far end of a room. Her hair hung down almost to her shoulders; stuck to the top of her head was a frosty, crystal bowl, filled with what looked like a mound of rainbow-colored gumballs. At first glance, he thought she might be wearing a hat, like a heinous version of the Chiquita banana woman. Her limp body was weighted down and seemed glued to the wall and seat; her face wore a dumb, empty stare.

A thought came that she might be in an electric chair, but she wasn't strapped in—her blank gaze and teary eyes seemed zombie-like, as if she had been hypnotized. Both her pants and shirt were purple in the style of prison or hospital garb; her feet were bare.

In a long sparkling robe, Azazel stepped *through* the wall on the right side of the room like a magician performing an impossible trick, first showing a hoofed foot, then the glistening shimmer of the cloth that wrapped around his bony shoulders. His oblong head, adorned with spiraling horns, approached Kia, who only stared forward as if watching Cashe from the other side, lost in a comatose trance.

With one step after the other and his posture ceremonially erect, the goat beast arrived at Kia's side. In both of his hairy hands, he grasped the bowl atop her head, bent over, and began chewing and swallowing the multicolored spheres like a ravenous hog digging its head into the slop of a trough.

Kia's eyes widened, and her mouth stretched open in agony as she strained and screamed uncontrollably, thick veins bulging from her neck and forehead. Though she seemed to be in pain, he heard nothing but muted shrieks coming from her mouth, which bore the slivers of the bottom and top rows of her white teeth. She wiggled and squirmed back and forth in the chair, trying to escape, but all the more, Azazel held a firm grip on the bowl and *ate*.

The goat-man lifted his head, and finally turned to the window, dropping pieces of the multi-colored spheres onto to the floor. He opened his jaws and held up his hands, mocking Kia in her apparent torment, then let out a laugh that Cashe could hear through the wall.

Two Steps Behind

THE SOFT RADIANCE OF DAYLIGHT coming through the blinds awakened Cashe gently, and his first thought of the morning had been that something was wrong. After lifting his cell phone off the windowsill, he checked the time on the display. It showed 8:45 A.M. He had overslept, and there would be no time to make it to the gym.

In all the rigmarole of the previous night, he didn't think to prepare for the next day; he had been rushed out of it, more concerned about Kia and what she might or might not be doing than his own needs. No matter how distracted he became from his dreams, by the opening and shutting of the doors to the spirit realm, or the sudden, harsh rivalry from his wife, he needed to find a way to concentrate on the simple, daily tasks of life. Upset with himself for forgetting to set the alarm, he climbed out the end of the bed so not to touch Kia, who still slept with her back to him.

The newness of the day almost made it feel as if last night had also been some type of hallucination. *And the dream.* Its details swirled in his mind and seemed more real than the fight with Kia before they had gone to bed. Azazel's scintillating purple gown overshadowed her spit that ran down his cheek outside the Giant Eagle parking lot, and the constant, incessant chomping from the crystal bowl, more substantive than the shattering of Cashe's plate on the floor next to the booth at Fridays.

In the shower, he tried to wash off his thoughts and memories as if they were sticky sweat. He wanted desperately to escape it all, to stay in the hot, steamy bathroom forever, to reside in a place where he couldn't be distracted or bothered. Refreshment was what he longed for, but unfortunately, over the past few days, he kept finding himself in situations that offered no rest. While dressing in the living room, trying not to distract Kia as she lay under the mound of covers, he checked to make sure he had everything he needed for another day of deliveries.

He left the apartment without speaking, figuring that it was just best to leave the events of last night alone for now. The closer he approached to his truck, the more he desired to call off from both Angelina's and Perfect Papa, to take a day to recover. But there was so much work to be done, so much necessary money to be made. *Money.* It seemed so insignificant now. So did paying the bills, and grocery shopping. And then there was the issue with the bank. He had almost forgotten. Sometime today, he needed to call or make a trip to PNC to get some answers as to why his cards hadn't worked.

As he started the truck and began to drive toward Angelina's, more of the details of his elapsed morning preparation ritual began to flood in. After patting his pockets, he realized that he left his cell phone in the apartment. Upon further inspection, he also found out that he hadn't taken his wallet and forgot to grab a pen.

At the light, he made a U-turn, and tried his best not to drive too far over the speed limit as he raced back up Shady Avenue. The space he had pulled out of near the steps was taken, and after a quick parallel parking job on the other side of the street, he crossed and jogged to the entrance of the building. Once inside, he grabbed his wallet, took two pens from the coffee table, his cell phone from the window and returned to the truck.

As if forgetting all the things he needed for work hadn't been enough, after turning the ignition, the orange glow from the instrument panel glared, and he noticed that the needle on the gas gauge rested just above the E. There was no way around it; he would have to make a stop at the gas station before heading to work, though the time on his phone displayed 9:45 A.M., and he knew making it there before 10:00 A.M. was an impossibility.

Cashe turned on Hobart Street for the second time, and then went left on Murray Avenue toward the Exxon at the very bottom of the hill. If for some reason he did run out of gas, at least he knew he could coast on fumes.

At 9:50 A.M., he turned into the gas station, weaving in and out of the crowded traffic, cautiously searching for an empty pump. All of them were taken, except number 1 at the other end of the lot. He steered around the cars, many of whose front bumpers were poked out into the lane, and finally parked. Prayerfully, he put his credit card into the slot as a long shot and waited for it to process, hoping to God that it would work as more of his overlooked morning routine came to mind.

Pray. Oh Lord Jesus, I forgot to pray this morning.

The electronic display blinked **Please See Attendant,** and immediately he knew his credit card had been declined. At once, two thoughts jumped into his brain. One, he would have to pray on his way to work; the other, a desperate wish that he might possibly have a few dollars in his possession. He hadn't thought to check the billfold in his wallet. Inside, he found the remaining twenty dollars he failed to give Kia in his hurried attempt to get into bed. With no time to celebrate, he stepped over the cement island and into the store.

Even though there were three people ahead of him, the attendant was diligently sending each customer in line methodically out the door. A young man wearing a thick, black, five-inch beard, the same length as the hair atop his head, lazily lifted his brown eyes after stuffing the register with a twenty.

"May I help you?" he asked.

"Fifteen on pump one please," said Cashe, beginning to feel the failure from his attempt to make it to work on time.

The cashier processed the payment, and after taking the receipt, Cashe gave a "Thank you," and returned to the pump, anxious get back on the road.

He put gas in the tank, then drove to the exit and stared at yet another hindrance—glowing red taillights formed a snake-line of traffic all the way up Murray Avenue to the apex of the hill in the direction he needed to go. Obstacle after obstacle circumstantially attacked him like the onslaught of an enemy, but if he was going to make it to work at all, he had no choice but to fight back. Instead of just sitting at the gas station stunned and dumbfounded, he began to drive.

Demonic Attacks

AFTER SIMULTANEOUSLY PRAYING and driving an unpredictable and erratic route to work—one that led him through Schenley park and down the cobblestoned Joncaire Street, parallel to the railroad tracks of Boundary Street—he found himself a block away from Angelina's at 10:20 A.M. Of course, there were no places to park on Alder, so he went into the back lot of the Highland Avenue Laundromat, then strolled silently through the entrance of the shop past Ingrid as she wiped down the glass doors of the Coca-Cola cooler. It was 10:30 A.M. when he entered the kitchen and his eyes opened to the spirit.

"Oh…my…God," said Marcus, while grinding out a ball of dough, and speaking loud enough for everyone to hear. A dark shadow spread over his shoulders, up his neck and over his head. "Here's Cashe coming through the door a half an hour late for work!"

"You're right, Marcus," Cashe answered, trying not to pay too much attention to the black mist floating behind him.

He clocked in at the computer terminal near the front of the kitchen, trying to convince himself that a half an hour was late, but really wasn't *that* late. This outburst made Cashe feel tense and on guard, as if Marcus had been *personally* offended by his tardiness. Like Marcus wanted to fight.

We fight not against flesh and blood. Lord help me.

"Guys don't last 'round here too long comin' in half *our*, or an *our* late for work, huh Trent?" asked Marcus trying to gain supporters, his thick Pittsburgh accent suddenly sounding lucid and unusually more pronounced.

"Shit happens," said Trent, not looking up from the slices of celery on the cut table.

"It's not a big deal," said Cashe. "You're more worried about it than I am."

"Well, we'll see what Miyad has to say 'bout that!" declared Marcus.

"Marcus, just dock your dough," said Cashe. "I'll worry about Miyad."

He turned around and tried to visually imagine what 10:30 A.M. at Angelina's was supposed to look like. Marcus and Keith were still grinding out dough. Trent was cutting up celery and broccoli on the make line. Hakan and Benyamin were probably finishing up salads and slicing tomatoes. For a moment, he thought about going back there to help them, but noticed the pile of dishes around the sink. Just before he began to prepare the dishwater, he was overwhelmed with the presence of fear in the room as Miyad appeared at the top of the steps.

"Cashe!" he yelled in his thick accent, emphasizing the *shh* at the end of his name. "Ware you bin man? It's elebin o'clock!"

Two bat-faced demons, cloaked in charcoal leathery wings like overcoats, mounted on Miyad's left and right. They both moved closer to him, and his eyes momentarily bulged.

The sight would have been terrifying if this had been his first time seeing them. But he was getting used to the spirits. He knew they only showed themselves. Reveal but don't touch. It was Miyad that he had to worry about. In that same instance, two angels from the meeting on the disc downtown swooped in through the ceiling in a crisscrossing pattern, swords drawn, sliced through each of the demons and then flew out the walls on either side of the room. The demons disintegrated into a black mist, then disappeared. Miyad was oblivious to the spectacle.

"It's only ten-thirty," said Cashe wanting to smack himself for forgetting to call. "I'm sorry, I ran out of gas and got caught into traffic."

"Dat's no excuse," he said. "Everybody here haz to deal wif da traffic. It's okay today, but next time dis happen, we hab to talk."

Miyad came down the steps and went to the front of the shop to Ingrid, who was now posted next to the registers. Cashe turned back to the sink and ran the water, hoping that doing the dishes might give him a break from the onslaught of accusations, but also knowing he would have to deal with maneuvering in the spirit.

By the time he finished, the *business* activity in the shop had significantly elevated and taken the attention off of him. While Ingrid answered the phones, Miyad steadily handed out orders until Cashe found himself as the only driver who hadn't left. Finally, Miyad called his name and assigned him two deliveries—one to Mike's Auto Body Shop on Meadow Avenue, the other to a residence on Stanton.

Cashe put the food in hot-bags, placed a two-liter bottle of Sprite on top, then carried the orders around the side of the building and through the alley to the laundromat parking lot. A tall man, in a green flannel shirt and blue jeans smoked a cigarette just outside the back door entrance. He tossed the butt to the ground, then snuffed it out with the toe of his boot.

Several bat demons flew in and out of the man, like a flock of sparrows checking on their hidden nests through a chimney of an abandoned building, or like swallows feeding on a swarm of bugs, squealing and squawking into the air in broken circles, following no particular pattern or course.

We will eat soon! Soon eat will we!

"Hey, you!" yelled the man. "Unless you're doing laundry, you can't park here!"

Cashe experienced several different emotions at once. For one, he wanted to challenge the man's authority; he had never seen this guy at the back door of the laundromat before and wondered if he really worked there. For two, at the same time, he clearly understood that this was a spiritual attack. Not only that, he knew he was at work and didn't want to get into any more trouble than he was already in with Miyad. He had to navigate through this carefully.

Besides, who knew? This guy could be the owner.

"Okay, I'm leaving now," he said, balancing the orders in one hand while opening the driver's side door of his truck with the other. He didn't like the way the man was talking to him, but seeing the demons, who he knew without a doubt had heightened the effect of his annoyance, somehow seemed to lessen the potency of his rudeness. Under normal circumstances, he might have gotten into a confrontation. Maybe he would have told him to go to hell.

"I mean it," said the man, the demons doing their best to provoke, "I don't want to see you parking in this fucking lot again. If I see your truck and you're not washing clothes, I'm calling the tow trucks."

He ignored the barrage of threats, stuck to his routine and drove out of the alley dizzy, weak and out of sorts, but without incident. It was similar to the Te' Café just before the crazy bag lady had yelled at him, and right after she put those figurines on top of the trash can while he stood next to Tulpehocken outside the library. Only the demons weren't on the way, they were here; he could sense their heavy, fluid presence growing, and his own confidence leaving. Cashe wondered if one of the employees had made a voodoo pile of garbage and hidden it somewhere in the store, like the items in his basement, and if that's what was really sucking away his resolve.

Outside Mike's Auto Body Shop, a row of broken-down cars and trucks lined the exterior of the establishment and the gravel lot across the street. He slowed down near the shop, surveyed the area and tried to find a place to park. Meadow Street was the kind of road where someone couldn't just stop in the middle of the street and put on their four-way flashers. Constant traffic from the East Liberty neighborhood used this two-lane passage as a shortcut. He paused while trying to decide whether or not to momentarily pull behind the three cars parked in front of the garage, which would block them from backing out, or to turn around and put his truck next to the fire hydrant at the corner.

"Get the hell outta the way!" someone screamed from the window of a car that had mysteriously snuck up behind him.

The man honked his horn violently and repeatedly, startling Cashe so much so that he thought he'd have a heart attack. With shaky hands, he quickly pushed the hazard light button and turned off to the shoulder.

In his rear-view mirror, he saw a man in a brown 80's model Chevrolet, filled with what looked like black smoke, hysterically punching the horn, even after Cashe had turned halfway into the gravel lot. The car looked like it was on fire, as if the driver might be hastily trying to speed around him to get down to the Allegheny River in order to quench its flames. But as he stared into the mirror, he knew that it wasn't smoke at all. Demonic spirits swam around the man in the car, swirling above his head, behind his back, in and outside of him. Erratically, the Chevy skidded out of control, spun its tires, painting the road with thick rubber marks, jolted forward and finally stopped on the side of Cashe's truck. Inside the car was a black man, wearing a Carhartt tossle cap and a plaid coat. He had rolled down his window and began screaming relentlessly, cursing and insanely spewing something about where Cashe might have gotten his driver's license. For a split second, Cashe began to get out of his truck to respond before he caught himself; he had even grabbed the door handle.

"Okay!" he yelled at the man, pointing down the street, "Just go!"

The man cursed one last *fuck you* and threw up a middle finger before taking off down the street; dark, misty spirits trailed as if in the wind. Cashe slid behind the parked cars at the garage, now unnerved, fumbled for the receipt to the order, read it and checked the price. For the very first time in all of this, he believed that the devil was trying to kill him.

A bell sounded as he pushed through the heavy metal door to the shop. A black and red "Open" sign hung from the square glass window, and inside, a pigtailed woman in an oily mechanic's uniform smiled as it closed behind him. A second man sat hunched over a corner desk, talking to a customer on the phone with one hand and holding a lit cigarette in the other.

"Pizza!" said the woman, raising both hands.

"I have a delivery here for Mike," said Cashe trying his best to smile back.

She pointed toward a shut door to the right.

"Mike should be somewhere in there."

On the other side was a spacious garage where several vehicles were held up in the air on top of hydraulic lifts. Tires had been stacked up along one of the walls, and long red hoses with what looked like guns attached to the ends lay indiscriminately on the floor. Every head turned toward Cashe, but no one moved or said a thing. He just stood there for second, not sure what to do.

"Hey, I'm looking for Mike!" he said, speaking to no one in particular, throwing his words forth, hoping they might elicit some type of response.

From the far end of the garage, a short white man in dirty blue jeans, work boots that seemed too large for his feet, and walking with a little too much cowboy swagger approached. Both of his thumbs were lazily slung into his pockets, and he seemed bothered, like someone had just jabbed him in the stomach with the end of a broom handle or plucked him on the crown of his forehead with a middle finger. The smoke from a spirit waved like a flame of a fire behind his head and shoulders, and Mike's foggy eyes danced around the room like he wasn't all the way there, as if his attention had been taken away by the assortment of objects in the garage.

"Mike?" asked Cashe after the man stopped in front of him.

"Yeah?"

"Hi, it's $24.97," he said. An odd silence passed while he waited for him to pay.

"You want to give me the goddamn food first?" asked Mike, rudely, in an unforgiving raspy voice, now looking only at Cashe. He thought that Mike might, for the hell of it, try to poke out his eyes.

It was supposed to be the other way around. The customer paid, then the driver handed over the food. It was a standard protocol that provided a sense of security and prevented the chance of robbery, according to his Perfect Papa handbook. But this was Angelina's, and there were no guidelines. Cashe became drunk with the hot urge to act out in response to his words, though he knew that it wasn't totally Mike speaking, but rather the dark spirit within him. Some of the other mechanics stopped what they were doing and slowly made their way over to where the two of them were standing, matching black flames waving behind their heads like flags.

"Sure, no problem," said Cashe and tried to hand Mike the two-liter of Sprite.

"Just put it over there on my desk," he said pointing to a messy chest of tools up against the wall. Cashe gritted his teeth and went to set the food down on top of the clutter. When he returned, Mike handed him a twenty and a ten-dollar bill.

"Thanks," said Cashe trying his best to maintain his composure, then hurried to leave the garage and the crowd of mechanic spectators, grateful that the anger he was feeling on the inside hadn't spilled out and possibly caused him to lose his job or go to jail.

"Jesus fucking Christ," said Mike before the now laughing arena of men, "Can I get my change please?"

"I'm really sorry about that," Cashe said, turning around, just before reaching for the door.

He dug into his pocket and leafed through several one-dollar bills until he found a five. There would be no wasting his time, predicting about whether or not the chances of giving five ones, opposed to a five-dollar bill might get him some type of gratitude. At this point, he knew he probably wouldn't take a $20 tip from Mike—demons or no demons.

Baldheaded Midgets

ALMOST AT HIS WITS END and more than ever considering quitting his career as a delivery driver, Cashe cruised up Negley Avenue, praying that the onslaught of repetitive attacks might soon come to an end. The license plate on the back of the car before him spelled out the name "MIKE," a vivid reminder of the experience he had just gone through at the auto body shop. Again, he thought about how he still hadn't had the chance to check and see if his credit and bank accounts would behave correctly today. The way things were going, he knew he might never get around to it.

He began to think of his wife and the image of Kia walking up the hill on the other side of the Homestead Gray's Bridge. She seemed so determined to make it home alone, without his help. Pictures of him lying down with his back turned to the living room also flashed in his memory, along with the sounds of all the bangs and clattering she had made before finally coming to bed. He thought of her balled-up body inches away from his on the futon underneath the comforter, being unable to hold her, unsure about how exactly to handle the matter.

Ten minutes had passed, and he parked on Stanton Avenue, having no problems whatsoever finding a space directly in front of the residence. To his right, he saw a silver storm door and noticed how it had been the only piece of metal on the weather-beaten wooden porch. Holding a hoagie and soda in his left hand, he rapped on the loose plastic window attached to the raggedy screen door, which made a clamor louder than expected. A middle-aged chubby woman answered with a smile, her chocolaty face making creases underneath round cheek bones.

"Here, come on inside," she said. "It's cold out there."

Though he usually denied offers to enter customer's homes, today was different; he was beginning not to *care* and would do anything and everything to expedite his shift's end at Angelina's, though it wasn't promised to get any better later on.

"Okay, sure," he said and stepped through the door and into the woman's house.

"I'll be back in a second. I have to go get the money. How much is it again?"

"It's $11.47," he answered and watched her climb a creaky flight of wooden steps.

"Don't mind the pets," she yelled as a cat leaned up against the banister, arching its back, then followed her upstairs, "They don't bite!"

An observation he had been privileged to study in almost every home he had the opportunity to look inside over the past two years while on deliveries—and on those rare occasions when he actually entered—was to see *how* the customers lived. Each home fell into the usual dichotomy; either they were neat, sparse and very clean or filthy, jumbled and filled with every kind of object imaginable.

The Stanton Avenue home was of the latter type. There were chairs and tables stacked one on top of the other, and clothing stuffed in boxes, strewn onto the floor and hanging off two filthy sofas. A trash can, halfway blocking the only path to the back of the room, overflowed with empty Burger King bags, lidless cups and wrinkled sandwich wrappers. Several golden Buddhas, cross-legged and frozen in place, had been placed on a ledge next to the steps. On the floor, a book of matches—with one single match inside—rested next to Cashe's left boot; a faded copper penny was next to the other. Thick green curtains prevented light from outside to enter in.

What he first thought to be another cat scurried from behind the trash can and took cover underneath a clutter of tables and chairs. He stared, waiting for it to come out and rub its body alongside the furniture's legs, for it to reach the top of its tippy toes and curl its tail around the side. Instead, a tiny, dark gray, leathery bald head peeked out from among the clutter, revealing its yellow eyes and stubby fingers; observantly, it gripped one of the legs of the chairs. Then, just as fast, it recoiled and darted deeper into the wooden maze with short, miniature strides and hid.

He had gotten a good enough look at the creature to know that it wasn't a dog or a cat and was unlike anything he had yet seen up until this point in the spirit world. Less than a foot tall, its thick, wrinkled grayish skin was rough and shiny, like the surface of an oiled-down elephant. It ran standing up, not on all fours, and had been totally naked. Rusty colored pubic hairs covered its groin and curled out from its armpits.

The room opened up further, and suddenly several little bald heads with sets of yellow eyes exposed themselves throughout the muddled room, from behind the piled-up boxes, books on the floor and other random objects.

"I'm so sorry for keeping you," the woman said, thumping down the steps. The creatures scattered at her arrival. All at once he noticed her thick gray sweater, sprinkled with reddish-brown colored snowflakes of the precise same hue as the creature's skin and hair.

"Here's fifteen baby, keep the change," she said, then took the food.

He thanked her, turned toward the screen door and the steps outside, listening to her shouts behind him.

"Move!" she said to her pets, "Get back! Get out of here!"

Prophecy Fulfilled

THE LAST THING CASHE EXPECTED to see after parking in an empty spot on Alder Street next to Angelina's was Kia's Ford Explorer. Everything he had been pondering during the ride to the shop concerning the spirit realm while on the drive back from Stanton Avenue disappeared as he scanned over the details of her vehicle. Yes, that was her plate number: *YSF-3588*.

He was transfixed by what was before him; he couldn't move and didn't want to. Several possible motives explaining her presence at his job came to the fore, but a solution hadn't. There absolutely was no reason for her to be there, unless something bad occurred. Maybe there had been an emergency. Perhaps something happened to Yousef.

But why didn't she just call?

He reached for the single empty hot-bag on the passenger side seat—it was the only thing he had to carry with him—and then came around the corner to the store's entrance. Inside, he saw his wife, leaning on the salad cooler, purse in hand, dressed in all black as if she were about to attend a funeral. *Maybe his funeral.* She wore black shoes and black slacks, creased with a straight line down the middle of her legs on the front and back, a black coat and black purse. Her black hair was pinned up into the back of her head with a long, black pin. Miyad was on the other side of the counter with both hands up on the cooler talking to her when he came through the door.

"Is there something going on?" Cashe asked Kia as he slowly rounded the corner, squeezing the blue hot-bag in his right hand.

Both she and Miyad glanced over at him but said nothing. Kia rolled her eyes, and quickly gave her attention back to his manager. Trent showed up in the doorway that led to the kitchen, as if on cue, with a hoagie roll in his hand.

To watch?

"Kia," asked Cashe again, stopping at her side and feeling a taste of fury under his tongue and in his chest. "What's going on? Why are you here?"

"Cashe, get back to work," said Miyad softly.

"Hold on, this is *my* wife," said Cashe, "I need to…"

"I said, get back to work!" he yelled.

"Fuck you, Miyad. Do your own work, I quit!"

Never in his life had he experienced such a consuming fire burning from within. Trent laughed out loud and returned to the kitchen. Kia still hadn't acknowledged him. She only smiled blankly. The room began to spin in a drunken vertigo.

"Kia, don't you hear me talking to you?"

She didn't move, and only continued to give Miyad her full attention.

"So, like I was saying," said Miyad in his thick accent, giggling with Kia as if Cashe didn't exist, "I'b been managing restaurants for over 20 years…"

The scene became surreal. Everything, his life, his job, his existence, all had suddenly become counterfeit. Nothing seemed real.

Cashe was not only embarrassed, but more surprisingly, for reasons beyond explanation, was *supernaturally* able to hold back an anger that was so unfathomable, so potent, he thought he might internally combust. It was like something had taken over his body and steered him in another direction, and for the first time in his life, he *wanted* to kill another human being.

His jaws loosened, and his mouth hung partially open as he watched both his boss and his wife pay no attention to him. He thought he might faint. The room began spinning faster, and his eyes opened up to the spirit. Suddenly, smoky black sheets of banshees flew past into the kitchen, in circles near the hood of the oven over Trent and Jihad's head and then out into the lobby of Angelina's.

As if in a trance, he silently stepped away from Kia and Miyad, from them, from *it*, that unexplainable, unidentifiable occurrence. That *thing*. He walked away from them and to the driver's station, caught in-between clocking in from his deliveries and returning to the lobby of the store. When he turned and looked over his shoulder, he could see directly to the salad cooler. A giant, purple anaconda-like snake wrapped itself around his grinning wife and intertwined with another pink serpent of the same size, slithering around the neck and body of an unknowing Miyad, spilling their thick muscles on top of the counter like living guts. Kia giggled. Miyad laughed.

"Cashe, what just happened?" said Jihad, his hulking frame standing next to him like a barricade, blocking the computer screen. "Did Miyad just play you like that in front of your wife?"

There was nothing Cashe could say, he had no answer and only remained silent, breathing slowly and heavily, trying not to pass out.

"That's fucked up!" said Jihad walking back to the pizza line. "You know what? Man, if I was you, me and Miyad would have to step outside."

Trent hysterically cackled in background, but the desire to keep going, to finish whatever this was, drove Cashe toward the computer screen.

Chapter Seventeen

CASHE REFUSED TO GO OUT to the registers and instead asked Jihad to take his money for the day. He walked past Kia and Miyad, knowing there was no other option but to ignore them. With his mind still twirling and revolving, he could do nothing when he arrived at the apartment. He couldn't even force himself to eat a peanut butter and jelly sandwich and a bowl of Ramen noodles. The thought of packing up his things and taking off came to him. *But to where?* Maybe going back to Angelina's and punching Miyad in the face was a better idea. Everything in the room reminded him of his wife, and he could no longer bear the thought of her behavior. It was making him contemplate dangerous and crazy schemes, things men shouldn't consider. There was no way in the world to just sit and relax, so he changed into his Perfect Papa uniform, pondering what the evening might entail, and left early for work. His shift didn't start until 5:00 P.M., but he decided that an hour of quiet time in the truck might be the perfect remedy to cure his now nonplussed state of being.

Like clockwork, right after he drove into the lot on the side of the building, Cleveland also turned in and parked next to him. Cashe didn't move but only watched him open his car door hesitantly, and then arrive at the driver's side window of his truck. He knocked twice, before Cashe rolled down the window.

"I really need to talk to you," said Cleveland, radiating an unnatural amount of sincerity.

"Sure, give me a second," said Cashe, putting the window back up and stepping out, beginning to sense some *relief,* an affirmation that he was indeed entering into the realm of his purpose, his destiny. Although he was hurting, it all seemed so déjà vu-ish and expected and he couldn't wait for what was next.

"What's going on?"

Cleveland stared away, up into the branches of the giant white birches across the lot, furrowing his brows reflectively. Usually, Cleveland had been the one to bring out the smiles, to show humor and break up tense situations on the job; mirth followed him around like a stray dog. But now, he carried a solemn disposition.

"Last night I had dream, Cashe," he said. "About you and me."

Immediately, he guessed it had something to do with the New Mafia, or Azazel. They way Cleveland was looking around as if he were searching for auras or hidden fairies, it wouldn't be a surprise if his eyes had finally opened to the spirit. Kris sped into the parking lot before Cleveland could go on, and before Cashe could even finish his thought, observing the two standing together over the top of his round framed glasses like the parking lot police, in anticipation of catching them committing a crime. With his left hand, he steered into a space; holding up his right, he flashed his ruby red ring, talking relentlessly on his cell phone. They both watched him get out of his car and walk toward the entrance of the store.

"I mean, I've never, ever, dreamt anything like this before in my entire life," Cleveland said, putting both hands in the air, using them to enhance his expressions.

"What was it about?"

"I dreamt that this angel took me way up in the air, over downtown," he said pointing to the sky.

"A dream?" he asked, knowing it was no dream. It really had happened.

Cleveland gave the alien smirk. "Yeah."

"Hold on one second," Cashe said, interrupting, realizing that he hadn't yet told Cleveland about his own angelic experience. "This may not seem important to you, but I want to ask you something before you go on. What did the angel look like?"

"He was a little boy, a Chinese little boy. He said his name was, and I'll never forget this, *Wissahickon*."

The details of Cleveland's story woke Cashe up a bit, but not much. Instead of being surprised, he was grateful. He had reached the point where he had become tired of being alone and welcomed these revelations with unabashed satisfaction. When he leaned back onto his truck, it was as if he had sunken into a cushioned sofa after a long, hard day of work. Finally, there was someone who would understand.

Cleveland recounted a story that paralleled his visitation on Shady Avenue. He described the white light, the marble disc, the international circle of angels, how the clear gel filled with flying sparks inside Wissahickon's hand had opened his eyes and how the cold flame had opened his ears.

"Then he told me that you and I have to go down to the South Side for the initiation tonight," said Cleveland.

"Wait a minute, what *initiation?*" asked Cashe. "What are you talking about?"

"Remember? The initiation? When the new inductees pass through that hazing ceremony to become members of the New Mafia. It's tonight."

"Tonight? What are we supposed to do?" asked Cashe deliberately, knowing that he had never been given specific instructions on *what* to do. It had always been where to go. Yet again, he was obliged that it was coming from Cleveland.

"Wissahickon said we will know what to do when we arrive."

Yes, they had contacted to him. Without a doubt. Cashe told Cleveland about Tulpehocken, Yousef and Kia and then silently, they looked away from each other, feeling the heavy peace of their common fate. Two wild doves flew into the middle of the lot, landed at their feet and began cooing.

"You in?" asked Cleveland.

"Yeah, I'm in," said Cashe.

Suddenly, Kris came from around the corner, scaring the doves into the trees.

"Hey fuckface," he said to Cleveland, "Sam told me to tell you that you have a delivery."

Chip Activated

CASHE'S FIRST DELIVERY of the evening took him to the Tower A Dormitory, one of the three cylindrical high-rise buildings positioned in the middle of Pitt's campus, which altogether made a giant triangle in-between Forbes and Fifth Avenues. Parking there was almost impossible. If it hadn't been for the lighted car topper above the roof of his truck, the police would no doubt mistake him for a derelict student and ticket him every time, despite his flashing hazard lights. He turned into a court called the Schenley Quad, directly in front of the Bruce Hall dormitory, and then carefully climbed the handicap ramp on the side of the three steep flights of steps up to the Towers.

Security prevented any deliveries from being made directly to a student's dorm room, so he called and waited in the crowded lobby for a girl named Jennifer to come and get her pizza. Hordes of college students passed by in jeans, hooded sweatshirts and backpacks, and he reminisced about all the times he had meandered through this same lobby, admiring all the blooming, fresh faces.

Did I really look that young?

A skinny, blonde-haired girl wearing fluffy house shoes that made it look like she had monster feet, and tiny shorts which revealed every inch of her tanned legs, bounced up to him with a glistening smile. She took the food, gave a five-dollar tip, and then waltzed back through the masses.

In the courtyard of the parking lot, Cashe noticed a blue neon sign advertising PNC Bank, and thought how now would be the perfect time to check and see if his account was working. He walked inside the glassed-in foyer, put his card in the machine, entered his PIN, and then pushed the button on the screen to check his balance. The display read: **Sorry, we're not able to process your request at this time.**

He gave it a second try, but only received the same response. Frustrated, he attempted to access his account by phone, but it too denied him. When he tried dialing the number to the credit card company, he found out that those accounts were also blocked. As he stood outside the bank in the Schenley Quad, listening to the automated rejections, he had never felt so defeated and helpless. The flow of students continued in what seemed like an endless herd, some playful, some serious, others drifting carelessly like loose fragments of leaves and branches down a flooded river.

Life had once been so easy. No worries. Just fun and friends.

Then someone called his name.

"Hey! What's the matter Cashe?" asked a voice booming from the other side of the lot. It sounded like Kris, but as he searched the crowd for a Perfect Papa uniform or car topper, neither could be found. He turned his back, thinking that maybe Kris's voice had bounced off the buildings and perhaps he was behind him.

"Fuckface! I'm over here! Come get at me!" echoed the voice again through the parking lot. A group of girls laughed. The sound of glass shattering from the far end of the lot was met with ooo's and ahh's, followed by a moment of hushed silence. As he made his way back to the truck, he noticed a couple approaching him from a gathering of students near the steps. They stood out like a bright light in the darkest part of wilderness. A shivering jerk went through his chest as his eyes gazed upon who he *thought* were Kia and Kris, walking side by side, holding hands. The instinctual desire to call out to his wife came and went as he realized that it wasn't her, and it wasn't Kris, but their doppelgangers, only younger *duplicates of the two*. The imposter wrapped his arm around the shoulder of his fake wife, then kissed her on the cheek the very second they passed next to him.

"She's my bitch now!" mocked Kris's voice from somewhere on the opposite side of the lot. "Ahhh, haaaa! Mine!"

He felt crazy, hearing a voice talking to him, but not being able to see who it was, or respond. If he yelled back, everyone in the parking lot might think he was insane. Cashe walked as fast as he could without running to his truck. Disoriented and out of sorts, he wondered if he would be able to drive back to the store safely. In his mélange of emotions, he thought he might cry. It was truly happening. Everything Cleveland had told him about the New Mafia in Uncle Jimmy's bar had come to pass. Maybe he was beginning to turn into a homeless lunatic.

As he came to the driver's side of his truck, he stepped over broken glass scattered on the ground. While he was checking his accounts, someone had apparently broken out the window of the car parked next his. Whatever had happened was now over with, and Kris's voice could no longer be heard.

Is Kris able to call me from another location? Do I really have a chip hidden underneath my skin?

When he turned out of the Schenley Quad onto Fifth Avenue, he almost ran head on into an oncoming Port Authority Bus speeding down the transit lane. Its horn wailed. Without thinking, he stepped on the gas, and sped in front of it, inches away from having his tail-end torn off, then swerved over into the middle line of traffic, avoiding a collision with an oncoming BMW. His eyes opened up to the spirit.

"Watch what the fuck you're doing, asshole!" screamed the driver to his right, after slowing down enough to look Cashe in the face. Three bat demons flew in different directions across the windshield of his truck, mocking him and howling chaotically.

Somehow, he had to regain his composure. Deep inhales and exhales temporarily eased him, but as he turned onto Bouquet Street and made a left at the light onto Forbes Avenue, he began to feel like the *enemy* wanted him dead like never before. He thought that if he could *just make it back to the shop*, there was a chance he might be able to establish some sense of normality. But he had hoped in vain.

Confirmation

"DID YOU HEAR WHAT I SAID TO YOU?" had been the first thing Cashe heard Kris say inside the store upon his return from the other side of the cut-table, his back turned, facing the make-line. His words sliced through the air and hit Cashe's ears like razor blades. He had to find out if Kris really had been talking him. Cashe threw his hot-bags underneath the driver's table and walked over to where he was standing.

"Did you say something to me Kris?"

"What?" he answered ignorantly, his voice filled with contempt. "No, I wasn't talking to *you*. I was talking to Brian. Anyway, niggas is *crazy*…"

Brian looked over at Cashe, paddle in hand, and scooped a pie out of the oven. The room had all of a sudden become small, and Cashe needed space to breathe. Several orders lined the computer screen. He snuck to the rear of the shop, into the bathroom and locked the door. Exhausted and now feeling himself beginning to mentally come down from what seemed like a skewed, evil mountaintop experience, he laid on the filthy floor, wanting to fall asleep.

Jesus, help me.

Back to Normal

THEN, THE STRANGEST THING HAPPENED. For the rest of the evening, the atmosphere around the shop amazingly returned so back to normal that after the final delivery of the night Cashe *almost* forgot about the incident at the Schenley Quad—but not totally. He talked with Cleveland while filling a mop bucket with water.

"Yeah, man," said Cleveland, "I'm starting to get excited about tonight."

"Wait a minute," said Cashe. "How much money does it cost to get into this place?"

"The cover at Utopia's, if I remember correctly, is usually ten dollars," said Cleveland who looked more like he was dancing than sweeping the floor. "But tonight's Free Draft Beer Night on the South Side so it might be more."

"Hey, listen. All that apocalyptic nonsense you told me about the New Mafia is starting to hit home," said Cashe.

"Why, did something else happen?" Cleveland stopped sweeping and put both hands on top of the broom handle.

"Yeah. Last night when I went out with Kia, I tried to use my credit cards to pay for dinner, but none of them worked. Even my bank card wouldn't go through, and I know I have money in the account."

"Are you serious?" asked Cleveland.

"I'm very serious," he answered. "And what sucks is that there's nothing I can do about it. I guess I'll just have to wait until they give me access, or show up personally at the bank tomorrow and find out what the hell is going on."

Cleveland gave an inquisitive smirk but kept silent about the subject.

"Hey, listen, do you have a problem with me driving tonight?" asked Cleveland.

"Not at all, as a matter of fact I prefer it that way. Just don't leave the South Side without me."

Cashe poured red floor sanitizer into the steaming hot water, tugged the handle on the side of the bucket and wrung out the mop. Sam always left it up to the two closing drivers to decide on who would sweep and who would mop. Of all the times they closed together, Cashe couldn't recall one occasion when Cleveland chose to mop.

"Do you think we'll see the devil tonight?" asked Cashe, leaning into the wooden handle, scrubbing out the caked flour that was stuck in the grooves of the square tiles.

"I wouldn't doubt it," said Cleveland, pushing the pizza cut table out of the way.

"What's her name?" asked Sam, surprising them all of a sudden from the back, clipboard in hand. They both let out fading laughs, and gave each other looks that said, *We have to be careful talking about this stuff.*

They finished cleaning, paid the store, and then met outside in the parking lot while Sam locked up. Cashe felt more like going home and sleeping than going out with Cleveland on special orders from Wissahickon. But at the same time, destiny had called and he *knew* more than ever that he was exactly where he was supposed to be.

"I'm going to go home and change," said Cashe. "Let's meet back here in about an hour."

"Got it," said Cleveland. "See you then."

South Side

AN HOUR LATER, in the Perfect Papa parking lot, Cleveland unlocked the door to his Toyota and Cashe slid into the passenger seat. At home, of course, Kia was nowhere to be found. He hadn't tried to call, but figured she was hiding out somewhere at her father's house. Hip-hop music boomed and seemed to rattle every loose screw in the car. The volume, for some reason, didn't irritate or bother Cashe. It sounded pleasant and made him feel as if he were beginning a dramatic scene in a film. But he understood that this was no movie. He knew the excitement would pass, and he surmised that the spirit world would be opening up to reveal itself soon.

As he looked around, he could see that it already had. The color-monster was as thick as a mirror. A matching burgundy Corolla with what looked like Cashe and Cleveland's twins inside—not exactly them, but some altered version from another realm—turned into the parking lot, sped around the store and exited onto South Millvale Avenue. Cleveland hit the gas and they rode through Oakland on Fifth Avenue toward the South Side, not speaking, only watching several other burgundy cars surround them along the way. Cashe began to feel inebriated; his senses grew, heightening to nearly an unbearable point the closer they came to the edge of the city. Just as he began to wonder if Cleveland was feeling the same way, Cashe heard him answering his thought, the way Tulpehocken had talked to him in front of the library.

Cleveland:

Yes, *Cashe. I do. I feel high. This shit is like a dream.*

Cashe:

Don't worry, everything will become clear.

Instead of looking at Cleveland as they traveled down Bates Street, Cashe looked out the window at the Monongahela River, wide and murky, shimmering under the streetlights posted along the bank. As they came around the bend, he saw a cluster of police and fire engines surrounding a building that had caught fire on some street on the hill over on the opposite bank. Its flames and smoke billowed and danced into the night and he remembered his dream from not too long ago.

As they crossed the Hot Metal Bridge, downtown Pittsburgh came into view. The sky above swirled with pink and purple clouds in the evening sky. Among them, the dark silhouettes of thousands of spirits circled, creating a cyclone, a spectacular spiritual fire burning near the heart of the city. The bottom of the funnel met the earth somewhere on the South Side.

Cashe:

My God, look at all those demons. Where are the angels?

Cleveland:

I don't know, but I hope they'd hurry up.

Cleveland ducked his head and gazed up out of the windshield to see the top of what looked like a tornado.

They made a right onto East Carson Street and immediately saw crowds of revelers packing both sides of the strip, creating a Mardi Gras atmosphere. Free Draft Beer Night seemed to attract ten times more than the usual clientele. They maneuvered at a turtle's pace around the traffic until they arrived at a cobblestone through-way on a random side street. Cleveland parked and they steadily blended into the jammed masses, peeking into the windows of filled-to-capacity pubs, clubs, restaurants, hookah bars and cafés. Down both sides of the road, buses and cars honked sporadically as they walked past throngs of clubbers standing outside rows and rows and street after street of nightclubs, storefronts and bars, and Cashe noticed that none of the people had auras. Like a surprise, about a block away from Utopia was the prophet, along with his two German Shepherds at his side, standing on a corner close to the bag lady who had tormented him outside the library, pointing an icy finger in her face and yelling vehemently. The old woman gazed at the prophet, as if she were paying more attention to his glaring, forceful eyes and the way the tip of his red beard bobbed up and down, than to what he might have actually been saying. Suddenly the prophet stopped as if he had just heard his name called, turned toward Cashe and Cleveland and screamed:

They are of the order of the two olive branches! Of the two that stand before the Lord!

Most of the people in the street only gawked at him. Some brave badass carrying on with his friends told him to shut the fuck up.

As they continued by the vagrant pair and approached Utopia's blue neon sign on the right, something caught Cashe's eye in the spirit. Down what normally would have been an unlit passageway between two buildings, he saw the yellow glow of radiant light coming from underneath a green dumpster at the far end of the passage. He nudged Cleveland with his elbow and nodding with his head, directed his attention down the narrow alleyway. They both looked straight ahead into what everyone else might have only seen as darkness, and as they neared the dumpster, stepping over bottles and using the brick wall of the buildings on either side as a guide, a fuzzy whiteout suddenly knocked them both into unconsciousness.

The Elders

ON A MARBLE DISC above downtown Pittsburgh, up in the sky centered in the core of a lavender fog of demons cackling in drunken laughter, Cashe and Cleveland awoke and found themselves sitting cross-legged, surrounded by twelve elderly men blanketed in swirling clouds. Each was from a different ethnicity, and had a long beard hanging down to the middle of their chest, waving wildly in the wind. Golden crowns encased with multicolored gems adorned the top of their balding heads. Two elders spoke, one after the other harmoniously, using the telepathic language of the spirit; their words echoed twice, doubling their statements.

Elder 1:

Now is the time.

Elder 2:

Now is the time…

Two followed in turn; then two more, one after the other from different parts of the circle.

Elder 3:

Walk out what is destined and don't be afraid.

Elder 4:

Walk out what is destined and don't be afraid…

Elder 5:

Use what will be given to you.

Elder 6:

Use what will be given to you…

Elder 7:

The Spirit of the Beloved will possess you.

Elder 8:

The Spirit of the Beloved will possess you…

Elder 9:

You will be filled.

Elder 10:

You will be filled…

Elder 11:

And the Father's purpose will come to pass.

Elder 12:

And the Father's purpose will come to pass…

The Initiation

WHEN THE VISION ENDED, Cleveland and Cashe found themselves no longer resting Indian-style on the floor but standing upright in the unlit alley. All was dark, except for the rays of light coming from underneath the dumpster. They turned their heads and gazed into each other's face, stunned and teary eyed, then moved forward. When they came to the green metal container,

Cashe dropped to his knees and looked underneath to see where the light might be coming from. On the ground within arm's reach were two garbage gifts sparkling with a spiritual glow: a pair of Glock pistols with four fully loaded cartridges stacked neatly at their sides. Cashe thought the weapons must have been left on the ground for them, just as the prayer rug, the basketball, the pizza box and Bible had just as inexplicably been set up like a shrine on the table next to the washer and dryer in his basement. He rose to his feet and handed a gun and a set of magazines to Cleveland.

Cashe:

Someone's helping, but who?

He thought of how the bag lady had put the action figure and angel on top of the trash can at the library, and envisioned both she and the prophet walking along like zombies, hiding the guns there as if under a spell. Instinctively, without thinking further about *how* they had gotten there, Cashe carefully studied the gun and ammo, loaded it with a cartridge, hit the safety button, then hid it and the other clip inside his coat. Cleveland did the same, tucking the weapon between his belt and stomach; he slid the extra cartridge in his pocket and then threw his shirt over the bulge.

Cleveland:

I guess we'll be needing these.

Outside Utopia's, patrons lazily smoked cigarettes. One couple groped each other unashamedly up against the wall of the building. They all seemed unaware that something out of the ordinary had just taken place less than a block away. In the spirit, two white flames sprung out of the sidewalk on either side of the club like geysers, both as high as the top of the door. As Cashe and Cleveland came near the entrance, each flame lifted into the air and hovered about a foot off the ground. One flew to Cashe's right, the other to Cleveland's left, and the fire went inside them, possessing them. They felt invincible, livid and *offended*. They could kill and wanted to.

Cashe opened the door, and Cleveland followed him inside. As they moved through the dense crowd, it was as if Cashe was in an intoxicating dream; the set up was just as Cleveland had described. Players from every Pittsburgh professional athletic team, politicians and local celebrities spotted the room. These were the people always talked about at work, and those always seen on TV—but there was more. Mixed among them were the familiar faces of the people in Cashe's life. Those he encountered and worked with on a regular basis. People he saw at the shop and customers he delivered to, day in and day out; all had gathered as if they were attending a sickening graduation party. From the bar, Lenny Smith, his manager from Coccelli's, raised a glass, toasting to him as if offering a congratulatory salute for making it this far. Mr. Reddy, his landlord, turned around from an island bar on the right and smiled. Hakan Selim and Benyamin Dini, his co-workers at Angelina's, looked on, grasped shoulders and gave each other high fives, their silent laughter masked by the blaring music of the club. Tony Jackson and Cliff Pataski from the YMCA eyed him as he approached, grinning and nodding their heads, eerily welcoming his arrival. Buck Alvarez sipped whiskey from a small glass at the bar with squinty eyes. Scantily dressed women in high heels and jewelry passed by periodically, whiffs of their perfume scenting their nostrils in soft waves. Lights flashed on the floors and the walls and the ceiling.

Cleveland spoke without moving his lips.

Cleveland:

We need to go through that red door in the back.

They slid past the gathering of revelers dancing in the aisles next to the island bars, brushing by and rubbing against them until they reached the crimson door leading to the basement. Cleveland opened it and Cashe followed, descending down a flight of red steps.

Three naked, baldheaded goblins materialized from the shadows and ran ahead of them like scurrying rats. Overhead, a swarm of maggot-like, hairy locust sprayed down the stairwell from above, towards the strobe lights near the landing, making the two duck to the floor until the very last one had passed.

Near the bottom, a mob of partygoers pulsated in a body locked orgy, swaying to the rhythm of the music, holding bottles of beer and lit marijuana into the air. A cloud of smoke hung thick in the basement as black shadows of demons flying above the people flashed among the white mist. Some of the women were topless, others wore eclectic costumes with strange shapes and colors, as if they might be in the lineup to walk the runway at a Paris Fashion Week show. The two pushed further ahead until a break in the crowd came into view and the roisterers began cheering and screaming wildly around an open circle in the middle of the dance floor.

As the strobe lights flashed, he could see glimpses of half-naked men in the center of the room. Black leather straps were tied across their torsos and around their backs, exposing their bare chests and stomachs, stiff, protruding penises and fleshly bare buttocks. Around the inner circle were other figures in hooded cloaks, looming over something near the floor.

Cashe couldn't see what was on the ground inside the opening, but as he continued on, he remembered what Cleveland had said would be there. The crowd began to cheer uncontrollably, throwing up their hands.

From the right corner of the room, he saw a glimpse of the top of the head of Azazel, his goat face and two horns curving toward the sky. There were others accompanying him, following in a procession, leading him closer and closer to the open ring in the middle of the club.

Near the center of the circle, he recognized more of the people who embellished his everyday life. Trent Blake and Marcus Tolman kneeled down on either side of a round, wooden platform, holding down the arms and legs of a woman splayed across a white star. A strobe light flashed in the face of Miyad Burek, as he stood to the side watching the scene transpire. Opposite Miyad across the circle, Sam Thomas' face lit up and Cashe saw his cross-armed bulky frame. The frog woman from the VA Hospital cackled insanely, waving a beer into the air. Mike, the worker at the auto body shop had either hand up the skirts of two drugged-up girls as they gyrated next to him to the music. The two black women from the hospice and the transvestite from Giant Eagle danced with one another in circles, holding hands.

Kris Williams was there. With his brown, sweaty bald head and ebony leather straps crossing his back, he gripped the woman on the platform as he rocked his hips back and forth, thrusting into her. Cashe pushed himself forward, with Cleveland at his side, and tried to see the woman's face.

Bent over underneath Kris was Kia, both of them clothed in their initiation outfits. Open mouthed and taking what Kris was giving her, Cashe saw her long, curly black hair spread out behind her like a natural halo. The sparkly purple dress she wore had been pulled above her waist. Azazel entered the circle opposite them, and Cashe suddenly felt Cleveland push through into the middle of the gathering, nudging him out of the way.

Anger and the feeling of wanting to destroy everything in sight overcame Cashe, just as it had done while watching Kia and Miyad together at Angelina's. Casually, he reached inside his coat as Cleveland simultaneously grasped near his waist and together they revealed their weapons.

Cashe hadn't shot a gun in years, but quickly recalled those times when he had been deep in the woods of Virginia while in the service, shooting off rounds at targets and into the sky as he held the hard plastic in his hand. His index finger lightly touched the trigger and he took the gun off safety.

"Die you motherfucking devil!" screamed Cleveland, rushing forward, gun drawn.

He fired at Azazel, who disappeared in a puff of black smoke, his purple robe dropping to the floor like a pile of dirty laundry. In the spirit, the angelic form of Azazel rose out of the cloud. His massive wings opened behind the visage of a black man whose ruby colored eyes glimmered through the shadowy club like dull moon beams. Just then, four Annunaki-like creatures entered through the ceiling and landed on either side of him. Their wings sounded like an explosion, and their bodies shone like blood light. Above their heads—which had four sides, each side having the face of a man, a bull, an eagle and a lion—was a circular screen which intermittently pulsated every color of the rainbow. A face of each creature turned toward Azazel—each being a different one of the four—and he let out his terrible, discordant cackling laugh, flapped his wings, then shot through the roof. The four creatures trailed behind.

In the same moment, a giant bat demon exposed its head from out of the back of Kris's neck, spread its wings and leaped at Cashe. Its red eyes and long, sharp teeth glared from its hairy face. He fired several rounds at the demon, but it too vanished as Kris's back and head tore open, spilling blood onto floor, exposed by the pulsating strobe light. Kris stopped moving and slumped to one side of the platform as the crowd dispersed, slowly pushing Cashe away from where the center of the circle had been. In a brief instance, he caught a glimpse of blood covering the stomach of his naked wife. She coughed and a scarlet eruption bubbled out of her mouth.

"Kia!" he yelled, helplessly, an unstable mix of emotions breaking through him; feelings of hatred and vindication, of grief and shock, of drunkenness and despair.

"No!"

The sound of the firing Glocks clapped as the music continued to play in the basement. He squeezed the trigger of the Glock over and over again, and those closest to him dispersed, creating a small space around him, giving him room to move and time to reload. *Clap. Clap, Clap, Clap. Clap, Clap.* But just as quickly, the gap of the disorientated, frantic crowd of people and spirits closed, moving him even further away from the platform until the circle of the ceremony had totally disappeared. In one instant, a screaming woman crashed into him, a second later, several demons flew past, sweeping up against him, some passing *through* him. Goblins tugged at his leg while gunshots popped into the mix of the rhythm until he could no longer distinguish the two. Many of the clubbers continued to drop to the ground from sheer panic, others from bullet wounds, until both Cleveland and Cashe were out of ammunition. Like the music and gunshots, they also lost each other in the stampede. Cashe hid the gun inside his coat, maneuvered toward an open door below a red exit sign in the rear of the room, with the empty clips knocking in his pants pockets, and then ran outside.

Coincidence

"THERE YOU ARE!" said Cleveland as they miraculously met outside Utopia's near the alley where they found the guns, like some schizophrenic coincidence. "We need to get the hell out of here."

Revelers scattered into the streets, some screaming, others jogging away. Cashe and Cleveland strolled down East Carson Street silently and coolly, toward the parked car. Once there, Cleveland unlocked the doors, and they both climbed in. Carefully, they drove out into the intersection, through the groups of people who packed the sidewalks and crosswalks until they became stuck in traffic.

"Cleveland, drive to the first bridge you can find," said Cashe. "We need to get rid of these guns. Do you still have yours?"

"Yeah, it's all right here," he said.

"Let's go back over the Hot Metal Bridge. I know exactly what we need to do."

Surprisingly, the congestion before them cleared in a matter of minutes. The flashing sirens of the police and fire trucks raged in the rear-view mirror. Smoke above Utopia swelled violently into the nighttime sky like a ghastly river. The club had somehow caught fire.

Evidence Disposal

WHILE CROSSING THE MIDDLE of the Hot Metal Bridge, they rolled down their windows and threw the guns and clips hard and far into the Monongahela River.

Sleep

"CLEVELAND, I DON'T THINK I want to go home tonight," said Cashe, as they walked back to his car. "Do you mind if I stay the night at your place?"

"No, problem man," he said. "It's not a problem at all."

He needed a new environment, a new atmosphere, and wanted to be as far away from anything that might remind him of tonight, of the shooting, of Kia, of work or *spirits*.

After they arrived at the parking lot of Perfect Papa, Cashe got into his truck and followed closely behind Cleveland. His body ached and longed for a bed. The spiritual high still lingered heavily, but he had no concerns. He didn't care about the police coming after him. Nor was he worried about them finding the guns. Whether Kia had survived or had gone to the morgue didn't matter. Nothing seemed important anymore. That night, he slept soundly, and for the first time in a long while, he didn't dream.

Epilogue

IN THE MORNING, Cashe left Cleveland's place, drove to Shady Avenue and parked his truck next to the young sapling across the street from his apartment building. Although he wasn't sure what had happened to his wife, if she were alive or dead, he *knew* she wasn't inside. He needed to come home; he needed to finish this ride. His work was done and now he had to think about what to do next.

On the ground below the door to their apartment, he saw a small wooden box, and instantly, he remembered where it was from. It was the one Yousef had given Sami during their visit to his home. He picked it up, unlocked the door and went inside. Immediately, he noticed that the place was empty. Everything—all the furniture, the dining room table and chairs, the bed, coffee table and lamps, his bike and clothes, everything—was gone.

He walked into the kitchen, leaned on the counter and opened the box. Inside was a gold ring with a sparkling blue stone. After he studied the design, the familiar, intricate patterns on its sides and the tiny engravings of angels underneath the octagonal gem, he slid it onto the middle finger of his right hand. And that's when it all came back to him. The shooting on Tennessee Avenue. The naked woman being kicked. The ring with the blue stone that the man in the white T-shirt wore on his hand.

Cashe jogged outside, started the ignition to his truck and turned on the radio. At the end of the song, a newscaster began to give a report about the events of the previous night.

Reporter:

Last night, at Club Utopia on the South Side, both a mass shooting and fire occurred, allegedly involving two unidentified gunmen. Over twenty people have been confirmed killed with the death toll still rising, in what is being called one of the deadliest tragedies in the history of Pittsburgh. So far, police haven't made any arrests…

He stared out the window in a wide-eyed gaze and watched who he thought was Kia coming up the right side of the street. They shared the same walk; hands tucked into her pockets, her long, black curly hair gathered back into a ponytail, a loose lock covering her right eye. The woman looked down at the sidewalk as she approached. When she came near the truck, she raised her head and gave a despondent grin. Her face emanated an expression that said, *I'm sorry it has to be this way, my love. I'm so sorry.*

As the woman passed, Cashe watched a white van speed up from the bottom of the hill, quickly cross the double golden lines in the middle of the street and park head-on in front of him. It happened so fast that he had no time to react. Three men wearing black ski masks got out and surrounded the truck. One stood near the hood, one outside his passenger door, and the third came to the driver's side door. He saw the man on his side pull out and point a gun at his head, motioning for him to get out.

Immediately, Cashe knew that the authorities must have caught up with him. They were going to arrest him and take him to jail. But these men didn't seem like police officers. Cashe's cell phone rang on the seat next to him. It was Cleveland, but he ignored the call.

"Is there a problem?" asked Cashe as he got out and raised his hands behind the open door to his truck.

Before he could respond, someone bear hugged him from the rear and pinned his arms behind his back. He watched the man in the mask hold a wet cloth over his mouth and nose as he struggled, but not for long. Gradually, he inhaled its fumes and drifted through the dark recesses of unconsciousness and into the unknown, weaving through the neon lines of purples and yellows and reds of his mind.

Afterword

I've always been fascinated with race, love and spirituality. So, first and foremost, *The Inescapable Consequence* is about the intertwining of ethnicities between two individuals who live in the same city, but have different and distant cultures. The protagonist, Cashe, comes from a mixed-race American family and falls in love with Kia, a second-generation Egyptian. As someone who has personally struggled with identity issues, I wanted to craft a story depicting characters who experienced the same type of uncertainties and challenges I had gone through in the past and continue to deal with each day. The idea was to tell a tale that could only be birthed out of the United States—living life in a black and white world, never feeling complete on either side and searching for oneself through *foreigners* residing in your own homeland. I always desired to read literature depicting this type of racial paradox, but those novels often seemed impossible to find.

Growing up, I knew without a doubt that the root of all the confusion concerning my identity centered around both of my grandfathers; my dad's father, who I had the opportunity to know, and my mom's father, a man I only learned of posthumously through photographs. Whenever I considered them as a youngster, I had an incredibly difficult time understanding *what they were* as far as their race and heritage was concerned. Both were very similar in a lot of ways. In my tender, naive eyes, they were pasty-skinned white men in plaid and sometimes solid button-down shirts, neatly tucked into buckled slacks. They had slicked back hair and a lit cigarette constantly dangling from a weathered hand. On their heads were old-fashioned hats and for the most part, both gave the impression of being very silent human beings. The one I knew while he was still living barely spoke, and when he did, it was always tremendously pointed, and always funny. These were shy fellows with reputations for being ladies' men, telling dirty jokes, and striking fear if their temper was ever roused. But as I looked around at the family, I also noticed how my grandfathers both seemed foreign and out of place, as if they were hiding amongst the rest of us with a dark secret. Trying to figure out how they fit in was like attempting to solve a complex puzzle.

Their wives were African American women who clearly faced no problem harmonizing into the diaspora. Clothed with coffee brown skin and powerful vernaculars, they were part and parcel with the fashion, music, food and culture of the time, and seemed to richly garnish the black community which saturated the inner-city blocks of their hometown and my place of birth in Fort Wayne, Indiana. But their husbands remained an enigma. Even though they were surrounded by siblings and other family members who shared the same *kind* of resemblance, the rest of the family, including their offspring of nieces and nephews, in-laws and the children from their wives' previous marriages, formed a hodgepodge of colors and complexions. Yet, despite the variety of hues, it also became clear to me—not only through the conversations I listened to while attending summertime gatherings in Fort Wayne, but also at home during my early years in Pittsburgh—that there were no *Caucasians* in the immediate family, which presented yet another conundrum.

To me, it seemed absurd to call my grandfathers African American. Anybody who wasn't blind could see that they weren't black. But at the same time, they just didn't have that crisp blue sparkle of the eyes, the clear skin and perfectly straight hair which would put them into the Aryan class either. *Some* of the features were there, but not all of them. When I humbly asked my dad about this after his father passed away, I was always taken aback with his smile and light laughter, as if he knew the answer but refused to come out with it. "Well, I've heard your great-grandmother was full-blooded Cherokee," he once said. "And rumor has it that your great-grandfather was half-white." I hit back with a pure response. "Then what did that make grandpa?" The grin returned. "Your grandpa was black," he said, obviously beguiling, unable to disguise the truth. "What do you think he was?" I could never answer that question; it silenced me for years. It just didn't make sense, especially when my mother countered with the same thing concerning her father—half German, half Indian, but black. They seemed like scripted, silly responses.

It wasn't until I moved out of my mother's house, grew into adulthood, and continued to educate myself in college and beyond that I began to seriously examine the person I saw every morning in the mirror. While doing work researching a family history project, I started to understand the dark past of what the *big deal* was, why the subject seemed so taboo and what was making everyone so uncomfortable. I learned that both of my grandfathers and my parents too, for that matter, were a product of a great American miscegenation experiment that began over 150 years ago. In the early part of the last century, we were called Mulattoes until violent racism and what might have been a threatening fear of a population explosion changed the laws so that giving birth to Mulatto children even became illegal in some states. In 1930, a change in practice forever erased the nomenclature from the U.S. Census. Indeed, I am the multi-generational offspring of a people in my country who now have no name. In our present day, being bi-racial, mixed-raced, more than two races or just "some other race" has not only become somewhat of a trend, but also a business when one considers the culture of self-identifying, marketing, advertising and the prevalence of the Internet. It still presents a huge swath of concern in America, especially considering the continued influx of immigrants versus the rise of White Nationalism as we have watched it again emerge with vengeance in the early part of the 21st century.

While in school, I met people from many far away countries of the world and became fascinated because we all looked alike, in a sense. I realized that there weren't just pockets of settlements here and there, filled with people who shared the same resemblance as me—like in the Hispanic and Puerto Rican neighborhoods in California, Chicago, New York and Philadelphia where I had visited or spent years living—but entire *countries*. Just like a black person in the United States could compare himself to a sub-Saharan African, or a white person could draw similarities to Europeans, in the same manner I found myself drawn to a generation of Latin Americans, North Africans, Middle Easterners, Indians, Asians and South Pacific peoples who originated in places where literally billions of others with the same complexion and exotic look thrived, with God-given characteristics that separated them from the historically black and white races often praised on this side of the Pacific and Atlantic. I learned to appreciate the subtle incongruencies between them, and found it fascinating just thinking of the genetic comparisons between people like, for example, Yazidis, the ethnic Kurdish minority group indigenous to Iraq and Tunisians, or Mexicans and the people of the Philippines.

I realized later that this innate attraction was an unconscious attempt to connect with something outside my border that I could not obtain within the purview of white and black America. The pull sought to establish meaning to my own self-identity and to that of my mysterious grandfathers, who existed enigmatically and virtually concealed in society, yet somehow remained extremely powerful, like the statues of statemen on the facades of government buildings or dotted inconspicuously throughout city parks. I believe these men did not reside in either of the two worlds defined in this country, and no doubt proved invaluable and precious because of their perspective. They belonged to a class of people with an identity that no longer existed at home, pushed to the limit of obscurity, separated from every American Indian tribe and-something-else-American. So, it was from this mold and historical perspective from which the main character Cashemente Tomás Alvin came to life, and provided inspiration for the role of Yousef, Kia's elderly father in the novel.

The Inescapable Consequence is also the tale of young marriage and true love unraveling. As most newlywed couples do, Cashe and Kia quarrel over the simple things of life, like who's taking up the most space in bed and finances, but their main contention revolves around religion. The animus which drove me to write about this type of relationship arose following the termination of my second marriage. Both unions lasted very short periods of time—the first two years and the second, only one—and afterwards, I truly couldn't understand the reasoning behind why they both had left. It literally seemed as though an ethereal force had suddenly placed a spell and subsequently led them away captive, out of my arm's reach. During this time of bewilderment, I turned to my Christian faith for answers, and an exhaustive study of biblical scriptures I had recently undertaken immediately prompted me to put the onus of responsibility of their departure on Satan. Whether he was truly to blame or not, the thought nevertheless led me down a surprising path and provided an interesting antagonist for the story—Azazel.

Everyone knows the original and oldest example of a wife being lured away by another was the tempting of Eve in the Garden of Eden mentioned in the book of Genesis, with her partaking of the forbidden fruit and then making matters worse, bringing her husband Adam in on the mishap. In the same book there is another story just as captivating. Abraham, recognized by many as the founder of modern faith in God, had a wife named Sarah who was stolen away by a king named Abimelech. The ruler only returned her after the Lord threatened to kill him.

But my focus fell on a briefly mentioned anecdote between these two accounts, a recounting of a sect of angels who left their proper positions appointed by God, and following the pattern of the fallen angel Lucifer, not only stole the wives of men, but also fathered children with them. The book of Enoch, written by Enoch, the father of Methuselah, the oldest man to ever live, and who was also the great-grandfather of Noah, recounted the same incident, but in much greater detail. Enoch resided in the ancient civilizations before the great flood, and spoke of a time when:

"… it came to pass when the children of men had multiplied that in those days were born unto them beautiful and comely daughters. And the angels, the children of the heaven, saw and lusted after them, and said to one another: 'Come, let us choose us wives from among the children of men and beget us children,'" Enoch 6:1-2.

This group of angels, known as the *Watchers* and who are also mentioned in the book of Daniel, carried out their plan and birthed children who grew into giants. One of these Watchers, a prominent fallen angel named Azazel, not only fathered offspring with the female species of earth, but also taught the forbidden secrets of heaven by crafting weapons and showing women how to beautify their appearance. Because of his crime, God bound him in prison for thousands of years, only to be released at the end of time.

Apart from theology, Azazel has recently been portrayed in popular culture through a slew of different media, including books, movies, video games and television series. In the late 80's, the science fiction author Isaac Asimov published the book *Azazel*, a collection of short stories depicting the corrupt angel as a two-centimeter tall genie-like demon who grants wishes. Though Azazel, usually seen as a historical figure in biblical literature, was presented as a lead role in Asimov's science fiction, the bridge he makes between fantasy and faith is worth noting. Ten years later, the film *Fallen* featured Azazel as an invisible spirit that jumps from person to person by touch. In the movie *The House with a Clock in Its Walls,* he makes a brief cameo as a Rumpelstiltskin-type character who sits around a campfire deep in the woods. He takes on a host of other varied appearances, from a Marvel Comics villain in *X-Men* to a crystal-line dragon in the video game *Tekken 6*. My version of Azazel keeps closer to his biblical visage, in a way. I wrote him as a fallen angel who transforms into a satyr-like goat-man only seen with spiritual eyes, and constantly haunts Cashe through his dreams to get to his wife Kia.

The Inescapable Consequence is also a novel about the end times. In the ninth chapter of the book of Revelation, four bound angels appointed to kill a third of mankind are released during a 'cere-mony' where divine seals latched around a closed book in the hand of God are opened. Though the angels aren't specifically named in this passage, it doesn't seem too far-fetched to assume that Azazel has a high probability of being one of the four, in that he is specifi-cally listed as an imprisoned Watcher in the book of Enoch. Again, as a life-long Bible student who has lived in the same century as the Holocaust, both World Wars, the Korean War, the Vietnam War, the Persian Gulf War, has watched the carnage of the Syrian Civil War, foreign and domestic terrorism, and now, as a new type of war in our midst, *mass shootings*—a peculiar problem that former US President Barack Obama said only exists in the frequency and scale that it does in America—which has sprouted like hellish blossoms all over the face of earth, I can only wonder whether or not those incarcerated angels at the great River Euphrates have been set free and are somehow behind it all.

Lastly, the novel addresses a topic I place in the center of all my work, the idea of the *spiritual awakening*. In my first book *Hades' Melody,* a memoir about the opening of my own spiritual eyes and ears during the summer of 2001 just before the 911 attacks, the entire narrative revolves around this phenomenon. Likewise, Cashe's vivification in *The Inescapable Consequence* also takes center stage. Placed in the setting of Pittsburgh's pizza delivery business—like most starving artists, it was a trade I spent years working in part-time when I wasn't making enough money writing—our main character, too, happens upon his own doorway into the otherworldly realm. He encounters both good spiritual beings, like his guardian angel Tulpehocken, and also evil entities, like the pesky bat demons.

    The Inescapable Consequence hopefully brings to light those unspoken presences—so taboo to the American culture—which can drive a person to act beyond their normal limits, and reveal not only a hidden and frightening landscape, but also, we must not forget, an intricately *designed* world of wonder.

J.D. Belcher
Lakewood, Ohio 2020

Acknowledgements

Special thanks to Samantha Ryan at Yorkshire Publishing, for her patience, perseverance and dedication in helping with the republication of *Hades' Melody*, and the publication of this novel. Also, I want to give my appreciation to those whose names I may never know, who worked so very hard behind the scenes to make this dream of mine become a reality.

CPSIA information can be obtained
at www.ICGtesting.com
Printed in the USA
LVHW091811080421
683893LV00022B/565/J